D0895389

IVORY TOWER COP

IVORY TOWER COP

A NOVEL

BY

GEORGE KIRKHAM

AND

LEONARD TERRITO

CAROLINA ACADEMIC PRESS
Durham, North Carolina

Library of Congress Cataloging-in-Publication Data

Kirkham, George.
  Ivory tower cop : a novel / George Kirkham and Leonard Territo.
    p. cm.
  ISBN 978-1-59460-656-4 (alk. paper)
  1. Police—Florida—Fiction. I. Territo, Leonard. II. Title.

PS3611.I754I96 2009
813'.6—dc22   2008052720

Carolina Academic Press
700 Kent Street
Durham, NC 27701
Telephone (919) 489-7486
Fax (919) 493-5668
www.cap-press.com

Printed in the United States of America

*FOR THE MEN AND WOMEN OF AMERICA'S LAW ENFORCEMENT
PROFESSION, AND OUR FELLOW CRIMINAL JUSTICE
EDUCATORS AND POLICE ACADEMY INSTRUCTORS
WHO PREPARE THEM "TO SERVE AND TO PROTECT"*

ACKNOWLEDGMENTS

Some debts can never be fully repaid. Such a debt is owed to two men, without whose courage and assistance the personal experiences that provided the inspiration for this novel would never have been possible. The late Dr. Eugene Czajkoski, Dean of the College of Criminology and Criminal Justice at Florida State University encountered strong opposition from many faculty members over the never-before-tried experiment of allowing a university professor to attend a law enforcement academy and then spend some months walking in the shoes of an urban police officer. Jacksonville-Duval County, Florida Sheriff Dale Carson experienced similar resistance from the staff of his agency over the prospect of providing a gun and badge to a "Berkeley radical." Both men shared a belief that the potential benefits of such an unorthodox form of research far outweighed its liabilities. Special thanks go to Jacksonville police Sgt. Sonny Connell, one of the senior author's undergraduate students, who first conceived the idea of what became nationally known as the "professor-policeman" project.

The authors were fortunate to receive valuable assistance from many experienced law enforcement professionals as they researched and wrote *Ivory Tower Cop*: these included our good friend and colleague of many years, retired Miami, Florida, Police Chief Kenneth Harms; Ken Katsaris, former Sheriff of Leon County (Tallahassee), Florida; Ed Gunther, Senior Crime Analyst with the Florida Department of Law Enforcement; Tony Potts of the St. Petersburg, Florida Police Department; Rich Walker of the Hillsborough County (Tampa) Sheriff's Office; FBI Special Agent Jody Cornwell; William Rykert, Director of the National Crime Prevention Institute at the University of Louisville; Sheriff Tim Dunning and Captain Bob Tramp of the Douglas County, Nebraska, Sheriff's Office; Captain Anthony Infantino and Detective Marilou Davis of the Omaha Police Department; Omaha private investigators Dennis Whelan and Rick Dunn helped obtain critical police records about the sexual assaults on which the story is based and arranged for the authors to visit the actual crime scenes, as well as interview victims, witnesses and law enforcement officers who were assigned to the case.

A number of medical professionals were of great assistance to the authors in developing and presenting technical aspects of the story: these include forensic pathologist and former medical examiner Dr. John Feegel; psychologist Dr. Max Dertke, and the late psychiatrist Dr. Bernard Diamond provided the authors with a psychoanalytic lens with which to examine the mind and behavior of the unusually dangerous type of serial rapist portrayed in the book; Rita Hall, a Nurse Practitioner whose background includes working extensively with sexual assault victims, provided a wealth of important information about the psychology of rape victims; Karen Murrell, M.S., R.N., Jamie Kirkham, R.N., and emergency medicine physician David Birdsall, M.D., provided essential information on the medical dynamics of physical violence; Lance LoRusso and Pete Fenton, both attorneys and former law enforcement officers, contributed valuable observations regarding police procedures relevant to the story. We are indebted to Dr. Esther Smith and the late Dr. Elton Smith, superb English professors, for their many thoughtful suggestions on ways to improve the flow of the novel. Dr. Margit Grieb of the University of South Florida's Department of World Language Education was kind enough to check the accuracy of our German to English translations, and the Aramaic Bible Society translated a passage from one of the Gnostic gospels into the dialect of ancient Estrangela.

When we set about writing *Ivory Tower Cop*, we found little in our backgrounds as academic criminologists and textbook authors that prepared us for the task of producing a novel, let alone developing a compelling story with interesting characters, imagery and dialogue. Belated thanks must go to Genevieve Young for patiently teaching the senior author the basics of creative writing some years earlier while she edited his autobiography, *Signal Zero*, at J.B. Lippincott. The authors were fortunate to have the assistance of two highly skilled and experienced "trade book" editors in the writing of this novel: Greg Lawrence, who was an assistant to the late Jacqueline Onassis while she was at Doubleday, provided invaluable guidance during our initial work on the manuscript, while Bill Greenleaf, helped greatly with the final revisions.

Our thanks to New York literary agents Bob Lescher and Mickey Choate for their encouragement and assistance, as well as to our publisher, Keith R. Sipe, and our publicist, Elizabeth McCurry of Phenix and Phenix, for making *Ivory Tower Cop* a reality. Credit also goes to Barbara Iderosa for her skillful editing, and to Pamela Crawford and Donna Burchfield for their careful study of the manuscript at various stages of development. Marianne Bell and Carole Rennick worked tirelessly in preparing early drafts of the book. Our proofreader, Sharon Ostermann, deserves special recognition for bringing to her work an eye for detail worthy of any detective or crime scene technician. Finally, if a picture is worth a thousand words, we are convinced that the talented graphics designer and photographer Christopher Bridge succeeded in capturing the essence of our story in his art work for the book cover.

It is the authors' hope that this book will prove enjoyable to readers who like reality based police/crime genre stories, as well as informative to those who share our professional interest in the complex process of criminal investigation and the many scientific advances that have been made in the field in recent years.

While this story is based on actual events, any resemblance of characters portrayed to persons living or dead is purely coincidental.

George Kirkham
Leonard Territo

Whoever fights monsters should see to it that in the process he does not become a monster.
                              Friedrich Nietzsche

PROLOGUE

Nearly a half hour had passed since he pried open the kitchen window and quietly lowered himself into the apartment. He had been standing beside the woman's bed the whole time, listening to the barely audible sound of her breathing and watching the rise and fall of her chest in the moonlight that filtered through the dusty curtains. He glanced at his watch as the familiar fantasy began swirling in his mind. It was almost time.

He could taste the perspiration on his lips beneath the ski mask as he placed a gloved hand on her shoulder. She moved her head on the pillow, murmuring something in the twilight of sleep. He brought his mouth close to her ear and whispered her name.

Her eyes flew open and her breath caught in her throat when she saw the gun in his hand.

"Who ... who are you? What do you want?" she gasped. He stood beside the bed and stared at her without speaking. "Please," she said, in a tremulous voice, "I only have a few dollars!" She motioned toward the dresser. "It's in my purse!"

She pressed her back against the headboard. Her eyes were wide with fear now.

He gazed at the large black crucifix on the wall above her head. The bronze figure suspended from it looked down on him with an agonized expression, the painted blood prominent on its hands, feet and side. The beginning of a smile tipped the corners of his mouth as he reached up and touched the face of Christ.

"Bridget," he said softly. "It's three o'clock."

CHAPTER

1

Sunlight streamed through the bay window of the three-bedroom, Spanish-style house in Coral Gables. Dr. David Roth padded across the cold tile floor in his bare feet and striped pajamas with the morning *Herald* tucked under his arm. The Mister Coffee was gurgling through the end of its brewing cycle as he gathered the remnants of last night's dinner—a congealed, half-empty carton of Moo Goo Gai Pan and some steamed rice—and dumped them in the trash, along with an unopened fortune cookie. The University of Miami criminologist yawned and sorted through the paper. An article in the lower right corner of the local section immediately caught his eye.

POLICE SEEK RAPIST

A 71-year-old woman was brutally beaten and raped early Thursday morning in her south Miami apartment. According to police, the assailant gained access to the victim's second-floor residence by climbing a garden lattice and opening a locked window. Police say that the attacker, who wore a ski mask and gloves, was armed with a small caliber pistol. He reportedly woke the victim by calling her name and told her it was three o'clock.

Roth's eyebrows drew into a frown. Why did he want her to know the time? He shoved his glasses higher on the bridge of his nose. He had worn the same full-moon, wire-rimmed lenses ever since he was a graduate student at Berkeley; bifocals were added to the prescription a couple of years ago, around the same time that flecks of gray began to appear in his beard and thick black hair. He stirred his coffee and returned to the *Herald*:

A security guard in the lobby responded to the woman's cries for help after she managed to free herself from the duct tape used to bind and gag her. Nothing was reportedly stolen from the apartment. The assailant is described as a white male in his late twenties to early thirties, six-feet tall, with an athletic build. Anyone with information about this crime is asked to contact Sergeant Maria Sosa of the Miami Police Department's Sexual Battery Unit at 305-555-8934.

An overweight tabby threaded himself between his legs in impatient, serpentine movements.

"Just a minute, Nine Lives," he said distractedly.

At forty-three, David Roth was an internationally-recognized expert on the behavioral profiling of serial rapists. He had developed the Roth Rape Typology several years before under a grant from the U.S. Department of Justice. The RRT was widely used by law enforcement agencies throughout the country, including the FBI's Behavioral Science Unit, to predict future assaults by serial rapists.

The tabby was clamoring to be fed. Roth opened a can of Little Friskies and scooped it into a bowl.

Getting back to the article, he could already discern important parts of this rapist's *modus operandi*. He was apparently drawn to older women and was a stalker of some kind. The fact that he knew the victim's name suggested that he had been watching her for a period of time, probably learning personal things about her. The criminologist pinched the corners of his mouth with a thumb and forefinger, noting with interest that nothing apparently had been taken from the victim. That meant the sexual assault wasn't the spontaneous by-product of a residential burglary gone awry. He had gone there to beat and rape her. But, why this particular woman when Miami was full of elderly females living alone in apartment buildings without security guards?

The method of entry reported in the paper suggested that this was no ordinary burglar. Roth suspected that the feat of climbing a building and silently opening a locked window in the middle of the night was beyond the physical prowess and skill of most periodic residents of the Miami city jail; breaking into any home at 3 a.m. was a risky thing to do in a crime-conscious city like Miami, where so many residents kept guns within reach.

He filled a bowl with Rice Chex and stared thoughtfully at the article. Whoever he was, the assailant had a criminal history in all probability. The gloves he wore said that his fingerprints were on file somewhere. By itself, the beating of the woman told him little; some form of violence, he had discovered, is a given in most rapes, regardless of the submissiveness of the victim. After examining police records on over one thousand sexual assaults during his career, he understood that a rapist's genitals are really just a weapon he uses to vent his anger against women. They are interchangeable with fists and feet, guns and knives.

He took a bite of cereal and propped his angular chin on his palm. This rapist would strike again. Probably soon, he mused. The duct tape, ski mask and gloves were pieces of a behavioral signature that would become clearer as the attacks continued. Picking elderly women as victims and making certain they knew the time of the assault would likely also be part of the emerging modus operandi.

He refilled his coffee cup. *What a strange MO.*

He often came across accounts of sexual assaults in the local press but rarely lingered over them. There was something particularly foreboding about this rapist. Going to a drawer, he rummaged in it until he found a felt tip pen, a notebook and a pair of scissors. He went through the article again, pausing this time to make notes and underline portions that appeared significant. It occurred to him that the police were probably aware of other details they hadn't shared with the media.

He cut out the article and wrote TIME MAN across the top of it before placing it in a brown accordion folder in his study. The folder was labeled RAPISTS AT LARGE and contained accounts of unusual sexual assaults he had culled from newspaper, magazine and Internet articles. Every attack in the folder had something unique about it. If the elderly woman's assailant was captured, he could use the RRT to compare the profile with those of other serial rapists he had studied. He had the uneasy feeling that more articles would be written about this rapist before then.

*   *

Later that morning, he was several blocks from the university when traffic slowed to a crawl and then stopped. Up ahead, he could see a trail of bright red flares in the road. Several patrol cars with overhead light bars pulsing had blocked off the street around a late model sedan that was upside down. He gripped the wheel tightly and looked away. Almost four years had passed since his wife and nine-year-old son were killed by a drunk driver. The memory of what had happened to his family was still as painful as it was surreal. He recalled the last time he saw them. It was in the kitchen on a Friday morning. Jacob was spreading blackberry jam on a piece of toast, grinning as he predicted a massacre at his team's upcoming soccer match. Sara was at the sink, loading the dishwasher. He remembered slipping his arms around her waist and feeling the swell of her belly beneath the fluffy, terrycloth robe. She was due in only a couple of weeks. Her long, black hair was pinned up and she smelled of lavender soap. Sometimes, when he closed his eyes, he could still taste the trace of toothpaste when he kissed her goodbye. That morning he was in the garage getting ready to leave for his first class when she called after him not to forget the dry cleaning on his way home. *Dry cleaning.* It occurred to him that life is made up of such small things.

The shrill blast of a whistle interrupted his thoughts. He followed the cop's hand signal and drove slowly past the wreck.

Until the death of his wife and son, David Roth was a deeply religious man. The son of a Rabbi, he had prayed daily and observed the Sabbath as faithfully as any Jew. All that changed after the accident. No syllable of prayer had passed his lips since then. In the bitterness that consumed him, he vowed never to enter a synagogue again.

The universe wasn't malevolent, he reflected, just indifferent to the fate of its elements. If there was a God, He had no interest in His creation: a supernova in its death throes billions of light years away; a tree split by lightning; Sara driving Jacob to his orthodontist on a sunny, May afternoon. It was all completely random. Meaningless.

His office at the university had become his world since the accident. Its lights burned late each night on the darkened campus as he wrote articles and papers, proofed galleys on texts and revised lecture notes—anything to keep from going home. He realized now that it was only by immersing himself in his studies to the point of exhaustion that he had been able to do what no amount of psychotherapy or Prozac had. Work had enabled him to skirt the edge of madness and pull himself back from the abyss of despair that threatened to consume him.

CHAPTER

2

Roth parked his yellow Volvo station wagon in the faculty lot and grabbed a bulging briefcase from the back seat. Cigarette smoke drifted above students sprawled in shorts and bare feet on the library lawn as he headed for class with a seersucker jacket slung over one shoulder. The armpits of his blue shirt already revealed damp half-circles of sweat. *Miami. Eternal summer.* He quickened his pace when the bell in the campus tower began tolling the hour.

After slipping into the auditorium through a side door, he walked briskly up a half dozen steps to the raised platform. He spread his notes on the podium, surveying the several hundred faces in front of him. Every seat was occupied, and a number of late arrivals were camped in the aisles. Victimology 3666 had been full every semester since the murder of thirty-three students and faculty members at the Virginia Tech campus the year before by a deranged student named Seung-Hui Cho. Until then, students on Miami's palm-dotted campus, like most Americans, had taken their personal safety for granted. Now, violence and potential victimization seemed to be on everyone's mind. Not just criminology majors, but students from many other departments regularly signed up for the course.

Dean Stafford joked that Roth would soon be competing with the Miami Hurricanes for the stadium if the chronically over-enrolled course continued to swell. In contrast to most of the other buildings on the campus, the Memorial Building had seen better days. The acoustic ceiling tiles were stained in various places from leaks brought on by the subtropical summer rains and the increasing number of hurricanes striking the Florida peninsula. A couple of them drooped precariously high above the heads of students. A few of the overhead lights had burned out, creating small pockets of darkness in the windowless structure, which students jockeyed to avoid. The antiseptic green walls hadn't seen a fresh coat of paint in years. A frayed, brown carpet, pounded by legions of feet each day, ran down the wide center aisle, separating cramped rows of desks on either side of it.

He unbuttoned his collar. The air conditioner was set as low as it would go but did little good. With so many bodies jammed in the room, it was still uncomfortably warm. The criminologist's rumpled suit was a half-size too large for his frame, and the bottoms of his trousers bunched above a pair of scuffed, cordovan Rockports.

Removing a pocket watch, he wound the stem several times before placing it on the podium. The old Elgin, with its scratched cover and faded Roman numerals, conspired with his neatly-trimmed beard, collar-length hair and glasses to give him the austere look of a turn-of-the-century schoolmaster.

The gooseneck microphone squealed in protest when he started to speak. "Before we get started, just a reminder: we have a midterm on Thursday." There were groans throughout the auditorium. An Irish setter, lying at the feet of a blind student in the front row, stared up at him listlessly.

"Today, we're going to pick up where we left off with sexual violence."

Turning, he wrote a single word in large letters on the blackboard with a piece of yellow chalk:

VICTIMOGENESIS

"Victimogenesis refers to the role that the victim plays in the chemistry of sexual assault." Laptop computers began to chatter throughout the auditorium. He dusted the chalk from his hands and leaned on the podium. "Why do you suppose a sexual assailant picks a particular woman as his victim?" he challenged.

The students' eyes fastened on him.

"Take Jack the Ripper, for example. Why did he select prostitutes to disembowel instead of, say, governesses or chambermaids?"

A hand shot up. Roth pointed to a youth with a fraternity logo on his T-shirt and a baseball cap cocked sideways on his head. The student removed a ballpoint pen from between his teeth and slouched in his seat.

"Doesn't it all boil down to opportunity?" he said. "Prostitutes were probably a lot easier to get to than other kinds of women."

Roth wrapped his long fingers around the edges of the podium. "The motivation behind most sexual assaults is more complex than that," he countered. "Victorian London had thousands of prostitutes to choose from. The Ripper picked the handful of females he did for some very specific reason. Many serial rapists go to extraordinary lengths to assault a certain kind of victim. There's something about a woman who's targeted for a sexual attack by a stranger that draws him to her."

"Like what?" asked a black student with a Jamaican accent in the sixth row.

"Well … it could be almost anything. Something about her appearance may arouse sexual hostility in him. She may remind him of someone in his past towards whom he feels anger." He thrust his hands in his pockets. "Maybe it's her tone of voice or the way she walks or dresses. In most cases, neither she nor her attacker has any awareness of what it is."

He glanced at his notes. "One of the chapters in my book, *Patterns of Sexual Violence*, deals with Theodore Bundy. He may have raped and murdered as many as one hundred women before he was caught. Nearly all of his victims were slender and in their twenties with long dark hair. Bundy was typical of most serial rapists in selecting the same type of victim each time."

He thought of the article in the morning *Herald*, wondering how long it would be before another elderly woman was attacked.

Another hand went up. "Yes," he said, calling on a woman in black linen slacks and a white blouse, who appeared to be a few years older than the other students. She had piercing blue eyes and short blond hair. Her body tensed when she spoke.

"Dr. Roth, are you suggesting that Bundy's victims were somehow responsible for what happened to them because of the way they looked?"

"No, of course not. It's just that …"

Her voice rose sharply. "I don't understand why we're talking about victims instead of the men who commit rape and what to do about them."

A murmur swept through the auditorium. A number of students turned in their seats and stared at her.

"Well … it's just that the victim is part of the equation. We have to consider …"

"Being raped isn't part of any *equation!*" she blurted angrily. A rush of blood mottled her complexion. "You might be a little less analytical if it happened to you!" She grabbed her books and ran crying from the room.

Roth's lips parted in stunned silence as a din of voices engulfed the auditorium. He raised his hands in a gesture for quiet. "As I was saying," he continued, clearing his throat, "there's a psychological connection between the victims of sexual assault and those who commit it. We must examine it to fully understand the anatomy of rape."

With some difficulty, he gradually regained his composure and finished the lecture.

* *

Late that afternoon, he sat at his desk in a large corner office of the Merrick Building that afforded a sweeping view of the campus. The room was tastefully decorated with burgundy carpeting, cream-colored drapes and a comfortable leather couch—perks of a full professor who had been awarded more research grants than any faculty member in the history of the School of Criminology. The steady stream of government funds gave him a reduced teaching load each semester as well as a full-time graduate assistant.

He watched a couple of shirtless students playing catch with a Frisbee on the lawn, still brooding over the incident in his class. How could anyone think he lacked compassion for women who had been raped? He had authored several books and dozens of articles on sexual assault and had attended conferences on the problem from Paris to Los Angeles. The month before, he had been appointed by Florida's Attorney General to serve as chairman of the state's Rape Prevention Task Force.

Roth's career as a scholar had afforded him no personal contact with rape victims. For all his research on sexual violence, he had no practical experience dealing with crime or criminals in any part of the justice system.

Like most of his colleagues in the School of Criminology, he came to the sun-drenched campus straight from graduate school with the expectation of spending twenty or thirty years lecturing and writing about something he had never witnessed firsthand.

During the short time when the female student's eyes met his, he had glimpsed a human dimension to sexual assault that couldn't be neatly catalogued or reduced to graphs and tables.

CHAPTER

3

He sat on a bench at Ocean Reef Park with a copy of Stephen Hawking's A Brief History of Time on his lap anxiously waiting for her to appear. She rounded the bend of the jogging trail a little after five with a woman about her age, just as she had every day this week. It was smart not to jog alone in such a densely wooded place, especially this late in the afternoon when there were so few people around. He could tell that she was a very cautious lady. She always carried a small can of pepper spray on her hip and a whistle on the key ring clipped to her waist. He watched her tan legs glisten in the hot afternoon sun as her Nikes pounded the ground. She drew closer, laughing and chatting with her friend, oblivious to his presence. The damp orange T-shirt with CLEM-SON lettered on it clung to her body, accenting firm breasts. He averted his eyes, reminding himself that women who look like that want men to watch them and have sinful thoughts. She had never so much as glanced at him, not even the time she paused to lace a shoe only a few yards from where he was sitting. He may as well have been a rock or a tree. That was alright. Soon, she would think of him every day for the rest of her life.

CHAPTER

4

Roth was standing in line at the cafeteria near campus where he usually ate dinner trying to decide between fish and meatloaf when he heard a familiar voice behind him. He turned and saw Frank Bailey, a Miami sexual battery detective, who was one of his graduate students.

"What brings you down here?" Roth asked.

"Oh, out crushing crime tonight," Bailey grumbled. "I had to give a talk on 'Stranger Danger' to the PTA." The handcuffs looped in his belt swung into view when he reached under the glass shield for a salad.

"Feel like company, Doc?"

"Sure." Roth liked the brash policeman. He was a tall, fit-looking, thirty-year-old with a deep, south Florida tan. The ridge of a two-inch scar on one cheek marred an otherwise handsome face. Bailey had been one of Roth's students while he was completing his bachelor's in criminology, and was a regular racquetball partner. Their shared interest in sexual violence often led to discussions that spilled into pizza parlors after class.

They settled into a booth and began unloading their trays. The policeman's presence reminded him of the article in the morning *Herald*.

"Hey, do you know anything about the rape of that elderly woman on the south side?" Roth asked.

Bailey had already dug into his lasagna and was eating wolfishly. "Oh, you mean the nut who told the victim the time before he put it to her?" he said, through a mouthful of food.

"Yeah."

"Maria Sosa's handling it. She's our unit supervisor. If anybody can

find the asshole who did it, she can." Bailey glanced around him and lowered his voice, adding, "The victim was a nun."

Roth looked up with surprise. "I thought this happened in an apartment building, not a convent."

"It did. She lives in a little efficiency above a rescue mission she runs
out on 8th Street." Bailey doused his entrée vigorously with Parmesan
cheese. "Nothin' sacred anymore, huh? I figure it was probably one of the
shitbirds who hang around there every day, lookin' for handouts. Most
of 'em have records. They're all scumbags."

No. This wasn't a street person.

"What happened?"

Bailey tore a roll in half and slathered it with butter. "The guy apparently jimmied a window while she was sleeping. The next thing she knows,
he's standing beside her bed in a ski mask, with a blue steel semi-automatic."
He wiped his mouth with a napkin and leaned forward as if about to im-
part something confidential.

"Get this. After he ties her up and gags her, he starts wailing on her
with a crucifix that was hanging on the wall."

"A crucifix?"

"Yeah. How's that for sick, huh? You ought to see the pictures. Her
face is swollen up like a pumpkin. He apparently got her on the floor and
kicked the shit out of her. Busted one of her arms, and a bunch of ribs.
A woman her age. She's lucky to be alive."

Something had thrown the rapist into a frenzy. The cross?

"That's not all," Bailey added disgustedly. "Fucking animal! He anally
raped her!"

Roth's eyes narrowed pensively. "Any vaginal penetration?"

The policeman shook his head. "Not from what I heard."

Odd. "Any leads?"

"Not yet," Bailey replied, signaling the waitress for a cup of coffee. "No
prints, but we have his DNA. They got a semen sample from her at Good
Samaritan."

Roth squeezed a slice of lemon over his Dover sole, wondering why
the rapist hadn't used a condom. This was obviously a carefully executed

crime. Why would anyone cautious enough to wear gloves to keep the police from obtaining his fingerprints leave the calling card of his personal DNA at a crime scene? The *deoxyribonucleic acid* in the rapist's sperm would be enough by itself to put him behind bars once he was caught. Surely, he knew that. The incongruity in the modus operandi bothered him.

Roth removed a notebook from his pocket and jotted a few lines. "Got anything else?"

Bailey speared a wedge of tomato. "I heard that the techs vacuumed a blond pubic hair from the bed sheets. If you're interested in the case, give Sosa a call. She can tell you a lot more about it than I can." He wrote his supervisor's number on the back of a business card and handed it to him.

CHAPTER

5

When he got to the university the next morning, Roth called the number Bailey had given him. He waited through several rings before there was an answer.

"Sexual Battery, Sergeant Sosa," a woman said crisply.

He could hear people talking in the background. "Sergeant Sosa, my name is David Roth. I'm a criminology professor at the University of Miami."

"Uh-huh ... hang on just a moment." There was a muffled sound as she said something with a hand over the receiver.

"What can I do for you?" she asked hurriedly.

"I understand that you're investigating the rape of the nun."

There was a long pause on the other end of the line.

"Who told you the victim was a nun?" Sosa demanded.

"Detective Bailey is one of my graduate students. He mentioned that you—"

"Goddamn him! He knows that information is confidential."

Her anger startled him. "I do research on sexual violence. The FBI uses a rape profile system I developed."

"Good for them," she responded coolly. "Just what's your interest in this?"

"Well ... I thought that I might be able to help if I knew a little more about what happened." He heard her breath over the phone.

"Let me tell you something, Professor ..."

"Roth."

"Miami's a big city. Women get raped here all the time. Right now, we have no reason to regard this as anything more than an isolated event."

He picked up a calabash pipe from an empty ashtray on his desk. It still held a trace of the Turkish blend that passed through it regularly until the university banned smoking in all campus buildings. "I think you've got a serial rapist on your hands," he said directly.

"How can you say that when we've only had one attack?" she shot back.

"His preoccupation with the time suggests a compulsive personality. The behavior of people like that tends to be repetitive."

"Oh," she said sharply. "I suppose you're a psychiatrist as well as a criminologist?"

He didn't tell her that one of the two master's degrees he held was in clinical psychology.

"This crime was far too methodical and well planned for a one-time event," he offered.

"You mentioned the FBI a moment ago. I assume you're familiar with ViCAP."

"Of course." Every criminologist in the country was aware of the FBI's Violent Criminal Apprehension Program.

"It might interest you to know that I e-mailed ViCAP a profile on the nun's assault and had them run it against their database. There's no record of a rape with these characteristics anywhere in the country."

He pressed the stem of the pipe against his lip. "This was probably his first attack," he mused.

"Look, the lady ran a rescue mission. She dealt with all kinds of unsavory people. Any one of them could have done it."

"Sergeant, when was the last time you saw a panhandler or wino scale the side of a building and open a locked window without making a sound? The kinds of people who hang out at rescue missions are lucky to know what day of the week it is, much less be able to pull off a rape at exactly 3 a.m. with a guard downstairs."

"There was no guard," she corrected. "The press got that wrong. He was just an old drunk who was a regular at the mission. The nun gave him a few bucks a week to sleep in the lobby because of some burglaries they'd had. There could have been rapists running all over the place that night, and he wouldn't have noticed. He was still half-bagged when I interviewed him."

Roth shifted in his chair, mulling over what she had just said. "His presence in the lobby still complicated things. This guy went to a lot of trouble to get to her."

"Oh, the beginning of a wave of terror against nuns, huh? Does your crystal ball tell you if he's going to keep assaulting Dominicans? Or should we tell the Carmelites and the Sisters of the Blessed Virgin Mary they need to worry, also?"

The shards of condescension in her voice made him bristle. "I doubt the fact she was a nun had anything to do with why she was assaulted, though I think his use of the crucifix to beat her is significant."

"I wouldn't read too much into that. It was probably just handy."

"So were his fists."

"Maybe he's a lapsed Catholic who had his knuckles cracked by a nun one too many times in parochial school," she scoffed. "Listen, I'm really kind of busy right now. Why don't I give you a call if it looks like we need any outside help on this, okay?"

Bitch!

"Fine," he said curtly, slamming down the phone.

CHAPTER

6

On Monday, Frank Bailey was waiting outside Roth's office when he returned from his graduate seminar in Criminal Sexuality.

"Frank, your sergeant has the disposition of a scorpion!" he said brusquely.

Bailey lowered his eyes and scuffed the floor with a shoe. "I'm sorry about that. I wouldn't have told you to call her if I had any idea she'd get so pissed! She really climbed my frame for talking to you. I told her I never mentioned the victim's name. You'd think I'd given an interview to the *National Enquirer!*"

"Why all the secrecy?"

Bailey followed him inside and dropped into a chair. "It's not the kind of crime the department likes to see publicized. Something like the rape of a nun scares the hell out of most women. If someone like that isn't safe, who is? Cases like this put a lot of heat on us."

Roth took off his jacket and draped it over the back of his chair. Beside his desk, waiting to be sorted and analyzed was a box of sexual assault records from the Wisconsin Department of Law Enforcement. Similar files arrived each week from police agencies and correctional institutions throughout the country.

"I think Maria was just having a bad day. She's really a helluva cop. You ought to watch her do an interrogation."

Roth said wryly, "What does she use to get them to talk, waterboarding?"

The policeman grinned and propped an ankle on his knee. "Hey, once she turns those big brown eyes loose on a perp, he can't wait to spill his guts."

Roth had difficulty reconciling his words with the image of a hydra-headed ogress he had formed. "She's attractive?"

Amusement flickered in Bailey's eyes. "Whoever said the Cubans never made anything worth wanting except cigars obviously never saw Maria. I asked her out a couple of times back when I was single. No dice. Everything with her is strictly business. She doesn't date cops. I don't know about professors. I can try to fix you up with her, if you like."

"No, thanks. Talking to her on the phone was more than enough for me."

CHAPTER

7

He could feel the heat radiating through the latex glove on his left hand as he reached up and twisted the yellow forty-watt bulb. It winked off after a half turn, plunging the porch of the one-story stucco house into darkness. He stood there for a minute, letting his eyes adjust. A cacophony of night sounds came from crickets and frogs in the dense foliage surrounding the home.

A hinge on the screen door creaked when he opened it. He cursed under his breath; for all the things he knew about the jogger from Ocean Reef Park, he had no idea how sound a sleeper she was. One of her sisters, who was a pharmaceutical sales rep for a company in Fort Lauderdale, also lived in the three bedroom home, but she was out of town on business this week. He removed a small, leather case from his windbreaker and unzipped it, studying its contents in the narrow beam of his penlight. His fingers glided over several tools before selecting a tension wrench and a stainless steel probe with a hook on one end that resembled a dental pick. He patiently raked the tumblers in the deadbolt cylinder until the pins fell into place, then turned the knob and eased the door open. The corners of his mouth drew into a smile when he felt the safety chain grab. He knew she'd have it latched.

He cut a link on the brass chain and stepped inside, moving silently down the narrow hallway toward a door that was partially open. He could see the outline of her body from the green glow of an aquarium in the corner of her bedroom. She was lying on her side beneath a single sheet, with her legs drawn up in a fetal position. He paused at the foot of the bed, listening to the soft whir from the blades of the ceiling fan.

"Diane."

Her body jerked at the sound of his voice. An instant later, she thrust a hand under her pillow and spun toward him, holding a chrome revolver. She was nude.

His eyes moved beyond the sheet gathered around her hips to the satin smoothness of her stomach.

"Don't move!" she shouted. She held the snub-nose .38 in the two-handed cup and saucer position of someone who was familiar with guns. He had no doubt that she could hit whatever she aimed at. The red numbers on the digital clock beside her bed flipped from 3:02 to 3:03.

"It's time," he said, barely able to contain his excitement.

Her breath came in quick, short gasps now. She reached for the phone without taking her eyes off him, knocking over a glass of water. He watched it roll off the nightstand and shatter, spraying jagged slivers across the hardwood floor. She jabbed the keypad urgently. *"Help! Police? Hello!"* She held the dead phone for several seconds before letting it slip from her fingers. He came closer, stopping abruptly when she cocked the gun.

"Your father was a pilot, too, wasn't he?" he said calmly. *"You must have been just a baby when his fighter jet crashed. They never brought his remains back from Vietnam, did they?"* A shiver passed through him. The thought of touching her made his skin crawl.

She choked back a cry. *"Stay where you are. I'll shoot! I mean it!"*

He smiled beneath the ski mask. *"You're not going to kill me, Diane,"* he said. *"You're going to fuck me."*

The weapon's firing pin made a hollow sound when it landed on the first of six empty chambers. She snapped the trigger repeatedly, the color draining from her face.

He removed a handful of cartridges from one of his pockets and let them clatter to the floor. *"I said you weren't going to shoot me, didn't I?"*

She dropped the gun and clutched the sheet in front of her. He could see that she was scared, but she still hadn't lost control. Her eyes darted rapidly from side to side, searching for a way out. He could imagine the same look on her face if she lost an engine over the ocean in the big Jay Hawk helicopter she flew for the Coast Guard.

He withdrew a small pistol from the back of his waist. "This one's loaded. Now, get on your stomach."

She made a plaintive gesture with one hand. "Listen to me. You don't want to do this!"

"Don't I?" He closed the distance between them with two quick steps and struck her hard in the face with the gun, knocking her back on the bed. "Cunt, I told you to get on your stomach!"

She raised herself on one elbow and touched her split lip. A bright red rivulet trickled down one side of her chin as she began to cry.

Now she was there, he thought with satisfaction. Somewhere on the far side of petrified.

"I ... I just started my period. I'm wearing a tampon!"

"Shut up!" he yelled.

He could already feel the constriction starting in his chest. Wheezing sounds emanated from behind the ski mask as his breathing became labored. He kept the gun on her and fumbled in a pocket of his jeans for a tube of Vancenase. The inhaler made a hissing sound as he sucked the Albuterol deep into his lungs. Slowly, his shortness of breath began to ease. His voice became a hoarse whisper as he pressed the gun against her temple. "Don't ... say ... anything ... not a fucking ... word!"

She stifled a sob and nodded.

His eyes lingered on the dark coronas around her nipples for several seconds before he grabbed a terrycloth robe that was draped across the foot of the bed and flung it at her. "Cover yourself, bitch!" he rasped.

The soft hue that had bathed the room was replaced by blackness when he unplugged the fish tank. His breathing was still labored as he moved to where she was lying face down on the bed and unbuckled his belt.

CHAPTER

8

Roth sat at his desk proofing an article he was co-authoring with a professor of endocrinology at the School of Medicine on the relationship between levels of the neurotransmitter serotonin and aggressive sexual fantasies of convicted rapists. He was about to leave the office when he noticed the drop slip that had appeared in his box earlier that day from the student who left his victimology class in tears. Withdrawal from a course this late in the semester was normally only allowed under extraordinary circumstances. He signed the form, checking the box marked "Student Illness" as the reason for approval.

When he got home, he kicked off his shoes and sprawled on the couch, just in time for the six o'clock news.

> *"Our lead story tonight at Action Central: A thirty-four-year-old woman living on a quiet residential street on the city's north side has become the second victim of a man Miami police are now calling the Wake-Up Rapist."*

He turned up the volume with a remote:

> *"The woman who was assaulted was apparently asleep when her attacker, described as a white man in his twenties, appeared beside her bed and confronted her with a gun. The attack was virtually identical to another one on the south side of the city last month when an elderly woman was assaulted. In both rapes, the assailant called the victim by her first name and told her it was three o'clock.*
>
> *"In other news ..."*

Roth switched off the TV and sat there staring at the darkened screen. Several weeks had passed since he and Bailey discussed the nun's rape. While he had expected another attack by the person he had begun thinking of as 'The Time Man,' the age of the latest victim surprised him. It was unusual for serial rapists to choose victims of such radically different ages. There was another curious detail. The rapist had shifted his hunting field to a different part of the city. The apartment the nun lived in was in a deteriorated section of Miami, while the latest attack took place in a middle-class suburb miles away.

* *

The next day he placed a call to Frank Bailey in the Sexual Battery Unit.

"I see that whoever raped the nun just hit again."

"Yeah. The three o'clock shit is strange, huh?"

Roth drew a deep breath. "Frank, I'd really like to get a look at the case files on both attacks."

"Jesus Christ!" Bailey exclaimed. "You must be trying to get me fired. Have you ever heard of the Rape Shield Law? It's a first degree misdemeanor to disclose the identity of a rape victim."

He was ready for the reaction to his request. "You could sanitize the files," he suggested. "Just black out anything that might identify either woman. What I'd be seeing wouldn't be any different than the records I get at the university every day from prisons and police departments all over the country."

Bailey groaned. "Maria would kill me."

"She doesn't have to find out."

"I don't know …"

"Look, this guy is going to keep right on attacking women. I may be able to get some idea of what he's doing if I can see the files." He waited anxiously as Bailey considered his request.

"I suppose you'll let me and my family move in with you after I wind up unemployed."

"Absolutely."

"Alright … Maria's going to a supervisors' conference in Orlando on Thursday. I'll copy the records while she's gone and redact anything that's confidential. I should have them to you by the weekend. Just remember, they didn't come from me."

"I've already forgotten where I got them."

CHAPTER

9

That weekend, Roth sat in his study, examining the investigative files Frank Bailey had dropped off at his house. He began with the sexual assault of the nun. Every reference to her name in both police and hospital records had been meticulously blacked out. She was identified only as *BK* in an interview Sergeant Sosa had conducted at the hospital on the morning after the rape. He read a portion of the transcript with particular interest:

MS: Did the man who assaulted you say anything that led you to believe he realized you were a nun?

BK: Yes. He called me 'sister' several times. He also knew that I had worked at a mission in Zimbabwe in the seventies. He talked about the deaths of Sister Agnes and Sister Helena there.

MS: What happened to them?

BK: All three of us were nurses. We were supposed to go to a village to inoculate the children, but I sprained my ankle and had to stay behind. Sister Agnes and Sister Helena were attacked by Mashona rebels on the way there. They were both raped and murdered.

MS: I'm sorry. That must have been very hard for you.

BK: We're all born to die, Sergeant. I know they're with our Lord now.

MS: Besides the things we've discussed, can you remember anything else he did or said?

BK: Well ... he was very polite and soft-spoken at first, even when he had the gun pointed at me. After he tied my wrists behind my back, he wanted to know if the tape was too tight. He said that he wasn't going to hurt me and that he just wanted to talk. I remember that he touched the crucifix above my bed and kept looking at it. All of a sudden, he put his face in his hands and began to cry. He shook his head and said something, but it was hard to understand.

MS: What do you think it was?

BK: It sounded like 'Ann … don't. Please don't!' Then, he grabbed the crucifix and began hitting me in the face with it.

MS: You said earlier that he was cursing as he struck you with the cross.

BK: That's right.

MS: Do you remember his exact words?

BK: Yes.

MS: What were they?

BK: I … I can't repeat them.

MS: Will you write it for me?

BK: Yes.

A piece of paper was stapled to the transcript with five words neatly printed on it.

Filthy cunt. Whore. Cock-sucking bitch.

Roth pondered the significance of the rapist's outburst. Strange insults to hurl at a woman who, according to Sosa's notes, entered a convent at eighteen and presumably had been a virgin her entire life.

He turned his attention to a trace evidence report from the state police lab. A sample swab of a dark smudge on the nun's bedspread had been taken by the evidence technicians and analyzed. It proved to be common *crankcase oil*.

He opened an envelope containing a dozen 8X10 crime scene photographs and began sorting through them. The first picture showed a bent drainpipe and a lattice on the side of the building, surrounded by a tangle of kudzu vines. The next was an interior shot of an open kitchen window; someone had drawn a circle around the window and written POE, for *point of entry.*

There were several photos of the small bedroom area where the rape and beating of the Dominican nun took place. One showed a chair tightly wedged against a pair of drawn curtains to hold them in place. In another, an evidence technician crouched on the carpet next to a broken crucifix. He held a tape measure in his gloved hands to show the dimensions of the unusual weapon. It was exactly eleven and a half inches long. The horizontal wooden bar of the cross was splintered and bloody, leaving the tarnished bronze effigy of Christ clinging to the vertical shaft by a single rivet through the feet. Rust-colored spots of dried blood were spattered across the wall behind the bed as well as on the carpet, sheets and pillow.

Why did he cry? Roth had seen accounts of serial rapists who experienced intense guilt reactions after their crimes. A few even turned themselves in when the knowledge of the things they had done became too much to bear. Others broke into tears after they were caught and questioned. But, he had never heard of a case where a rapist wept *before* attacking a woman.

He opened the second file folder. It revealed that the Wake-Up Rapist's most recent victim was a helicopter rescue pilot at one of two Coast Guard stations in the Miami area. Like the nun, she was also anally raped and savagely beaten. He underlined a sentence in Sergeant Sosa's report where the victim recounted how her assailant made her put on a robe and turned off the light on an aquarium before raping her.

A photocopy of Sosa's handwritten case notes was paper clipped to her report. In them, she mentioned: "V worked pt-time as a fashion model when she was in college. Pictures of her appeared in both *Vogue* and *Cosmopolitan,* 10-12 years ago."

He leafed back through the nun's file to the statement about the chair that was shoved against her curtains. Why would a man whose face was concealed by a ski mask need to darken the rooms of women he was about to rape? Even if he was repulsed at the prospect of sexually assaulting a seventy-one-year-old woman whose hospital records showed was suffering from advanced osteoporosis, that didn't explain why he made the former fashion model put on a robe before he raped her.

He massaged his forehead with the tips of his fingers. Even more baffling was why the rapist apparently suffered an asthma attack when the younger woman told him, as a ruse to keep from being raped, that she was menstruating.

The criminologist paused to make some notes. It was clear from the unloaded gun under the pilot's pillow that the Wake-Up Rapist's modus operandi involved burglarizing the homes of his victims sometime prior to the night of the assault. It was probably during those entries that he had come across personal letters, diaries or newspaper clippings that contained details about the murders of the nun's co-workers in Africa and the death of the pilot's father in Vietnam.

He clicked his pen absently. It was hard to imagine two more different women than an elderly Catholic nun living above an inner city rescue mission and a junior grade Coast Guard lieutenant flying rescue missions out over the Atlantic. The rapist had selected them both from the hundreds of thousands of women in Miami for some reason.

The beating of the nun with the crucifix led him to wonder if the other victim was also Catholic. He found that Sosa had already explored that possibility. The Coast Guard pilot told her she had been an atheist all her life.

He put the case folders aside that night with far more questions than answers about the Wake-Up Rapes.

CHAPTER

10

He stood in line on a balmy Saturday evening at the Miami AMC Theatre behind a middle-aged black woman who was about to buy a ticket. This was the first time since he began watching her that he had seen her engage in any kind of recreation. She worked long hours every day and regularly took work home with her, even on weekends. As far as he could tell, she had no social life. Her children were grown and lived on the west coast. While they seldom got to Florida to visit her, they'd all be booking flights to Miami in a panic before long.

Three films at the multiplex were scheduled to start within minutes of one another. He wondered which she would pick. Anything with much violence seemed unlikely for someone in her line of work. Ditto explicit sex. That left the British comedy. Sure enough, she bought a ticket to it. Such a sweet movie for a lady with diabetes. He had found the insulin while going through her refrigerator earlier in the week. While he already knew a great deal about her, there were many other things he needed to know before they met. The constant presence of the Rottweiler in the fenced yard around her house complicated things. He had only been able to get inside once, on a day she took the dog to the vet.

He loitered in the theatre lobby, pretending to play a video game, while she bought a small popcorn and a diet Coke, then followed her inside and took a seat a couple of rows behind her. The number of scenes in the film she apparently found funny surprised him. Laugh while you can, Georgia.

CHAPTER

11

Roth and Bailey sat in a booth at a bar near the campus, cooling off after a Saturday afternoon game of racquetball. Their conversation soon turned to the 3 a.m. attacks.

"You know, you're really getting into this case, Doc," Bailey said, after ordering a draft beer. "I've got a wild idea. Why not come over and work with us for a while in the Sexual Battery Unit—as a cop."

Roth stopped sipping his beer and looked up at him.

"You're kidding."

"No, I'm not," Bailey insisted, his voice rising a register.

Roth chuckled.

"Look, you really want to understand sexual violence? Then you need to see it up close and personal, the way we do day after day. Believe me, you'd learn more about rape in a few months with us than in years of reading about it in your ivory tower." He ran a thumb and forefinger reflectively along the edge of his chin and continued.

"Hell, anthropologists go off and live with primitive tribes to learn their folkways, don't they? Sociologists have masqueraded as patients at alcohol and drug rehab centers to study addiction. I even read about a guy at NYU who cruised gay bathhouses to gather material for his doctoral dissertation. Why couldn't a criminologist study rape the same way? Someone like you could ..."

"Wait a minute," Roth said, with a palms-up gesture. "I'm no anthropologist. I don't do that kind of research."

"But you could, couldn't you?"

Roth peered at him over the rim of his beer mug. "I suppose so, but ..."

"But what?"

He wagged his head. "I'm basically just a numbers cruncher. I collect data on serial rapes and massage it looking for profile patterns. I don't know anything about police work."

"So, you could learn. You know, you already think a lot like a cop."

"What do you mean?"

"All that stuff you do at the university, digging through police files analyzing MO's—that's detective work. The main difference between us is that I carry a gun and badge and don't give a fuck about doin' a multivariate analysis on some dirt bag, like the one who raped the nun. I just want to find his ass and lock it up!"

Bailey's eyes narrowed reflectively. "Didn't you tell me that you just got a new grant?"

"Yeah, from Health and Human Services. Why?" Roth said, draining his glass and putting it down.

"Well, why not use it to work as a sexual battery detective?"

Roth waved a hand dismissively. "Come on … This is crazy!"

"What's crazy about it?" Bailey volleyed.

"Well, for one thing, no chief of police is going to let a criminology professor just walk into his department and do something like that."

"I'll bet you're wrong," Bailey said. "I think Crenshaw would go for the idea. He's always ready to try new things."

Roth was aware that Miami's Chief of Police had the reputation of being one of the most progressive law enforcement administrators in the country. He had become something of a political lightning rod by actively recruiting gays right along with other minorities.

"Of course, you'd have to go through the academy just like any other cop," Bailey added.

Roth stroked his beard. "And how long, pray tell, is the academy?"

"A thousand hours."

"A thousand hours!" Roth exclaimed.

"Wouldn't it be worth it to do something no criminologist ever has? You told us in our research methods seminar how hard it is to find new things to do in the social sciences."

Roth sighed. "Yeah, but ..."

"What could be more original than doing something like this?" Bailey pressed.

Roth grunted. "Tell me, just how many cadets over forty have you got in the Miami Police Academy right now?"

"Okay, so you'd be the first one," Bailey conceded. "You're still young enough to do it!"

"You sound like an Army recruiter trying to sign someone up for a hitch."

Bailey held his eyes. "Give me one good reason for not at least looking into it!" he said.

Roth gestured toward the policeman's hip. "You know how I feel about guns. I don't like them."

"I know ... I know," Bailey said, rolling his eyes. He pulled his jacket back slightly exposing the semi-automatic pistol on his waist. "Look, I've been in the department going on eight years now, and I've never fired this thing off the range. Despite what you see on TV, detectives rarely shoot anybody."

"That's really comforting," Roth said sarcastically. "Even if I was willing to do something like what you're suggesting and both the chief and my dean went along with it, how could I work in Sexual Battery? Don't all recruits go directly into uniformed patrol after the academy?"

"Most of them do," Bailey replied, "but it's really up to the chief where any new cop is assigned. One of the guys in my class went straight into narcotics and began working undercover without ever spending a day in uniform." He unclipped the gold and silver shield on his belt and put it on the table between them. "If Crenshaw wanted to, he could hand you one of these the day you graduate from the academy and assign you to the Sexual Battery Unit."

Something about the idea was beginning to intrigue Roth. He started to say something when Bailey's cell phone rang.

"Hold on. That's Sosa," he sighed. After speaking with her he said, "Off-duty isn't part of Maria's vocabulary. I gotta go."

Roth walked with him to the parking lot. "You really think your chief would be interested in a research project like that?" he said.

Bailey stood beside the open door of his unmarked car. "There's only one way to find out," he grinned. "Why don't we ask him?"

"You're persistent, aren't you?"

The detective stuck a toothpick in his mouth. "I'm a cop. I get paid to be pushy. What do you say? Do you want me to talk to the chief?"

Roth shrugged his shoulders. "Sure, why not?"

CHAPTER

12

It was a little after one when the figure in the ski mask threw several pounds of raw hamburger over the chain link fence at 5116 West Kendall Drive. The Rottweiler attacked the meat ravenously, making low, guttural sounds as it ate. When it had finished the food, the dog leapt against the fence, panting contentedly. Its pink tongue lolled across rows of jagged yellow teeth as it watched its benefactor.

The neighborhood was dark, except for a cone of golden haze coming from a street light. The man who had thrown the offering sat in the shadow of a large oak tree with his arms wrapped around his knees. He hummed softly, taking in the sweet scent of night-blooming jasmine.

A few days before, he had picked up a mutt at the Miami-Dade County Animal Shelter that was about the same size as the Rottweiler. He fed it an identical quantity of ground glass and hamburger, noting how long it took to kill the animal. Other than whimpering and groaning, the dog from the pound made little noise before it collapsed and died. The experiment was important, since silence was essential tonight.

A burst of police radio traffic came from the earpiece tucked beneath his mask. He cocked his head, listening attentively. Just a minor traffic accident miles away.

His eyes roamed up and down the block. Nearly an hour passed before the Rottweiler began to pace the yard restlessly. It threw itself on the grass when the hemorrhaging started, flailing from side to side, trying to escape the torment that consumed it. Foam sputtered from its mouth and nostrils, and its body began to convulse in spasms of bloody diarrhea and vomiting.

He knelt on the damp grass beside the fence, captivated by the drama that was taking place. The animal was on its side now, breathing heavily and shuddering. He thought of the hundreds of tiny, sharp cuts the glass was making as it churned through the dog's intestines.

The swelling in his groin surprised him. He unzipped his jeans and touched the sticky film of pre-ejaculate in his shorts. He had no idea that seeing the woman's dog dying would be so exciting. The animal's breath gradually became shallower, and then stopped. He watched the glassy eyes of the lifeless form for a long moment before putting on his gloves and vaulting the fence.

CHAPTER

13

Roth had been putting off meeting with Chief Crenshaw to discuss Bailey's professor-policeman project. Unconscious resistance, he guessed. As fascinating as the idea was, he was sure it would be an incredibly difficult thing to pull off. Even if the chief was willing to go along with such a novel form of research, the City of Miami and the university might not be. A criminology professor becoming a cop to study rape? He could imagine the knee-jerk reaction of his peers at the prospect of one of their number violating, however briefly, the time honored tradition of scholarly isolation from the outside world. Learning of the second attack by the 3 a.m. rapist helped him resolve his ambivalence. He called the chief's office the following morning and made an appointment.

"Well, I did it," he told Bailey, after reaching him at the Sexual Battery Unit. "I'm going to meet with Crenshaw on Friday."

"That's great! I was about to give up on you."

*　*

Roth inched along in a stream of traffic toward his one-thirty appointment with Chief Tom Crenshaw downtown. Off to his left, a group of pelicans rode the thermals above Biscayne Bay, swooping low over the water in search of food. He could see the brightly-colored sails of windsurfers through the breaks in the natural wall of sea grapes and bougainvilleas that lined the expressway; a lone cigarette boat skipped across the blue-green water, registering in his ears like the whine of an angry mosquito.

He switched on the radio. "¡Venga aqui hoy. La vendada termina mañana (Come on in today! The sale ends tomorrow)!" an announcer said excit-

41

edly. A bumper sticker on the Econoline van in front of him, proclaiming, CUBA LIBRE! (FREE CUBA!), underscored the reality that Anglos were now officially a minority in Miami.

*　*

He waited in the foyer of Crenshaw's office until a slender black secretary approached him. "The Chief will see you now, Doctor."

She ushered him into a large room with dark wood paneling and plush carpeting. The city skyline loomed beyond the windows of the twelve-story building.

Chief Crenshaw's eyes fastened immediately on his visitor. "Ah, Dr. Roth, it's good to meet you!" he said, with a trace of a southern accent. He gripped Roth's extended hand firmly.

Miami's Chief of Police was a man in his late-fifties with silver gray hair. The well-tailored pinstripe suit, white shirt and burgundy tie he had on made him look more like a stockbroker than a police chief. Roth recalled seeing him on the cover of *Parade Magazine* a few months before in a dark blue uniform with a row of four gold stars on each shoulder. The *Parade* article described how Crenshaw's department had achieved the best police civil rights record in the nation under his leadership.

Crenshaw had been hired as chief some years before to clean up notorious corruption in the wake of a scandal that the media had dubbed the "Miami River Cops Case." During his first year on the job, seven city officers were indicted and convicted of stealing narcotics from major drug dealers and then murdering them.

The walls of the office were filled with awards and badges from other police departments where he had served. A laminated copy of the front page of the *Miami Herald* showed Crenshaw in a sweat-drenched shirt, rallying his officers with a bullhorn during one of the city's worst riots. The headline read 'ONE RIOT—ONE CHIEF.' In other photographs, he was standing with prominent political and entertainment figures; one showed him greeting the President of the United States and First Lady as they stepped off Air Force One at Miami International.

"Detective Bailey tells me you're interested in coming over here and working with us for a while," Crenshaw said directly.

Roth nodded. "I guess it goes without saying that the chance to get a firsthand look at rape as a police officer would be quite an opportunity for any criminologist," he replied. He had started to say *cop* but caught himself.

"I agree. Frankly, I'm surprised that no one in your field has done it before."

Roth settled into the high-backed leather chair, trying not to appear too eager. In a highly technical era, when most criminologists spent their days at computers doing armchair research, this was a chance to get access to a completely new perspective on sexual violence: to interact with victims in the aftermath of a brutal act he and other criminologists had so far only studied from a distance.

"I've already talked with my dean about the project," he began. "He's all for it, except ..."

"Except what?"

"A university sabbatical is usually a year, but nine months is the most release time I can get right now. We're really short-handed in our department."

Crenshaw frowned. "Hell, Doctor, the academy alone is six months."

"I know."

The chief looked at him intently.

"Are you really sure you want to do this?" he asked.

"Yes, I am," Roth replied firmly.

Crenshaw leaned back in his chair and clasped his hands on his chest.

"Hmm ... there may be a way to shorten the training in order to give you more time in the Sexual Battery Unit."

"How?"

"Even though our academy is a thousand hours, state law only requires that a recruit successfully complete half that much training in order to be certified as a police officer. If you attended the first three months, I could waive the rest and have you sworn in."

"You could do that?"

Crenshaw tugged at a wattle of flesh under his chin and smiled. "It'd raise some eyebrows, but, yeah, I could. That would give you six months as a sexual battery detective. You could learn quite a bit in that length of time."

Roth was barely able to contain his excitement.

The chief raised a cautionary hand. "Even if we cut it in half, the academy still won't be easy. The PT alone is a ball-buster."

"PT?"

"Physical training," he explained, eyeing Roth appraisingly. "What kind of shape are you in?"

He shrugged. "Pretty good. I, er … play racquetball."

"You need to understand you'd be going through rigorous conditioning every day with men and women who are half your age."

He felt a little intimidated.

"Ever been in the service?" Crenshaw asked

He shook his head.

"I was a marine," Crenshaw said. "Our PT program reminds me of the boot camp I went through at Parris Island. Right after I took over the department, I put a former leatherneck in charge of it." He chortled. "Meanest son-of-a-bitch I could find."

"When does your next academy begin?" Roth asked.

Crenshaw checked his calendar. "In a little over two weeks. Could you be ready that soon?"

"I believe so," Roth said resolutely. "My dean mentioned it to our president recently. He likes the 'hands-on' community service appeal of a project like this."

"I think it would be good for us, too," Crenshaw opined. "A lot of people think of police as some kind of secret fraternity. We don't have anything to hide from anyone in this department. Letting an outsider like you have the run of the place for six months would be pretty convincing proof of that."

Roth's mind was racing. He was sure he could talk another faculty member into covering his graduate seminar in Criminal Sexuality, and his teaching assistant could take over his victimology course for the rest of the semester. With a little guidance, Greg Hastings, his senior graduate assistant, could keep his grants running until he was back at the university.

Crenshaw buzzed his secretary and had her bring him an application packet. "We can sidestep a lot of this stuff," he said. "Two weeks wouldn't normally be anywhere near enough time to process a police application. Just checking employment and character references can take a couple of months by itself." He crossed out a number of sections on the application form and initialed them. "Just put me down as a reference," he said. "By the way, how many degrees do you have?"

"Four. Why?"

He smiled. "Just checking. We have a two year college requirement." He handed Roth the mass of forms. "You'll find a lot of bureaucratic bullshit in there that there's no way around. Personnel will want a complete physical, including a stress EKG. They'll give you a battery of psychological tests and set up an interview for you with one of our shrinks. He'll ask you questions about everything from how you feel about your mother to your thoughts about germs on doorknobs. We'll also need to schedule a polygraph as soon as possible. I assume you're not wanted anywhere."

Roth worked his hands together uneasily. "There is one thing I should mention," he said.

"Oh ... you mean the arrest while you were a graduate student at Berkeley?" the chief said casually.

Roth blinked in astonishment. "How did you ..."

Crenshaw picked up a paper on his desk. "I ran a records check on you as soon as Bailey told me what you had in mind. Berkeley PD faxed a copy of the arrest report."

"You don't think that will be a problem?" Roth said hopefully.

Crenshaw tossed the report on his desk. "Shit. Blocking traffic during a campus sit-in to protest acid rain twenty years ago? It was only a misdemeanor. Besides, it's ancient history. Don't worry about it."

Roth hadn't thought about the disorderly conduct arrest in years. Looking back, he was surprised that he was only arrested once, given the number of protests he took part in. He cleared his throat. "I also smoked quite a bit of grass back in those days," he said sheepishly.

A ripple of mirth showed on the chief's face. "Any more confessions?"

"No."

"You'll be relieved to know that it's rare these days to find a police applicant who hasn't at least experimented with marijuana; as long as you're not still getting high or growing hemp in your backyard, you'll be fine."

He covered a few more points before walking Roth to the door. "Okay, here's the deal," he said, resting a hand on his shoulder, "you bring me passing scores for the first half of the academy, and I'll make you a detective third grade and assign you to the SBU for six months. Fair enough?"

"Fair enough."

Crenshaw's voice grew serious. "Remember, if you fail any part of the course, we won't be able to do this."

"I understand." Roth's pulse quickened as he left the chief's office. *Am I really going to do this?*

CHAPTER

14

Roth tore the envelope open quickly when he saw the familiar palm tree logo of the City of Miami. It was the letter he had been waiting for, appointing him as a cadet in the next academy class. His enthusiasm faded when he came to the last paragraph:

Cadets will appear in uniform promptly at 0800 hours on the first day of class with their hair worn above the collar. Sideburns will not extend below the middle of the ear. Facial hair of any kind is prohibited.

He stroked the full beard he had worn since he was a sophomore in college. It had become part of his identity over the years. Even his wife had never seen him without it. He wasn't going to be working in uniform. Why did he have to shave his beard to become a sexual battery detective for six months?

Of all the asinine ... ! He let the thought pass. No big deal. It would grow back.

* *

On the day before the course was scheduled to begin, he sat on a bench in the academy locker room, surveying the mountain of supplies he had just been issued; ironically, much of it was for use in the second half of the program. He examined each item carefully before stowing it in the gray, metal locker. Among the things he had received were a black five-cell flashlight; a lightweight, bulletproof vest; a yellow raincoat that said MIAMI PO-LICE; and a set of templates for working traffic accidents. Three short-sleeved khaki uniform shirts had the word CADET stitched above the left pocket, with City of Miami police patches on each sleeve. He placed the uniforms in the locker, along with a pair of shiny black shoes, before inspecting the table of contents in the study manual.

His hands grew clammy when he took the lid off a box that held the new .40 caliber semiautomatic pistol he had signed for. This was the closest he had ever been to a gun. He wiped his palms on his pants. The firearms portion of the course would be coming up soon. He had to find a way to overcome his lifelong aversion to guns if he was going to make it through the academy. All he had to do, he told himself, was desensitize himself to the weapon for a short period of time. He would do it the same way many people overcome their fear of airplanes and elevators: by repeated exposure to the dreaded object under carefully controlled conditions. For several minutes, he sat looking at the blue-steel pistol in his lap, as if it were a snake that might strike without warning.

Finally, he set his jaw determinedly and began reading the instruction manual that came with the gun:

Operation of the Glock .40 Caliber Semiautomatic Pistol. Step One: Eject the magazine.

The empty clip dropped into his palm when he located the release button and pressed it. *That was easy enough.*

First, insert cartridges into the magazine until it is full.

He took a brass cartridge from one of the ten boxes of ammunition he had received for the course and held it between his thumb and forefinger, reminding himself that it was just an inanimate object. Without the malice of a human will, it was incapable of harming anyone. Emboldened by the thought, he dumped a fistful of bullets into his hand and began loading them one by one.

Oh, so they go in this way. He was surprised at how quickly the bullets were swallowed by the magazine. It was as if the mechanism he had just released from its cocoon was thirsty. He shoved his glasses back on the bridge of his nose and continued reading.

<u>Next, insert the loaded magazine into the weapon.</u>

He did that.

<u>To chamber a round, pull the slide back with your free hand.</u>

He gripped the slide and drew it back.

<u>Now, release the slide, allowing it to feed a cartridge from the magazine into the chamber.</u>

The gun made a sharp, metallic sound when he let go of the slide.

<u>Caution: The weapon is now ready to fire.</u>

"Oh, no!" he exclaimed. His pulse began to race. He put the gun on the bench and stepped back from it. His mouth went dry as he turned the pages in the manual, trying to find out how to unload the pistol. He took a deep breath, telling himself not to panic. Minutes passed. Frantic now, he walked the length of the locker room, looking for someone who could help. The place appeared deserted. The last of the other cadets had left a half hour before.

Carefully putting the gun back in the box, he started down the hall with it. A light was coming from beneath one of the doors. The nameplate above it said SGT. J.T. AKERVIK. He rapped tentatively.

"Yeah," a gruff voice responded.

He cracked the door a few inches and peered inside. The walls of the office were bare, except for a dartboard and a plaque bearing the globe and anchor insignia of the U.S. Marine Corps., with the phrase Semper Fidelis inscribed on it. The steel barrels of a row of twelve gauge shotguns gleamed menacingly behind the glass of a locked cabinet. Pieces of police equipment were stacked around the room: canisters of pepper spray; helmets with face visors; and 'body bunkers'—shields that officers can crouch behind during riots to protect themselves from rocks and bottles.

When Roth entered, Sgt. Joe Akervik was unpacking a box of ASP batons—short, inconspicuous metal tubes that can be telescoped into formidable striking weapons with the snap of a wrist.

"Excuse me ..."

Akervik glanced at him with obvious annoyance. "Who are you?"

"My name's David Roth ... I'm a cadet."

Akervik put his hands on his hips. "You're shittin' me!"

"I have my appointment letter right here," he said quickly. He tucked the box with the loaded Glock under his arm and handed the sergeant an envelope.

Akervik read the letter with a disinterested grunt. "Oh, yeah," he said sarcastically. "You're the chief's ninety-day wonder. I got a memo on you." The sergeant's face suddenly contorted. He sneezed loudly.

"Gesundheit," Roth offered.

Akervik drew the back of his hand across his nose. "Fuckin' pollen," he muttered.

He was a short, stocky man in his mid-forties with ugly features that included a wide mouth, a large, vein-streaked nose and a wine-colored birthmark that covered much of the left side of his face. He regarded Roth with close-set, mean eyes. "Little old for a cadet, aren't you, buddy?"

"I'm going to be working in the Sexual Battery Unit for six months as part of a research project."

"So, what do you want?"

Roth's fingers tightened on the box. "Sergeant, I'm afraid ... well, uh, I've loaded this gun, and I can't figure out how to ..."

Akervik looked at him agape. "You *what?*"

"I was trying to ..."

"You fuckin' moron! Put that box on the desk right now!" he snapped. His face became livid as he removed the Glock from the box and inspected it. "Jesus H. Christ!" he muttered, ejecting the magazine and racking the slide. The live round that had been in the chamber spun through the air and landed near his feet.

"I'm really sorry about this," Roth said miserably.

Akervik's nostrils flared. "Tell me, thumb dick, can you read?"

"What?"

He pointed to a sign in bold red letters above his door.

ABSOLUTELY NO LOADED FIREARMS
OFF THE RANGE AT ANY TIME!

Akervik picked up the bullet from the floor, glowering at Roth. He emptied the gun's magazine and scooped the cartridges into a pile on his desk. The cords in his neck stood out when he spoke. "Listen, fuzzy, I don't know what you're doing here, and I don't give a shit! I don't care if you're the chief's brother. You ever do a dumb fuckin' thing like this again, I'm going to personally shove my hand down your throat and rip your spleen out!"

Roth swallowed hard, folded the appointment letter and put it back in his pocket.

"We expect cadets to make mistakes ... but not with guns. A gun's the worst thing you can screw up with in this business!"

"I ... I understand."

"You better! The academy hasn't even started yet, and you're already on my shit list." He put the semiautomatic back in the box and handed it to him. "Now, try to make it back to your locker without having an accident." Roth's hand was on the door when the sergeant called after him. "And lose that fuckin' beard by tomorrow!"

He left the academy in a daze. *Thumb dick? Moron? Fuzzy?* His face flushed with anger. Who was this knuckle-dragging Neanderthal to speak to him like that? Until today, he had been *Doctor, Professor* and *Sir* to other people. In a matter of seconds, the gargoyle in uniform had stripped him of the professional identify it had taken him years to build.

What have I gotten myself into?

CHAPTER

15

The Miami Police Department's triangular banner hung limply beneath the American flag in the still morning air. The cadets milled around on the parched grass of the drill field, awaiting instructions. Roth stood off by himself, feeling out of place. He hadn't worn a uniform since he was a cub scout in Brooklyn; he was already having reservations about the project after his not-off-on-the-right-foot encounter with Sgt. Akervik. A number of the other cadets stared at him, obviously curious about what a middle-aged man was doing in their midst. A few whispered remarks or giggled. About half of the class was made up of women, and a third was black or Hispanic.

He ran his hand over the smooth surface of his cheek. The visage he saw in the mirror that morning when he put down his razor shocked him. The face staring at him in the harsh glare of the bathroom light seemingly belonged to a stranger. He suddenly appeared much older than he thought of himself as looking. The dark, full beard had masked faint creases and a clutter of age lines that now seemed prominent.

At exactly 8 a.m., Sgt. Akervik emerged from the main academy building wearing dark blue, military-style fatigues and a wide-brimmed campaign hat. He stood rigidly while several instructors assembled the cadets into four rows.

Akervik took two steps forward and positioned himself squarely in front of the class. "I am Sgt. Akervik, senior self-defense instructor and range master here at the academy," he announced in a magisterial voice. "Let me say that you are, without a doubt, the sorriest looking bunch of assholes I've ever seen out here!"

He walked slowly along the row of cadets, shaking his head disgustedly.

"Any former-marines?" he asked. Two hands went up; one of them belonged to a muscular black man in his mid-twenties; the other belonged to a stocky Cuban American who looked a little older than the other recruits.

"Two out of fifty; that's just fuckin' great!" He paused in front of a loose-lipped youth with sunglasses and a complexion that showed traces of acne. He tapped the cadet's chest with his swagger stick. "What's your name?"

"J-Joel Fenwick," the cadet replied in a timorous voice.

Akervik brought his bulbous nose within an inch of his face. "That's Joel Fenwick, Sergeant!"

"Joel Fenwick, Sergeant!"

"Take off those faggot sunglasses when I'm talking to you, boy!" The cadet snatched the yellow-hued aviator sunglasses off his face and stuffed them hurriedly in his shirt pocket. Akervik scowled. "You aren't a fairy, are you, Fenwick?"

"No!"

"Goddamnit! That's 'No, *Sergeant!*' How do you expect to become a police officer if you can't follow simple instructions?"

"I ..."

"Drop and give me twenty-five!"

"Sir?" Fenwick said, with a perplexed look.

"Push-ups, you idiot!" the sergeant thundered.

Roth was already thankful to be in the last row. He and the other cadets watched Fenwick get down on his knees and struggle through fifteen push-ups. His arms began to shake, and his cheeks puffed out. He grunted through half of the nineteenth one before giving up and collapsing on the grass.

Akervik shook his head. "Pathetic!" he said.

He moved on to the second row. "Stand up straight!" he barked at a pudgy recruit with dull eyes and tousled hair. "Get those shoulders back! Suck in that gut!"

The cadet took a deep breath and held it. The sergeant's eyes narrowed to slits. "Better chain the refrigerator, porky! You keep stuffing Twinkies and potato chips into your fat face, you won't last a week out here!" He knocked the cap off the recruit's head with his stick. "Pick it up!" he ordered. The cadet's face reddened as he bent and retrieved his hat.

Roth was aghast. *God in heaven! What is this, a concentration camp?*

Akervik stopped when he came to a short, female cadet. "What's your name, little girl?" he said in a feigned dainty voice. The woman looked straight ahead with a stiff, blank face.

"Rita Fuentes, Sergeant!"

Akervik leaned forward and cupped a hand to his ear. "I can't hear you!"

"Rita Fuentes, Sergeant!" she shrilled.

"I still can't hear you. C'mon Fuentes, sound off like you've got a pair hangin' down there, even though you don't!"

There was a catch in the woman's voice as she shouted her name again.

Roth's stomach plummeted like a runaway elevator when Akervik stepped in front of him. The sergeant grinned malevolently. "Well, now, fuzzy, you look almost human without that beard. You haven't shot your dick off yet have you?" Akervick's face was so close that Roth felt a droplet of spittle hit his cheek.

"No … Sergeant."

Akervik turned to one of the other instructors. "This guy's a college professor," he said. "Can you believe that? The department's going to hell. I wonder how much longer it'll be before they start hiring transsexual midgets as cops."

The sergeant finished the inspection and stood in front of the class. "See this?" he said, pointing at the birthmark on his face. "Ugly, isn't it? I've been on the job nearly twenty-two years. Can you imagine how many IA complaints I'd have in my personnel file by now if I'd punched out every drunk who made a smart-assed remark about it?" His eyes shifted to Joel Fenwick, Rita Fuentes and the cadet he had called 'porky.' "A few of you just got a taste of our stress desensitization program. Like a lot of other parts of the academy, it's not real pleasant, but there's a good rea- son for it. We don't want any of you opening up somebody's head with a nightstick just because you got your feelings hurt, especially with every asshole and his brother out there runnin' around with cell phone cameras, ready to put the whole thing on CNN."

Even at the early hour, the subtropical heat and humidity were merciless; a dark butterfly of sweat covered the front of the sergeant's shirt. "You better have skin like a fuckin' rhino by the time you leave here, or you'll never make it on the streets!" he roared. "That's why we're gonna try as hard as we can to piss you off."

Roth's jaw tightened. *Fascist bastard! You've already succeeded with me!*

"If you think you can't take the pressure, do us all a favor and quit right now. You want a job where people are glad to see you? The fire academy is right across the street," he sneered, jerking a thumb over this shoulder. He walked over to one of the other instructors. "They're all yours, Corporal," he said.

The man he addressed clapped his hands and shouted, "All right, everybody, fall out and muster on the track! On the double! Let's go! Move your asses!"

The cadet jogging alongside Roth shot him a glance. "Lotsa fun, huh?" he said.

"Yeah ... never had such a great time!"

⋆   ⋆

The PT phase of the academy proved far more grueling than what Roth had imagined. He had already begun to dread the sight of the asphalt track shimmering in the morning sun. The academy day began each morning at 8 a.m. with a two-mile jog. During it, Akervik and the other instructors mercilessly taunted the recruits. The severity of the hazing alone caused several cadets to drop out during the first few days.

Joel Fenwick was one of them. By the end of each run, sweat burned the professor's eyes, and his feet were sore from the struggle to keep up with his younger peers.

After the daily run came a punishing series of sit-ups, push-ups and jumping jacks, followed by classroom lectures and practical exercises designed to test the recruits' grasp of what they had been taught. Roth practiced 'speed-cuffing' while an instructor hovered over him with a stop watch; he learned how to remove a belligerent drunk from behind the wheel of a car by applying fingertip pressure to the mandibular joint and hypoglossal nerves in the head; he practiced CPR on a dummy nicknamed 'Ressuci-Annie'; and he swung his ASP baton at a six-foot rubber man known as 'Numb John' until his arm felt as if it was about to fall off. By the end of the second week, he was half-convinced that Akervik was the reincarnation of Torquemada from the Spanish Inquisition. Any doubts he may have had about that were eliminated during the next phase of the PT program. Department regulations required that all cadets personally experience the physical effects of being sprayed with a canister of "OC" (Oleoresin Capsicum, a caustic derivative of cayenne pepper), a substance which they would be carrying as patrol officers. Even though Roth would never spend a day in uniform, "OC familiarization" was still part of the five hundred hour training curriculum he had to pass. He recalled the chief's warning that failing any part of the course would mean the end of the "professor-policeman" project.

He stood nervously in line with the other cadets while a couple of instructors began hooking up garden hoses. As soon as they were turned on and the water was flowing freely, one by one the recruits were subjected to a blast of OC in the face. Sgt. Akervik stood to the side of each cadet victim, calmly pointing out the debilitating effects of the chemical weapon to the rest of the class.

The line inched steadily forward on the parched grass. Roth's stomach drew into a tight knot when he heard the female cadet in front of him breathing heavily and trying to stifle tears just before she was sprayed. When his turn came, as soon as the searing mist hit his eyes he began to claw at the air, flailing about in blind panic, unable to see or breathe as his throat constricted. It felt as if a swarm of yellow jackets had somehow gotten beneath his eyelids and was stinging him furiously. One of the instructors directed a stream of cool water into his face. "More ... more!" he croaked, frantically rubbing the inflamed orbs of his eyes. He had never experienced anything as terrifying and painful in his life. His eyes and face still burned for hours afterward.

"Sheeet, man … I'd rather have my balls slammed in a car door than ever go through that again!" the cadet next to him confided as the class shuffled off the field.

*　*

The "OC" ordeal was followed a couple of days later by the introduction to the class of yet another non-lethal weapon in the police arsenal. This time it was the "electronic control device" (ECD). The object that Sgt. Akervik pointed at Roth's chest from a distance of about eight feet looked a little like a TV remote. He heard a faint clicking sound when Akervik fired the ECD. An instant later, two razor-sharp barbs attached to thin strands of wire penetrated his gym shirt, delivering a thunderbolt of 50,000 volts that knocked him off his feet and left him writhing helplessly on the ground. He lay there dazed, like a beached whale, with no muscular control for seconds that seemed an eternity.

*　*

That night he soaked in a tub of Epsom salts. Every muscle in his body ached from the spasms he experienced after being jolted by the ECD. He draped a steaming wash cloth across his face, wondering if he could survive another week at the police academy, let alone nine.

CHAPTER

16

Sgt. Akervik placed a life-sized replica of the human head on a table in front of the class and motioned toward the neck with a laser pointer. "The CRT or carotid restraint tactic involves shutting down the flow of blood to the brain by applying pressure to a person's throat with your forearm and bicep," he explained. "It's dangerous as hell. Keep in mind that the decision to use a CRT on a resisting suspect is damn near as serious as shooting him. If you don't let up as soon as he blacks out, you can cause permanent brain damage, even death."

Roth thought to himself, *Finally, something I can really use! Next time I have a problem with anyone in the Contracts and Grants office at UM, I'll just choke them out.*

Roth was only half listening as Akervik droned on. He had been in a funk all day over having to miss the annual convention of the American Society of Criminology because of the academy.

"Fuzzy, are you paying attention?" Akervik scowled.

Roth stiffened in his seat suddenly like a grade school student who'd been caught throwing spitballs. "Yes, sir."

"Get up here," Akervik ordered. "You, too, Pee Wee," he called out to a tall, black cadet in the back of the room.

The sergeant had a demeaning moniker for every member of the class. While Roth hadn't worn a beard since the academy began, he had been 'Fuzzy' ever since the incident with the loaded gun.

"Okay, now, listen up," Akervik announced to the class. "We're gonna do a role play using the CRT. Here's the situation: Me and Washington have just been dispatched to a domestic violence call. Fuzzy's old lady comes to the door and tells us that her asshole husband is pumped up on angel dust. From the bruises on her face, it looks as if he mistook her for a piñata. We tell him he's under arrest, but he says he ain't goin'."

He turned toward Roth. "C'mon, let's see a little hostility."

Roth shrugged. "Sorry, but I'm not going with you guys," he said.

"For Chrissakes!" Akervik bellowed. "You're supposed to be whacked out on PCP. Act like it!"

Roth crouched in a boxer's stance and clenched his hands. "You'll have to fight me," he said.

Akervik rolled his eyes. "You'll have to fight me," he mimicked in an effeminate voice.

"Roth, you're such a pussy!"

"Go fuck yourself!" Roth shouted. Shock registered on the faces of the other cadets.

Even Akervik appeared stunned. He reflexively took a half-step backward. "Okay, now try to hit me," he challenged.

Roth swung his fist as hard as he could directly at the sergeant's face. Akervik proved remarkably agile for a short, stocky man. He deflected the blow, then spun and clamped a hairy, tattooed arm across Roth's throat. Roth grabbed his forearm with both hands, trying in vain to loosen the grip that kept tightening on his neck. He was aware of feeling lightheaded just before he blacked out; the next thing he knew, he was sitting on the floor with his hands cuffed behind his back. After Akervik uncuffed him, he made his way back to his desk on wobbly legs.

The rage that had momentarily consumed him left him badly shaken. For the first time in his life, David Roth had *wanted* to harm another human being—not just hurt him, but smash his face in! Even more disturbing was the realization that the prospect of injuring Akervik had been, in some strange way, pleasurable. As much as Roth hated the drunk driver who took his family from him, he had never been conscious of a desire to injure or kill the man. The training exercise had just awakened something primordial that frightened him. He recalled that Mark Twain once said that every man is like the moon, with a dark side he keeps hidden. He vowed that he would never lose control of himself like that again. *Never.*

＊　＊

The following week's training schedule at the academy held a sur-prise: Monday afternoon included a two hour lecture on rape investigation by Sgt. Maria Sosa. Roth was sitting in a sea of khaki uniforms when she entered the classroom in a pair of slacks, a white silk blouse and a navy blue blazer. Bailey hadn't exaggerated; she was a strikingly attrac-tive woman in her mid-thirties with smooth olive skin, medium length coal-black hair and high cheek bones; her full lips curved slightly down-ward, giving her mouth a sensual, petulant look.

"Most of you probably don't think of uniformed officers as detectives," she began, "but the truth is that most rape investigations start the moment a patrol car arrives. You're usually going to be the first contact victims have with the police. Whether you're warm and sympathetic, or come across like an old *Dragnet* re-run, can affect a woman's ability to recall the details of what happened as well as her willingness to cooperate." She turned off her cell phone when it rang, briefly exposing a slender hip. "I'm going to give you some handouts on the different types of serial rapists that have been identified," she told the class. "We'll be talking briefly about each of them today."

One of the documents she passed out held the logo of the FBI's Be-havioral Science Unit. A footnote on the first page indicated that the ma-terial was based on a Department of Justice research project conducted by David A. Roth, Ph.D. It was strange to be sitting in a classroom as a stu-dent listening to someone lecture on his rape typology.

At one point during Sosa's discussion of Stalker Rapists, Roth raised his hand.

"Yes?"

"Sergeant, aren't many stalkers also fetishists who take things from their victims?"

Sosa's eyebrows arched. "Yes … that's true." She explained to the class, "A fetish is a trophy or memento that the Stalker Rapist later uses to recre-ate a particular sexual assault in his mind. He needs some physical object to psychologically reconnect himself to the rape; it doesn't have to be anything explicitly erotic, like a pair of panties or bra. It might be something very ordinary, such as the victim's address book or toothbrush."

The police reports Roth had seen indicated that nothing was taken from either of the Wake-Up Rapist's victims; he wanted to urge Sosa to have both women check again carefully for anything that might be missing, no matter how small.

She kept glancing at him during her lecture. He was sure she was wondering what a man his age was doing in a cadet uniform, let alone why he was asking questions about sexual fetishism. He assumed that, after their run-in on the phone, Frank Bailey had been reluctant to tell her about the 'professor-policeman' project that was already underway.

When the class was over, other cadets gathered around her with questions. Roth wanted to talk to her about the Wake-Up Rapes, but that would have involved revealing things that could only have come from Bailey.

CHAPTER

17

Roth stood on the seven yard line of the pistol range with the .40 caliber Glock strapped to his waist. This was the moment he had been dreading for weeks; he was going to have to fire the gun today. He wiped a film of sweat from his forehead with the back of his hand and fixed his eyes on the paper target.

"Most police shootings take place at short distances, just like this," Akervik told the class. "Looks easy, doesn't it?" He snorted. "Keep in mind these targets aren't trying to kill you. If somebody ever points a gun at you, believe me, you'll be scared so shitless, you'll be lucky to hit anything, no matter how close you are or how good a shot you may be. The average number of hits for a cop in a combat situation is only 3 out of 10 shots."

A lanky range instructor with a weathered face threw in, "Spray and pray—that's what it comes down to on the streets."

Roth put on his ear protectors and waited tensely for the sound of Akervik's whistle. As soon as he heard the shrill blast, he jerked the Glock from its holster. Popping sounds were already coming from the guns of cadets on either side of him. He held the pistol with both hands, trying to stop shaking long enough to align the sights on the paper man.

Akervik raised the protective muff on one of Roth's ears and bellowed, "What the fuck are you waiting for? For Chrissakes, shoot!"

Roth slowly drew back the trigger, closing his eyes when the Glock recoiled with a flash. He missed the target completely with his first few shots; as the afternoon wore on, however, shafts of light finally began to poke through scattered holes on its surface.

Akervik squinted disapprovingly at the crimninologist's target. "Look how your shots are pullin' to the left. You're jerkin' the trigger. Stroke it gently—like it's a woman's tit." He squinted at Roth suspiciously. "You have touched a woman's tit haven't you, Fuzzy?"

"Yes, sir." *Asshole*, he thought, firing again.

Akervik shoved his ball cap back on his head and spat on the ground. "You still don't have a single round in the kill zone," he complained. "You *do* know where it is, don't you?"

"Yes, sir. *K-5*," Roth replied, referring to the innermost circle on the paper man's chest.

"Good! How about trying to hit it?"

His shooting continued to improve throughout the week, though his overall marksmanship remained dismal. On Friday, he managed to meet the minimum qualifying score after three tries.

＊　＊

The class spent the second week of the firearms course on a portion of the range called 'Hogan's Alley.' The alley resembled a Hollywood movie set. Its narrow streets were lined with the facades of stores and houses. Booby traps lurked everywhere in the form of remote-controlled paper men. They hid behind cutaway cars and lurked in stairwells, alleys and darkened doorways, always ready to pop up at Akervik's command.

During a robbery-in-progress exercise, Roth ran with a shotgun toward the side of a building; he had nearly reached it when he slipped. The shotgun went off with a deafening roar when he pitched forward and landed on the ground. He scrambled to his feet with his ears still ringing, racking a fresh shell and firing at a paper man that sprang from behind a parked car. The shotgun blast bruised his shoulder and left the acrid smell of cordite hanging in the humid air.

Akervik tore off his ball cap and threw it on the ground. "Fuzzy, you dumb fuck! What part of 'always keep your finger off the trigger when you run' didn't you understand?" he yelled. "You're a goddamn college professor! Why can't you grasp something that simple?"

Roth inspected the raspberry abrasion on his knee beneath the torn uniform pants while Akervik continued ridiculing his performance to the rest of the class.

*   *

On the last day of the firearms course, Roth swabbed the barrel of his Glock with a clean, white patch; somehow, he had made it through what for him was the most daunting part of the academy; he had put five hundred rounds through the .40 caliber semiautomatic. It was no more mysterious or frightening now than any of the computers he regularly worked with at the university. He put the weapon back in his locker and looked at the black residue of gunpowder on his hands. *What a stupid waste of time for a six-month career as a sexual battery detective.*

*   *

A criminalist from the state crime lab was lecturing the cadets on trace evidence the following day when a secretary entered the room and handed Roth an urgent message from the dean's office. The professor who had been teaching his Criminal Sexuality graduate seminar had just called in sick. Roth glanced at his watch. If he left now, he could make it in time to cover the class.

He took a shortcut to the campus and parked hurriedly in the faculty parking lot. A couple of minutes later, he dashed up the front steps of the Memorial Building in uniform, with his cadet cap in hand amid the stares of students. He had just picked up his lecture notes and locked his office when he heard a familiar voice behind him.

"Well … well, I do believe it's Officer Roth."

His spirits sank when he turned and saw Professor Wayne Phelps. His hopes of slipping on and off campus undetected by any of his peers were now dashed. Like Roth, Phelps was one of five full professors of criminology at the University of Miami. He was a slightly built, meticulously groomed man with snow white hair and quick, liquid eyes. At sixty-seven, he was the oldest member of the criminology faculty as well as the most outspoken critic of the kind of 'hands on' research Roth was now conducting.

Phelps flashed a sardonic grin. "To what do we owe the honor of this rare sighting of UM's answer to Dirty Harry?" he asked.

"Janet had been covering my afternoon seminar," he explained. "She's out sick."

Phelps' bushy eyebrows rose. "Surely, you're not going to teach it wearing *that*?"

"I didn't have time to change."

Phelps pointed to the plastic nameplate on his khaki shirt that said D.A. Roth. "You know what they say, old boy: if you're still wearing a name tag after thirty-five, you've probably made a bad career move somewhere along the way," he chortled, drawing him to one side. "Tell me, are you packing heat?" he asked in a hushed voice.

"I'm a cadet, Wayne. Cadets don't carry guns. Look, I've got to go. I'll be late for class."

"Well … *ciao!*" Phelps called after him.

* *

It was the first time he had been on campus since the research project began. Nine graduate students were seated around a long table in the conference room when he entered. "Professor Collins is ill. I'll be with you today," he explained, still catching his breath after running up three flights.

The students looked as if a stranger had just entered their midst. The familiar, musty scent of the room immediately enveloped him; the pale green walls that had absorbed the verbalizations of generations of faculty and students comforted him like the appearance of an old friend. A slat on the window blinds was crooked, just as it had been thirteen years before when he came to the university as a freshly-minted Berkeley Ph.D. The trash can in the corner overflowed with soft drink cans, candy wrappers and other detritus onto the coffee-stained floor. How good it was to be back in his own world again, if only for an hour.

"Where did you leave off last time?" he asked.

A male student with retro-looking sideburns said, "Dr. Collins was talking about the relationship between sexual violence and homicide. She had just mentioned the 'Stalker Sadist' from your rape typology."

"Okay," he said, opening his notes. He slipped off one of the shiny, black patent leather shoes under the table and unfastened his clip-on tie. "The Stalker Sadist, or *SS*, as I refer to him in my typology, is by far the most dangerous of all sexual predators," he began. "You might call him the Great White Shark of serial rapists. I was able to find only sixty-four documented cases throughout the country during the last century." He clasped his hands. "Rapists who stalk their victims, of course, are quite common. What makes this particular subtype of stalker so unusual is that his sexual gratification comes to depend entirely on the infliction of pain. Almost all *SS*'s begin killing their victims, sooner or later."

Several students began writing in spiral notebooks. A couple of others opened laptops and turned them on as he continued. "For the Stalker Sadist, torture is an end in itself," he explained. "To him, the act of rape often becomes superfluous. It's not unusual for an *SS* to become so aroused by, for example, mutilating a victim's genitals or breasts, that he experiences spontaneous ejaculation without intercourse."

He noticed the fingers of one of the female students dig into her arms. "The behavior of most Stalker Rapists doesn't change much over time," he said. "That's not true of the Stalker Sadist. Torture becomes a narcotic to him. He has to keep experimenting with higher doses of it in order to become sexually satisfied; his behavior is constantly mutating, like a retrovirus."

He turned a page in his notes. "Let me tell you about a Stalker Sadist who terrorized women in Manhattan back in the eighties. Ronald Craine was a forty-five-year-old plumber who became known as 'The Acid Man' because of the grisly nature of his attacks. He raped and tortured a total of eleven women before he was finally caught. While he had only a grade school education, his crimes displayed the intelligence and cunning that's typical of an *SS*." He leaned back in the chair and pushed off the other shoe with his toes, feeling the coolness of the linoleum radiating through his socks. "Like most *SS*'s, Craine had a very distinctive MO. Part of his signature involved tying his victims with electrical cord that was always knotted in a double half-hitch. After gagging a woman to muffle her screams, he would put on a surgical mask and thick rubber gloves; then, he would begin swabbing her genitals with sulfuric acid. Each time, he spontaneously climaxed when he saw the victim's pain was becoming intolerable." A male student at the other end of the table grimaced as he went on. "Craine's attacks were always slow and methodical. All of his acid victims died horrible, lingering deaths from toxic burns. The fumes at some of the crime scenes were so intense that police and paramedics had to be treated."

He paused and drew a deep breath. "Most SS's don't torture their victims in the beginning. Sexual sadism is something that gradually appears as the assaults continue. Craine is a good example. He only inflicted bites and minor cuts on the first few women he raped. Then, he began doing things like binding his victims with barbed wire and using cattle prods to shock them. Like most Stalker Sadists, his torture was primarily focused on the genitals."

He swiveled his chair and picked up a piece of chalk, drawing an ascending line on the blackboard behind him. "If you were to graph the level of violence in Craine's attacks, you'd see it steadily inching closer to homicide. When an SS begins killing, there are no fast, merciful deaths. Most of them revive their victims as many times as possible before murdering them."

A male student in Banana Republic shorts and a tank top raised his hand. "How do they go about picking victims?"

"Very selectively," he said. "The assaults are never random. They only target women with whom they can act out particular sexual fantasies. There's always a clear victim profile with an SS." He glanced back at his notes. "All of the women Craine attacked were tall and between twenty-eight and thirty-five years old; curiously, they were all foreigners, though they were of different nationalities."

"What was his thing about tall, foreign women?" a student asked.

Roth shrugged. "None of the psychiatrists who interviewed him before he was executed were able to answer that question. I doubt that Craine himself had any idea why he stalked the women he did."

"What about his criminal history?" another student inquired.

"Before being arrested and charged with murder, he'd never had so much as a parking ticket. That's true of most SS's"

One of the students opened a cassette recorder and inserted a fresh tape.

"An *SS* will usually watch a prospective victim for some period of time before he attacks her. The stalking can go on for days, weeks or even months; some will sit in a car all night in front of the victim's house or follow her around during the day; others take temporary jobs as janitors or parking lot attendants just to be close to the women they plan to attack. They go to great lengths to learn everything they can about them. Some scavenge through their trash. What kind of food does the victim like? Does she drink wine or beer? What credit cards and debts does she have? Who does she write to? He may even burglarize her home to get more information."

A petite student in her mid-twenties raised her hand. "Was Ted Bundy an *SS*?"

Roth shook his head. "While Bundy was discriminating in his choice of victims and stalked many of them, there was never evidence of systematic torture in any of his murders. That's the hallmark of an *SS*."

Lines appeared on the forehead of one of the female students. "I don't understand why they want to know so much about these women," she said.

Roth fingered the brass MPD insignia on one of his collars and replied, "The more they know about a victim, the more pleasurable the torture becomes."

He turned next to a demographic profile of the Stalker Sadist rapist he had developed. "Most *SS*'s are white and divorced; they're usually loners in their late thirties or early forties, with no history of either drug or alcohol abuse; some have collected violent pornography for years. They commonly pose and photograph or video their victims before and after torturing and killing them. After their arrests, police often find elaborate torture chambers set up in their homes, trailers and vans, as well as various fetishes or trophies they've taken from the victims."

He leafed through his notes. "This is interesting," he observed. "Forty-three percent of the Stalker Sadists whose psychiatric records I studied reported homosexual experiences, and one-third were actively bi-sexual at the time of their arrest." His eyes drifted beyond the small room's single window to the steady flow of students entering and leaving the library.

"Stalker Sadists often regard the efforts of police to catch them as a game," he said. "Their intelligence usually enables them to elude apprehension for a long period of time. Craine was at large for almost a year after his torture-murders began."

He pressed his lips together thoughtfully. "Most *SS*'s are college educated, and some even have graduate degrees. Listen to these occupations: accountant, geologist, trial lawyer, aerospace engineer, investment banker, social worker, plastic surgeon and urban planner. One was even a CIA agent involved in counter-espionage work. Many *SS*'s are ..."

He glanced at his watch. "I guess we're out of time," he said disappointedly. The hour had passed too quickly. After the last of the students left, he remained in the room for a couple of minutes, trying to break the grip of nostalgia.

CHAPTER

18

Roth's scores on written tests at the academy were consistently the highest in his class, but his performance on practical exercises, such as arrest tactics and self-defense, was marginal at best. He was more than a little chagrined to receive the "Cone Head Award," a humorous plaque presented to the member of each class who knocked down the most orange traffic cones during simulated vehicle chases.

As busy as the academy kept Roth, the Wake-Up Rapes were always in the back of his mind. The word from Frank Bailey was that the investigation was at least temporarily stalled for want of leads.

The oldest cadet in the history of the Miami Police Department was cleaning out his locker after his final day of training when he felt someone's eyes on him. He turned and saw Sgt. Akervik. "Well, it looks like I did it," he beamed.

Akervik regarded him with a look of amused wonder. "Fuzzy," he said, shaking his head, "you wouldn't make a pimple on a cop's ass if you went through a dozen academies!"

Roth continued gathering his personal effects, thankful to finally be free of his tormenter. He told himself he'd sooner accept a dinner invitation from Osama Bin Laden than spend another minute around Joseph T. Akervik.

* *

On the Saturday night before he was scheduled to report for duty at the Sexual Battery Unit, he attended a faculty party at the Key Biscayne home of Dean Henry Stafford. The spacious ranch-style house was nestled on a small piece of property surrounded by coconut palms, gumbo limbo trees and flowering shrubs.

"David!" Elise Stafford said cheerfully, hugging him as soon as she opened the door. He proffered a bottle of pinot noir.

"If I come in, will you promise not to try and marry me off to anyone?" he joked.

She took his arm. "I don't know. You're getting so damned handsome. I may run off with you myself." She led him through a softly lit, marble foyer and sunken living room to the patio out back. All twenty-one members of the School of Criminology faculty were chatting amiably in small clusters around a shear descent waterfall that cascaded into the swimming pool.

"Henry, look who's here," she called out. Henry Stafford was a large, gregarious man in his mid-fifties, with a ruddy face and a sizable spread around his middle. The renowned criminal psychiatrist had been dean of the University of Miami, School of Criminology for many years. Both he and his wife had become good friends of the Roths shortly after the young couple arrived in Miami. Even after Sara's death, they remained close to Roth. Elise Stafford had sought tirelessly—if unsuccessfully—to pair the eligible widower with a number of her friends and acquaintances.

"Ah, the Spartan arrives, bloody but unbowed!" Stafford said, pumping Roth's hand. "I see you survived the academy."

"'Barely' is the operative word," Roth confessed. He ordered a Heineken from the white-jacketed Cuban American who was tending bar and began mingling with the others. Although his colleagues greeted him with forced half-smiles and nods of civility, the reaction of most of them to his appearance at the party was discernibly cool. He realized that his enrollment at the academy and the six-month career as a detective he was about to begin had generated more than a little controversy on campus.

"What happened to your beard?" a new assistant professor inquired.

"A small sacrifice in the pursuit of knowledge," Roth replied, sipping his beer.

"How's the new book coming?" another colleague asked.

"I've had to put it on hold until I finish the police project."

"Not much time for academic duties these days, eh?" Professor Wayne Phelps blurted loudly from a half-dozen feet away. Dean Stafford had mentioned that Phelps had written a letter to the president's office, denouncing the police research project as 'unscientific and indecorous.'

"Just how much longer is this cop bullshit going to go on?" Phelps slurred. The ice clinked against the side of his fourth Cutty and water as he made his way to where Roth was standing.

Apparently sensing the imminent outbreak of hostilities, the dean sought to intervene. He placed a hand on Phelps' shoulder. "Wayne, you're drunk," he said amiably. "Now, be a good boy, or I'll throw you in the pool."

Phelps pulled away from his grasp. "Maybe I'm just drunk enough to say what's on everyone's mind."

"That's enough," Stafford said firmly.

"No, wait," Roth said, "I want to know why what I'm doing is bullshit!"

Phelps gestured expansively, spilling some of his drink. "You're an embarrassment to us all!" he said.

"Why?" Roth demanded.

"Good Lord, man! A full professor running around the campus in a police uniform ... it's ... well, it's unseemly."

Roth set his jaw. "What I find unseemly," he snapped, "are criminologists like you who never do anything about crime except talk about it!"

Phelps' voice rose with indignation. "We're scholars, not practitioners! We have reputations to uphold!"

"Reputations for what? Irrelevance? My field is sexual violence. Until this semester, I'd never spoken to a rape victim — not once in thirteen years at the university." His eyes moved across the faces. "Don't you see how out of touch we are? This is criminology, not medieval history! We're supposed to be coming up with answers to crime. How are we going to do that, sitting on our asses on the campus?"

He turned toward a statuesque woman about his own age. "Marjorie, you've been teaching criminal law at UM ever since you graduated from law school, yet you've never spent a day as either a prosecutor or defense attorney." She glanced at him uncomfortably but said nothing.

He motioned toward a man standing next to the dean. "Stan, you've become a nationally recognized expert on prisons without ever actually working inside one. How can you possibly understand the problems a warden faces?"

Henry Stafford broke the uneasy silence that followed. "David, please ... this isn't the place ..."

"I'm sorry, but I don't belong here," Roth said. He put down his beer and left abruptly, feeling torn between the two worlds he now occupied.

On his way home, he pulled off the Rickenbacker Causeway and sat watching the lights of Miami sparkle across the water. The ordeal of the academy was behind him now. He would soon be a sexual battery detective. He felt a mixture of excitement and apprehension, wondering what the second half of his exodus held.

CHAPTER

19

Detective Frank Bailey pulled alongside Roth's Volvo in his unmarked car and handed him the case records on the latest Wake-Up Rape. "I copied everything we've got so far on this one so you'd have it before you start work on Monday," he told him. Roth was already eagerly reading Sergeant Sosa's report before Bailey's car had left the Burger King parking lot. The rapist's third victim was a forty-two-year-old black elementary school principal.

> *After killing V's Rottweiler, S entered her single-story house by slipping the lock on a patio sliding glass door. Woke V and told her the time (3 a.m.). Armed with small blue steel semi-auto. Forced V into the bathroom, where he began running hot water in the tub. V told him that she had no cash on hand but offered to get money from a nearby ATM. S gagged and bound V with duct tape and forced her onto her back in the tub. Held her head underwater repeatedly, pulling her up by the hair just long enough for her to breathe. S laughed and told her he was going to drown her.*

A chill passed through Roth. What he had just read sounded like the pre-shock tremors of a Stalker Sadist rapist who was beginning to experiment with torture. He resisted the idea, searching for some other explanation. The near drowning could have been a fluke. The victim may have done or said something that enraged her assailant, though he doubted it. He kept reading.

> *V stated that, just when she was certain he was going to kill her, he pulled her out of the tub and anally raped her on the floor.*

Why wasn't he picking easier targets? Why go after a woman who has a hundred-pound Rottweiler guarding her home or a Coast Guard pilot who sleeps with a gun under her pillow? As different as the victims seemed, they had to be connected in some way. He was certain of that.

He had never seen anything like the attack pattern that was taking shape. Picking the same type of victim each time was the closest thing to a universal law of physics he had found when it came to serial rapists. Why wasn't this guy following it? His victims were all over the board demographically: young and old; black and white. They lived in different parts of the city. Even their physiques—known in profiling as *somatotypes*—were dissimilar. Police records described the nun as short and frail, the Coast Guard pilot as tall and slender and the school principal as a 'stout' woman of average height. Sosa's report indicated that she had showed all three women pictures of one another. They were total strangers.

Another anal rape. The absence of either penile or digital penetration of the victims' vaginas puzzled Roth. So did the fact that the assailant hadn't forced any of the women to either perform oral sex or submit to it. The lack of any kissing of the victims or fondling of their breasts, hips or thighs also represented unusual behavior for a rapist.

The police reports disclosed another curious anomaly. Most of the serial rapists he had studied were talkers who spoke to their victims during the sexual assaults. They terrorized them with threats of death or injury, ordered them to do and say certain things or sought compliments on their sexual prowess. Not this man. As conversational as he was when he first confronted the women, he never spoke another word once the rapes began.

> *S knew where V had gone to college and graduate school, as well as the fact that she was divorced and had three children, one of whom died in a hiking accident.*

Knowing so much about each victim was consistent with the modus operandi of an emerging Stalker Sadist rapist. Only one thing didn't fit: the absence of any form of contact with the victims' genitals.

CHAPTER

20

Maria Sosa finally gave up trying to sleep after repositioning her pillow a half-dozen times. She threw the covers aside with a Spanish expletive, surrendering to the gravitational pull of the office. Fifteen minutes later, she was still standing in the shower with her eyes closed when the water began to turn tepid. She couldn't get the Wake-Up Rapes out of her mind. Her cop's instincts told her that another attack was coming soon.

She got out of the shower and toweled her hair. Maybe he'd skip this month. She reminded herself that the man she was after could be in jail right under her nose, on some charge completely unrelated to sexual violence. For all she knew, he could be dead or off inflicting his hatred of women on the population of some other city.

Dawn was just beginning to break behind a ragged bank of clouds when she left her condo at Brickel Point and headed downtown. A laser eye at the entrance to the police garage read the bar-code sticker on her windshield and the steel gate opened. She nosed the unmarked Ford Taurus into a parking space marked CID ONLY in the police garage, then clipped her gold sergeant's badge to her belt and rode the elevator to the Criminal Investigation Division on the third floor.

In a couple of hours, the cavernous structure that housed CID would be bustling with over a hundred detectives and staff. It was all but empty now. One of the midnight detectives going off-duty responded to her smile with a slack-jawed nod of fatigue.

The lights of a police scanner flickered ominously on a file cabinet in one of the outer offices. Its dozen red eyes blinked sequentially as it scanned patrol frequencies throughout the city. Tourist season was in full swing now.

As the day wore on, the radio would begin chattering like a magpie with coded pronouncements of human misery. Many of them would eventually work their way into the overcrowded pipelines of the Miami Police Department's detective bureau.

After brewing coffee in the break room, she sat at her desk, holding a steaming ceramic mug that said, COPS DO IT UNDERCOVER.

'*You've got mail!*' her computer announced in a disinterested, mechanical voice. Her eyes skipped down the list of e-mail messages and stopped at one. She clicked the cursor:

CONFIRMING RECEIPT YOUR FD-676 SUPPLEMENTAL IN-QUIRY. BE ADVISED NO CURRENT PROFILE MATCHES IN ViCAP DATA BASE.

She stared at the characters on the screen, puffing out her cheeks in frustration. *Still no help from the feds on the Wake-Up Rapes.* She pressed the delete key and watched the message from the FBI's Violent Criminal Apprehension Program evaporate. The terse response meant that never, during the more than twenty years the Bureau had been compiling nationwide data on violent sexual offenders, had its computers detected such an unusual combination of traits in a serial rapist. She had submitted three revised profiles to ViCAP in the last sixty days. The FBI still had come up with nothing that would help her on the rapes of Bridget Kearney, Diane Whitaker and Georgia Griffin.

*   *

Within an hour, the multi-celled organism of CID began to come to life as other workaholics trickled in. Even with her door closed, she could hear voices and phones through the wafer-thin walls. Around nine, the intercom on her phone buzzed.

"Sergeant, Captain Wilcox would like to see you," the division commander's secretary said. Sosa was now number one on the promotion list for lieutenant. Sometime during the next few weeks or months, the division captain would summon her to his office with the news that she was no longer just the acting lieutenant of the Sexual Battery Unit. Once she made lieutenant, the squad of ten detectives would become her full-time responsibility. In the meantime, she had the task of overseeing the work of all five investigative teams while still carrying active cases of her own.

A man with wire-rimmed glasses was sitting outside the captain's office. He looked vaguely familiar to Sosa, though she couldn't place the face. At first, the steno pad on his lap led her to assume he was a reporter. His suit had made one too many trips to the cleaners and the brown penny loafers he had on looked as if someone had gone over them with a warm Hershey bar. Then she noticed the unmistakable bulge of a gun in a shoulder holster under his jacket. He didn't look like a cop. What agency could he be with?

She entered Wilcox's office and closed the door. The CID commander had the look of a middle-aged wrestler gone to seed, with big rough hands and a beer gut that partially obscured the snub-nosed .38 on his waist. He smelled of stale cigarettes and had red-rimmed, watery eyes that fueled rumors of alcoholism. Wilcox held out a half-empty box of Krispy Kreme Donuts after she took a seat.

"No thanks."

"How about some coffee?"

She shook her head. The offering from the viscous reservoir of the captain's personal coffee pot confirmed her suspicion that something was wrong. The Hal Wilcox she had worked for over the past five years was never this pleasant.

"So what's up?" she asked.

Wilcox bit into a powdered donut. "It looks like we're going to have someone from UM with us for a while," he said, his words slightly garbled from the food.

"You called me in here to tell me that?" she said in a puzzled voice. Student interns had been common at the department for years.

"This guy is one of the criminology professors over there."

She made a face.

"You're not talking about that character who called me after the nun's attack?"

Wilcox nodded, wiping his mouth with the back of his hand. "Yeah. Seems he's interested in the Wake-Up Rapes. Since it's your case, I thought you could ..."

She was on her feet instantly. "Oh, no, you don't! You're not sticking me with a goddamn intern!"

"He's not an intern. He's a cop."

"What?"

He handed her a memo from Chief Crenshaw confirming Roth's appointment.

She looked at it incredulously. "Detective, Third-Grade! What the hell's going on?"

Wilcox shoved the rest of the donut in his mouth and slouched in his seat. "It's some cockamamie research thing the chief has going with the university. I'm afraid there's nothing we can do about it."

She put her hands on her hips. "Just what am I supposed to do with him?"

Wilcox shrugged. "I understand he's a rape profile expert. Maybe you can use him."

"Captain, most of the people over there can't walk and chew gum at the same time."

Wilcox got out of his chair with a grunt. He walked around his desk and stood beside her.

"Maria, I really need your help on this," he said with a hangdog look. "My ass is in a sling. I got a call from the chief yesterday. He wants us to use Dr. Roth on the Wake-Up case."

She crossed her arms defiantly and turned toward the window.

"Look, he's only going to be here for six months."

"*Six months*?" Her mind flashed to the man she had seen sitting outside the door. "Oh, God! That nerdy looking guy outside your office. That's him, isn't it?"

"Shh ... he'll hear you," the captain cautioned.

Suddenly it hit her. She knew where she had seen him before. The forty-something cadet who kept asking questions during her rape lecture at the academy.

"Son of a bitch!" she exclaimed.

"I promise, I'll unload him on someone else the first chance I get." The captain walked to the door and opened it.

"Professor Roth," he said warmly, "please come in."

"This is Sergeant Sosa. She's in charge of the SBU."

She extended her hand coolly. "I believe we've already met."

"I was just telling the sergeant that you'd like to get involved in the Wake-Up investigation while you're with us," Wilcox said.

"Yes, I would," Roth said quickly.

"I'm sure your expertise could be a real help," Wilcox ventured.

Sosa glared at the captain without speaking. Hal Wilcox looked nervous, like a salesman who was afraid the deal he'd just put together might fall through.

"Why don't you show Dr. Roth to Jack's old office. He can use it for now."

"Follow me," she said with a conspicuous lack of enthusiasm.

She led him down a long hallway, past rows of offices with plastic nameplates affixed to them. Secretaries and clerks with laminated photo ID tags moved along the corridor like worker bees in a hive. Glimpses beyond the open doors revealed men and women wearing the silver and gold shields of detectives; some were on the phone, while others leafed through files or tapped computer keyboards.

"This is the SBU," Sosa announced when they rounded a corner and came to another group of offices. A cork bulletin board on the wall displayed an assortment of wanted posters beneath the acronym BOLO: Be On The Lookout.

She led him into a cramped room with a frosted glass border. "This will be your office," she said in a businesslike voice. "Mine is three doors down on the left."

The cubicle was sparsely furnished with an old metal desk and a couple of chairs covered with a film of dust. Last month's calendar was taped to the wall. Someone had left a ballpoint pen and a chipped coffee cup on the desk.

Roth spotted an anemic looking plant in the corner. "Hey, it's a Mimosa peduca!"

"A what?"

He crouched beside the clay pot and stuck a finger in the soil. "It needs water. Looks like it could use a little fertilizer, too."

She cocked a hip and leaned against the doorway. "I think the guy who had this office was trying to kill it. He used to pour coffee on it."

He touched one of the bayonet-shaped leaves with the tip of his finger; it snapped shut instantly. Every other leaf on the stem followed its lead like a Rockettes' chorus line. "Isn't that incredible?" he said.

"What?"

"Its consciousness."

"You think that thing is conscious?"

He adjusted his glasses and looked up at her. "All living things react to their environment in some way. That's consciousness."

She picked an imaginary fleck of lint off her blouse. "You don't talk to plants, do you, Professor?"

"Only the more interesting ones," he deadpanned.

CHAPTER

21

Roth checked out a cell phone and portable radio before going to Sergeant Sosa's office. She was on the phone when he arrived and motioned for him to take a seat.

"I'm afraid there isn't a lot I can tell you about the Wake-Up Rapes right now," she said after hanging up. "This guy has been hitting once a month like clockwork. There doesn't appear to be any pattern to what he's doing." She massaged the back of her neck, adding, "He might be a 'spree rapist,' who does a few and gets it out of his system for a while."

Roth shook his head dubiously. "I don't think so."

She shoved a stack of papers to one side of her desk as a detective in his late-twenties with sandy hair and boyish features poked his head inside.

"Sergeant, I've got my probable cause affidavit ready on Becker."

She put on a pair of half-shell reading glasses and inspected the three-page report he handed her.

As soon as the other detective left, Roth removed his pipe from his jacket.

"You can't light that in here! The whole building's non-smoking."

"Oh, I don't smoke it much anymore. I just chew on it sometimes out of habit when I'm thinking."

She raised her chin and said icily, "Doctor, most of us spend at least three years in patrol before we're even eligible to apply to CID. How the hell did you make detective without even finishing the academy?"

"That would have taken six months and I only had a nine month sabbatical. The chief gave me a special appointment so I could spend as much time here as possible."

Lucky us!

She noticed the thin gold band on his hand. "How does your wife feel about you doing this?"

His face darkened. "My wife and son were killed in a car accident four years ago," he said quietly.

Nice going, Sosa!

She felt the heat stealing into her cheeks. "I'm sorry."

Several seconds passed before he spoke. "What do you have to go on so far?" he asked, opening a tablet on his lap.

She fingered a tendril of hair. "Not a hell of a lot," she sighed. "I've got DNA from ejaculate in all three rapes. It's great courtroom evidence, but it doesn't bring me any closer to finding the guy." She tugged at the hem of her skirt when she noticed his eyes shift to her legs. Men had been looking at them the same way since she was fourteen.

Her head was starting to throb. She found a container of Advil in her purse and washed a couple of them down with water from a cooler in the corner. "The only thing I can tell you for sure about this character is that he doesn't have a sexual battery record anywhere in Florida. We had the Florida Department of Law Enforcement lab check out the DNA from sperm in the first rape and run it against their database in Tallahassee. They've got DNA records on every sex offender who's been convicted in Florida in recent years. We also checked his DNA against CODIS."

"What's that?"

"*Combined DNA Indexing System.* It's a nationwide data counterpart to our state sex offender records. It's so new that a lot of the other states still have a huge backlog of DNA data that hasn't been entered into the pipeline. He could have a sexual assault record in a lot of places and we wouldn't know about it."

He studied his pipe. "Anything else in the way of evidence?"

"Nothing really useful. This guy is very careful. He always wears gloves. No one's seen his face, so we can't get a composite sketch. The duct tape he uses on his victims could have come from any Home Depot or hardware store in south Florida."

The ringing of her phone interrupted their discussion of the case a couple of times.

"I'm sorry, but I have to be in court in an hour. Look, why don't you have our unit secretary pull the case files. You can review them today, and we'll talk in the morning. Okay?"

He looked at her blankly.

"You *do* want to see the files, don't you?"

"Oh, yes … yes, of course."

*   *

Roth's desk chair squeaked in protest as he sank into it. *Cubicle hell.* The room felt more like a walk-in closet than an office. He began sorting through the official SBU case folders, knowing that the only thing that would likely be new to him would be the names of the women. The briefcase next to him held two legal tablets filled with notes he'd already taken from Frank Bailey's copies of the same records. He jotted down the name of each victim, along with her age, occupation, and the date she was attacked:

KEARNEY, BRIDGET, 71, CATHOLIC NUN, RAPED 11/8
WHITAKER, DIANE, 34, PILOT—USCG, RAPED 12/7
GRIFFIN, GEORGIA, 42, SCHOOL PRINCIPAL, RAPED 1/6

Once a month and always at 3 a.m. What was it about that hour that made it so special to this man?

He propped his chin on his hand and began doodling in the margins of a tablet: triangles, rectangles, circles. He shaded each one with the side of his pencil, soon filling the page with an assortment of geometric shapes. It was as if he might render calculable whatever the Wake-Up Rapist was doing if he could somehow draw it into the ambit of geometry, with its precise angles and measurements.

CHAPTER

22

The sight of the tall, well built young man standing near the cockpit door caused one of the flight attendants to look up from the drinks she was pouring in the first class galley. She returned his smile when he motioned to the OCCUPIED light above the john. He had always been good at putting people at ease. Ever since they left L.A., he had been stealing glances at the woman in the bulkhead seat across the aisle from him, unable to take his eyes off her hands. Such beautiful alabaster hands. How many times had he watched those fingers fly with grace and precision across a keyboard? It was obvious she didn't recognize him, even though he had stood only a few feet from her at the reception that followed her last concert.

He could tell by the way she was fidgeting that she was dying for a cigarette. She had been ever since they lifted off. Vantage Lights, as he recalled. She had been on the airfone eight or nine times before they were over New Mexico and was already nursing her second Stoly on the rocks while talking animatedly to her agent, a whiny little sycophant with a pallid complexion and rose-tinted granny glasses. They were returning to Miami from a west coast conference with the producer of her hugely successful new CD, The Romantic Chopin. He had followed them to the meeting and from there to a power lunch with several recording executives at Spago's in Beverly Hills.

She responded with an icy glare to the twenty-year-old flight attendant who timidly approached and asked for her autograph, then grudgingly signed her name. So very busy. So important. Her music and all the attention it had brought her would soon be just a painful memory. See you on the ground, Laura.

CHAPTER

23

When Sosa arrived at the SBU the following morning, Roth was at his desk in a short-sleeved striped shirt, a pair of tricolor suspenders and a bow tie. The shoulder holster that held his .40 caliber Glock was draped over the back of his chair along with his jacket.

She rolled her eyes. "Dr. Roth, your weapon is supposed to be on your person at all times when you're on duty," she said sharply. He looked up distractedly from the case file of Sister Bridget Kearney. "This is a police building, in case you haven't noticed," she added sarcastically. "We bring prisoners in here every day. A lot of them are looking at long sentences. You step out to get a cup of coffee or use the john and some three time loser who's just been popped for violation of parole sees your piece hanging on the chair. The next thing we know we've got a hostage and barricaded gunman situation on our hands. Do you follow me?"

She could see that he was embarrassed.

"I'm sorry," he said awkwardly. "It's a little hard to get used to carrying a gun." He slipped his arms through the shoulder harness and adjusted the strap.

"Well, solve the case yet?"

"Not quite."

She picked up a piece of sheet music from his desk that contained the lyrics to *Three o'clock in the Morning*. "What's this?"

"Just something I found on the Internet last night. That time must have some emotional significance to this man. I was reminded of a movie where the killer was obsessed with a particular song."

She snapped her fingers. "*Sea of Love*, with Al Pacino and Ellen Barkin."

The corners of his mouth tipped in a smile. "You know your movies, Sergeant."

She pulled up a chair and sat beside his desk. "I played around with the time thing myself for a while. Last call at the bars down here is at two. At first, I had this image of some guy who keeps putting it away until they close the doors, then goes out and unloads his hostility on women."

"Hmm ... interesting."

"Yeah," Sosa said, flipping a pen between the fingers of one hand. "Except that none of the victims reported any signs of alcohol, and the kind of break-ins this nut's been pulling must take the skill and concentration of a goddamn neurosurgeon."

CHAPTER

24

Laura Kelce was trembling. Tears glistened in her white-ringed eyes. The man beside her bed removed a serrated hunting knife from a mustard-colored gym bag and cut a four-inch strip of duct tape from a roll, pressing it firmly against her mouth with his gloved hands.

"We have to be very quiet," he said in a hushed voice. "We mustn't wake Rosalie."

One of the straps of her nightgown slipped off her shoulder when he eased her head back onto the pillow. He replaced it gently and brushed a wick of auburn hair away from her face.

"You don't have to be afraid of me, Laura," he said softly. "I'm one of your greatest admirers. I was at your concert in Rome last month." A hint of sadness crept into his voice. "I can tell you don't believe me."

He licked his lips nervously behind the ski mask and sat on the edge of the bed.

"You and Rosalie had lunch at Portofino's on the Via Del Corso on the day of the concert. It's always been one of my favorite places. Your performance that night was at the Esposizione di Roma, and your first piece was Chopin's Polonaise *in A-Major."*

"Let's see...," he said, running a finger along his lower lip. "I remember you wore a sleeveless, floor-length, black gown with pearls. You played on a Steinway. It had a slightly brighter sound than your baby grand downstairs." He giggled. "I'm afraid I was naughty. I played it one afternoon when you and Rosalie were out."

A tear coursed down her cheek.

He raised her chin with his finger tips. "There, there," he said, sooth-

ingly, wiping away the tear. "Do you know what an Erard is?" he asked,
folding his hands in his lap.

Her head bobbed nervously a couple of times.

"I learned to play on one as a child," he said proudly. "I still have it.
I love Beethoven's sonatas, especially the Adagio Cantabile. *Your rendition*
of it in Rome was so...," he made a circle with his thumb and forefin-
ger, " ... so bellissimo!" A moment later, he kissed her forehead impul-
sively. "Did you know that Beethoven was nearly deaf when he composed
it? Poor thing. He was only thirty at the time. Imagine creating some-
thing of such beauty and then not being able to ... to ..."

He stopped speaking and stared fixedly at the gym bag for a minute
or more before reaching inside it. Laura Kelce's eyes widened in horror
when she saw what was in his hand. A short, strangled cry rose in her
throat. She arched her back and threw her head from side to side,
struggling vainly to free her wrists. He picked her up and carried her
from the bed, humming the prelude to Adagio Cantabile.

CHAPTER

25

The ringing of the phone slowly permeated Roth's consciousness. He extended a hand from the warmth of the covers and groped for the receiver. It was Sergeant Sosa.

"Our guy just did a woman in Coral Gables," she said, in a voice still thick with sleep. "I'll pick you up in twenty minutes. Be ready."

*   *

He was sitting in his living room, listening to the tattoo of rain on the metal roof when Sosa's headlights sliced through the darkness. It was a little after five. The Ford's wipers slapped the windshield in a rapid cadence as he jumped in and wiped the rain from his face.

"What did he do?" he asked, already afraid of the answer.

Her mouth became a thin line. "I don't know yet, but it must be bad. Wilcox is on his way. I just heard him on the air." Roth ran a hand across the stubble on his face.

"I didn't have time to shave," he said self-consciously.

"Relax. We're not big on grooming codes, especially this time of the morning. You can lose the jacket, if you want."

He tossed his coat on the back seat, surprised at how pretty she was even with no makeup and little sleep. She had on a pair of gray slacks, a peach-colored blouse and sneakers. A barrette held her black hair in place.

He watched the lights of passing cars, wondering what was waiting for them at the scene of the fourth Wake-Up Rape.

*   *

They drove through the rain to Gables Estates, an affluent residential community many miles from the locations of the earlier attacks.

A deafening peal of thunder reverberated inside the car when Sosa rolled down the window and showed her badge to the guard on duty at the entrance kiosk. After the metal gate rolled open, they followed a wide, curving ribbon of pavement flanked by neatly trimmed ten-foot ficus hedges that partially hid the elegant homes beyond them.

"Pretty pricey real estate," Roth observed.

"Yeah. I worked a few off-duty details here back when I was in patrol. You couldn't touch anything in Gables Estates for much under a million and that was some years ago."

A white Bronco with a rotating yellow light on its roof slowed on the opposite side of the street, running its spotlight across the front of a huge home with a three-car garage.

Sosa said, "This place has more guards per square inch than any residential development in the city. I don't think they've ever had so much as a stolen bicycle."

Rain raked the car in wind-driven sheets. They could see the glow of emergency lights up ahead. Several cruisers, an unmarked car and an evidence van were parked in the circular driveway of a residence that was set far back from the street. Their flashing red and blue lights created an eerie kaleidoscope in the darkness.

Torrents of water ran off the edge of the roofline and splashed onto the ground. Roth and Sosa walked briskly towards a cluster of uniforms, shielding their faces from the rain. They found Captain Wilcox standing under an eave. An evidence technician knelt beside him, using dental stone to get a cast impression of a single footprint next to an open burglar alarm box.

"What have we got?" Sosa asked.

Wilcox turned up the collar of his raincoat. "Same MO as the others, with one major difference. This time, he amputated the victim's fingers with a pair of garden shears."

"¡Madre de Dios!"

It's started. The very thing Roth had dreaded since the near drowning of the school principal had just happened. The Wake-Up Rapist had entered the torture phase of the Stalker Sadism syndrome.

The tip of the captain's cigarette glowed brightly in the dark. "The housekeeper was asleep downstairs," he told them. "She heard a noise around four and went to check on it. That's when she found her."

"What about her fingers?" Roth said. "Is there any chance they can …"

Wilcox shook his head. "The paramedics couldn't find any trace of them. Looks like the bastard cut them off in the bathroom and flushed them! There's blood all over the floor around the toilet."

"Who's the victim?" Sosa asked.

Wilcox drew a deep breath. "That's the *really* bad news. It's Laura Kelce."

"The pianist?" Roth said.

"Yeah."

He and Sara had heard her perform at Carnegie Hall six years before.

Wilcox turned to Sosa. "Can you imagine what a shit storm there's going to be when this gets out?"

Roth said, "Won't the Rape Shield Law keep her name from being released?"

Sosa explained, "When it comes to someone this prominent, there's no way to keep a lid on it. Too many people know what happened— the ambulance crew, hospital staff and security guards. It's bound to leak out."

Roth watched the evidence technician finish lifting the only footprint that apparently hadn't been washed away by the rain.

"Christ," Wilcox said, angrily, "by morning the *Herald* and every TV station in town are going to be all over us. Maria, you're going to need more help on this one."

She nodded. "First thing in the morning, I'll pull McNees and Walker off that Internet kiddie porn thing they've been handling with the feds."

"Work this one hard!" Wilcox said forcefully. "We've got to find this asshole fast."

Roth followed Sergeant Sosa past a handful of uniformed officers in rain slickers.

"Where are your gloves?" she asked, after they ducked under the ribbon of yellow crime scene tape circling the house.

"I'm afraid I didn't bring any," he replied awkwardly.

She slipped on a pair and tossed him the car keys. "You'll find some extras in the trunk. When he returned, she drew him to one side. "Don't touch anything when we get inside, understand?"

He pressed his lips together, resenting being treated like a child whose parents are worried he might break something at a friend's house.

Inside the spacious home, they ascended the steps of a spiral staircase and made their way to the master bedroom on the second floor. A camera flash bounced off one of its pastel walls as they entered. Skylights in the vaulted ceiling admitted the dull haze of early morning through broken clouds.

A torn, silk nightgown on the white Persian carpet and a bloodstained down comforter on the bed were the only signs of the savagery that had taken place a couple of hours before. Freshly cut, yellow roses in a crystal vase sat in front of a large window that afforded a panoramic view of the Intracoastal Waterway. A delicate china tea cup with traces of lipstick on its rim rested in a saucer beside the bed. Pictures of the internationally acclaimed pianist and her family were neatly arranged on the mantelpiece. A signed Picasso sketch in an ebony frame hung above them.

An evidence technician in a blue jumpsuit finished photographing a crumpled aluminum foil wrapper on the floor near the bed. He was placing it in a plastic bag when another ET stuck his head out of the bathroom.

"Sergeant Sosa," he called out. "There something in here you need to see."

The master bathroom was the size of an average bedroom. A long, mirrored wall behind the Jacuzzi made it seem even bigger. Roth followed the sergeant's footsteps as carefully as if he were entering a minefield.

The bathroom looked like a slaughterhouse. Crimson smudges covered the toilet and the Venetian marble around it. The bloodstained jaws of a pair of green-handled garden shears yawned in an open position beside the bidet. The technician who had summoned Sosa pointed to an unrolled condom on the counter between the two sinks. A milky fluid fogged the tip of it.

Sosa bent and examined it. "He's never used a rubber before," she said. "Why start now?"

Roth looked out the window at a tug pushing a barge slowly down the Intracoastal. "It's a gauntlet," he said. "He wants us to know that it doesn't matter if we have his DNA because we'll never have him to compare it to."

* *

After they left Gables Estates that morning, he told her what he had learned about this particular kind of rapist during his years as a criminologist specializing in sexual violence. He explained that of all the types of serial rapists he had identified from his research, the Stalker Sadist was the rarest and most dangerous.

"Sooner or later, most Stalker Sadists begin killing," he told her.

"How much time do we have before that happens?" she asked tensely.

He knuckled the fatigue from an eye. "Judging from what we saw back there, I'd say, one ... maybe two more attacks."

* *

He slept fitfully for several hours that morning before returning to the department to meet with Sosa and the two additional detectives she was assigning to the case. They were all in the SBU briefing room when he arrived. Detective Jim McNees was an avuncular figure with thick tortoise shell glasses and a Panama hat shoved high on his freckled forehead. His partner, Alvin Walker, was a tall, lean black man in his early thirties with skin the color of hot tar and a gold earring.

"Okay, let's get started," Sosa said. "We've got a lot to do." She turned first to McNees.

"Jim, go out to Gables Estates and get a copy of their gate log. I want to know everything that came through there yesterday— visitors, Fed Ex, flower deliveries. Check it all. Also, talk to the guards on their roving security patrol who were on duty last night. One of them may have seen something."

She paused to make a note. "Alvin, get with forensics and find out how soon they'll have something back on that footprint. Also, see what they can tell us about the shears this guy used and the condom wrapper the techs picked up."

Alvin Walker pushed his lanky frame back from the table. "I'm on it," he said.

She grabbed her radio and purse. "We're going to Mercy to try interviewing the victim. We'll also talk to the live-in assistant. She was so hysterical last night that the patrol guys didn't get much out of her."

CHAPTER

26

The doctor treating Laura Kelce had limited the interview with her to fifteen minutes. The forty-one-year-old woman in the bed at Mercy Hospital's Intensive Care Unit bore no resemblance to the vibrant, attractive musician Roth had seen play at Carnegie Hall. Her face was drawn and pale, and she spoke haltingly through the torpor of painkillers. Sosa had to bring her face close to the thin, bloodless lips each time she asked a question in order to hear the response.

Laura Kelce slowly described, in a barely audible voice, how the Wake-Up Rapist amputated her fingers, digit by digit, while he held her on the bathroom floor. He had gone about his gruesome work methodically—like someone pruning a rose bush. Each time she passed out, he crushed an ampoule of ammonia under her nose, to make certain that she remained conscious throughout the ordeal. He grabbed her by the hair and made her watch as he flushed away the remnants of lithe fingers that had evoked the beauty of Chopin and Beethoven, Mozart and Brahms, throughout the world.

Roth stared at the bandaged stumps that had been hands. *How could one human being do something like this to another?*

Laura Kelce told them that she had just returned from a European tour a couple of weeks before. The two SBU detectives exchanged an incredulous glance when she said that her assailant had apparently attended her concert in Rome.

"He ... he told me that he learned to play the piano as a child on an ... an Erard," she murmured.

"What's that?" Sosa asked.

"It's a very … ornate French piano. I don't think they've been made since the late 1800's." She hesitated, barely able to continue. "He also said he'd played the baby grand in my home one day when my assistant and I were out."

"Anything else about him you can recall?" Sosa pressed.

"Yes … there was … a smell …"

"What kind of smell?"

"Cologne of some kind … I know I've been around it before …"

Roth rubbed his chin, trying to gauge how Sosa might react if he asked a question. He waited while a nurse adjusted the IV drip beside the bed, and then said, "Was there anything unusual about his speech or appearance?"

Laura Kelce thought for a moment before slowly inclining her head toward him on the pillow. "I … I remember seeing the tip of a red handkerchief in the front pocket of his jeans."

*   *

They went directly from Mercy Hospital to a modest home in Coral Springs where Laura Kelce's live-in personal attendant of many years, Rosalie Olivares-Popoca, was now staying with relatives. Fear still showed on her face. Sosa conducted the interview in Spanish, hoping to relax the woman and elicit more details about the night of the attack. While she had accompanied her employer on the European tour, she could recall no problem with any of the pianist's many fans and well wishers or anyone who even vaguely matched the description of the Wake-Up Rapist.

Sosa slid behind the wheel. "I've seen a lot of strange stuff over the years, but nothing like this. A rapist who follows a woman around Rome, watching where she eats, noting the music she plays, and the clothes she wears. Then he waits until she gets back to Miami and…. Why?"

CHAPTER

27

Late the following day, they met again with Walker and McNees at the SBU.

"The garden shears are a common brand," Alvin Walker reported. "They could have come from just about anywhere. Techs say there were no prints on the window he came through or anywhere in either the bedroom or bathroom."

"Gloves again. What a surprise," Sosa said facetiously.

"He may not care about us having his DNA, but he obviously doesn't want us to get his fingerprints," Roth offered.

Sosa nodded agreement. "Have the techs process her piano very carefully," she told McNees and Walker. "He told the victim he'd played it one day while she and her assistant were out."

Alvin Walker's face brightened. "Maybe our boy got careless while he was ticklin' the ivories, huh?"

"Maybe," Sosa said. "We're sure as hell overdue for a break of some kind." She had found during her years as a detective that most criminals fail to realize how much modern law enforcement can do with the most subtle forms of trace evidence. Even without the Wake-Up Rapist's sperm, they still could have extracted his DNA from the lone pubic hair vacuumed from the nun's bed sheets. Although the blond follicle lacked an intact root with a nucleus, a recent breakthrough in *mitochondrial DNA testing* made it possible for labs to extract DNA from non-nucleated cells on the hair shaft itself.

It occurred to Sosa that, when the Wake-Up Rapist played Laura Kelce's piano during his visit to her home days or weeks before the attack, he may have removed his gloves. Perhaps he wanted to feel the smooth black and white keys against his fingers as he played.

He would have reasonably assumed that the police would never process the entire eight-thousand square foot home in their search for physical evidence. Indeed, the crime scene investigation so far had been primarily focused upstairs in the immediate area of the attack.

The victim had told Sosa and Roth that she sometimes practiced for hours each day on the piano in her living room. The frequent placement of her hands on the keyboard would make it a poor candidate for recovery of any latents belonging to the rapist, but it was possible that his ungloved fingers or palms had come in contact with another part of the instrument's polished ebony surface—perhaps someplace that the pianist rarely touched. He may have shoved the bench back a few inches to accommodate his six-foot frame or raised the keyboard cover with his finger tips.

Just a moment's carelessness. One tiny slip. That was all she needed. It would happen sooner or later. Sosa was certain of that. The only question was how many women would be tortured or killed before then.

"By the way," Jim McNees said, "the alarm this guy beat was an AV-TEK Millennium."

"Yeah … so?" Sosa said.

"Well, the guys in Burglary say it's state-of-the-art stuff—supposed to be 100% tamper-proof. A couple of them were out there with one of the engineers from the company today. They still have no idea how he managed to bypass it."

Sosa drummed her fingers impatiently on her desk. "What about the shoe print beside the alarm box?"

The black detective balanced himself on the back legs of his chair. "Our people haven't had any luck with it, so they sent the cast over to the FDLE lab to see what they can come up with."

McNees explained that he had gotten the gate log and was in the process of running registration checks on every vehicle that had entered Gables Estates during the twenty-four hour period preceding the rape. He had already talked to all of the guards who were on duty that night. No one remembered seeing anything unusual.

Sosa checked off a couple of items on the list of leads she had made. "How about the condom?" she asked.

Walker told her, "Forensics was able to ID it from the manufacturer's lot number stamped on the wrapper. It's made in Hong Kong and distributed in the states by an outfit called G & R Productions in Laredo, Texas. I knew I recognized the name the moment the lab guy mentioned it. It's called Buttmaster—they're in vending machines in gay bars all over the city. The guy I talked to told me that gay clubs are just about the *only* place where this brand is sold."

McNees chuckled. "I'll bet a gay stud like Alvin has got one of them in his wallet right now."

"I'm strictly a Trojan man," Walker responded drolly. "You won't catch me wrapping my willy in a two bit piece of shit like that." He handed Sosa a sheet of paper and said, "I pulled some information about this particular rubber off the Internet."

Sosa propped her chin on one hand. "A ribbed, cherry-scented, anal lube, latex condom with ten percent benzocaine."

McNees threw in. "I put some ointment with benzocaine on a sore gum once. That stuff numbs anything it touches. I sure as hell wouldn't want it anywhere near my dick!"

"At your age, what difference would it make?" Alvin Walker gibed. Everyone laughed, except Roth.

For all of his technical knowledge about rape, the criminologist's background had left him with little personal experience when it came to sex. He had never used a condom or had anal sex. Indeed, with the exception of a couple of heavy petting sessions as an adolescent and a brief affair with a music major while he was at Berkeley, he had never been with anyone besides his wife. He had no idea that an entire segment of the condom industry was devoted to the kind of erotica Alvin Walker had just described.

"How many gay bars in Miami have vending machines with Buttmaster condoms?" Sosa asked.

Alvin Walker had already learned the answer to her question from the sales rep at G & R Productions. "Twenty-three in the metro area," he reported.

She shook her head. "Talk about looking for a needle in a haystack."

Jim McNees turned to a portion of the crime scene report he had high-lighted. "Listen to this. The ET's found a thread caught on the sill of the window he came through. It was *lamb's wool.*"

Roth frowned. "Who wears anything made of lamb's wool in this heat and humidity?" he said.

Sosa pursed her lips thoughtfully. "We know this guy travels. It could be static cling from a sweater or overcoat in his closet."

She had plenty of physical evidence in the case. The problem was that none of it told her anything useful at this point. Once they had a suspect in custody and knew where he lived, the lamb's wool thread might pro-vide a wealth of information. A criminalist would be able to make a pho-tomicrographic comparison of it with any woolen garments owned by the accused, checking such things as the numbers of fibers per strand, their dye content, plus thickness and direction of twist. With each new at-tack, the Wake-Up Rapist was unwittingly adding to a forensic noose that would eventually tighten around his neck.

CHAPTER

28

Several days passed before the crime lab was able to identify the type of footwear that produced the print beside Laura Kelce's alarm box. That afternoon, Roth and Sosa displayed their identification to the FDLE clerk on the other side of a bulletproof glass partition.

"I didn't realize that Walker is gay," Roth told his partner after an electronic lock clicked, admitting them to the state crime laboratory.

"You'd be surprised at how many cops are out of the closet today," she said matter-of-factly. "He lives with a guy who's a chopper pilot with the highway patrol. They've been together for years. I couldn't care less what someone does in bed, as long as they do the job." They went to the third floor of the Forensic Services section and located a bald man in a lab coat with a picture ID clipped to his lapel.

"Mike, what have you got on my shoe print?" Sosa asked.

Mike Owens looked up from the comparison microscope he was hunched over. "Well, first, it isn't a shoe print. It was made by a boot." He opened a drawer beneath the black slate table he was seated at and removed one of a number of dental stone casts with labels on them. "We had quite a time with this one. The FBI couldn't come up with a match on it, either. They thought it might be foreign, so they e-mailed a scan of the cast to New Scotland Yard. The Brits have just come up with a shoe print computer system called SICAR—Shoeprint Image Capture and Retrieval—that catalogues thousands of types of footwear from all over the world. That's how we got the hit."

She sat on the stool next to him. "What can you tell us about it?"

Owens' shiny pate gleamed beneath the rows of overhead fluorescent lights as he turned the cast over and inspected it. "It's a Garibaldi boot—made in Venice."

Something he picked up in Italy while he was following Laura Kelce on her concert tour?

"Nothing like this in my closet, I can tell you that," Mike Owens said. "A pair of Garibaldis retails for around six hundred bucks."

"Who sells them?" she asked.

"Lots of upscale men's shops around the country—Rodeo Drive and Worth Avenue kinds of places. They're also sold all over Europe."

"Anything else noteworthy about the boots?" she inquired.

"Yeah. Looks like the guy you're after is a biker."

Sosa's forehead creased. "Why do you say that?"

"Here, I'll show you." He switched on a high intensity halogen light and centered a large magnifying glass on a pulley over the cast. The two detectives peered into it. "The Garibaldi that made this print is almost new. Notice the horizontal scratches where the sole and heel meet. Those are wear marks made by one of the metal pegs where a motorcycle rider rests his feet."

Roth asked, "What about the scratches in the middle of the impression?"

"They were produced by friction strikes of a metal brake pedal."

"Couldn't the marks have come from something else?" Sosa asked. Owens shook his head.

"Nothing but a motorcycle produces this kind of wear pattern."

"Can you tell what kind of bike it came from?" she asked.

Owens kneaded his scalp. "Well, it's not a rice burner."

"What's that?" Roth inquired.

"The Japanese bikes—Hondas, Suzukis, Kawasakis. They all have rubber sleeves on their pegs. Harley-Davidson is the only company I know of that still makes some of its bikes with exposed metal pegs."

Roth recalled the smudge of crankcase oil on the nun's sheets.

CHAPTER

29

They returned to Gables Estates the next morning. Not surprisingly, a check with the management office revealed that none of its residents owned a motorcycle. Nor was there any record at the front gate of a visitor entering the complex on a bike the night Laura Kelce was assaulted.

The pianist's estate looked very different than it had during the rainstorm. Huge oaks loomed majestically along the front of the property, obscuring much of the house from the street. The imposing, two-story, Mediterranean structure with pecky cypress trim appeared to have been built in the twenties. The stacks of three fireplaces were visible on the barrel tile roof—an unusual feature for a home in the subtropics. Behind the house, a thirty-foot yacht rocked gently at its dock on the Intracoastal.

The detectives went to where the burglar alarm had been. A company representative from AV-TEK had already unbolted the unit and shipped it to their home office for testing, no doubt in anticipation of a major lawsuit.

Roth looked at the eave above where the footprint was found. The overhang had apparently extended just enough to protect the imprint of the Garibaldi boot from the heavy rain.

"It all makes perfect sense," Sosa said sarcastically. "When this guy isn't stalking women around Rome in six-hundred dollar designer boots or playing sonatas on his antique Erard, he wears oily jeans and rides a Harley. I wouldn't be surprised if he moonlights at Jiffy Lube to pick up extra change. That's probably where the oil on the nun's sheet came from."

The contradictions facing them in the aftermath of the fourth Wake-Up Rape were mind-numbing. They were looking for an obscenity-spewing, sexual sadist who rode a motorcycle and had an impressive knowledge of classical music, as well as expensive taste in footwear and enough money to travel abroad.

They looked through the partially open drapes of the bay window where the intruder had entered. Roth ran a finger along the sill, which was now smudged with black graphite powder from an earlier attempt by the ET's to recover latent prints. He recalled the solitary lamb's wool fiber that was found snagged on the window sill. Where had it come from? The victims all said their attacker was wearing jeans, a sports shirt and a windbreaker.

Sosa scuffed the soft earth with her shoe. "He may ride a bike, but he sure didn't use it that night. It poured from midnight on. Even if the gate guard was asleep, one of the roving patrols would probably have spotted a guy on a motorcycle in the rain."

Roth's eyes shifted to the thick canopy of trees bordering the property. "Maybe he came in another way."

"There isn't any. The Intracoastal Waterway runs along the back of the entire development."

Roth paused and gazed at the wide expanse of water behind the concert pianist's home.

"He could have used a boat," he suggested, motioning toward the slip where Laura Kelce's Sea-Ray was tied up.

"Not likely," Sosa responded. "Security out here is so tight that they have their own 24/7 boat patrol on the Intracostal." She explained that every boat docked in the Gables community was listed in its security database. A maritime intruder would probably have been quickly spotted.

When they returned to the car, she pointed to a dark trickle that was creeping from beneath it. "I call this heap the *Exxon Valdez* because it leaks nearly as much oil as that tanker in Alaska." She leaned in the window to get her radio, exposing the faint outline of a pair of bikini panties beneath her slacks. "418 to Miami … show me as a two-officer unit until further notice." She released the transmit button momentarily and looked over her shoulder at Roth. "Hey, what's your badge number?"

"What?"

"It's not a trick question, Doctor," she said dryly. "Communications needs it for their computer."

"Oh, sure. It's ... ah ..."

"Standby, Miami," she said, rolling her eyes.

He fumbled with the shield clipped to his belt, squinting at the numbers stamped on it. *What a shlump I am! A detective who doesn't know his own badge number.* "It's 714."

The starter on the *Exxon Valdez* churned gratingly for several seconds before the engine turned over.

"Where are we going now?"

"To Saks Fifth Avenue at the Bal Harbour Shops. We're about to conduct what you could call an olfactory lineup. I want to see if Laura Kelce can recognize the cologne the rapist was wearing."

*   *

On the way to the mall, Sosa phoned Laura Kelce's personal physician and explained what she wanted to do. After getting permission to revisit his patient that afternoon, they went directly to the men's section of Sak's Fifth Avenue. She had one of the clerks there spray a series of nine cards with her best fragrances. She carefully labeled each one and placed them in separate plastic evidence bags.

One of the floor nurses at the hospital escorted them to Laura Kelce's room, where they found the maimed pianist more alert than the last time they saw her.

"Ms. Kelce, I've brought some samples of men's colognes with me. Do you feel up to seeing if any of them was what this person was wearing?"

She nodded slightly. The nurse eased a pillow behind her back and elevated the bed a few degrees. Sosa passed the first scent card in front of her face. No reaction.

"Just close your eyes and try to relax."

Laura Kelce moved her head from side to side after the next card. Sosa tried another one. Still nothing. Her response was the same to the next three cards.

As soon as Sosa removed the sixth one from its bag, Laura Kelce's eyes shot open. "Oh, God! That's it!" she sobbed, turning her head away.

Roth looked at the brand name Sosa had written on the card. *Pasha de Cartier.*

CHAPTER

30

They left the hospital and were on their way back to the Sexual Battery Unit when Sosa spotted a shirtless boy threading his way between cars with an armful of Spanish language newspapers. She motioned him over and bought one.

¡UN DEMONIO TORTURO MUJER! the headline blared.

"Fiend Tortures Woman!" she translated.

Even in the Cuban community, the latest Wake-Up Rape was front-page news. She tossed the paper on the seat. "Shit rolls downhill," she said. "The Mayor and City Commission raise hell with the chief. He puts it to Wilcox. Wilcox dumps on me."

The portable radios on the seat between them crackled sporadically as they drove. "A guy who uses one-hundred-fifty dollar an ounce cologne and rides a Harley," she said. "What do you make of it?"

Roth was reluctant to tell her what he was thinking, knowing how absurd it would sound.

"I think the man we're looking for is ..."

"Is what?"

"Remember what Alvin found out about the vending machine condom?"

She shrugged. "So, the guy's AC/DC. Big deal. Lots of rapists are bisexual."

Roth leaned back in the seat and folded his arms.

"He's not bisexual," he said.

She shot him a baffled glance. "What do you mean?"

"That he's gay."

An amused look crossed her face. "You're putting me on."

"No, I'm serious. I'm sure the Wake-Up Rapes are the only form of sexual contact this man has ever had with a female."

"A homosexual rapist. Isn't that sort of an oxymoron?"

He flipped down his visor. "Not really. Being gay doesn't make a man incapable of having sex with a woman."

"Maybe I'm missing something here," she said tongue-in-cheek. "I thought gay men weren't attracted to women."

"Most aren't."

"Not to be indelicate, Doctor, but do you mind telling me how a gay rapist goes about getting it up with a female?"

"He uses homoerotic ideation."

"What?"

"He fantasizes that he's having sex with another man during the rapes."

"Oh, give me a break!"

"The mental process isn't much different from that of a husband or wife who pretends they're making love to a movie star instead of their spouse," he countered.

She draped her wrist over the steering wheel. "No offense, but that's the silliest goddamn thing I've ever heard."

"Really?" he sniffed. "Why do you think he always darkens the room before each rape?"

She glided to a stop at a red light. "Lots of people like to do it in the dark."

"How many rapists have you seen make an attractive woman like Diane Whitaker put on a robe before they have sex with her?" he asked. She looked at him without replying.

"And how do you account for the fact that he only rapes his victims anally?" he added.

"Anal rape isn't that unusual. I see it all the time. It's just another way of degrading a woman."

"Of course it is, but most rapists have at least *some* contact with their victim's genitals. This man never does."

"So, that makes him gay?"

He turned toward her and said earnestly, "Look, most men are highly visual when it comes to having sex with females."

"I guess I'd agree with that," she smiled, pulling away when the light changed.

"But this man isn't! It's as if the sight of a woman's body disgusts him. When most Stalker Sadists move into the torture phase, their violence is centered on distinctively female parts of the victim's body—usually the genitals. Why do you suppose that he mutilated Laura Kelce's hands instead of her vagina?"

"That's easy to explain," she said, turning on the wipers as a light mist of rain appeared on the windshield. "He wanted to punish her by taking away her musical talent. I'd say that's consistent with sadism."

"With sadism, yes, but not with sexual sadism," he volleyed. "This rapist avoids the genitals of his victims because he's phobic about them—the way other people are about spiders or open spaces."

She made a face. "Why would he be afraid of a woman's vagina?"

His reply was interrupted by the sound of Alvin Walker's voice coming over the radio.

He told them that a thorough check of Laura Kelce's piano had revealed no prints except hers and those of her maid and piano tuner. Despite the grisly mutilation of the concert pianist's hands, Walker was able to obtain a set of comparison prints from the Canton, Ohio School District, for which she worked briefly as a music teacher after graduating from college.

"Let's get back to this phobia thing," Sosa said. "What makes you think this rapist is frightened of female genitals?"

"Remember the asthma attack he had the night he raped Lieutenant Whitaker?"

"What about it?"

"It was brought on by her reference to menstrual blood."

"Now, you've really lost me."

The night before, he had read an article called "The Genesis of Castration Anxiety" in the *Journal of Abnormal Psychology*. It described several cases of men who experienced such intense fear of female genitalia that the sight or thought of a woman's vagina made them completely impotent.

"On an unconscious level, he views women as castrated men. Someone with his kind of neurosis thinks of a vagina as a wound that's produced by castration. Knowing that female genitalia bleed periodically reinforces both the neurotic fantasy and his childhood fears of emasculation."

"Really ... this is so far out!"

Traffic ahead of them had slowed to a crawl. In his side view mirror, Roth saw a tow truck with flashing lights working its way along the grassy shoulder toward a wreck in the distance.

"How much do you know about the Oedipus complex?" he asked.

"Not much. We touched on it in a child psych class I had in college."

"Let me tell you about where it fits into our case."

"Gosh, should I be taking notes?"

What chutzpah! He drew a deep breath. "Freud believed that a child's penis first becomes a source of pleasurable sensations around six. About the same time, he develops a strong, emotional attachment to his mother and begins to see his father as a rival for her affection. When a little boy discovers that girls don't have a penis, he unconsciously concludes that they've been castrated as punishment for the same kind of incestuous feelings he has toward his mother. He goes through a brief period where he's afraid the same thing will happen to him. That's the Oedipus complex, in a nutshell."

He hoped he didn't sound like he was lecturing. Sara used to accuse him of having chalk dust in his veins. "Unconsciously, this rapist has probably dreaded castration his whole life."

"This is a smart guy. Why would he believe something so ridiculous?"

"It's no more ridiculous than being frightened of the sound of jets or not stepping on cracks. People carry around all kinds of irrational baggage from childhood."

He watched a couple of kids racing each other on skateboards down the sidewalk. "Most males, regardless of whether they become straight or gay, work their way through the Oedipal period. Something went terribly wrong in this man's childhood. Whatever it was, it left him with a level of castration anxiety that's off the charts."

"Have you ever heard of a gay guy raping a woman?"

"No," he admitted.

"Even if one could, why would he want to?"

"The same reason as any other rapist—anger towards females."

She pulled into the entrance of the police garage. "This guy is apparently in his late twenties or early thirties. Why would he just now be 'coming out' as a rapist?"

"Something must have happened to produce the violence against women we're seeing."

"Gays don't limit themselves to anal sex," she pointed out, angling the *Exxon Valdez* into a parking space. "If he's as terrified of female genitals as you say, why doesn't he make his victims go down on him the way other rapists do? A mouth in the dark is pretty impersonal. Couldn't he just pretend another guy is giving him a blow job?" She looked at him expectantly, waiting for an answer.

Roth cleared his throat. He wasn't used to being around women who talked about sex as graphically as Maria Sosa. "He avoids fellatio because he can't take the chance that a victim might speak or start crying while he's having sex. The sound of a woman's voice during a rape would make him impotent. That's why he always gags his victims."

She grinned. "Professor, you've got one hell of an imagination!"

He said no more about his homosexual rapist theory that day.

CHAPTER

31

An altar boy in a loose fitting cassock shook a tinkling gold bell when the priest elevated the host in front of the congregation. "May the body of our Lord Jesus Christ preserve your soul to life everlasting," the clergyman prayed aloud.

Kneeling in one of the pews, he repeated the words to himself in Latin, words he had spoken thousands of times before: *Corpus Domini nostri Jesu Christi custodiat animam tuam in vitam eternam.* Latin had always been one of his favorite languages. What a pity it had been eliminated from the mass. A feeling of melancholy came over him. Why had the Church destroyed and suppressed so much that was good and beautiful?

He slid back in his seat to allow others in the pew to join the Sunday communion line that was forming in the center aisle. One of them was an attractive woman in her mid forties with silken blond hair and delicate features. He had been watching her for almost a week now. How demure she looked in her knee-length skirt and white turtleneck. What would her superiors say if they knew she was spreading her legs regularly for a doctor on her staff who was married and had three children? Hypocrite!

She returned to the pew after communion with her eyes downcast and her hands clasped in front of her. When he raised the kneeler to let her pass, she smiled, glancing at him with haunting gray eyes. Was that the look that had persuaded her lover to dishonor his marriage vows? He shuddered inwardly with anger. If thine eye offends, pluck it out, Nina.

CHAPTER

32

On Wednesday, Roth accompanied Sosa to a lecture on rape investigation she was giving at a regional training seminar in Miami Beach. As soon as he fastened his seat belt, he felt the familiar weight of the shoulder holster against his side. He chafed at the thought of carrying a gun for six months.

"Ever seen Liberty City?" Sosa asked after they left the police garage.

"No."

"You're about to get a quick tour. We're taking a shortcut through it." Minutes later, they turned off Northwest 27th St. onto Dr. Martin Luther King Jr. Boulevard.

Roth's only prior exposure to Miami's largest ghetto had come from news coverage of the crime that abounded in it. He took in the tableau of poverty around him. Atlas Pawn. Bennie's BBQ. Jake's Bail Bonds. A line of black men and women waited patiently in front of a convenience store to buy Florida lottery tickets—a twenty-three million to one long shot at The American Dream. The windows of every shop they passed were covered with burglar bars, and the fronts of some buildings were pockmarked with bullet strikes from the last major riot.

Men and women sat on wooden stoops in the bright sunlight. Some leaned against parked cars while others moved torpidly along the crumbling sidewalks. Stubby beer cans in the gutters had holes punched in their sides to transform them into crack pipes, marking a trail of despair that led nowhere. Most of the men, women and children on Martin Luther King didn't need anyone to tell them that The Man was on the block. The Ford's black-wall tires and the small antenna on its trunk said that the couple inside were cops.

"LC was my beat for two years when I worked patrol." She slowed and rolled down her window.

"Hi, Albert!" she called out to an old man in a frayed, camouflage jacket, pushing a shopping cart filled with empty aluminum cans. He smiled, flashing a mouthful of yellow stumps. The *Exxon Valdez* idled behind a bus while it disgorged several passengers.

PUSSY

Someone had sprayed the word in large red letters on the back of the bus. Roth was reminded of the things the nun's attacker had called her. Why had men coined so many hostile sexual terms for women? As a psychiatrist, his dean found the sexual epithet '*pussy*' significant, suggesting that its frequent use in the street language of men speaks volumes about their unconscious fear of the opposite sex: beneath a purring cat's warm, soft fur, are sharp teeth and claws that can rip into flesh if the animal becomes angry or excited.

He leaned against the headrest, pondering the cruelties meted out to women throughout the ages: foot binding in ancient China; coercive veiling in the Middle East; the barbaric practice of clitoridectomy in sub-Saharan Africa. Rape seemed to be just another in a long list of atrocities visited on females. He was about to say something when he noticed two black youths walking rapidly toward his side of the car. The taller one had a boom box propped on his muscular shoulder, and the other was carrying a brown lunch bag.

"Hi," he said pleasantly, rolling down his window.

"Yo, man ... I got somethun' fo' you!" the man with the bag said, thrusting his hand inside it.

Sosa suddenly lunged across the seat with her pistol pointed at Roth's open window. "That's close enough, bro'!" she warned.

Roth flattened himself against the seat, startled by the abrupt appearance of her gun. The two men froze, glancing at each other for a moment before sprinting away.

"Wh ... what's happening?"

She holstered her Glock, still breathing rapidly. "Those zombies were so coked-out they probably thought we were a couple of lost tourists."

His head swiveled toward the receding figures. "You … you mean they were going to rob us?"

"Or worse. The little guy probably had a piece in the bag."

She glared at him. "Why weren't you watching? They were on your side!"

"I'm sorry. I just didn't …"

"This isn't a goddamn classroom!" she snapped. "You could have gotten us both killed! You can't ride around an area like Liberty City with your head up your ass!"

The rebuke stung. They rode in silence for almost a mile before he spoke.

"I've been thinking," he said. "A lot of stalkers are fetishists who take things from their victims. We should have our victims check and see if they're missing anything."

She swerved to the curb and jammed the car in park. "Goddamnit! Don't tell me how to run my investigation!"

"I'm only trying to help!"

The tires scratched on the pavement as she punched the accelerator.

"Fine! Then stay the hell out of my way and keep your bullshit theories about the case to yourself!"

* *

After work that day, Roth knelt in his wife's garden, troweling the damp earth before planting a row of plumbagos, pentas and hibiscus. He plucked some crabgrass and tossed it aside. Brushing the dirt from his hands, he surveyed his efforts. No matter how hard he tried, he could never get Sara's garden looking the way it had when she tended it. She used to say that nurturing new life is a 'chick thing' that comes naturally to women.

His mind returned to Liberty City. Sosa was right. He could have gotten them both shot. The experience of being only a few feet from a crack head with a gun introduced a new element in his life, something he had never known in all his years at the university. The moment he saw the pistol in Sosa's hand, he was afraid.

CHAPTER

33

The flashing red and blue strobe on the *Exxon Valdez* swept across darkened office buildings along Flagler Boulevard as Roth and Sosa rushed to the scene of Miami's fifth Wake-Up Rape. The instant black coffee he'd zapped in his microwave just before she picked him up sloshed onto his hand.

"For God's sake, slow down!" he complained. "You want to have an accident?"

She gripped the wheel defiantly and nudged the speedometer needle up another ten miles. They were both frustrated by their lack of progress on the case. The call that had jolted them out of their sleep forty-five minutes earlier didn't help.

The latest assault took place at a Miami Beach high-rise called Sea Dunes. Several patrol cars and an evidence van were already in the condo parking lot when they arrived.

They took the elevator to the twenty-sixth floor and went directly to the victim's apartment. A stiff breeze was blowing into the three-bedroom unit through an open sliding glass door that looked onto the ocean. Sosa located the uniformed sergeant who was in charge of the crime scene. He was a solidly built man in his mid-forties with wide shoulders and a dark mustache. He explained that the victim this time was the forty-five-year-old Chief of Staff at St. Joseph's, the largest Catholic hospital in the city.

"How did he get in?" Sosa asked.

"The condo next door is empty. Looks like he picked the lock on it and then jumped from one balcony to the next."

"At twenty-six stories?" Roth said. The five-foot gap between the balconies meant certain death for anyone who failed at such a leap.

"This asshole must think he's Spiderman, huh?" the patrol sergeant said. "It's hard to believe anybody in his right mind would risk a jump like that."

Roth stood on the balcony and looked down at the white sand and dark water below them. The first light of morning was beginning to seep into the eastern sky. A sliver of moon and the flickering pinpoints of stars were still visible above the calm surface of the ocean.

"People leave their sliding doors open when they go to bed so they can hear the ocean," the sergeant said. "Up this high, you'd think it would be safe."

He led them to the bedroom where the attack took place. Everything on the white French provincial dresser had been swept onto the carpet: hairbrushes, combs, powder and bottles of lotion were scattered everywhere. "The victim woke up and saw him beside her bed in a ski mask with a gun. He told her it was three o'clock and made her get on the floor," the patrol sergeant explained.

Roth took a step back when he felt something crunch under one of his feet. It was a piece of glass from the broken oval mirror above the victim's dresser. Sosa shook her head in exasperation. "Aren't things bad enough without you walking on evidence?"

Shards of mirror were strewn across the cream-colored carpet. A few jagged fragments still clung to the frame. "Looks like seven years' bad luck for somebody," the patrol sergeant observed.

Roth noticed some red smudges on a couple of the larger pieces. "Blood?" he said, bending to get a better look.

Sosa knelt beside one of the fragments. "No, it's lipstick," she reported, pointing to a shiny gold tube that had rolled against the baseboard.

"Looks like he wrote something on the mirror before he broke it."

"Maybe the lab can tell us what it was." Roth said.

"Maybe."

"The neighbors heard a racket a little after three and called 911," the patrol sergeant told them. "When our people got here, the victim was running around in just her pajama tops, shouting that she was blind." He crouched beside an eyedropper and a small glass vial on the floor. "He put whatever was in that in her eyes." The dark brown bottle still held a small residue of fluid.

"Any other injuries?" Roth asked.

"Not that we could see. She said he pinned her to the floor, then bound and gagged her."

"With duct tape," Sosa supplied wearily.

"Yeah. Then he started putting the drops in her eyes. She apparently passed out from the pain."

"Did he rape her?" Roth asked.

"We're not certain, but, if he didn't do her, he was damn sure getting ready to. When she came to, she was face down on the floor with her pajama bottoms off, and he was on top of her. She managed to get the tape off her mouth and started screaming. That's when he beat feet out the door."

A slightly-built evidence technician entered the room lugging a bulky case. *First, Laura Kelce's fingers. Now, this woman's eyes.* The Stalker Sadist was continuing to restrict his torture to gender neutral parts of his victims' bodies.

"Got anything else?" Sosa inquired.

The sergeant shoved his uniform cap back on his head with a thumb. "Oh, just one other little thing," he said casually. "The victim says she knows who did it."

Sosa's lashes flew up in surprise. "What?"

The patrol sergeant leafed through a couple of pages on his clipboard. "I had one of my guys ride in the ambulance with her. She didn't want to go to the ER at St. Joe's. Too embarrassed, I guess. So, they took her to Mercy. She ID'd the perp on the way as Donald Vincent. He worked at the hospital as an orderly until she fired him a few days ago for coming on to one of the nurses."

Roth raised an eyebrow. "A *female* nurse?"

The patrol sergeant gave him a puzzled look. Sosa whispered in his ear just loud enough for Roth to hear. "He thinks this rapist is gay."

"Sure, he is!" the uniformed sergeant grinned.

Sosa asked, "What makes her so sure it was Vincent?"

"She says she recognized his voice. He also called her 'boss lady' a couple of times."

"Does he match our guy's description?"

"Get this," the patrol sergeant responded. "Vincent is around thirty, blond and blue, six feet, maybe one seventy."

"Sounds like our boy!" she said eagerly.

"Looks like he's got a real bad temper. The victim said he broke a lamp on her desk the day she fired him. He told her she'd be hearing from him. Her secretary had to call hospital security and have him removed from the property."

Sosa's eyes roamed around the room. "Any witnesses?"

The patrol sergeant shook his head.

*   *

After leaving Sea Dunes, they went to the personnel office at St. Joseph's Hospital, where Sosa had a clerk pull the employment records on Donald Allen Vincent. "Jackpot!" she exulted, holding up a copy of the parking permit the former orderly had been issued. "Look! It's for a motorcycle!"

Roth inspected the form briefly. "Yeah, but it's a Kawasaki. The guy at the lab said the peg marks on the boot came from a Harley-Davidson."

"So ... ? He could have switched from a Kawasaki to a Harley before he raped Laura Kelce."

Roth wagged his head. "I don't see a hospital orderly wearing six-hundred dollar boots or jetting off to a piano concert in Rome, do you?"

"The job may be just a front. Anyone as skilled as this rapist could be doing break-ins all over town that give him plenty of money. After today, I'd say pulling cat burglaries at luxury condos along the beach is a real possibility." She copied Vincent's address and made arrangements for immediate surveillance of his Coconut Grove apartment.

On their way across town to interview the latest victim, Roth ran a Bureau of Criminal Identification check on Donald Allen Vincent, WM, 33. Communications advised that he had two prior convictions: one for driving under the influence and the other for burglary of an occupied dwelling.

Sosa said mischievously, "Looks like Donnie left out a couple of things on his employment application."

Roth didn't find the BCI information very persuasive. "The burglary conviction is almost five years old," he pointed out.

"I don't care. I'm telling you, he's our guy!"

"How much do you want to bet?" he challenged.

"What about breakfast?"

"You're on," he said, reaching for the hand she offered. His stomach did a somersault when he felt the warmth of her palm against his.

CHAPTER

34

Clear plastic tubes curled from bags on IV poles on either side of Dr. Nina Pulaski's bed in the Intensive Care Unit; they fed a continuous drip of saline solution onto gauze pads beneath her eyelids. The hospital's poison control center had already determined that the substance her assailant put in her eyes contained sodium hydroxide, a caustic chemical found in household products, such as Drano. The prognosis was bleak. The cornea of her left eye was badly seared, leaving her completely blind in it; even with surgery, it was unlikely that she would ever recover more than fifty percent of the vision in her other eye.

The two detectives entered the room quietly and stood on either side of her bed. "Dr. Pulaski, I'm Sergeant Sosa from the Miami Police Department," Maria said softly. "My partner, Dave Roth, is here with me." Roth did a double take, caught off guard by the introduction.

Partner? Did she really say 'partner'?

The woman turned toward the sound of Sosa's voice, trying to raise herself on her elbows.

"Have you caught Vincent?" she asked.

"Not yet, but we will," Sosa assured her. Over the next half hour, she led Dr. Pulaski carefully back through the attack, asking only the questions that needed to be answered immediately. Her years of experience as a sexual battery detective showed; she chose her words carefully, gauging the impact of each one. She reminded Roth of a dentist doing a root canal, probing a little deeper each time and watching to see if more anesthetic was needed. The spindles of the microcassette recorder beside the bed rotated slowly as the interview continued.

At one point, Nina Pulaski grasped the crisp, white sheets with both hands. "My God, I'm blind! I don't want to live like this," she cried.

Sosa spent several minutes calming her. Roth heard the hesitancy in the sergeant's voice when she came to her last question. "Dr. Pulaski, there's something I have to ask every victim," she said gently. "Please don't take it personally, but I need to know if you had sexual intercourse within twenty-four hours of the time you were assaulted."

Shock and outrage registered on the physician's face. "How dare you say such a thing to me!" she seethed.

"Please, I …"

"Get out of here! Get out!" A young Cuban-American nurse rushed into the room with a look of alarm.

"It's alright," Sosa said, with a palm-up gesture. "We were just leaving."

Several new arrivals were being wheeled into the ICU as Sosa and Roth walked down a polished green corridor to the parking lot.

"I hate asking a woman that, but it's the first thing any defense attorney will key on."

Roth put his hands in his pockets. "So, now I'm 'Dave,' huh?"

"Well, I just thought we may as well dispense with titles since it looks like we're going to be working together for a while."

"Fine with me."

"I gather you don't like 'Dave.'"

He waited for the wail of an inbound ambulance to subside. "My friends call me David."

"Okay, David it is, and I'm Maria—or Sosa, if you like. Just *please* don't call me 'Sarge.' It makes me feel as if I should be wearing Aqua Velva and have hair under my arms."

CHAPTER

35

Sosa walked into Roth's office with the lab report on Dr. Pulaski two days after they interviewed her.

"This can't be right!" he said after reading it.

She looked at him in quiet triumph. "They checked all three ports of entry in the good doctor's body. Her mouth and anal cavity were both clear, but there were enough motile sperm in her vagina to impregnate every female in Miami. So much for your 'vagina phobia' theory."

He recalled from an investigative text Frank Bailey had loaned him that the presence of live sperm in the vagina is considered presumptive evidence of sexual intercourse within three hours.

He handed her back the report, still mystified. "But he put her on her stomach for anal sex, just like the other victims."

She smirked. "You can also have vaginal intercourse in that position, or didn't you know that?"

He felt himself blush. "Maria, this guy couldn't have vaginal sex with a woman if his life depended on it. There has to be some other explanation!"

She leaned against his desk and crossed her arms. "Why do you have to be so pig-headed? This homosexual rapist thing is becoming an obsession!"

"The sperm in her vagina could have come from someone else. Maybe she has a boyfriend."

"Who just happened to get it on with her a few hours before she was attacked? Come on!"

"It's possible. That would explain why she was so upset when you asked if she'd had sex that night. The rapist could have been watching the condo, waiting for him to leave, and ..."

123

She threw up her hands. "David, you're hopeless!"

He removed his glasses and wiped them with a handkerchief, then said, "Didn't the lab extract DNA from sperm in the nun's rape to check against the state database on sex offenders?"

"Yeah … why?"

"Well, why not compare that rape DNA with DNA from the sperm in Pulaski's vagina?"

"Read my lips," she said, silently mouthing, 'N-O!'

"Why not?"

"I'll give you a couple of good reasons. DNA testing is expensive and time consuming. We don't need any more of it until we've got a suspect in custody. We've already got plenty of probable cause. There isn't a judge in the county who wouldn't issue an arrest warrant on Donald Vincent right now." She ticked off the elements of 'probable cause' on the fingers of one hand. "Here's a guy with a bad temper and a clear motive who matches the description of the Wake-Up Rapist perfectly. He also just happens to ride a motorcycle."

"Damnit! I keep telling you, it's the wrong kind of bike. Why won't you listen?"

She raised her chin haughtily and looked away as if she hadn't heard him. "The victim also recognized his voice. He called her 'boss lady.' What the hell more do you want?" she said.

"Some vague link to the other attacks would be nice," he shot back. "We can't tie Vincent to any of the women except Nina Pulaski."

"We'll worry about connecting the dots once we've arrested him. I'm telling you, this guy is the Wake-Up Rapist!"

"Let me suggest another explanation," he said reflectively.

"I'm listening."

"Let's suppose you're Donald Vincent. You're furious at Pulaski for firing you. You want to get even with her."

He stared out the window, absorbed in thought. "You just happen to be a white male with blue eyes and blond hair. You're also in your thirties, with the same general build as the Wake-Up Rapist."

She pursed her lips. "You think Vincent is a copycat?"

He moved his chair closer to hers. "Maria, the media has been covering the MO for months: the ski mask, the hour of the attacks, gagging the women with duct tape. The last *Herald* story even mentioned that he'd begun mutilating his victims. There's nothing that Pulaski's attacker said or did that he couldn't have gotten from TV or the newspapers. There's only one thing he wouldn't have known."

"The fact that our guy only rapes women anally."

"Exactly."

He thought he detected a glimmer of interest in her dark brown eyes. "Well, there's an easy way to find out if you're right, and it's a lot faster than doing a DNA comparison." He listened attentively as she went on. "We know from the rape kits that we're after a secretor. With secretors, you can determine blood type from bodily fluids, like sweat, saliva and semen. I'll have the lab run an *absorption inhibition test* and compare the blood type of the semen they extracted from Pulaski's vagina with the blood type in our anal rapes." She reached for the phone.

"How long will it take to get the results?"

"We could know something by tomorrow."

The long hours they had been working since the Pulaski attack and the sleep deprivation were beginning to catch up with him; his eyes were burning, and he had a sour taste in his mouth. "Now what?" he yawned.

"We need to relieve McNees and Walker on the stakeout at Vincent's apartment."

No rest for the wicked. He guessed that the chances of seeing his bed any time soon were slim.

*   *

Detective teams had been conducting continuous surveillance of Donald Vincent's apartment ever since Dr. Pulaski identified him as her attacker. The stirring of palm fronds portended rain when Sosa and Roth pulled alongside McNees and Walker, who were parked beside a blue dumpster. Sosa rolled down her window.

"Anything yet?"

"Nope," Alvin Walker reported, slouched behind the wheel.

His partner leaned across the seat and threw in, "We got his recording when we called."

As soon as McNees and Walker left, Sosa backed into their parking spot. She took a small pair of Nikons from the glove box and focused them on the drawn curtains of Donald Vincent's upstairs apartment.

"We'll get a search warrant as soon as we bag him. I'd give anything to see what's inside there."

Roth braced a knee against the dash and peered through the film of dust on the windshield.

"You're thinking a ski mask and duct tape."

"Among other interesting items, like a small caliber pistol," she replied, handing him the binoculars. After entering a code in her cell phone to block caller ID, she got the number for the manager's office from directory assistance and dialed it. "Hi … uh … my name is Cindy Scott," she said in a ditsy voice. "I'm a friend of Don Vincent in 203. I'm only in Miami for a couple of days, and I didn't want to miss him. I keep getting his answering machine when I call. I thought he might be out of town." A moment later, she flashed a 'thumbs up' sign.

"Apparently, he's around," she said, after hanging up. "The manager has seen him a couple of times this week." She kicked off her flats and rubbed her eyes. "Now comes the fun part … waiting. Believe me, surveillance is only exciting on TV shows."

She stretched languorously, revealing the fullness of her breasts beneath the blouse.

"You need two things for a stakeout. Lots of patience and a strong bladder. By the way, how's yours doing?"

He squared his shoulders. "Fine," he said, knowing that, with all the coffee he'd been drinking to keep awake, he was good for only another half-hour at most.

"It could be a long night. If you have to pee, there's an empty Gatorade jar in the trunk."

He looked at her aghast.

"Oh, Jesus!" she laughed. "You should see the expression on your face. I'm just kidding! There's a gas station just down the street."

She trained the binoculars on a UPS truck that had just pulled into the lot. The driver turned on his flashers and took the steps two at a time; he left a package several doors down from Vincent's apartment and drove off.

People came and went over the next hour, but there was still no sign of the man they were waiting for. A Hispanic gardener arrived and began working in the flowerbeds with a weed eater that rasped like sandpaper on gravel. The humidity was fierce; the still air inside the car was worsened by the smell of overripe garbage wafting from the dumpster beside them. Roth finally decided that whoever held the department's bladder distention record could keep the title.

"I'm going back to the gas station," he announced. "Will you be okay?"

"Oh, I think I can manage to survive without you for a few minutes."

Why did she say things like that? It seemed that every time they started getting along she was in his face with some smart-assed remark.

"Hey, how about picking us up something to eat while you're back there," she said. "I think I saw a Kentucky Fried Chicken."

"You can *eat* in a place like this?"

"Hell, I've eaten at autopsies," she said casually. "This isn't so bad."

He stopped her when she reached for her purse. "My treat."

* *

He thought about Donald Vincent on his way back to the car with chicken, French fries and Cokes; even if he wasn't the Wake-Up Rapist, if he was Pulaski's attacker, there was a good chance he'd be armed. Most people would surrender when confronted by two police officers; but, suppose he didn't? He tried to put the thought out of his mind.

"God, I'm starving!" Sosa said when he returned with the bag of food. They both ate ravenously.

She wrinkled her nose when he squirted ketchup on a drumstick. "You put ketchup on chicken?"

"Doesn't everyone?"

A few yards away, a black and white cat prowled through the debris of the dumpster.

"Were you a criminology major?" he asked.

"Business administration," she replied, dabbing her lips with a napkin. "Right after I graduated from Florida State, I got a job as a management trainee with IBM in Atlanta. They laid me off when Big Blue started downsizing. Miami PD had just started recruiting women and minorities. I wanted to be down here with my family, so I took the test. Here I am, still a cop, eleven years later."

He glanced at her as he tore open a packet of salt and shook it on his fries. She didn't wear a wedding ring. *He had to know.* Now was as good a time as any to find out.

"Is there a Mister Sosa and maybe a little Sosa or two?"

"No and no. I was married for a couple of years to a guy I grew up with. He was a very traditional Cuban male who wanted his wife at home with children, not running around the streets with a gun and badge. One day, he gave me an ultimatum: quit the job or else. So, I walked—end of story." He thought he detected a trace of sadness in her voice.

"Do you want kids?" he asked, knowing the question was too personal.

She drew the last of her soda through a straw. "Of course, I do. A boy and a girl. I'd also like Santa to find me the love of my life and make me deputy chief over the next few years. We learn to live with what life gives us."

We learn to live with what life gives us. He remembered how excited he and Sara were when the sonogram showed the baby she was expecting was a girl. They were going to call her Esther, after Sara's mother.

The ringing of Sosa's cell phone interrupted his thoughts. He couldn't tell what the call was about from her end of the conversation, but she wasn't happy.

"Are you sure? Uh-huh ... I see ... thanks." She flipped the phone shut.

"Bad news?"

"That was the lab. Are you in the mood to gloat?"

He gathered the trash from the front seat and prepared to toss it in the dumpster. "I don't gloat well when I'm this tired."

"Your hunch was right. The Wake-Up Rapist has Type O blood. They got Type *AB* from the semen in Pulaski's vagina."

It now seemed certain that Donald Vincent was a copycat who had adopted the Stalker Sadist's MO to keep himself from becoming a suspect in the rape and torture of his former employer. Sosa slapped a mosquito that had gotten inside the car. "He may not be our guy, but he's still going down for what he did to that woman!"

A couple came out of one of the downstairs apartments and passed in front of the unmarked car without noticing them. Roth's eyelids were getting heavy. He tried counting bricks on the building to stay awake. His chin slumped on his chest as a gray mist of fatigue enveloped him.

His eyes jerked open when Sosa poked him.

"You were snoring."

"Oh … I'm sorry."

"Armando, my ex-husband, used to snore. That ought to be a second degree felony in a marriage." Her eyes seemed softer for a moment, and the rapier edge was gone from her voice.

Residents of the complex were coming home now. The lights in apartments began to flick on. Roth kept shifting in his seat, trying to find a more comfortable position.

"You still think he'll show?"

"Everybody comes home sooner or later."

A little before eleven, his body tensed at the sound of a motorcycle roaring into the parking lot. They both ducked on the seat with their heads inches apart. She was so close that he could smell the shampoo in her hair.

"Is it him?" he whispered, as if whoever was on the bike might somehow hear him.

"I don't know …"

She eased her head above the dash and focused the binoculars on the motorcycle. A moment later, she keyed her radio and ran a registration check on the plate. In less than a minute, dispatch confirmed that the bike was registered to Donald Allen Vincent.

She handed Roth the binoculars. He could see that the rider was tall; the full helmet and dark face shield hid his features, giving him a menacing appearance.

"Sergeant, do you need back-up out there?" the dispatcher asked.

"Negative. 714 is with me."

Roth's throat went dry. *I'm her back up!*

She grabbed her three-cell Maglite off the seat. "Okay, let's do it."

They had only taken a few steps toward the man on the bike when he looked over his shoulder at them.

"Uh-oh … we're burned! Quick! Come here and put your arms around me!" Sosa told him.

"What?"

"Just do it. Act like we're lovers."

He closed the distance between them with wooden steps and slipped his hands around her waist; she draped her arms over his shoulders and nuzzled her cheek against his face. His heart was pounding.

"Hold me closer," she whispered in his ear.

Freeze frames from a memory flashed in his mind; for a moment, he was a clumsy, sixteen- year-old kid again with braces and zits, trying desperately to control an erection while he kissed a girl named Susan Gordman goodnight on her front porch. Back in reality, he could feel the suppleness of his partner's breasts pressing against him as she watched the rider.

"It's working," she reported. The man on the bike cut his engine moments later and set the kickstand. "You can let go now … David?"

He released his grip when her hands pressed against his chest, then fumbled with his badge case and ran beside her toward the man on the bike.

"Police!" she called out, with her hand on her gun. "Hold it right there!"

The motorcyclist casually removed his helmet and hung it on the handlebars. He was wearing a tan windbreaker, jeans and a pair of black boots with metal tips.

"Are you Donald Vincent?" Sosa asked.

"I might be. Why do you want to know, baby?" A grin played on his face and his sinewy form gave off the humid smell of liquor mingled with sweat.

"We need to talk to you," Sosa said.

"Well, maybe I don't want to talk to you!" he said, defiantly notching his thumbs in his jeans. He towered above Sosa by a good seven inches.

She slipped the short Maglite out of her back pocket and stepped closer to him.

"Listen, shitbird!" she said firmly. "Would you rather talk here or downtown?"

Vincent threw his hands up in mock surrender. "Okay ... okay. No need to get your panties in a bunch!"

"Where were you Saturday morning around three?" she demanded.

"You mean you don't know?" he chuckled. "Here, I'll show you." He reached for his back pocket.

Roth caught the blur of Sosa's flashlight out of the corner of his eye an instant before she drove it into Vincent's solar plexus. The motorcycle rider's jaw dropped; he gaped at her, wide-eyed, and then dropped to his knees, clutching his stomach and trying to get his breath. Sosa grabbed his arm, taking him to the ground in a swift motion.

"Jesus!" he cried, when she planted a knee in the middle of his back. "You're gonna break my fuckin' arm!"

"Frisk him," she instructed.

"Oww!"

Roth checked him quickly for weapons, starting at his neck and working his way down to his ankles. "He's clean."

She jerked a pair of handcuffs from the back of her waist and snapped one of the loops on Vincent's wrist.

He raised his face an inch above the asphalt. "Hey, what the hell is this?"

"You're under arrest," she said.

"For what?"

"Oh ... how about burglary, mayhem and sexual battery, to start with. Read him his rights."

Roth took a laminated Miranda warning card from his ID case.

"You have a right to remain silent. You have a right to an attorney ..."

"Hey, you got the wrong guy, lady!"

Sosa attached the other handcuff and they got him to his feet. "I suppose you don't even know who Nina Pulaski is, do you?"

Vincent strained against the handcuffs. "I know the bitch. I ought to. She fired me!"

Sosa's eyes hardened. She snatched the front of his jacket, pulling him close to her face.

"And you decided to play catch-up with her Saturday morning, didn't you?"

"I don't know what you're talking about! I've been in your goddamn jail since Friday night." The detectives exchanged a bewildered look.

"I got busted for drunk driving around midnight. See for yourself. The ticket's in my back pocket."

Roth found a yellow Florida Highway Patrol traffic citation in Vincent's jeans and unfolded it. "It's true. A state trooper arrested him for DUI at 11:27 on the night of the attack. He impounded his bike and booked him into the Metro Dade County Jail."

"That's what I was trying to tell you when you hit me. I didn't make bail until a couple of hours ago."

He rubbed his wrists after she removed the cuffs. "I'll have your goddamn badges for this!" He paused halfway up the steps to his apartment and shook his fist at them. "I'm going to sue this mother-fucking city for every cent it has!" The door to the apartment they had been watching for so many hours slammed shut behind him.

As soon as they got in the *Exxon Valdez*, Sosa put her forehead against the steering wheel and closed her eyes. "Oh, shit," she groaned. "I was sure he'd done Pulaski."

"Me, too," Roth said dispiritedly.

On the way to CID, they pieced together what had happened. It apparently was a busy twenty-four hours at the Metro Dade County Jail on the night Dr. Pulaski was assaulted. Donald Vincent's recent arrest for driving under the influence still hadn't been entered in the BCI computer when Roth ran his criminal history check.

"You were apparently right about somebody else making it with her a few hours before the assault," Sosa said.

They passed a grove of Australian pines filled with screeching macaws. "Why didn't she just tell us she'd had sex that night?" Roth asked.

"That's not hard to understand. She's a single woman who's chief of staff at a Catholic hospital."

They drove down Biscayne Boulevard, past the American Airlines Arena, toward the new, ultramodern Intercontinental Hotel. Neatly planted rows of palm trees flanked both sides of the wide boulevard. The sidewalks were bustling with late night tourists, wandering in and out of bars and nightclubs.

"This is the first time everything hasn't gone exactly the way he planned during an attack," Roth reflected.

"What do you think he'll do?"

He watched a cluster of old men playing shuffleboard on a lighted court, turning the question over in his mind. "He could try to get to her in the hospital."

"Christ! You think that's possible?"

He ran a hand through his hair. "People this compulsive don't like leaving things unfinished."

Sosa had apparently heard enough; by the time they got to the SBU, she had placed a twenty-four hour police guard on Nina Pulaski's hospital room.

* *

They sat in a Waffle House off the freeway, eating breakfast. The air was thick with the smell of grease and coffee; the conversation of people at the counter and in the booths around them blurred into a steady din. Roth's eyes felt puffy with fatigue.

"You know, if I go a little longer without sleep, I think I can break the habit," he yawned.

"I really must look like hell," she said, brushing the hair back from her face.

He ate the last bite of his watery, scrambled eggs. "You look fine."

She smiled tiredly. "Professor, you just got a C minus in female psychology."

"Why?"

"No woman ever wants to hear that she looks 'fine.' Fine means 'so-so.' We want to be told we're beautiful."

He looked at her for a long moment. "You *are* beautiful."

He saw her face flush slightly, realizing that he had held her a second too long in the parking lot.

She reached for the check. "We … we'd better get some rest."

CHAPTER

36

Maria found Roth in the police gym doing bench presses.

"Hey, the lab just finished its Humpty-Dumpty number with the broken mirror," she reported. "The lipstick was badly smudged, but they managed to reconstruct what he wrote. It was a name: *Jan*."

He sat up and wiped his face with a towel. The front of his gray t-shirt was damp with sweat. "I wonder who she is," he said pensively.

"It could be a man."

"I wonder if it's *his* name."

"You think it might be?"

"It's possible, though he may just be playing games with us," he said, adding another ten pounds to the weight stack. "Stalker sadists like to do that with the police."

"The first time I spoke with Sister Kearney, she told me the rapist said something that sounded like '*Ann, please, don't!*' It must have been 'Jan.' " She looked perplexed. Why write a name on a mirror and then try to rub it out?"

"Something may have frightened him," he said, shoving the weight bar off his chest with a grunt.

* *

Later that day, Captain Wilcox called Sosa to his office. "Good news, I'm taking the professor off your hands," he beamed.

"What?"

"I thought you'd be glad."

"Well … yeah. Of course, I am," she said, still taken aback by the sudden news. "What are you going to do with him?"

135

"I'm loaning him to Crime Prevention on Monday."

"Crime Prevention? Why?"

Wilcox rubbed the back of his neck with one of his big hands. "The goddamn press is all over us with these Wake-Up Rapes. The chief's balls are in a vise. He wants the Crime Prevention Unit to put on a series of rape seminars for women all over the city." The captain smiled. "Now, is that a natural assignment for a criminology professor or what?"

She folded her hands in her lap and studied them. "I suppose so…," she replied in a subdued voice.

"Look, I know how tough this case is. Starting Monday, you'll have a regular detective taking Roth's place."

"Who?"

"Al Renfro just put in for a transfer to the SBU."

"Oh, Jesus, Captain!" she said, rolling her eyes. "Renfro's a narc. He doesn't know squat about rape!"

"I'm sure he'll pick up what he needs."

"Are you kidding? He's as dumb as a post. The high point of his career has been scoring nose candy from 'gen-x-ers' along South Beach." Her posture stiffened. "Sir, I'm sorry, but I just can't work with him."

"Why the hell not?" Wilcox scowled.

"I've known him for years. We went through the academy together. He couldn't find his ass with both hands … and, by the way, I don't want him feeling mine."

"What do you mean?"

"He's notorious! He's put the moves on every female partner he's ever had."

"Surely you don't want to keep working with Roth."

"I don't mind," she said, touching her cheek idly. "Actually, he's been coming up with some pretty good ideas."

CHAPTER

37

Roth was standing at a map that showed the location of the Wake-Up attacks when Sosa arrived at the office. He looked different this morning. It was the first time she had seen him without a sports jacket, bow tie and suspenders. He was wearing a well-tailored, charcoal gray suit that looked as if it had come from one of the better men's stores in town.

"Strange...," he said.

"What?"

He motioned toward the map. "Every one of our assaults has been inside the city limits."

"Gee, I guess that's why they call him the Miami Rapist, huh?" she quipped.

He touched a red push-pin that showed the location of Nina Pulaski's assault and traced his finger outside the metro area.

"The population of Miami is only around 500,000," he said. "We've got another two million people out in the county. Why isn't he hitting there?"

"Maybe he hates MPD. He must realize he's busting our chops."

* *

That day, they followed up on the question of why all of the Wake-Up attacks so far had been concentrated in Miami by sending an e-mail profile of the crimes to every police department and sheriff's office in Florida. If there had been any recent sexual assaults with even vaguely similar characteristics in other parts of the state, they would soon know about them.

On Friday, around noon, Sosa received a call from a detective named Luther Williams with the Riviera Beach Police Department, ninety miles to the north. He told her that RBPD was working a rape-homicide that took place the same night Dr. Pulaski was attacked. It involved the anal rape of a black prostitute whose body was dumped beside the narrow inlet that separated Riviera Beach from Palm Beach Island, the wealthiest community in the nation.

*   *

Roth was eating a hard-boiled egg on his salad platter when Sosa entered the building cafeteria. He reacted skeptically when she told him about the Riviera lead.

"You're talking about a prostitute. All of our victims so far have been professional women. Besides, Riviera Beach is too far away for it to be him."

"No, it's not," she countered. "The ME estimates the time of death at between six and eight a.m. If our guy left Pulaski's condo around three-thirty, he could have made it to Riviera Beach easily before sunrise."

"Yeah, but ..."

"David, the victim was anally raped."

He tried putting himself in the mind of Dr. Pulaski's attacker. It was possible that the dead woman in Riviera Beach was a psychological *proxy*, a stand-in for the victim he had been unable to finish brutalizing that night. It occurred to him that raping and murdering another woman— any woman—might have enabled the obsessive-compulsive personality to mentally complete the violent sequence of events that was disrupted when Nina Pulaski came to and began screaming.

Sosa reached across the table and plucked a grape from his plate.

"If he wanted to assault another woman after he left Pulaski's, why drive almost a hundred miles to find a street walker?" he said, thinking out loud. "It's tourist season in Miami. The streets are full of them at all hours of the night."

She smiled. "It's a nice day. Want to take a ride up to Riviera Beach?"

*   *

The homicide report the Riviera Beach detective faxed them before they left indicated that the prostitute who was working with Amber Semple on the night she was murdered got a good look at the man who picked her up. On the way to Palm Beach County, Roth studied the Compusketch the Riviera cop had created. In the new millennium, the once tedious practice of having police artists work with victims and witnesses for hours to produce a suspect likeness had given way to law enforcement computer programs like Compusketch. Using a combination of multiple-choice and open-ended interview questions, detectives were now able to sit at a computer with the victim and quickly assemble an on-screen approximation of a criminal's appearance from an image library containing over 40,000 features.

The face Roth was looking at belonged to a handsome man in his late twenties or early thirties with a cleft chin, deep-set blue eyes and thick blond hair.

Sosa glanced over at the Compusketch as she drove. "Looks a little like Robert Redford when he was young," she said.

If the man in the computer-generated sketch was the Wake-Up Rapist, it would be a major break in the case. Up to now, no one had seen the face behind the mask.

The voices coming over their portable radios began to break up as they drove beyond range of Miami's repeaters.

"So, where did you grow up?" Sosa asked.

"I'm not sure I ever really have."

"Come on, which is it, New York or Jersey?"

"Brooklyn," he confessed.

"Aha, I knew it!" she said, snapping her fingers.

He feigned a wounded look. "I don't sound like a Northerner! You don't hear me say things like 'I'm wearin' a new shoit,' and 'youse guys, c'mere,' do you?"

She laughed. "No, but you're the worst kind of *yanqui*! At least the *tourista* have the decency to leave when the season's over."

Forty-five minutes after leaving Miami, they were in Palm Beach County, the largest unincorporated area in Florida, with a land size roughly equal to Delaware. They exited I-95 at Blue Heron Boulevard and crossed a bridge that arched high above the Intracoastal Waterway; on the other side of it was a blue and white sign showing a sailboat and a swordfish. On it was the greeting, 'Welcome to Florida's Friendliest Beach!' *Not for Amber Semple.*

*   *

A secretary at the police department directed them to the desk of Luther Williams. He was a clean-shaven, well-built black man in his forties with close-cropped hair that was graying at the temples. The pocket of his starched white shirt with French cuffs bore the monogram *LTW*. An old-fashioned, military Colt .45 with pearl handle grips was canted at a rakish angle on his hip.

"I sure hope we can help each other on this one, folks," he said, in a concerned voice. He motioned the Miami detectives to a couple of chairs beside a wall air conditioner that vibrated intermittently. "Peaches Brooks was the girl who was with Amber the night she was killed. She's on her way over here now. I figured you'd want to talk to her."

"Thanks," Sosa said. "I filled my partner in a little on the way. What else can you tell us, Luther?"

The black detective massaged a muscular bicep. "Amber and Peaches were in the stable of a local pimp named Hogshead."

"Maybe he's the one who did her?" Sosa ventured.

Williams shook his head. "Naw. I've known Hogshead for years. Busted him a couple of times myself. He's just a small-time hood. He's not above slapping a girl around if she shorts him on the night's receipts, but murder is a little out of his league." He removed a green file folder from a wire basket on the corner of his desk and opened it. "Besides," he said, "the skin the ME got from under Amber's nails came from a Caucasian."

Roth saw his partner's face brighten. The killer's DNA could be compared to DNA in the Miami rapes.

"Robbery certainly wasn't a motive," Williams continued. "It must have been a good night. She had almost four hundred bucks on her. It was still in her tote bag when we found her." Roth and Sosa traded a glance, their interest piqued now. The Wake-Up Rapist was no thief.

"What did the lab get from the rape kit?" Sosa asked.

"No semen. But they found *lycopodium* on her butt and traces of *benzocaine* in her rectum."

Benzocaine! The same analgesic that was on the anal lube condom the rapist left on Laura Kelce's bathroom counter.

"What's lycopodium?" Roth asked.

Luther Williams explained, "It's a powder that condom manufacturers use on rubbers to keep them from sticking when they're unrolled."

"Maybe she had anal sex with one of her tricks that night," Sosa suggested.

"According to Peaches, Amber refused to have anal sex. She said it was just too painful." The Riviera Beach detective turned a couple of pages in the homicide report. "Something else," he said. "We couldn't find her panties."

"Lots of hookers don't wear them on busy nights," Sosa remarked.

"We know she had on a pair when the perp picked her up. Her girlfriend told us they'd done a 'twofer' in a motel room an hour before with a john who wanted to get it on with two women. Peaches is sure that Amber was wearing lavender panties."

The murderer must have taken the victim's underwear as a fetishistic trophy.

Williams removed a stack of color photographs from the file. He selected several and shoved them across his desk. "Thirty-six stab wounds in all," he said somberly.

Roth's spirits sank. The violence in the Wake-Up attacks was highly focused; what they were looking at here was a case of crazed overkill. He examined a close-up morgue shot of the body, noting a number of 'defense wounds'—slashes inflicted along the victim's forearms and palms when she apparently raised her hands to protect herself.

In addition to the sheer ferocity demonstrated by the multiple stab wounds inflicted on Amber Semple, the crime scene technicians had taken close-up photographs of deep bite marks on her bloody left buttock. The medical examiner later carefully excised the soft tissue surrounding the bite and preserved it in a compound called formalin. While not as precise as DNA or fingerprint evidence, the bite marks could provide an important potential link to the young woman's attacker. Once a suspect was in custody, a search warrant could be obtained for his bite impression and a comparison of it then made with Amber Semple's wound by a forensic odontologist. Such distinctive features as misaligned or chipped teeth could become significant supplemental evidence.

Roth's jaw bunched when he came to a picture of the gaping wounds in the young woman's upper chest and throat. He had seen many graphic photos of rape-murder victims in the police records he regularly examined at the university, but this was different. The body had a name. Amber Semple. It was all a little too personal.

"You can see she put up a hell of a fight for such a small woman," Williams said.

Watching her try to protect herself from the knife thrusts must have excited him. That's why there were so many stab wounds.

A cut from some type of edged weapon in the victim's left upper back suggested that she might have been trying to get out of a car when she was first stabbed, then turned toward her attacker. One frontal blow was delivered with such force that it severed her left carotid artery. If the murder took place in a car, the resulting arterial spray would almost certainly leave blood traces on the floor and upholstery that no amount of scrubbing could remove. Sosa began making notes.

"The ME is certain from the angle of the wounds that the perp is left-handed," Williams told them. "Looks like he used a serrated blade that was six or seven inches long, probably a hunting knife of some kind." He handed them some more photos and said, "There were no signs of subdural trauma or bruising around her anus."

"What does that mean?" Roth asked.

Sosa said bleakly, "That she was already dead when he raped her."

No need to gag her for the homoerotic fantasy.

Roth told the Riviera Beach detective, "We can place our suspect leaving a condo on Miami Beach somewhere around 3:30 a.m. He could have made it up here in plenty of time to rape and murder your victim before sunrise."

Williams shrugged. "Wouldn't have mattered much if it was light or not. The area where we found the body is pretty remote. She could have screamed her lungs out, and nobody would have heard."

Sosa leaned forward intently. "You don't understand, Luther. It has to be dark for this guy to rape a woman."

"Sounds like a goddamn vampire," Williams sniggered. "Maybe we should start handing out garlic and crosses to the hookers."

Roth started to say something and stopped, remembering how hard it had been to get Sosa to even consider the idea of a gay rapist; he wasn't about to try and sell his theory to Luther Williams.

"Did your techs *glue fume* the body for latents?" Sosa asked.

Williams nodded. "He obviously wore gloves," he said, explaining that technicians had sprayed the dead woman's clothes with a film of *Leucocrystal Violet*. The substance, after being mixed with hydrogen peroxide, turns violet when it comes in contact with the hemoglobin in blood. The LCV mist revealed extensive violet-hued glove marks on Amber Semple's light-colored slacks; curiously, however, her blouse held no such imprints. Luther Williams told them that, while the body was naked from the waist down, none of the buttons on the bloody blouse had been undone.

"Kind of strange behavior for a rape-homicide, huh?" he said.

"Yeah," Sosa agreed.

Williams detached the evidence report from the case file and handed it to her. Roth scooted his chair closer and read over her shoulder. The ET who inspected and photographed the body of Amber Semple found evidence of blood transfer from wounds on her chest and throat to her bare buttocks. The assailant had left numerous smudges on her hips in the process of repositioning the body for post-mortem anal intercourse.

Even though the killer had taken the precaution of wearing gloves when he removed the victim's slacks and panties, it was possible that he had succumbed to the desire to feel the ebbing warmth of her flesh in his hands when he had sex with the corpse, perhaps unaware that forensic technology has developed the ability to lift fingerprints directly from human skin. Technicians had tried without success to bring out latent fingerprint ridges on the bloody skin by spraying it with a substance called *tetrameytholbenzidine* (TMB) and blotting the surface with Krome-Koat paper; they also scanned both sides of the body with an ultra-violet lamp in a futile effort to detect such subtle forms of trace evidence as light-colored fibers, semen, saliva and urine.

Luther Williams waved to a young black woman who had just entered the detective bureau.

Laquita Brooks, a.k.a. 'Peaches', sashayed between the rows of desks in a short skirt that looked as if she'd gotten into it with a shoehorn. She was a big-bodied woman with a heavy bosom and ample hips. A double strand of imitation pearl beads, yellow vinyl boots and a wig that was somewhere between red and orange in the color spectrum completed a hooker ensemble straight from central casting. She moved through the detective bureau with the aplomb of someone who was no stranger to the sight of guns and handcuffs.

"Hi, good lookin'!" she called to Williams. The broad grin that followed revealed a prominent gold tooth behind a pair of full red lips. She let her tote bag slide off her shoulder before dropping into a chair and checking a run in one of her fishnet stockings.

"Peaches, these officers are from Miami. I'd like you to tell them just what you told me about the night Amber was killed."

She removed a wad of gum from her mouth and wrapped it in a napkin. "I'll do anythin' I can to hep you get that cocksucker!" she said emotionally.

Sosa said, "Why don't you start by telling us about when you first saw this man."

"Me 'n Amber had jes' quit fo' the evenin'. Musta been 'round five. We was walkin' 'long Federal on our way back to Hogshead's crib when this Rolls pulled up 'long side us."

Sosa frowned. "Are you sure about the car?"

Peaches seemed mildly affronted. "Honey, I know my cars, 'specially the real 'spensive ones. I oughta! Limp-dicked ol' fuckers come over in 'em alla time from the island, lookin' t' get sucked off fo'a fifty."

Roth was listening attentively.

"It was kinda dark out. I couldn't quite make out the color—coulda been cream or maybe white. I 'member it had a black roof."

"A Rolls-Royce and Bentley look almost the same," Sosa pointed out.

Peaches eyed her slyly. " 'Cept a Bentley don't have that silver lady on the radiator and a Rolls do," she said, with a hint of defiance. Pendulous earrings danced along the side of her face as her head moved animatedly.

"I'm tellin' you this was a late model Rolls-fuckin'-Royce, Honey!" she said, shaking an inch long, red fingernail with gold flecks on it at Sosa. "And you can take that to the bank!"

"She could be right about the car," Williams said. "There was a lot of moist sand on the bank beside the body. We got a good tire impression." He paused and put on a pair of reading glasses. "The lab says it came from a Dunlop Cross-Ply 285/45R21."

"What's the significance of that?" Roth asked.

"It's a British tire. The technician I talked to said anything with a ply rating that high must be on a car that weighs close to six thousand pounds. We know the print wasn't made by some big-assed SUV like a Hummer, and a Caddie or Lincoln tops out around four thousand pounds. Rolls-Royce and Bentley are the only cars I know of that heavy."

Peaches raised her chin triumphantly. "Said it was a Rolls, din't I?"

Sosa told Roth, "In most places, knowing you're looking for a light-colored, late model Rolls would be the next best thing to having a license plate number. Unfortunately, Rolls-Royce is the Toyota of south Florida."

Williams threw in, "I once read that there are more of them down here than anywhere in the world, except Saudi Arabia."

"Maybe so," Peaches Brooks said, "but the Rolls I seen was from Palm Beach island."

"How do you know that?" Sosa asked.

Peaches unwrapped a fresh stick of gum and popped it in her mouth. "I seen a little green palm tree in the middle of the plate while Amber was leanin' in the window, talkin' to the dude."

For many years, residents of Palm Beach island had been able to purchase special 'vanity plates' that separated them from other drivers in the state.

"Well, that narrows it down some," Williams said. "But, there are still a helluva lot of Rolls-Royces on the island."

Roth adjusted his wire rimmed glasses. "Can you remember any of the letters or numbers on that plate?" he asked.

"Naw. 'Fraid I didn't pay no mind to that."

Sosa said, "We understand you got a good look at him."

"Sho' did. Couldn't a been no mo' than fifteen feet from him the whole time."

"But you said it was dark," Roth reminded her.

"Yeah, but the roof light inside the car come on when Amber opened the door to get in. That's when I seen him. Won't never forget that face. He looks jes' like the drawin' I he'ped the po-lice make." She smacked her gum loudly, adding, "He was real nice lookin'. Tan—like a dude you see at the beach. Eyes jes' as blue as that sky out there. Had sorta wavy blonde hair. I 'member that." She uncrossed her legs and adjusted her skirt.

"So, you'd have no trouble recognizing him if you saw him again?" Sosa said.

Peaches choked back a sob. "Jes' you catch that sucker and put him in a line-up and watch me pick his sorry ass out!" She dabbed at her eyes with a balled-up Kleenex. "That low-life mother fucker killed my home girl!"

"This guy is extremely dangerous," Sosa said. "He must know you saw him."

"Sheet!" Peaches opened her purse and took out a straight razor, snapping it open deftly with a flick of her wrist. "I ain't afraid o' that asshole! Ah'll cut his nuts off!"

"Put that thing away!" Luther Williams ordered. "Christ Almighty! Carrying a concealed weapon into a police station! I oughta book your ass!"

Peaches' thigh rippled like Jell-o when she slapped it. "C'mon, Luther," she laughed, dropping the razor back in her purse, "you ain't gonna bust a workin' girl jes' fo' carryin' a little protection, are you?"

After Peaches left, Sosa picked up the Riviera Beach lab report. "How about it, Luther?" she said in a sultry Lauren Bacall voice. "Wanna comingle DNA?"

The black detective's eyes twinkled with amusement; then, he said seriously, "Let's give it a try. What have we got to lose?"

* *

The Miami detectives paused on the steps of the Riviera Beach Police Department watching the sails of a white catamaran flutter in the distance as it crept out of its slip at Palm Beach Marina.

Sosa said, "First the handmade Italian boots, then the Cartier cologne. Now a Rolls." She looked across the water toward the affluent island community. "Our perp must be one of the beautiful people over there."

"Raping and murdering a street walker in Riviera Beach that night begins to make sense if he was on his way home," Roth said.

She clucked her tongue. "From a Harley-Davidson to a Rolls-Royce. Now that's what I call upgrading your wheels!"

Roth thrust his hands in his pockets and jingled some change.

"You're getting that worried look on your face, David."

"This thing just doesn't add up," he complained. "A motorcycle, dirty jeans and vending machine condoms hardly fit with the typical Palm Beach lifestyle."

"Yeah. That bothers me, too."

"How long will it take to get the DNA comparison back?"

"I'll have the lab expedite it. We should know something in a day or so. If it is him, letting Peaches see his face and car was a major screw-up. Why would he take a chance like that?"

Roth recalled the lipstick on the mirror. "Maybe he's trying to help us catch him."

Sosa scoffed, "If you really believe that, I've got a bridge in your hometown I'd like to sell you." She put on a pair of Ray-Ban sunglasses and handed him the keys. "Do you mind driving back? I'm really beat."

The heat from inside the *Exxon Valdez* hit them like a blast furnace when they opened the doors. Roth decided to take the Sawgrass Expressway back to Miami, opting for the panorama of swaying Bahia grass and grazing cattle over the urban clutter of zero lot line houses and condos off the freeway.

Within minutes of leaving Riviera Beach, Maria was asleep. Strands of hair fluttered across her face as her head lolled on the seat. He stole a glance at her, wondering fleetingly what she slept in.

Madness!

He jerked his eyes back to the road, rebuking himself for leering at her like a testosterone-crazed undergrad in one of his classes. The few moments he had held her in the parking lot awakened a part of him he thought was buried with Sara. It was more than just sex, though he longed to sleep with her. He suddenly wanted it all back: the love of a woman, children, and a home to come to each night instead of just a house; he wanted everything life had taken from him. He told himself he had no chance with a woman like her. Before long, he'd be back at the university and out of her world; he wasn't about to make a fool of himself in the meantime.

He bumped the speedometer up to seventy-five, hoping that Amber Semple's killer wasn't the Wake-Up Rapist. He thought of the frenetic stab wounds, the multiple deep bite marks and the rape of the corpse. Whoever the prostitute's murderer was, something inside him had snapped. His sexual gratification would be linked to homicidal violence from now on.

They would know soon enough if the blood and skin under the dead woman's nails belonged to the Wake-Up Rapist. Roth was awed by DNA: millions of genetic codes—for everything from a person's eye color and height to intelligence and personality—all jammed into one trillionth of a gram in every cell of the body.

The shadows of tall buildings along Biscayne Boulevard were lengthening by the time they returned to Miami; shoppers, some of them sporting recent sunburns, lugged the day's purchases along crowded sidewalks like pack mules.

Maria stirred at the sound of a Metromover roaring above them on the rails of an elevated platform. "Umm." She stretched and rubbed her eyes. "How long have I been out?" she asked, through half-closed lids.

"Over an hour."

She turned the AC up a notch and smoothed the hair back from her temples.

"You know," she said sleepily. "If Peaches had seen even part of that license plate, we could have run registration checks on every Rolls on the island and narrowed it down to probably very few cars."

The germ of an idea suddenly dawned in his mind.

"Maria, we just passed a billboard for Princess Cruise Lines. Do you remember the phone number on it?"

"Of course not. I get paid to watch things that are suspicious."

"But the sign was on your side of the car. You had to see it!" he insisted. "You don't remember the number because it wasn't important at the time. Your eyes took a snapshot and fired the image off to a dusty shelf in your unconscious. Everything about that ad—including the phone number on it—will be stored there for the rest of your life, along with trillions of other undeveloped negatives of things you've seen."

Her brown eyes widened. "So, if Peaches saw the palm tree in the middle of that license plate, she must have seen the letters and numbers on either side of it."

"Right!" he replied excitedly. "I've got a friend in the psych department at UM who's a hypnotherapist. If anyone can pull that plate number out of her psyche, he can."

She clapped her hands in delight. "Roth, I swear, if you weren't driving, I'd kiss you!"

Cheap, city cars. Never a cruise control when you need one.

* *

Sosa spotted Roth getting off the elevator around ten the following morning. "Wow, talk about banker's hours," she said wryly.

"Believe it or not, I've been on the job." He walked with her to the SBU. "Maria, until today I couldn't understand how Laura Kelce's attacker managed to get in and out of a community as well guarded as Gables Estates without being seen."

She paused in the doorway of her office.

"You were right about the rapist not riding a motorcycle the night he attacked Laura Kelce," he told her. "He used the Rolls that Peaches saw Amber get into."

"And just how do we know this?"

"Remember what the techs found snagged on the window sill at Kelce's house?"

"It was a fiber of some kind, wasn't it?"

"Not just a fiber," he said, raising a forefinger instructively. "It was lamb's wool." He unfolded a colorful Rolls-Royce brochure that was tucked under his arm and opened it to a page he had marked.

"Thinking about trading in your Volvo?" she joked. Her lips parted when she read the paragraph he directed her to:

> *Pamper yourself in the new Rolls-Royce Phantom with such standard features as Conley English leather, a hand-selected burled walnut interior and lamb's wool carpeting throughout ...*

"Lamb's wool!" she exclaimed.

"Did you know that Rolls-Royce is the only car in the world that comes with lamb's wool floor mats and carpeting? The rapist's boots were wet because of the rain. One of them must have picked up a fiber and deposited it on the sill when he climbed through the window."

She smiled approvingly. "We may just make a detective out of you yet. Where did you get this?"

He adjusted his tie with an exaggerated gesture. "The title 'Doctor' works wonders sometimes. On my way in this morning, I stopped by the Rolls dealership in Miami Beach. I guess it was the northern accent that convinced them I was a serious sales prospect. The guy couldn't wait to give me everything he had about Rolls-Royce." He followed her into her office and pulled up a chair.

"That's why none of the guards recalled seeing anything unusual that night," she said. "Luxury cars come and go out there at all hours. Hell, with the storm, the old duffer on the front gate probably opened it without even glancing at the driver as soon as he saw a Rolls. He would have just assumed it was one of the residents coming home."

"You have to admit, most criminals don't drive around in three-hundred-thousand dollar cars."

* *

Later that afternoon, the Florida Department of Law Enforcement laboratory in Miami finished its comparison of the DNA from the Riviera Beach homicide with the DNA from the Wake-Up Rapes. Sosa and

Roth waited impatiently while the SBU fax machine churned the report out:

DNA WAS EXTRACTED FROM FOREIGN SKIN PARTICLES EMBEDDED BENEATH ONE OF THE FINGERNAILS OF DECEDENT AMBER SEMPLE. DNA BANDING PATTERNS WERE COMPARED WITH PREVIOUS DNA SPECIMENS HARVESTED FROM SPERM RECOVERED AT THE KEARNEY, GRIFFIN, KELCE AND WHITAKER CRIME SCENES, USING THE RESTRICTION ENZYME HINFL AND FIVE SINGLE LOCUS PROBES (MS1, MS31, g3 AND YNH 24). THE STATISTICAL PROBABILITY OF THE DNA BANDING PATTERNS OBSERVED IN ALL FIVE ASSAULTS COMING FROM OTHER THAN A SINGLE CAUCASIAN DONOR IS APPROXIMATELY ONE IN ONE HUNDRED MILLION.

They stared at the report for several seconds and then looked at each other.

"My God, it's him," Sosa said grimly.

CHAPTER

38

A secretary at the Department of Psychology told Roth that Dr. Jack Belk was attending a convention in Washington, D.C. all week. He was able to reach him by phone at the Hyatt Regency. Plans were made to bring Peaches to his campus office for a hypnotherapy session that might yield the license plate of the Rolls-Royce she saw Amber Semple get into.

Roth had yet to receive anything in his mailbox at the Sexual Battery Unit. This morning, however, was different. An envelope was tucked in the pigeonhole above his name. It was neatly addressed in peacock-colored cursive and had no return address:

> Officer 714
> Miami Police Department
> Municipal Justice Complex
> 400 NW 2nd Ave.
> Miami, Florida 33101

He looked at the vanilla-colored envelope, wondering how anyone outside the police department would know his badge number. After rummaging in his desk, he found an opener and slit the envelope.

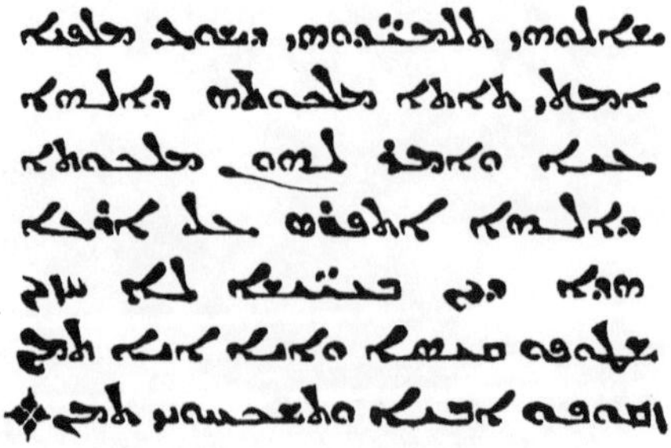

[handwritten text in Syriac script]

"What the … ?" He stared at the strange writing for several seconds in bewilderment. A rush of adrenaline hit his bloodstream when he saw the postmark:

TOWN OF PALM BEACH, FL

Moments later, he was in Sosa's office, waving what he had just received. "Maria, I think I just got a letter from the rapist!"

She reacted doubtfully. "What makes you think it's from him?"

"Look at the postmark," he said, holding out the envelope.

"Palm Beach!" she said in a startled voice. "Put it down, for God's sake! You're smearing your prints all over it!"

He dropped the letter and envelope on her desk as if they were hot coals. In his initial excitement, it never occurred to him that he might be contaminating important evidence.

She put on a pair of latex gloves, using a tape dispenser and a box of staples to flatten the letter on her desk. "What the hell kind of writing is this?" she said, bending over it.

"It looks like some kind of Arabic," he ventured, adding, "How could he have gotten my badge number?"

"That would have been easy. You can buy a scanner with a list of all MPD's frequencies at any Radio Shack in town. We're both on the air every day. He must be listening to us." She got an evidence bag from a drawer and put the envelope and letter inside it; then, she sealed and labeled the bag, noting the date and time.

"Why wouldn't he have sent this directly to me?" she puzzled. "He must know I'm in charge of the investigation."

"That's another reason I'm sure it's from him. He wouldn't communicate with you just because you're a woman."

She puffed out her cheeks. "We get a lot of nut mail up here. Before we knock ourselves out on this, let's try to make sure it's from him."

"He's been very careful about not leaving any fingerprints," he reminded her. "I doubt that we'll find any on the letter."

"Probably not, but maybe he accidentally left us something else." She held up the plastic evidence bag, "If he licked the envelope flap we can get DNA from his saliva."

A few minutes later, Roth took the evidence bag to the lab and had them make him a copy of the letter before going to the University of Miami Department of Linguistics.

Sosa's phone rang shortly after he left. It was Captain Wilcox. "Sergeant, I need to see you in my office right away." She could hear the edge in his voice.

*　*

The CID commander looked as solemn as the farmer with the pitch-fork in Grant Woods' *American Gothic* painting when Sosa entered his of-fice. Two other men were in the room with him. She recognized one of them. It was Ernie Fladd from Internal Affairs. He was a tall, scarecrow of a man with a bushy mustache and a prominent Adam's apple. *Head-hunters. What do they want with me?*

She took a seat after Fladd introduced his partner, Tom Cochoran. "What's going on?" she said. Fladd cleared his throat and started to speak.

"Just a minute," Wilcox said, interrupting him with a raised hand. "Maria, you have the right to have a union representative present before you talk to these guys."

Her pulse quickened. "Captain, I don't need a PBA rep. I haven't done any-thing." She faced Fladd and Cochoran squarely. "Now, what's this all about?"

Cochoran spoke first. He was an overweight man in his mid-for-ties with a sluggish, gouty look. Disheveled mousy-brown hair half hid his ears. "Sergeant Sosa," he began officiously, "you and Detective Roth were on a stakeout at the El Camino Apartments last Wednesday night."

"That's right," she replied. A wave of relief passed over her. *Donald Vincent.* So, that's what this was about. The prick! He said he'd have their badges. He must have filed an IA complaint alleging false arrest, brutal-ity or some other bullshit. The Rat Squad was just following up on it; she was already glad that she and Roth had submitted detailed reports on the incident. In hers, she had explained that she struck Vincent because she thought he was reaching for a gun. At the time, she had every reason to believe that they were dealing with an armed felon. *Just let Internal Affairs try to make anything out of this!*

"Sergeant," Cochoran continued, "it's my duty to inform you that we have reason to suspect you of violating General Order 9201.03."

She made a face. "What the hell is that?" With well over a hundred General Orders in the department, no one knew more than a handful of them by number.

"Fraternization with subordinates," Ernie Fladd piped.

"What?"

"Come on, let's not play games," Cochoran told her.

She met his eyes defiantly. "I have no idea what you're talking about."

The IA detectives exchanged a knowing look. "I assume you realize that Dr. Roth is no different from any other member of the department while he's here," Fladd said elliptically.

"Of course. So what?"

Cochoran interlaced his fingers in front of his paunch. "We understand that you recently declined Captain Wilcox's offer to replace him with a regular detective."

"That's right."

"May we know why?" Cochoran asked.

She raised her chin. "Personal reasons."

A monkeyish grin flashed on Ernie Fladd's face. "I'll just bet they're *real* personal," he snickered.

She glared at him. "Just what are you accusing me of, asshole?"

Wilcox slammed a beefy palm on his desk. "Goddamnit!" he thundered. "Just show her the pictures!"

"What pictures?" Sosa said.

A crooked smile played on Cochoran's face. He removed an envelope from his jacket and handed it to her, with the expression of a man who had just laid down a royal flush against four of a kind.

Sosa's breath caught in her throat when she saw the first 4 × 6 color photo. There were seven pictures in all, each one obviously taken with a telephoto lens. They showed Sergeant Maria Sosa and Dr. David Roth standing beside their unmarked car in what could only be described as a passionate embrace.

She leafed through the pictures in disbelief. "Wh … where did you get these?" she managed, realizing how flustered she sounded.

Cochoran bored in now. "We'll ask the questions, *Sergeant*," he said condescendingly.

"You don't think that we…."

"Of course not," Fladd said derisively, holding up another set of the photographs. He walked over and thrust one of them in front of her face. "How could anyone possibly conclude after seeing these that you're fucking a subordinate officer?"

She brushed his hand away roughly. "Don't try treating me like a perp!" she told him through clenched teeth. She explained to Captain Wilcox how she'd hit on the ruse of making it look as if she and Roth were lovers when it seemed Donald Vincent was about to run.

"Very creative story," Ernie Fladd said. "I'll give you that."

"If you don't believe me, ask Roth."

"You think we're idiots?" Fladd said, raising his voice. "I'm sure you told him to feed us the same horseshit!"

Fury welled in her. "This charge doesn't have anything to do with the fact that I happen to be a woman, does it?" she said icily. Fladd started to speak but she cut him off. "Tell me, has the department *ever* accused a male officer of violating the fraternization rule?"

Cochoran retorted loudly. "We don't have to justify anything to you, lady! You're the one who got caught on Candid Camera!"

"Okay … fine," Sosa volleyed, "let's go down to polygraph right now. You can put me on the box. If I flunk, you can have my shield and gun on the spot. Fair enough?" The complacent expression on Cochoran's face faded. "You know what I'm going to do after I pass the polygraph?" Her eyes shifted to the captain. "I'm going to make a list of every superior officer who's come on to me since I joined the force. I think I'll talk to some of the other women in the department. I'll bet we can generate enough sexual harassment complaints between us to keep both you guys busy until you retire!"

Hal Wilcox appeared acutely uncomfortable. "Hey, look," he said. "This is obviously a misunderstanding."

The IA detectives left several minutes later. As soon as the door closed, Sosa wheeled on Wilcox with the photographs clenched in her hand. "Goddamnit! How many years have I worked for you?"

He averted his eyes with a pained look. "I'm sorry," he said sheepishly, "but when I saw the pictures, I …"

Several of the photos hit him in the chest when she threw them across his desk. "If I was having an affair with Roth or any other cop, do you think I'd be dumb enough to be making out in public on a goddamn stakeout?" She stormed out of his office and slammed the door.

* *

Roth went directly to Sosa's office when he returned from the campus. He noticed the troubled look on her face.

"Well, don't just stand there!" she snapped. "What did you find out about the letter?"

"They couldn't translate it," he told her, still wondering what was wrong. "All they could tell me is that it's some kind of middle-eastern dialect. None of the linguists I talked to had ever seen anything like it."

"That's just fucking great!"

"They're sending a copy to a specialist at Princeton. He may be able to tell us something."

She gazed distractedly out the window, seemingly not listening.

"Want to tell me what's going on?"

She broke the pencil in her hand and threw it at the wall.

"What's wrong?"

She told him about the photographs and the confrontation with the IA detectives. "They accused us of having an affair! Can you believe that?"

God forbid! He suppressed a smile.

"Who the hell took those pictures?" she said.

He thought for a moment. "Well, we were in a city car. Maybe somebody at the apartments spotted us and figured there was hanky panky going on at the taxpayer's expense."

"Somebody who just happened to have a 35 millimeter camera with a telephoto lens in their lap? I don't think so."

He filled a paper cup with water from the cooler. "You're about to make lieutenant. Anyone around here who might not want to see that happen?"

"Sure, but nobody who feels strongly enough to spend hours watching me in a parking lot."

He crushed the cup and tossed it at the trashcan, missing by a couple of inches. "Okay, then how about a reporter with the *Herald* or one of the TV stations. Maybe someone is doing a story on the professor-policeman project."

"Listen, if the media ever got hold of anything that juicy, you can bet it'd be all over page one and the six o'clock news. 'UM Prof-Cop and Police Sergeant Caught Boffing on Duty!'" She bit a nail nervously. "Whoever took those pictures had no way of knowing we were suddenly going to provide them with a photo op like that. David, someone's watching us."

He slapped his forehead.

"What is it?"

"The rapist took the pictures and sent them to IA! It had to be him!" he exclaimed, rising from his chair.

"Are you kidding? We're the last people in the world he wants to be anywhere near!"

"That's the whole point," he said earnestly. "This is a game to him. He wants us to know that he's not afraid of us, that he can stalk us just as easily as we can him. We know he has a scanner. He must have heard us check-out at Vincent's place when we relieved Walker and McNees on the stakeout."

She began pacing her office. "Talk about brass balls," she seethed. "The nerve of the bastard!" The anger on her face gave way to an anxious look.

"This guy's a killer!" she said. "He could just as easily have used a gun as a camera that night."

Roth shook his head. "Maria, he doesn't want to kill us," he said evenly. "He just wants us to keep playing."

CHAPTER

39

Whoever mailed the letter with the Palm Beach postmark hadn't licked the envelope, eliminating the possibility of obtaining a saliva swab that could yield DNA. The envelope was disappointing from an evidential standpoint. Its surface was a useless maze of superimposed fingerprints laid down by postal employees, clerks and secretaries who handled it before it reached Roth's mailbox.

The stationery proved to be a high-quality linen fiber that was, unfortunately, all too common. The sender had obviously worn gloves when he penned the letter's cryptic message. Once the file prints of Detective David Abraham Roth were eliminated from the sheet of paper, only a single latent remained on it; the solitary fingerprint was made by the first joint of a left forefinger and was located on the right side of the page, directly below the last line of the strange writing. The careful positioning of the print suggested that it was left intentionally as a *forensic signature*. The latent appeared as a bright red whirl under the laser light, standing out as distinctly as a luminous galaxy against the black void of space. No booking officer at any jail in the country could have rolled a better fingerprint. There were no breaks or blurs anywhere on the pattern. Virtually every loop, whorl and ridge was easily discernible without computer enhancement. Lab analysis revealed traces of *formaldehyde* on the paper around it.

Once the print was developed, its minute ridge endings, bifurcations and contours were scanned and digitized by the Automated Fingerprint Identification System. In a matter of minutes, the electronic brain of AFIS compared the latent against millions of criminal and application fingerprints on file in its databank. The lightning-fast analysis stopped when the computer came to a print taken many years before during a routine application for an Ohio teacher's license. AFIS had a '*hit.*' It proclaimed, with a 99.82% probability, that the latent print had come from the hand of a woman named Laura Elaine Kelce.

"The sick son of a bitch!" Sosa said. "He kept one of her fingers as a sexual fetish!"

Roth observed, "He probably took mementos from the other women, too. Most likely small things they wouldn't miss."

She smiled weakly. "You tried to get me to follow-up on that once before."

"I did? When?"

"The day we were coming back from the lab, and I got so pissed."

"You're always *k'vetshing* at me for something," he said, ducking when she flicked a paper clip at him.

They called the other victims, asking each of them if anything had disappeared around the time of the attacks. Diane Whitaker said that when she got out of the hospital she found that a silver lieutenant's bar was missing from the collar of one of her uniform shirts in the closet. Georgia Griffin told them that an onyx letter opener had mysteriously vanished from the desk in her study. Nina Pulaski's sister mentioned that the doctor's Phi Beta Kappa key was gone. Sister Bridget Kearney couldn't locate a small replica of Michelangelo's *Pieta* that was given to her by her parents the day she took her vows.

CHAPTER

40

Roth had been expecting the call from Professor Paul Brashears at Princeton University.

"What kind of writing is this?" he asked eagerly.

"It's a form of ancient Aramaic called Estrangela. It hasn't been spoken in almost two thousand years."

What the hell?

"Well ... what does it say?" Roth asked.

"Here, I'll read you the translation."

> "THE DISCIPLES OF JESUS ASKED HIM, 'MASTER, WHEN WILL THE KINGDOM OF GOD APPEAR?' HE ANSWERED, 'THE KINGDOM OF GOD IS SPREAD UPON THE EARTH BUT MEN DO NOT SEE IT. CLEAVE THE WOOD, AND I AM THERE. LIFT UP THE STONE, AND YOU WILL FIND ME THERE.'"

A biblical passage.

Roth made some notes as Brashears continued.

"The quality of the writing is amazing. Every character is perfectly formed. There's a natural flow to it, almost as if the person were writing in his native tongue."

"Who can read and write this kind of thing?"

"Very few Aramaic scholars. I'm the only one at Princeton who can. It took me a while to decipher this. It's an unusually archaic, very difficult form of the dialect. I don't believe there are any linguists at either Harvard or Yale who can translate Estrangela."

"Can you tell me anything about this particular piece of scripture?"

"I'm afraid biblical literature is a little outside my area of expertise. I have a colleague in Canada who's a theologian as well as a middle-eastern linguist. I can put you in touch with him, if you like."

"Please!"

* *

The pressure on the Miami Police Department to solve the Wake-Up Rapes was steadily increasing. Channel 7 had just aired the first of a three-part segment called '*Women at Risk*.' MPD's Public Information Office was being inundated each day with calls, letters and e-mails from terrified women all over the city. Sosa and Roth met in the SBU briefing room with McNees and Walker to discuss the peculiar letter from Palm Beach.

"Okay, guys, think," she urged. "Why send us something like this?"

Alvin Walker straddled a chair and wrapped his arms around the back of it.

"He's just messing with our heads," he said.

"I don't think so," Roth opined. "The letter must be a clue of some kind."

"If it is, why send it to us in this mumbo-jumbo?" Walker responded.

Roth said thoughtfully, "Maybe either the quotation or the odd language it's in has something to do with who he is. He could be a linguist, like the prof I talked to at Princeton, or even a minister or priest."

Sosa propped her chin on her hand and said, "A Palm Beach clergyman with a Rolls-Royce and a Harley-Davidson who can write in ancient Aramaic?"

Roth picked up a copy of the letter and said, "He chose this particular passage for some reason. The references to 'cleave the wood ... lift up the stone and you will find me' may mean that he's right under our noses. Like the Kingdom of Heaven, we just don't see him."

"Could be," Sosa said. "He must want us to know that he lives in Palm Beach. That's why he postmarked the letter from there."

Jim McNees loosened his tie. "If this is his idea of a clue, it's sure as hell not worth much. There are thousands of people on the island. He could be any one of them."

"There may be more messages now that he's started communicating with us," Roth speculated.

McNees snorted. "What are we supposed to do while we're waiting for them, just watch the bodies pile up, or start knocking on doors in Palm Beach asking who understands this weird dialect?"

His partner added, "We don't have any legal authority up there. Even if we did, we couldn't pull over every light-colored Rolls on the island just because some hooker thinks the guy who offed her girlfriend drives one. Half the folks in that town are on a first name basis with the governor." He jabbed Jim McNees in the shoulder and said, "Can you imagine what's going to happen the first time someone in a Rolls gets blue-lighted on their way to afternoon tea or a polo match?"

"We won't have to do anything like that," Roth said. "Once Peaches is hypnotized on Saturday, we may have his license plate."

"Suppose the shrink can't get her to remember it?" Walker said.

Sosa took a sip of black coffee and said, "These attacks have been going on for months. Why start writing us now?"

Roth turned the question over in his mind for a few moments and then said, "This is the first time he's killed anyone. I think sending us a biblical quotation is a reflection of the guilt he's feeling."

"Oh, yeah!" Jim McNees said bitterly. "He's so torn up about what he's doing that he kept that poor woman's finger in formaldehyde and put her print on the letter right below the words of Jesus."

Alvin Walker said, "This is one sick puppy, but criminals writing the cops is nothing new. The Boston Strangler left notes behind at some of his murders."

"He didn't write in a dead language," Sosa said.

Roth opened his laptop and turned it on. "I picked up a New Testament software program and downloaded it right after Professor Brashears called with the translation. I found plenty of references to conversations between Jesus and his disciples about the '*Kingdom of God*' and the '*Kingdom of Heaven*' but nothing about it being spread upon the earth and men not seeing it." He scrolled down the screen past a large number of offerings from both the Protestant King James and Roman Catholic versions of the New Testament. Maybe there's something wrong with the software."

"Well, so much for the marvel of computer technology," Sosa said. "The passage has got to be there somewhere … anybody got a Bible handy?"

Walker snapped his fingers and grinned. "Damn! Must have left mine at the revival last night." He volunteered to go next door to the Miami-Dade County Superior Court building and returned fifteen minutes later with four copies of the New Testament he'd located in empty courtrooms.

"They may have a little trouble swearing in witnesses on the second floor tomorrow," he said, passing out Bibles to the others.

Each detective took one of the Four Gospels and began searching for the quotation. Not finding the passage anywhere in the Gospels of Matthew, Mark, Luke or John, they turned to the remainder of the New Testament: Corinthians, Galatians, Ephesians, Colossians …

Jim McNees was the last to clap his Bible shut. "It's just not here," he said with frustration.

Sosa rubbed her eyes. "If it's not in the Bible, where did it come from?" she said, looking at the others.

"Like I said earlier," Walker responded, "he probably just made all that shit up."

"In a language that nobody's spoken for a couple thousand years?" Roth supplied.

CHAPTER

41

The following day Roth received an e-mail from Professor Brashears' colleague, the Reverend Jean LeClainche at the Jesuit Seminary in Montreal, suggesting that he contact Monsignor Pietro Garofalo, a specialist in ancient medieval codices at the Vatican Archives in Rome. When he called, the monsignor's secretary explained in halting English that Garofalo was in Genoa on business and wouldn't return until the end of the week. Roth faxed a copy of the Aramaic letter along with a note saying it was urgent they speak with him.

* *

Several days passed. A conference call was finally arranged with Monsignor Garófalo on the Saturday they were to take Peaches Brooks to the University of Miami for the hypnosis session. The two detectives waited anxiously in the SBU briefing room while the international operator put them through.

Sosa picked up the phone on the first ring and put it on speaker. "Did you get our fax, Monsignor?"

"Yes ... I did," Pietro Garofalo replied, in a thickly-accented voice. "May I ask who is there besides you, Sergeant?"

"Just my partner, Detective Roth."

"Are you recording this?"

"No," Sosa replied with surprise. "It's against the law in Florida to tape any conversation without the consent of the other party."

"I see ..." Garofalo said guardedly.

'WHY SO PARANOID?' Roth scratched the words on a tablet and shoved it in front of her. She shrugged.

165

"Where did you get this?" Garofalo said sternly.

Sosa brought her face closer to the speakerphone. "It was sent to us by a man who's been raping and torturing women here in Miami. He's already murdered at least one person that we know of."

They heard a sharp intake of breath on the other end of the line. "Holy Mother of God … !" Garofalo whispered. There was no mistaking the emotion in the archivist's voice. It was *fear*.

Roth's eyes moved across the neatly penned Aramaic characters in front of him. "We couldn't find the phrase we sent you anywhere in the New Testament," he said.

"You wouldn't," Garofalo said gravely. "What you have is an excerpt from the Gnostic Gospel of Matthias, specifically, Chapter 9: Verse 31."

Sosa jotted the numbers with a frown. "I thought there were only four Gospels—Matthew, Mark, Luke and John."

"Those are the canonical Gospels, which are recognized as part of Holy Scripture. There were also a number of unorthodox Gospels that were examined and rejected by the early Church as heresy. The Gospel of *Matthias* was one of them."

Another detective momentarily opened the door to the briefing room before realizing it was in use. Sosa motioned for Roth to lock it.

"The Gospel of Matthias was officially condemned by the Council of Nicea in 325 A.D.," Garofalo explained. "The entire text was missing for centuries. Biblical scholars assumed that the work was destroyed by the early Church fathers after it was banned. We would never have known anything about its contents had it not been for some Arab boys playing in a cave in Upper Egypt in 1995 who found a sealed earthenware jar that contained a *palimpsest*."

"What's that?" Sosa asked.

"It's a trace text buried beneath later, superimposed writings. A great many such documents were created throughout the Middle Ages. Writing material was in such short supply that parchment and papyrus were often scraped and reused."

A medieval recycling program. Roth wondered what possible relevance any of this could have to their case.

"Years passed before an Egyptian archeologist recognized the potential importance of the scrolls in the jar and had them sent to St. Stephen's Monastery in Heidelberg for examination. The monks there are among the finest papyrologists in the world. They've been examining ancient codices since the 1300's. The Abbot contacted us as soon as they identified traces of Aramaic Estrangela beneath Semitic mercantile writings from the ninth century. Three of us here at the Archives were sent immediately by the Holy See to Germany. We spent six months at St. Stephen's, deciphering the trace text as the papyrologists uncovered it. Most of the scrolls were badly decomposed. The process of excavating the original document was as delicate as microsurgery. Even the slightest pressure would have obliterated the underlying Aramaic."

His voice grew animated as he went on. "While we had no way of verifying its actual authorship, the document was intriguing, to say the least. You see, the four accepted Gospels were all written in Greek and appeared long after the time of our Lord. *Matthias* was written in Aramaic Estrangela—which was the dialect scholars believe Jesus most likely spoke. Moreover, Carbon-14 dating of the papyrus containing the Matthias gospel places it very close in time to the crucifixion." Garofalo paused for a moment before continuing.

"You have to realize that over ninety-percent of the Roman Empire was completely illiterate during the lifetime of our Lord, and that rate would surely have been much higher in Galilee. The followers of Jesus were lower class, Aramaic-speaking peasants who almost certainly couldn't read or write. Even the apostles are described in the New Testament as unschooled, ordinary men. It's unlikely that any of them would have been able to produce the kind of flawless Estrangela we see in Matthias."

Sosa adjusted the volume on the speakerphone as Monsignor Garofalo went on. "Very few specimens of Estrangela have survived over the centuries. Only a handful of words and sentences here and there—isolated fragments of a dead language. That's why Matthias was such an incredible discovery. It's nearly as long as the gospels of Matthew and Mark combined. In addition to containing much of the same material as our four canonical gospels, it provides a wealth of information about the life of

Jesus before His public ministry. Without doubt, whoever wrote it knew Him well."

Sosa nodded when Roth pointed at his watch. They were supposed to be in Riviera Beach in an hour and a half to pick up Peaches.

"Imagine!" the monsignor said effusively. "Protected from the aridity of the desert in that cave for all those centuries, and buried beneath a layer of inconsequential ancient business notes."

Roth and Sosa heard someone enter the room on other end of the speakerphone. "Ah, my colleague, Father Salvatore Tomasella, has just joined me," Garofalo said. "He was one of the translators who accompanied me to Germany to study the *palimpsest*. We were discussing your fax earlier. Frankly, we're at a loss to understand how anyone could have obtained what you sent us."

Sosa looked at her partner. "Why is that?"

"One moment ... please." The men on the other side of the Atlantic spoke in hushed Italian for perhaps a minute. Garofalo cleared his throat. "You see ... no portion of the Gnostic Gospel of Matthias has ever been made public."

Astonishment registered on Sosa's face. "What?"

"Because the Church has regarded it as heresy for almost seventeen hundred years, his Holiness instructed us to bring the *palimpsest* to Rome once we finished our work. The papyrus scrolls, along with their translation, were placed in a hermetically sealed vault at the Archives as soon as we returned from Heidelberg. They have been here ever since."

Both detectives were thunderstruck. *Biblical palimpsest. Rape and torture*, Roth wrote, staring at the words, trying to imagine the connection.

They heard Garofalo's chair squeak loudly as he shifted in it. "The passage you sent me is pure blasphemy!"

"Why?" Roth asked.

"Bene Jesu!" Garofalo exclaimed. "To suggest that the Kingdom of Heaven is spread upon the earth is to make a mockery of our Faith and its sacraments! What need would there be for the Church our Lord established to guide us to eternal salvation if heaven were attainable in this world? 'Cleave the wood and I am there ... lift up the stone and you will find me.' Indeed!"

It wasn't difficult to understand why the Gnostic Gospel of Matthias had been ordered sealed. The leaders of any faith would likely react in much the same way to the appearance of a document suggesting that organized religion is unnecessary in man's quest for God. Roth's mind was reeling.

How could a wealthy, young, sexual sadist, thousands of miles from Rome, have gotten hold of such a thing?

"Very few people in the world can read and write this particular dialect and only a biblical scholar would appreciate the significance of the passage you sent me."

"Monsignor, what language did you translate the *palimpsest* into?" Roth inquired.

"Latin."

"There must be a great many scholars at the Archives who can read it," he said.

"Certainly. Hundreds."

"How about Aramaic Estrangela?" Sosa asked.

"Perhaps a dozen, including myself and Father Tomasella."

"Maybe someone there got a look at either the translation or the *palimpsest*," Roth suggested.

"That's impossible," Pietro Garofalo replied confidently. "The *Matthias* Gospel was sealed *ad eternum*—for all time—the very day we returned from Germany. No one has had access to it. Our security is quite stringent, as you might imagine. We are entrusted with the safekeeping of thousands of ancient documents that are irreplaceable."

Roth said, "You must have discussed something this momentous with your colleagues."

"Never!" Garofalo said forcefully. "Besides the three of us who translated the scrolls, only the Holy Father and his closest advisors knew what they contained. From the time we arrived in Germany, until we returned to Rome with the *palimpsest*, our only contact was with the Holy See. We never spoke of our work outside the manuscript room at St. Stephen's. Even the Abbot knew only that we were translating some early Aramaic codices. Until we received your fax, we never mentioned the Gospel of Matthias after we left Germany." His voice began to break.

"There are no words to tell you how upset I was when I saw what you had sent, nor how horrified I am by the things you have just told me."

Roth massaged his temples, searching for some explanation. "Someone must have seen either the scrolls or the translation while you were in Germany at the monastery," he concluded aloud.

"There is no way that could have happened!" Garofalo declared. "They were both kept locked in a safe in the manuscript room, along with all our notes, the whole time we were there. I personally oversaw the opening of the safe each morning and was there when it was locked again at the end of the day."

"You mentioned notes," Sosa probed. "What happened to them?"

"They were all destroyed before we left St. Stephen's. I collected them and burned them myself."

What about the papyrologists at the monastery who worked on the scrolls? They must have been around the *palimpsest* constantly," Sosa said.

"You needn't worry about them. They were all Trappists."

"Monsignor, I'm a Catholic, but I'm afraid I really don't know anything about the Trappists."

"Their formal title is The Order of Cistercians of the Strict Observance. Every Trappist monk takes a lifelong vow of silence, fasting and hard labor as penance for the sins of mankind."

"They don't speak at all?" Roth said in amazement.

"Only in the confessional. A Trappist brother never leaves the monastery from the day he enters it until he dies. His only possessions are the board and straw pillow he sleeps on and the robe he wears. During all the months we worked alongside them, I never heard any of the brothers utter a syllable. It's a difficult life. Few of us in the Church are blessed with the self-discipline and patience being a Trappist requires. These are simple men who live only to serve God. The brothers who uncovered the trace text never knew what it was."

It was hard for Roth to believe there were people that selfless anywhere on earth—or others as brutal as the man they were after. He thought of the Rolls-Royce, the Cartier cologne and the designer boots. How different the life of Amber Semple's killer was from that of the monks at St. Stephen's.

Sosa said in her cop's voice, "A moment ago you mentioned the Carbon-14 dating of the *palimpsest*? Who did that?"

"Dr. Hovin at the Radiometric Dating Institute in Zurich. The Vatican has used him for many years to help us determine the age of religious codices."

"Could he have … ?"

"We sent him only a few centimeters of the papyrus to analyze. Neither he nor his staff had any way of knowing what they were working on."

She fingered an earring. "Monsignor, you said that a third translator went with you and Father Tomasella to Heidelberg."

"Yes, Father Galgano. He died in January. He was only sixty-four, God rest his soul."

The ringing of her cell phone interrupted them. She turned it off quickly. "May I ask how old you and Father Tomasella are?"

The priest paused and said something in Italian. They heard chuckling in the background.

"I'm eighty-one and Father Tomasella is seventy-seven. I hope we're not suspects."

"Of course not."

Roth sipped coffee from a Styrofoam cup, wondering why she had asked the question. They were looking for an American in his late twenties or early thirties with the strength to climb the side of a building and leap between balconies at a high-rise condo.

"Will you help us find this man?" Sosa said plaintively. Garofalo paused, speaking again to the other priest in Italian. The second man responded with obvious agitation, lapsing into silence when the monsignor's voice grew angry. Garofalo said, "I'd be endangering my immortal soul if I didn't do everything I could to help you bring this evil to an end, but I must tell you, if I am ever asked, this conversation never took place. Do you understand?"

"We do," Sosa assured him.

"This … this just isn't possible," Garofalo murmured.

Roth stood and leaned on the table. "Monsignor, we didn't imagine this Aramaic passage. Someone sent it to us."

For several seconds, they heard only the hum of the speakerphone.

"Not someone…," Pietro Garofalo said, " … some thing."

CHAPTER

42

The conference call to Rome took longer than Roth and Sosa had expected; they grabbed their radios and prepared to leave for Riviera Beach.

"I'm not sure the Archives are as secure as the monsignor believes," Sosa said as they hurried down the hall. "Sealing a document that important must have created some kind of paper trail at the Vatican. Someone there either knew or found out what those priests brought back from Germany. Whoever it was had access to the vault where the *palimpsest* and its translation are stored and told our guy about them."

"But why?"

She smiled. "You would have to ask that."

A couple of homicide detectives passed them in the garage with a handcuffed prisoner as they walked briskly to the car. After telling dispatch that they were leaving the city, Roth clamped his pipe between his teeth.

"What are you thinking about?" Sosa asked.

"Who says I'm thinking about anything?"

"I'm getting to know your habits. Whenever the pipe comes out, you've got something on your mind. Come on, give!"

He scraped the crusty bowl of his pipe with a key. "I think this man was probably a devout Catholic at one time."

"I don't see how you can jump to that conclusion just because we've now got some kind of link to the Vatican."

He watched traffic backing up above them on a cloverleaf leading to the airport. "It's not just the *palimpsest*," he told her. "There are other things."

"Like what?"

"The rapist cried before he attacked Sister Kearney. Knowing he was about to assault a nun was obviously traumatic for him."

"If it was so damn traumatic, why did he do it?"

"I don't know, but it's significant that he didn't have that kind of emotional reaction with any of the other women." He ran a thumb distractedly around the rim of his pipe. "Sister Kearney said he kept looking at the crucifix before he grabbed it off the wall and started hitting her with it."

"What do you make of that?"

"I think it indicates deep-seated ambivalence about his religion. It's something he both loves and hates." He opened the glove box and rummaged in it until he found a pack of Life Savers.

"It's interesting that he chose the little replica of Michelangelo's *Pieta* as a sexual fetish. The things he took from the other victims were all emotionally neutral objects: a letter opener, a Phi Beta Kappa key, an insignia of military rank—even the pianist's finger had no personal significance to him." He handed her a Life Saver and popped one in his mouth. "The statue portraying the dead Christ in the arms of his mother had special meaning for him."

"Because of the Oedipus thing with his own mother?"

"Undoubtedly."

They passed a state trooper on the side of the road who was writing a ticket to a scofflaw with a Pennsylvania license plate.

"You think we could be looking for a rogue priest who's gone off the deep end?"

He shook his head. "How many men of the cloth have that kind of money?"

They rode in silence for another ten miles. Great Blue Heron, Osprey and Snowy Egrets perched on the gnarled branches of trees beside the highway.

"Let me run a scenario by you," Sosa finally said. "Imagine a rich, young, gay living on Palm Beach island, who hates women for reasons we still don't understand."

"Not just women," he corrected. "Professional women."

"We know our man is no stranger to Rome," Sosa continued. "He told Laura Kelce that the restaurant where she and her assistant had lunch on the day of the concert had *always* been one of his favorite places. You can hop on a jet at Miami International and be in Rome in about nine hours." She moistened her lips. "Suppose that, during one of his jaunts across the pond, he meets a guy—maybe a priest, a researcher, a secretary—someone who works at either the Vatican or the Archives and knows about the *palimpsest*."

"A gay lover?"

"That would be my guess." She slowed and took the Blue Heron exit for Riviera Beach. "Something like *Matthias* isn't the kind of thing you talk to just anyone about. I'm thinking that our perp developed a *very* close relationship with this person." She fingered a thin gold chain with a crucifix that dangled against her neck. "So … maybe one night over a candlelight dinner and a little too much vino, this hypothetical Vatican insider lets something slip about the Matthias Gospel. Our guy is immediately intrigued. Think about it! If you're right about the rapist having a strong Catholic background, wouldn't owning a document written by someone who actually knew Jesus be more exciting than having the Mona Lisa, the Shroud of Turin and every piece of White Star Lines china salvaged from the Titanic?"

"I'd say so."

"Our guy decided that he had to have a piece of the Gnostic Gospel of Matthias," she continued, still fleshing out her theory.

"Chapter 9, Verse 31, I take it."

"Correcto."

"But, how could he have gotten at the sealed scrolls?"

Her mouth curved into a cynical smile. "This creep is rich. There are very few things in the world that the right amount of money can't buy. Who knows how much he paid whoever his contact was. Maybe a guard was bribed, or they greased the palm of the right staff member at the College of Cardinals. It doesn't matter how he got it. The point is he obviously did."

Roth gazed pensively out the window. "But even if he found a way to get to the *palimpsest*, how did he create the handwritten copy of the chapter and verse he sent us? Professor Brashears told me that only an Aramaic scholar could write Estrangela that well." They stopped at a drawbridge spanning the Intracoastal Waterway when red lights began flashing and a black and white striped arm lowered in front of them.

"Garofalo said there are other people at the Archives who can read and write that dialect," she reminded him. "Whoever his accomplice was must have copied the passage he sent you. The Wake-Up Rapist is smart, but I doubt that he can anymore read and write ancient Aramaic than we can."

Roth ran a finger along his lower lip contemplatively. "If someone else wrote that passage from *Matthias,* why aren't the person's fingerprints on the letter?"

"He must have worn gloves, just as the rapist did when he planted Laura Kelce's print on the paper."

He watched the tall mast of a sailboat glide beneath the raised bridge, then said, "If you're right that someone in Rome copied the passage and the rapist later mailed it to me from Palm Beach, why are both the Aramaic Estrangela on the letter and the address on the envelope written in the same peacock-colored ink?"

"Good question" she conceded. The tires of the *Exxon Valdez* hummed across the metal span of the bridge.

"Can the lab compare the writing on the letter with what's on the envelope, to see if they were written by the same person?" Roth asked.

"I already checked on that. English and Aramaic are too dissimilar to make any comparison."

"South Florida has five or six million people. We had no idea where to start looking for him until we got that letter. If you're a wanted murderer living on an island with only twenty thousand inhabitants, why send the police an envelope postmarked from there, unless, of course, you're trying to get caught?"

"It's all a power trip, David, just like the pictures he took of us. You said yourself that he thinks of this as a game. Having us know that he lives in Palm Beach makes it more exciting to him. The island is full of wealthy people with Rolls-Royces. He knew when he mailed the letter that it wouldn't help us. He realized that even if we tracked the Aramaic passage to Rome, we'd never in a million years find out who told him about the *palimpsest* and copied the passage for him. The letter was a red herring all along."

He cocked his head. "But why send us an excerpt from a sealed biblical document that so few people had access to?" he persisted. "He could just as easily have mailed us a blank piece of paper with Laura Kelce's fingerprint on it in an envelope with a Palm Beach postmark? He must be trying to tell us something about himself."

Sosa shook her head. "He sent us that quotation because he wants us to appreciate the kind of mind we're up against. David, this is someone who managed to get hold of one of the most closely guarded objects in the history of Christendom!"

They were well into Riviera Beach now. Weekend traffic was heavy along the two-lane road that separated the community from the beach.

"I think Garofalo was being straight with us," Roth opined.

"So do I. He believes that the entire *palimpsest* they brought back from Germany is still sealed in the vault, but, I'd be willing to bet a month's pay that the piece of papyrus containing 9:31 is gone. A little scrap like that wouldn't be missed. Remember, we're not talking about a bank with an audit system. Garofalo said the *palimpsest* was sealed *ad eternum*—that means buried and forgotten." She coasted through an intersection on a yellow light.

"Once we get this guy and toss wherever he's living, we're going to find that fragment of papyrus, right along with the fetishes he took from our ladies," she predicted.

"I don't suppose there's much chance of getting a search warrant for the Vatican Archives to test your theory, huh?"

She laughed. "The odds of being struck by lightning would be a lot better."

She glanced at her watch. "Better give Peaches a call and let her know we're running a little late."

He dialed the number Peaches Brooks had given them and waited through four rings before her voice mail kicked in. He left a message saying they were about twenty minutes away from her apartment.

"I wonder why she didn't pick up?" he said.

Sosa's face conveyed uneasiness. "You don't think she got cold feet and split, do you?"

"I sure hope not." He felt a momentary queasiness in the pit of his stomach.

Knowing that the outcome of the entire investigation could hinge on the dependability of a prostitute who carried a straight razor in her purse was less than comforting.

They continued along the main drag of Riviera Beach, past flimsy shops jammed up against one another. Signs advertising everything from rubber sharks and pink conch shells to ice cream and suntan lotion cluttered the store windows. The sound of Reggae music and the click of pool balls floated from crowded open-air bars with long wooden decks.

They took a left and headed inland, stopping at a bait shop to get directions from an old black woman with knobby knees and a tattered straw hat. After several more turns, the *Exxon Valdez* bumped through rain-filled potholes onto Peaches' street.

They found the Ocean Vista Apartments just beyond a rundown trailer park. The name proved to be a misnomer; there was no view of anything except an auto scrap yard across Dixie Highway filled with the rusting carcasses of old cars. The Atlantic Ocean lay a full six miles to the east. An assortment of cans, bottles and fast food wrappers winked at them from the recesses of St. Augustine grass and weeds. A couple of children playing on a tire swing beneath a large oak ran away quickly when they saw the unmarked car. Roth guessed that cops were a familiar sight on Spinnaker Drive.

The subtropical sun had bleached the two-story building from whatever its original color was to a dull, sandy hue. Lush vines grew in untended profusion on either side of the cracked sidewalk, their tentacles coiled around a half-dozen warped steps leading to the second floor. Roth shielded his eyes from the sun, stepping over a tricycle that was missing its handlebars. An emaciated mongrel barked at them a couple of times when they started up the stairs. The screen door of Peaches' apartment was torn and hanging by a single rusty hinge. Roth was about to knock when he felt Sosa's hand on his arm.

She raised a silencing finger to her lips, and then whispered, "Those are fresh pick marks on the lock." Now he saw what she was talking about: almost imperceptible shiny scratches on the oxidized surface of the deadbolt cylinder.

Sosa already had her gun out. He reached beneath his jacket and drew the Glock. The swollen wood of the door resisted when he turned the knob and pushed. He jolted it hard with his shoulder a couple of times before it sprung open. They stood on either side of the door, listening.

"Peaches, it's Sergeant Sosa!"

Silence.

The weapon felt large and awkward in Roth's hand. They moved cautiously inside with their guns in front of them.

The air in the one-bedroom apartment smelled strongly of mildew. Roth was breathing faster now. His eyes skipped around the living room. Newspapers, pillows and wrinkled clothes were strewn on the floor. The furnishings were uniformly ugly: a nappy old red sofa with stains on it; a couple of battered end tables and cheap ceramic lamps. A picture of a bowl of fruit hung askew on the wall. He could hear Oprah's voice drifting from a television set in a room at the end of the hallway.

The planks beneath the worn Berber carpeting creaked noisily with each step they took. Sosa's gun swept back and forth in an arc as steady as a metronome as they moved cautiously past the kitchen. The stainless steel sink was piled high with dirty dishes; several roaches feasted on the remnants of a crusty plate.

Sosa paused and called out again when they reached the dimly lit hallway. Images from the TV screen flickered through a partially open door at the opposite end of it. She gave Roth a hand signal to take the right side. A paroxysm of fear seized him: *the Bermuda Triangle of police work.* That was what one of his academy instructors had called narrow hallways, like the one they were about to start down. Too many cops died in them. There was no cover—no doorway to dart into if someone suddenly jumped out of the room at the end with a gun. If that happened, Maria could easily wind up in his line of fire. If he turned to run in such a nightmarish situation, he would probably be shot in the back. For an instant, he imagined himself lying wounded on the floor, waiting for the *coup de grace* to the back of his head.

The armpits of his shirt were drenched. He flattened himself against the wall, trying to get his breathing back under control. They inched closer to the bedroom, listening for sounds of movement. Sosa gave him a tight-lipped glance then kicked the door open.

"Oh … no!" she cried.

He was at her side instantly. A cold tremor spread through him when he saw Peaches Brooks. She was sprawled diagonally on the queen-size bed in a pair of polka dot pajamas, with her head hanging over the side. Her dilated eyes and open mouth created an expression of horror, co-mingled with disbelief. Her arms were extended gracefully toward the floor, as if in a grotesque parody of some ballet movement. The open blade of the straight razor she displayed in Luther Williams' office gleamed wickedly a few inches from her fingertips.

Sosa sidestepped to the bathroom, training her gun on the shower curtain. Roth ripped it back, popping several clips off the rod.

They moved quickly back into the bedroom, past the body. Sosa slid the mirrored closet door open, exposing a jumble of high-heeled shoes and garishly colored clothes. Without saying a word, she lowered her gun and pointed it at the bed behind them. Roth knew what she was thinking. The week before, a couple of Miami patrol officers found a burglar hiding under a bed in the house he had just broken into. He swallowed hard, then bent and raised one corner of the blue and green spread, resisting the thought of a bullet crashing into his skull.

"Clear," he said shakily, still in the grip of adrenalin. Sosa knelt beside Peaches and went through the formality of feeling for a pulse they both knew wouldn't be there. She flipped her cell phone open and called the Riviera Beach police operator, stating who she was and that she was at the scene of a homicide in their city.

Roth stared at the dead woman while Sosa went to the car to get crime scene gloves. The boundary between life and death had seemed so permeable since he lost Sara and Jacob. He remembered the minutes after he arrived at the hospital on the day they died. Two uniformed officers were waiting for him in the emergency room lobby. They backpedaled ahead of him, trying to get him to stop and listen to what they were saying. Finally, they grabbed his arms and held him when he tried to force his way through the double doors that led to where his wife and son were. One of them blurted that Sara's car caught fire after it was hit. Several people had tried to help, he said, but the flames were too intense. He remembered the pleading sound of the cop's voice: "*Sir, please, you don't want to go back there!*"

"David …" The sound of his partner's voice interrupted his thoughts. He turned toward her numbly. "You can put your gun away."

He looked down, realizing he was still holding the Glock at his side.

"Are you okay?"

He nodded, holstering the weapon. A moment later, he slammed his palm against the wall in frustration. "Goddamnit! We should have gotten her to a safe place!"

She put her hand gently on his shoulder. "This lady wouldn't have gone, believe me, and there's no way we could have forced her."

"We could have tried …"

"Come on, help me," she urged, kneeling beside the body. "Let's see what we can find out while we're waiting for the local PD to get here." He pulled on the gloves she handed him and stood behind her while she drew back the bedding and examined the lower half of the body. "No signs of sexual assault." She turned the black woman's wrists and examined them. "It doesn't look as if she was bound."

"He didn't come here to rape or torture her. He was just eliminating a witness," Roth said. His eyes moved around the bedroom. A thick roll of currency with a rubber band around it was on the nightstand; so were a pack of Kools, a red Bic lighter and a can of Schlitz Malt Liquor. He counted seven cigarette stubs in the ashtray; all held traces of lipstick. Barbeque potato chips from a half-empty bag were scattered on the bed.

He looked at the razor. She must have heard someone in the apartment and tried to …

Sosa beckoned to him. "Come here and feel her skin."

His feet felt as if they were nailed to the floor. He took a tentative step and stopped.

"Come on. She's dead. She won't bite you."

He edged around the body and placed a gloved hand on Peaches' forearm, jerking it back as if he'd touched a live wire. "She ... she's cold."

Sosa felt the dead woman's jaw, then one of her elbows and knees. "You don't see this kind of advanced *rigor mortis* unless a person has been dead ten to fifteen hours."

"How did you learn all this working sex crimes?"

"I was in homicide for almost a year before I transferred to the SBU. In a lot of places, that wouldn't mean much, but, in Miami, it translates to a lot of bodies."

He could hear the faint wail of sirens now. Sosa pulled back the collar of the victim's pajamas and pointed at her throat. "See that thin line running across her larynx? It continues on either side of her neck."

"Ligature strangulation?" he ventured, recalling something from an academy lecture.

"Yeah. Some kind of garrote. Probably a very thin wire, judging from the width of it."

"Maybe a piano wire from an old Erard?"

"Could be. Whoever did it was very strong. See how deeply the ligature cut into her neck?"

"What are those little red marks in the whites of her eyes?" he asked.

"That's petechial hemorrhaging. The strangulation caused an elevation in blood pressure in her head that burst the vessels in her eyes."

They turned toward the window at the sound of brakes being jammed. Two marked patrol cars slid into the lot, followed moments later by a fire rescue vehicle. Luther Williams and another Riviera Beach homicide detective arrived not long afterward.

* *

A couple of hours passed before the body of Peaches Brooks was zipped in a bag and wheeled on a gurney to a black van with **PALM BEACH COUNTY MEDICAL EXAMINER** on its sides. By the time Roth and

Sosa left, the door to the dead woman's apartment had been sealed with crime scene tape, and the crowd of onlookers that initially numbered thirty or more had dwindled to only four or five people.

As soon as they got in the car, Roth said, "If he's spending time in Rome, he could be victimizing women there, too."

"We'd better send a profile to Interpol as soon as we get back and see if they've had anything in or around Rome that matches our attacks."

"Why not fax the Compusketch to Monsignor Garofalo. Someone at the Archives might recognize the face," he suggested.

"Sure. It's worth a try." They hardly spoke during the long drive back to Miami.

"Well, so much for the license plate lead," he sighed. He watched a cruise ship with waving passengers at its railings steam out of Port Everglades toward the open water.

"What do we do now?" he asked.

"I wish I knew."

CHAPTER

43

The message light was blinking on Roth's phone when they got back to the SBU. They were running so late after the conference call with Garofalo that he hadn't checked his voice mail before they left for Riviera Beach. 'ONE MESSAGE' it announced. In a couple of seconds he heard the throaty laughter of a man's voice, followed by a disconnect sound.

The caller ID indicated that the message came in at exactly *3:26 a.m.* from (561) 277-7268. He recognized the area code as Palm Beach County. His heart skipped a beat when he dialed the number and heard the familiar recorded message on the other end: "Yo ... this is Peaches. Sorry, I can't come to the phone right now. Jes' leave a number when you hear the beep and I'll get back to you." He clutched the phone tightly, realizing that the killer had placed the call from the dead woman's apartment after strangling her. The Wake-Up Rapist was still letting them know he wasn't afraid of them.

* *

That evening, while Sosa sat at her desk preparing a report for Captain Wilcox on the latest homicide, Roth e-mailed their suspect's profile and the Compusketch to Interpol headquarters in Lyon, France, along with a letter explaining their concern that the Wake-Up Rapist might be victimizing women in Rome. After he finished, he stood at the window in Sosa's office, watching traffic flow past the building.

"I was just thinking about one of Voltaire's plays I read when I was in college," he said distractedly.

She looked up from her report and took off her reading glasses. "Okay, I'll bite. Just how did we get from this case to the French Enlightenment?"

He unrolled his sleeves and began buttoning them. "This particular play is about an alien who visits earth. After seeing the things we do to one another, he concludes that the rest of the universe must be using the planet as a madhouse."

She smiled thinly. "I've been doing this kind of work long enough to agree with him."

He pressed his forehead against the cool surface of the window and closed his eyes. "He'll kill every victim from now on," he said.

CHAPTER

44

On Monday morning, Sosa convened the first meeting of the Wake-Up Rapes Task Force. The main conference room at the Florida Department of Law Enforcement was filled with investigators from police and sheriff's departments throughout Miami-Dade and Palm Beach Counties. The FBI sent two of its most experienced ViCAP profilers from Quantico. They had already met with Sosa, Roth and Captain Wilcox earlier that morning.

After introducing herself, Sosa pulled down a wall map behind her and said, "Palm Beach PD has had a BOLO out for a light-colored, late model Rolls with a dark top ever since we learned that one was involved in the murder of Amber Semple. The island is only a few square miles. The fact that they haven't been able to turn up the car by now probably means that he's moved it to the mainland. He may very well have already gotten rid of it."

A detective from North Miami Beach raised his hand. "Where do we look for this guy?"

"We're pretty sure he hangs out at gay bars in the area," Sosa replied.

Roth caught her eye. After her last remark, every investigator in the room would assume that the rapist-murderer was bisexual. The profilers from ViCAP had agreed that to get into details of the Stalker Sadist's sexuality and the bizarre likelihood that he was gay would only complicate an already difficult manhunt. The case was sensational enough without having the media get hold of something like that.

"Tell your people to be very careful approaching this guy," she cautioned. "He's armed and extremely dangerous."

Luther Williams raised his hand. "He must be feeling a lot of heat after this last murder," he said. "The Compusketch has been all over the news. He could have altered his appearance."

"We're thinking the same thing," Sosa replied. Roth began passing out computer-generated variations on the original Compusketch. They depicted the suspect with different hairstyles, as well as with beards, mustaches and glasses.

"Many of you are aware that my partner, Detective David Roth, is also a criminologist at the University of Miami. He's been working in our Sexual Battery Unit as part of a research project. I'm going to ask him to fill you in on what we know about the suspect so far."

Roth stepped to the microphone while she finished handing out the Compusketches. "The man we're looking for is young, bright and apparently wealthy. He plans each attack down to the smallest detail and has no trouble getting past even the best security measures: locks, guard dogs— even a victim who slept with a gun under her pillow. Whatever it is, he finds a way to get around it. During one of his assaults, he managed to deactivate what was supposed to be a tamper-proof alarm system. The people who designed it tell us that he must know a great deal about computers." He scanned the faces in the room, wondering if his words carried any more weight because they were coming from a criminologist who was also a cop.

"He has a strong interest in scripture and religious objects. It's possible that he's a present or former priest, although his obvious wealth makes that seem unlikely. We believe he spends time in Rome and may have friends there. We've passed that information on to both Interpol and the Italian *Carabinieri*."

Special Agent Marcie Crosby of the FBI spoke up. She was a prim-looking woman in her early thirties with hazel eyes and short blond hair. "How do you know he hasn't left the country by now?"

"He may have, but even if he's out of the U.S. right now we believe he'll return next month to resume his attacks. We're dealing with an obsessive-compulsive who has an intense hatred of professional women."

He adjusted his glasses and continued in a measured voice. "This guy enjoys playing cat and mouse with the police. He's been using a scanner to monitor our operations and even took pictures of us one night while we were staking out a place where we thought he might be living." He twisted his wedding band absently, remembering how he had held Sosa in the parking lot that night.

A murmur swept through the room. The Wake-Up Rapist didn't fit the mold of any known type of sexual predator or serial killer. It had been an accepted principle of criminal psychology for over a century and a half that most felons try to stay as far away from the police as possible.

He added, "We're encouraged by a couple of things: he likes taking chances, and he's starting to make mistakes. Letting the last woman he murdered see his face and live long enough to describe him to us was a big one. We're sure there'll be others. He recently mailed us a letter postmarked from Palm Beach."

"What did it say?" a husky detective from the Miami-Dade County Public Safety Department asked.

"It was a biblical passage, written in an ancient language that very few people can read."

Another hand went up. "Any idea what the connection is between the professional women he's been assaulting?"

"Absolutely none," Roth confessed.

CHAPTER

45

"Hey, nice tie," Sosa said when Roth walked into her office. "I like the colors with your shirt."

"Thanks." He was hoping she'd notice. It was one of several he'd picked out at a Hart, Schaffner and Marx store over the weekend. He felt like a kid trying to impress a girl.

What was next—a handstand?

"Uh-oh," she said.

"What's wrong?"

"Looks like you've got a coffee spot on it."

"Damn! Happens every time I wear anything light." He rubbed the stain vigorously with his handkerchief. "Are all cops as observant as you?"

"I think it really has more to do with being a woman. We're just better at noticing details than guys."

"Why are you smiling?"

"You make such a straight-looking, Joe Friday cop. When you were speaking at the meeting yesterday, I kept trying to picture you at Berkeley with a beard and hippie beads, marching in a Vietnam war protest."

"Vietnam? You make me sound ancient! I was still in grade school when Saigon fell."

She eyed him mischievously. "Oh, I guess I thought you were a lot older."

"I'll have you know, *Sarge*, that I'm only six years and three months older than you."

"And just how do you know my age?"

Oops ... One day, when she got out of the car to help a stranded motorist, he saw her wallet sticking out of her purse on the seat and sneaked a look at her driver's license.

"I'm a detective," he said, with mock officiousness. "It's my business to know things. Your birthday is July 21st." He dropped into a chair beside her desk. "If you're good, I might get you something really nice. Which would you rather have: a box of Black Talon hollow points or a pair of chrome handcuffs?"

She giggled. It was the laugh of a schoolgirl.

Are we flirting?

"What were you arrested for at Berkeley? Throwing rocks at cops, I'll bet."

"I'm a pacifist. Pacifists don't throw rocks—not if they're *kosher*."

"Oh, but I suppose it's okay for one to carry a piece?"

"You haven't seen me shoot anyone yet, have you?" He patted the Glock in his shoulder holster. "This thing may as well have come from Toys-R-Us. It's just a prop for the role I'm playing."

CHAPTER

46

Roth received a fax from Monsignor Garofalo promising to circulate the Compusketches immediately at the Archives. An e-mail from Interpol the same day indicated that the organization had no record of any assaults in Europe matching the profile of the Wake-Up Rapist.

He was surprised to find three items in his mailbox that day. The first was a belated memo from the personnel office, appointing him as Detective Third Grade for a period of exactly six months at a starting salary of $0000.00 per month. He smiled to himself. *Well, the withholding on that shouldn't be too bad.* He pitched a computer-generated invitation to join the Police Benevolent Association in the wastebasket, recalling Groucho's maxim about never joining any organization that would have him as a member.

The final piece of mail was a manila envelope addressed in black ink. He felt a momentary surge of anticipation before noticing that the handwriting was very different from that of the Wake-Up Rapist. The envelope had been postmarked in Delmar, one of Miami's suburbs, and carried both a name and return address:

> J. Nasargiel
> 3158 Gulfstream Ave.
> Apt. 11
> Delmar, Florida 33444

His graduate assistant had been collecting and responding to most of his routine correspondence during the research project. The envelope had been rerouted from the university to the police department only because the sender had written: **Personal — Please Forward** on it. Inside was the dust jacket from the most recent edition of his book, *Patterns of Sexual Violence*. A handwritten note on lined paper torn from a three-ring binder was paper-clipped to it:

Dear Professor:

I just wanted you to know that I enjoyed your book. There was a lot of real intresting stuff in it.

J. Nasargiel

Real intresting. Roth clucked his tongue. *You'd think students would learn to spell and use decent grammar by the time they reach college!* He glanced at the $89.95 price tag stamped on the cover, concluding that the note was obviously from some undergrad with too much time and money on his hands, trying to impress one of his professors. He threw the envelope, along with the note and dust jacket, in his trash can.

While he thought no more about the letter from Delmar that day, some subterranean part of his mind had apparently fastened onto it. He tossed restlessly in bed that night, unable to fall into a sound sleep. *Intresting ... intresting.* The word kept running through his mind. What was *intresting* about a two-inch tome filled with highly technical language and enough graphs and charts to put even the most dedicated graduate student into a soporific trance? Suddenly, it hit him. *The appendix!* The appendix to *Patterns of Sexual Violence* contained an exhaustive description of methods of torture used by Stalker Sadist rapists: whipping, bondage, electrocution, burning, and asphyxiation. That was what the writer of the note found *intresting.* The smeared word on the broken mirror in Dr. Pulaski's condo leapt into his mind. *Jan! J. Nasargiel!*

He put on his glasses and squinted at the clock on the nightstand. It was almost one-thirty. He dialed the SBU, hoping to catch whoever was working the graveyard shift. After eleven rings, someone finally picked up.

"Sexual Battery ... Detective Webley," a bored voice said.

"Hi, this is David Roth," he said, unable to recall Webley's first name. "Sorry to bother you at this hour. I'm the guy from UM who's working with—"

"Yeah, I know who you are," Webley responded gruffly. "Whaddya need?"

Maria had told him that Webley regularly volunteered for the midnight shift out of a combination of innate laziness and an inability to get along with people. Roth sat on the edge of the bed in his boxer shorts.

"I need a favor," he said anxiously. "It's really important." Webley grunted but said nothing.

"There's a manila envelope and a couple of other items in my trash can that I don't want thrown out."

"If the stuff's so all-fired important, then what's it doing in the trash?"

"I … I didn't realize it might be evidence until just a few minutes ago."

"The janitors are here now. It may already be down the chute."

His spirits sank when he heard the whine of a vacuum cleaner in the background. "I'd really appreciate it if you could check and see if those things are still there."

"Lemme get this straight," Webley volleyed. "It's one fuckin' thirty in the morning, and you want me to go dig in your trash can?"

"I realize it's an imposition."

"No way!" Webley laughed. "I'm no garbage man."

Roth took a deep breath. "Okay, then how about just putting the wastebasket on my desk with a note saying not to empty it?"

"Now, that I'll do," the midnight man said. "Hold on." Roth heard the phone clatter on a desk.

Webley returned after several minutes. "Okay, the trash can's on your desk with a note taped to it. You sure I can't do something else—maybe come over and wash your car or make you breakfast?" He made a monosyllabic noise and hung up.

*　　*

Roth was waiting in Sosa's office with the manila envelope and its contents in an evidence bag when she arrived the following morning.

She frowned when she read the note. "This is from Delmar—not Palm Beach—and the handwriting is nothing like our guy's."

"I had communications check the city directory. The address on the envelope is a vacant lot and there's no phone listing for a 'J. Nasargiel' in Delmar or anywhere else in Dade or Palm Beach County."

"It could be a college prank. A lot of kids at the university must know you're working here."

"Maria, *Eleven* was Peaches' apartment number."

"Probably just a coincidence. How many 'Apartment 11's do you think there are in a city the size of Miami?"

"I'm sure it's from him!" he said.

She smiled indulgently. "What are we talking here, a hunch? Tea leaves? I thought you were supposed to be a scientist."

He met her eyes. "Please, indulge me on this. Just send it to the lab."

*   *

Sosa received a call from the Florida Department of Law Enforcement laboratory as soon as they finished their analysis of the material from Delmar. While the note and book dust jacket contained no fingerprints besides Roth's, whoever mailed them had licked the envelope; saliva on it yielded a DNA banding pattern that matched that of the Wake-Up Rapist. And, that wasn't all. The Chief of the Documents Section at FDLE asked that Sergeant Sosa come to her office as soon as possible.

*   *

Sheila Allen was studying an exemplar of handwriting at a comparison microscope when Sosa and Roth arrived. She was a gray-haired woman with soft features and a strong, southern accent. At fifty-seven, she had been in charge of the Documents Section for as long as anyone could remember.

"The letters you've received were written by two different people," Allen declared bluntly. *No way!* Roth told himself. They *had to* have come from the same person! The Palm Beach letter held an unmistakable latent print from one of Laura Kelce's severed fingers, and the envelope from Delmar contained the Wake-Up Rapist's DNA. The two detectives exchanged a bewildered look.

"Are you sure?" Sosa said.

"There's no question about it. The Palm Beach cursive has a distinctive slant to it, while the characters on the note from Delmar are almost perfectly vertical."

"What does that mean?" Roth asked.

"Whoever sent you the Aramaic letter is right-handed. The Delmar note was written by a left-handed person."

Roth recalled the medical examiner's conclusion that Amber Semple's killer was left-handed.

"Couldn't this be the same person just trying to disguise his handwriting?" Sosa inquired.

Allen shook her head. "Even a master forger couldn't produce two pieces of handwriting this dissimilar."

Roth suddenly felt like Alice passing through the Looking Glass. "I thought you couldn't compare Aramaic and English handwriting," he said.

"We can't. The writing on the envelopes was what we compared."

She centered a wide magnifying glass on a swivel above the two envelopes, then switched on a high-intensity, halogen lamp and peered at the enlarged images. "The turquoise ink on the Palm Beach envelope was produced by a fountain pen, while the black ink on the Delmar letter came from a ball point."

"Quite a few people own more than one pen," Sosa said flippantly.

"Yes, but regardless of the writing instrument used, the pressure variations in the connectors and pen grooves should match if they were written by the same person. They don't."

She brought the magnifying glass closer to the two specimens. "The heaviness of the ascending and descending strokes varies significantly from one envelope to the next. There are a lot of other subtle variations: the 't's' in 'Police Department' are crossed at the top on the Palm Beach envelope; but, the 't's in 'University' and 'Important' on the Delmar envelope are crossed in the middle—same thing with the misspelled word, *'intresting'*. Also, the loops that the two writers make in their '*p*'s and '*e*'s are very different." She pushed her chair back.

"Here, see for yourselves." The detectives brought their faces close to the magnifying glass. "Look at the '*i*' in *David*," Allen urged. "It's dotted high and off-center on the first envelope, but low and directly overhead on the second."

They followed her as she walked with a slight limp to a computer across the room. "Now, I'll show you something really amazing." She adjusted her heavy-framed glasses and tapped a series of keys; then, she angled the split-screen display so they could both view it. "On the right side of the screen is an enlarged photo of the envelope that the Aramaic letter came in. To the left of it is a blow-up of the picture we took of the re-assembled piece of the broken mirror with the name '*Jan*' on it." She shifted the blinking cursor to the address on the Palm Beach envelope. "Watch what happens when I drag the higher case '*J*' and the lower case '*a*' and '*n*' from the Palm Beach envelope and superimpose the letters on the word '*Jan*' from the mirror."

"The writing looks the same," Roth observed.

Allen looked at him over the top of her glasses. "It *is* the same. The right-handed person who addressed the Aramaic letter also wrote '*Jan*' in lipstick on the mirror."

* *

On their way to the police department, Roth reflected on the latest bizarre development, trying to make sense of it.

"She has to be wrong," Sosa declared as she drove. "That's all there is to it."

Roth watched a group of children jumping delightedly through a six foot geyser from an open fire hydrant.

"Suppose she's right," he said. "What if the letters *were* written by two different people?"

"What the hell are you talking about? We've got …"

He interrupted her with a raised palm. "Up until now, we've had all these contradictions in the case we haven't been able to explain. How can someone who knows Beethoven's history be unable to spell a simple word like '*interesting*'?" He turned toward her. "One minute, this guy is riding a motorcycle in dirty jeans and the next he's cruising along Federal Highway in a Rolls-Royce. Talk about inconsistent behavior: he replaced the nightgown strap on Laura Kelce's shoulder just before he cut off her fingers and made sure the tape on the nun's wrists wasn't too tight before he beat her half to death."

"Where are you going with this?"

"Maria, I think we're dealing with a multiple personality!" he said forcefully.

"You mean, like '*The Three Faces of Eve*'?"

"Yeah."

"It would sure as hell explain a lot of things. Can multiple personalities alter their handwriting?"

"I don't know, but, I think I know someone who will."

CHANGE

47

Roth had the Registrar's Office at the university check his class rosters for the past five years. He had never had a student named Nasargiel. Moreover, there was no record of such a person ever having attended the University of Miami. He concluded that it was a pseudonym the Wake-Up Rapist had made up. He tried all day to get the name out of his mind but couldn't.

The next morning, he was shaving when it occurred to him that *Nasargiel* had a vaguely middle-eastern ring to it. On an impulse, he placed a call to his father in Brooklyn.

Rabbi Samuel Roth recognized the name immediately. He explained that *Nasargiel* was a demon from an old Hebrew myth. Now Roth knew where he had heard it before: it was in a mythology course he took at Yeshiva University during his freshman year. *More mind games.*

Later that day, he checked out a book at the university library called *The Devil in Antiquity.* He was engrossed in it when Sosa walked into his office.

"I know who Nasargiel is," he announced.

"Who is he?" she asked excitedly.

He grinned. "I'm afraid we might have a little trouble taking him into custody. He's a demon." He showed her the book. "According to Hebrew legend, Nasargiel was an angel who corrupted his holy essence by coming to earth and lying with a mortal woman. For his sin, he was condemned by God to spend eternity roaming the earth as the Angel of Destruction."

"Sounds like Lucifer."

"There's one very important difference between them. Nasargiel isn't an equal opportunity devil. It seems that he only preys on women." He

197

turned to a page he had marked and began reading aloud: "Every other fortnight, Nasargiel comes forth from the bowels of the earth in the blackness of the third hour to punish women for the evil in their hearts."

"The third hour ... Jesus!"

He glanced up from the book. "Every other fortnight is once a month. That's the attack pattern in the Wake-Up Rapes."

He went on: "'He hangs them by their hair and breasts because they uncover them in the presence of men so that they conceive desire and fall into sin. He burns their flesh, lashes their bodies with chains and breaks their teeth with fiery stones.'"

Sosa tucked her hands under her arms. "Sounds like a perfect role model for a sexual sadist."

"Listen to this. 'Nasargiel blinds the eyes that invite lust and severs the fingers that beckon wickedness from the loins of men.'"

Sosa's eyes widened. "My God, that's Nina Pulaski and Laura Kelce."

CHAPTER

48

Sosa was adamantly opposed to consulting with Roth's Dean, Dr. Henry Stafford, on the issue of whether or not Miami's Wake-Up Rapist was a multiple personality. Her resistance had nothing to do with the qualifications of the internationally-renowned forensic psychiatrist. It stemmed rather from the fact that he had served as a defense expert in the infamous murder trial of O.J. Simpson. After failing to persuade the trial judge to accept a *motion in limine* to exclude the testimony of detectives about a dream Simpson recounted in which he killed his ex-wife, Nicole, the defense team had recruited Dr. Stafford in an effort at spin control.

Stafford appeared as an expert witness at the lengthy trial, providing testimony that dream fantasies of violence are rarely translated into action. To buttress his claim, he gave a number of examples of former patients who had dreams of murdering their spouses yet never actually harmed them. Media interviews with the predominantly black jury after Simpson's acquittal revealed that Stafford's testimony served to dispel their initial concerns about the dream. It was clear that the dean of the University of Miami's School of Criminology had played a vital role in helping the ten-million dollar defense juggernaut demolish the prosecution's case.

* *

Sosa glared at her partner during a meeting in the captain's office. "This guy Stafford is nothing but a hired gun who helped set a murderer free! How can either of you even think of asking him to work with us?"

The captain set his jaw. "Listen, if this guy keeps raping and killing women down here, the roof is going to fall in on us. Dr. Roth says that Stafford has experience dealing with multiple personalities."

"But, he ..."

"Goddamnit!" Wilcox bellowed. "I don't care if he was a cheerleader at the crucifixion! I want you to reach out to him! Understand?"

Sosa nodded grudgingly. She was doing a slow burn by the time they left the captain's office. Her eyes tore into Roth like shrapnel. "Well, you heard him!" she said sharply. "Go ahead! Call the whore!"

CHAPTER

49

Roth personally delivered the case files on the Wake-Up Rapes to Henry Stafford at his university office and spent nearly an hour briefing him on things that weren't in the records, including the passage from the Gnostic Gospel of Matthias and the pictures they believed the Wake-Up Rapist sent to Internal Affairs. The next attack window was rapidly approaching; because of the urgency of the situation, Stafford agreed to expedite his analysis of the files.

The two SBU detectives went to the campus on Friday afternoon to meet with him. Roth could hear the sound of a typewriter on the other side of the door when he rapped on it.

"Come on in," a familiar voice called out.

Henry Stafford was pecking at the keys of an old-fashioned black Olympia with his forefingers when they entered. A knit tie hung loosely around his collar, and his glasses were propped on his mane of bushy white hair. He looked up from the clutter of books and papers around him.

"Ah, David!" he said, shaking hands warmly with Roth. "And you must be Sergeant Sosa."

She reacted to his greeting with a forced smile.

The shelves in the office were filled with texts on different aspects of criminal psychopathology. More than a few had been authored by Stafford. Roth's attention was drawn to the spine of a thick, green hardback on the dean's desk:

Multiple Personality and the Criminal Mind
by H. Raymond Stafford, M.D.

The Wake-Up files rested on a credenza behind him. Post-it notes in various colors interspersed throughout them said that Stafford had examined each page with characteristic thoroughness.

"I've heard a lot about you," Sosa said coolly.

Stafford smiled. "I hope it hasn't all been bad."

Her posture stiffened.

"I watched your testimony during the Simpson trial."

"Do I detect a faint note of disapproval?" the psychiatrist said genially.

"The son of a bitch was guilty!" she blurted. Roth shut his eyes. *Damn her!*

The dean's smile vanished. "Yes ... well, fortunately, I wasn't asked to opine on his guilt or innocence but merely the significance of a dream."

Roth saw the look of frosty annoyance on Stafford's face and nudged his partner's foot. Her remark had struck a raw nerve; even years after the Simpson trial, the dean's well-publicized testimony continued to haunt him.

"I see you've had a chance to study the files," Roth said, eager to dispel the tension in the room.

Stafford took the records from the credenza and placed them on his desk.

"Is this a multiple personality?" Roth asked directly.

"There's no doubt about it," the psychiatrist responded, pulling his glasses down on the bridge of his nose. "This man has two distinct personas. You've received a letter from each of them: *J. Nasargiel*, the alter personality, is the one who's committing the rapes and murders."

Sosa removed copies of both letters from a folder in her lap. "Can multiple personalities vary their handwriting like this?"

"Oh, yes," Stafford replied. *Multiples* also often have completely dissimilar IQ's and lifestyles. Everything from their voices to their physiology can be radically different. It's not uncommon for the heart rate, blood pressure and EEG of an alter ego to look nothing like that of the host personality. The alter may do things, like smoke, drink or use drugs, while the host doesn't." He paused and asked his secretary to hold his calls.

Sosa said, "When David started talking about multiple personality, I immediately thought of *The Three Faces of Eve*. Is there usually more than one alter?"

"There can be many. It's entirely possible that other alters will appear in this man as time goes on. I once had a homicidal female patient with four distinct alters—each with her own menstrual cycle!"

Sosa smoothed the sides of her slacks. "Surely the people around a multiple personality must notice the changes in their behavior when they shift identities."

Stafford grasped the arms of his chair and rocked gently in it. "Most *multiples* manage to keep their alters pretty well hidden from others. There's usually nothing that would alert an average person to the existence of the condition. The Stalker Sadist part of this man's personality probably only surfaces when it's necessary to plan and carry out his attacks."

Sosa asked, "Just how many multiple personalities have you dealt with?"

"Seven," he replied. "That doesn't sound like a lot until you stop to consider that there are only about two hundred authenticated cases in the annals of psychiatry. By the way, the technical label for the condition is *dissociative identity disorder.*"

Sosa tugged at an earring. "Someone this bright must realize we're going to get him sooner or later. Maybe he's setting up an insanity defense. Couldn't a clever criminal just pretend to be a multiple personality?"

"Certainly, but most people who fake the condition don't start displaying signs of it until they've been caught." He aligned the edges of the case files on his desk. "I've never known a criminal to show such convincing evidence of multiple personality while he was still at large." He picked up a Mont Blanc pen and rolled it between his thumb and forefinger.

"Let's call the primary personality *Robert,* since we don't know his real name yet," he suggested. "He's the one who sent you the biblical passage. Mailing the piece of scripture says a great deal about him. Quite apart from the question of how he obtained the Aramaic quotation, it's clear that religion plays a major role in his life."

Sosa removed a cassette recorder from her pocket. "Mind if I tape this?"

"Not at all."

She placed the recorder on his desk and turned it on.

"It's obvious from the meticulous planning of the attacks that he's extremely intelligent."

Sosa sneered. "I'd hardly call leaving his DNA at crime scenes smart."

"Ah, yes … we'll come back to that," Stafford assured her. "Robert is obviously a well educated person with refined tastes. He's also very shy and reclusive. I would imagine that he has few if any close friends. He's almost certainly *anhedonic*."

"What's that?" Sosa asked.

"An anhedonic is someone who regards pleasure of any kind as wrong or sinful. You may recall that he described himself as 'naughty' for playing Laura Kelce's piano without her permission. That's typical of the way anhedonics upbraid themselves over even the smallest sensual indulgences. They're like bulimics throwing up. On a psychological level, they try to purge themselves of anything remotely pleasurable."

Sosa cocked her head. "If this guy is anhedonic, how do you explain the Rolls-Royce and the one-hundred-fifty-dollar-an-ounce cologne?"

"Those aren't his," Stafford said quickly. "They belong to the alter ego, Jan Nasargiel. The car and the other trappings of wealth are a good indication of the extent to which the alter has invaded the host personality's life. While Robert obviously has money, he probably leads a fairly austere existence. Extravagant creature comforts have no place in the life of any anhedonic."

"What about sex?" she asked.

The psychiatrist touched his cheek thoughtfully. "When it comes to sex, anhedonics have moral codes rigid enough to put a Puritan to shame."

"David thinks he's gay."

An enigmatic smile appeared on Stafford's face. "Well, he is and he isn't," he told them. "Robert has no erotic interest in either men or women. His severe morality requires that he see himself as completely asexual. The alter ego is the part of the psyche that goes to bed with other men and rapes women. You see, Jan's existence allows Robert to engage in homosexuality without being aware of it. He's completely amnesic about his alter's gay lifestyle."

"Is he phobic about vaginas?" Sosa asked.

"Oh, yes," Stafford said resolutely. "Even the thought of a woman's genitals generates intense castration anxiety in him." Roth shifted his handcuffs to the side of his belt when he noticed the dean staring at them.

"Why did he call Sister Kearney a 'filthy cunt'?" he asked.

"Male anhedonics often regard female genitalia as a source of sin and evil. That's why the assaults have been confined to anal rape. The alter has learned to fantasize that he's having sex with another man during the attacks. That's the only way he can develop an erection and ejaculate with a female. Anal intercourse is simply a reflection of the dominant role he plays in gay sex." The psychiatrist turned and pulled the paper he had been typing out of the Olympia, setting it to one side. "To return to the sergeant's question, while the primary personality isn't gay, he is very 'artsy.' No doubt, he has mannerisms that come across to others as somewhat campy or effeminate." He paused and took a stick of licorice from a jar on his desk.

"Please go on," Sosa said, with obvious interest.

"Jan and Robert are dramatically different in every respect," he said, taking a bite of licorice. "Indeed, judging from the postmarks on the two envelopes, they even live in different places—Jan down here in Delmar, and Robert an hour and a half away on Palm Beach Island."

Henry Stafford inclined his head toward the files and continued. "Your Wake-Up Rapist is a macho caricature of the Marlboro Man in jeans and boots. He rides a motorcycle, uses vending machine condoms and likes rough sex. He also enjoys the attention he gets being seen behind the wheel of a Rolls-Royce. The kind of crude language he uses with his victims would never enter Robert's mind. Unlike Robert, Jan isn't overly bright, though he thinks of himself as a master criminal." He chortled. "I doubt that he could hotwire a car without getting caught if he didn't have access to Robert's intelligence and skill."

Real intresting.

"What causes someone to develop a multiple personality?" Sosa asked.

"It's usually brought on by some form of intolerable emotional stress. In this man's case, being both gay and anhedonic produces overwhelming guilt. The alter personality came into being as an unconscious mechanism for resolving the conflict."

"Is Robert aware of the rapes and murders his alter ego is commit-ting?" Roth asked.

The dean moved the brass lamp on his desk closer and flipped through several pages of notes. "There are moments during the assaults when Robert is present and knows what his alter ego is about do, but he can't stop him. The attack on Dr. Pulaski is a good example. Robert managed to gain the upper-hand just long enough to write Jan's name on the mirror at the condo. Jan then seized control again and tried to destroy the evidence by smearing the lipstick and breaking the mirror. Robert also 'got out' briefly during the attack on Sister Kearney. He was the one who kept looking at the crucifix on the wall and who cried before the rape. Sexually assaulting a nun and beating her with an object that's sacred to the host personality would have appealed to Jan's sadism."

Roth said, "Robert also came out during the attack on the pianist, didn't he?"

"Yes. It was Robert who discussed her concert in Rome. Jan wouldn't know Beethoven from the Beatles."

"Why can't Robert control Jan?" Sosa asked.

The psychiatrist tented his fingers contemplatively. "The amnesic wall the host personality erected between the parts of his psyche worked only as long as Jan remained an outlet for his repressed homosexuality. Once the alter ego began raping and torturing women, the balance of power shifted. While Robert is amnesic about the crimes of his alter ego most of the time, he senses that he's being used to do terrible things. That's why he sent you the Aramaic letter. He hoped it would lead you to him."

"How?" Sosa asked.

"I wish I knew the answer to that."

Exasperation showed on the sergeant's face.

"I don't buy it," she said cynically. "If he isn't playing games, why doesn't he just pick up the phone and tell us where he is?"

"He can't. Jan's much too strong to allow that to happen. He wants to remain free as badly as Robert wants him to be caught. The clue Robert sent you represents an unconscious compromise that his ego has worked out between telling you where he is and doing nothing."

For all the useful clues he could have provided about his identity, why send a passage from a two-thousand-year-old piece of scripture that only the pope and a handful of people in Rome knew about? The question kept eating at Roth.

Sosa said, "Doctor, what I don't understand is why the alter ego began attacking women?"

Stafford's blue eyes crinkled alertly. "Something traumatic involving a professional woman must have happened just before the rapes began. Whatever it was produced tremendous anger in Robert. Since that's an emotion that's unacceptable to him on a conscious level, it was channeled through the alter." Stafford poured himself a glass of water from a pitcher on his desk. "Think of the alter as a pressure valve," he continued. "Whenever an unacceptable emotion like sex or anger threatens to become conscious and overwhelm the host, Jan emerges and vents it."

"It sounds like the alter is basically just a thug," Sosa said.

Stafford gazed out the window. "The alter ego is a sadistic trickster. He enjoys pranks. That's why he called you from the dead woman's apartment and sent the pictures to Internal Affairs. He and Robert had very different reasons for writing you. You'll get no help from Jan."

Sosa asked, "Does the alter really believe he's this demon, Nasargiel, who goes around punishing women for seducing men?"

Stafford shook his head. "That's just something he apparently pulled out of Robert's knowledge of ancient mythology. He's been commandeering his host's intelligence right along with his financial resources. Conforming the attacks to the legend of a medieval devil who tortures women in the middle of the night no doubt amuses him."

Roth thought of the dust jacket of *Patterns of Sexual Violence* that Jan mailed him. The alter wanted him to know that he planned to use the appendix as a recipe book for new forms of torture. "Any idea what he— or they—are going to do next?" he asked.

"The two parts of the personality are at war, so to speak. While Robert will undoubtedly continue trying to help you, Jan realizes that he represents a serious threat to his existence. He can't let him keep interfering with the attacks or send more clues to the police. The alter is tired of being let out of the bottle only a few hours each month to do the dirty work of the psyche. Committing two murders so close to where Robert lives was clearly an act of defiance. So was using a high profile car like the Rolls when he killed Amber Semple and brutalized Laura Kelce. He's determined to destroy Robert and take over his entire personality."

Alarm registered in Sosa's eyes. "Can he do that?"

"I'm afraid so," Stafford said ominously. "The dynamics of the personality are changing rapidly. As the murders demonstrate, the sadistic component of the psyche is metastasizing. It's growing stronger with each attack. Robert has unwittingly created a monster he can't control. The psychiatrist's face darkened. "Jan has acquired a taste for blood. He's discovered that he enjoys killing women more than just raping and torturing them."

"There is one benefit to having Jan eliminate Robert," Stafford offered.

"I'd sure as hell like to know what it is," Sosa said. "It sounds as if he'll become even more dangerous without Robert around to control him."

Roth added, "Not to mention that we won't be getting any more help from the host personality."

"Keep in mind that if your rapist-murderer eliminates Robert, he'll lose access to his intelligence. That should make him much easier to catch. Every time Jan goes off on his own, he gets in trouble. He's a thrill seeker. He likes pushing the envelope. That's why he let the prostitutes see his face and car and risked getting close enough to you to take the pictures. Letting the police have his DNA was foolish. I'm sure he never stopped to think of the consequences. Left to his own devices, he'll screw up. You can count on that."

"Dr. Stafford, you'll pardon me if I say that all this really seems far-fetched."

The psychiatrist chuckled. "I understand. Whenever I start talking about multiples, people look at me as if I'm someone who sees UFO's. Some of my colleagues react the same way." He handed her his text on multiple personality. "Take this with you. It may help answer some of your questions."

She turned the recorder off. "What do you suggest we do now?"

"I'd concentrate on finding Jan. He's the weak link in the chain."

"We're already keeping an eye on gay bars, but there are so many of them," she said.

Stafford stroked his chin meditatively with a thumb and forefinger. "You're casting your net too wide. I'd concentrate on SM bars, as well as porn shops and those hole-in-the-wall theatres that cater to men who are into leather and bondage."

Sosa pressed her lips together. "That's still a lot of places. Miami has to be the kink capital of the country."

The forensic psychiatrist walked them to the door. "A word of caution about alters. There's a natural tendency to start thinking of them as real people. They aren't. Remember, an alter ego is nothing but a psychotic shadow cast by the dominant personality. Jan couldn't do or say anything that didn't already exist somewhere in Robert's unconscious mind."

CHAPTER

50

Roth was sipping a Pepsi in the break room when Sosa walked in. She dropped some change in one of the vending machines and got a candy bar.

"What do you know about Delmar?" he asked.

She tore the wrapper and took a bite. "Well, it ain't exactly Palm Beach. We have a saying in the department: 'If your lawn furniture can double as your living room furniture, you *must* be from Delmar.'" She pulled up a chair and sat beside him. "It's so rough that we ride two-officer cars there even on the day watch. *Mucho violencia!*"

"Sounds like a place where a guy on a Harley would fit right in. Any SM bars there?"

She was about to speak when her cell phone rang. "Sister Kearney! How are you?"

He saw a glint of apprehension in her eyes.

"Oh.... Okay, sure. You don't have to come down here. My partner and I will be right there." She closed her cell phone and looked at him.

"What's going on?"

"Something's wrong. Sister Kearney wants to see us."

*　*

Roth's only prior exposure to Catholic nuns had been as a youth growing up in Brooklyn. He had watched the Sisters of the Immaculate Conception walk past the brownstone where he and his family lived, on their way to and from St. Mary's Convent. He still remembered the stiffly starched, black and white habits and the heavy rosaries around their waists.

To his child's eyes, the figures rustling past had seemed menacing, wraith-like forms with hands and feet but no bodies.

The appearance of Sister Bridget Kearney failed to accord with such memories. Until today, he had only seen the digital photos Sosa took of her at the hospital. When he met her he was struck by the secular appearance of the rail-thin woman Sosa introduced him to at the Sacred Heart Rescue Mission. Her short, gray hair was neatly trimmed and combed. She wore a plain, cotton blouse that was open at the neck. The white flesh of stork-like legs protruded from the bottom of a checkered, mid-length skirt. Only the small crucifix around her neck gave any indication of her connection with a religious order.

The nun sat on a couch between them with an envelope in her lap. Her blue-veined hands worked restlessly as she spoke. "Maria ... there's something I thought you should see. This came today."

Roth noticed the bold type in the upper left corner of the envelope.

CITY OF MIAMI
DEPARTMENT OF PUBLIC HEALTH

"Our order sends each of us for an annual physical. The doctor who examined me last week pointed out that I hadn't been back for any ..." She hesitated, lowering her eyes, " ... any follow-up test since I was discharged from the hospital. He had me go to the public health department for some lab work."

Shock registered on Sosa's face as she read the report. "Oh ... no," she said in a barely audible voice, handing it to her partner.

REPORT STATUS: FINAL HUMAN IMMUNODEFICIENCY VIRUS: AB SCREEN RESULT: REACTIVE HIVI (LTLV-111) ANTIBODIES HAVE BEEN DETECTED IN THIS PATIENT SPECIMEN

Sister Bridget Kearney of the Order of St. Dominic was infected with the AIDS virus. Sosa seemed to be searching for the right words but not finding them. Tears welled in her eyes. It was strange, but Roth never thought of her as someone who ever cried.

The nun took her hand in both of hers. "It's alright. I'm not afraid. I was worried about the other women."

They now knew that the Wake-Up Rapist's ejaculate was as dangerous as a gun or knife. The anal intercourse that had become his signature carried a substantially greater risk of bleeding and infection than vaginal rape. Past and future victims could easily share the nun's fate.

Sister Kearney forced a smile. "Well, if it's true that the Lord doesn't call us until our work here is finished, I should be around for quite a while."

Neither detective had been prepared for anything like this. They both wondered how many more women he might infect or murder.

There was no way of knowing how long he had been harboring the disease. Roth thought of the basketball star, Magic Johnson, who had been HIV positive for years without displaying a single symptom. Jumping between the balconies at Nina Pulaski's condominium and garroting a strong, young woman like Peaches Brooks weren't the acts of a sick man.

He wondered if Death had manifested itself yet to the multiple personality in the form of any of the telltale symptoms of AIDS, like the purple skin lesions of Kaposi's sarcoma. Whoever he was, his financial resources would enable him to afford cutting edge medical treatment that might stave off debility and death indefinitely.

*   *

They paid a visit to the other victims the following day. The women reacted very differently to the news that their attacker had AIDS: Georgia Griffin wept but said nothing; Lieutenant Diane Whitaker was the calmest of all. It was as if she were dealing with an in-flight emergency. She peppered them with questions: How long would it take her to develop antibodies if she was infected? What were the risks of developing AIDS from a single act of unprotected, anal intercourse? Was there any preventive medication she could start on now?

The reaction of Laura Kelce was by far the most extreme. Despite the assurance of both Sosa and Roth that the chances of her contracting the disease were negligible because the rapist had used a condom, she began to hyperventilate as soon as she heard the word AIDS. A live-in nurse held a paper bag over her mouth and nose. The former concert pianist clutched at it frantically with the prosthetic claws that were now her hands. She had been convinced ever since the attack that her assailant would return to kill her and was never out of sight of one of the off-duty police officers she had hired as bodyguards.

CHAPTER

51

Alvin Walker told Sosa that while there were no SM or leather bars in Delmar, there was a skinhead nightspot called '*Steel*' that was popular with bikers. She and Roth decided to check it out.

They got to the bar on a Wednesday night a little after nine. A flashing neon sign in front of the place cast multicolored reflections on an assortment of motorcycles in the parking lot. Choppers. Hogs. Rice burners. They noticed a couple of Harleys on their way inside. The acrid smell of cigarette smoke greeted them when they stepped through the double doors. Johnny Cash was belting out 'Folsom Prison Blues' on an old Wurlitzer juke box well above the hundred-thirty decibel level at which hearing loss begins to occur.

A number of white men in their twenties and thirties sat around a horseshoe-shaped oak bar. All wore standard biker attire: high leather boots, cut-off T-shirts, vests and grungy blue jeans. Most had their heads shaved, though a couple sported ponytails. Some had motorcycle chains wrapped around their waists in lieu of belts. Gaudy tattoos seemed to be 'in.' A few were hunched over video games and pinball machines, while others shot pool on beer-stained tables.

Roth's breath caught in his throat when he saw the wall behind the pool tables. A large red banner with a black swastika hung in the center of it. On either side of the flag was a montage of photographs from the war years. He had seen most of the pictures before: a jubilant Hitler dancing a jig after learning of the surrender of France; elite troops of the German *Schutzstaffel* goose-stepping under the *Arc de Triomphe* in Paris; a Messerschmitt shooting down a Spitfire over the English Channel; Panzers crashing through the Ardennes Forest.

One picture showed Jewish men, women and children with raised hands being herded out of the Warsaw ghetto. In another, a Nazi officer in a trench coat pointed his pistol at the head of a man kneeling at the edge of a mass grave.

Hostile eyes tracked their passage through the bar. A barrel-chested figure with a walrus mustache and an Iron Cross dangling from his neck looked up from his pinball game and said something to a man who was wearing a Wehrmacht-style German helmet. *What have we stumbled onto, the Delmar Chapter of the Neo-Nazi Party?* All the place lacked was the strains of *Deutschland Uber Alles* booming from the Wurlitzer.

Roth doubted that the men inside *Steel* knew much about the ideology of hatred behind the symbols that were everywhere. It was enough that the sight of them would outrage most people. They were like the 'in your face' costumes the biker crowd wore. Identifying with the Nazis made them different. A man with a Reich Eagle tattoo on his bicep glanced at them and spat on the floor. The message was clear; outsiders weren't welcome at *Steel*.

Roth cupped a hand to his partner's ear. "Think they know we're cops?" he said over the noise of the jukebox.

"Are you kidding? That's probably the only reason they haven't tried to gang-bang me on one of the pool tables."

He followed her to the counter where a bartender about fifty was drying and stacking beer mugs. The man took his time walking over after she motioned to him. He had a full beard and a flaccid face with oversized comical-looking ears.

She laid her badge case on the counter. "Do you work here regularly?"

"Every night but Sunday. I own the place."

Roth showed him the Compusketch of the Wake-Up Rapist. "Ever see this guy before?"

The bartender peered at him through watery eyes. "Nope."

"How about looking at it before you decide," Roth said irritably.

The man picked up the sketch and grunted. "Answer's still the same."

Sosa shoved her business card across the bar. "How about giving us a call if anyone who looks like this shows up?"

"Sure," he replied, with a fatuous grin. He turned his back on them and resumed wiping glasses.

Roth's eyes roamed around the twenty or more faces in the bar. The only blonde in sight was short and potbellied. A slurred voice called out from the back of the room, "Hey, baby … come over here and sit on my face!" The remark was followed by sucking sounds and laughter.

Sosa shot a defiant glance over her shoulder on their way to the door. "Assholes … !" she said, under her breath. "Half the people in here probably have active warrants for something. I'm sure my card is already in the trash."

They spent the next several nights sitting in a darkened corner of the parking lot, watching the rogue clientele rev their bikes as they entered and left. Roth's shoulders sagged around two on the last night of the surveillance. "We're just wasting our time here," he sighed.

CHAPTER

52

"I hope I didn't wake you," Roth said when he heard Sosa's voice on the other end of the line, suddenly aware that it was after eleven.

"That's okay. I was just unwinding with a glass of wine," she replied. "What's up?"

He propped his bare feet on the desk in his study. "I think I know how to find out what the connection between our victims is."

"How?"

"A questionnaire."

She laughed. "I guess I should have known it would come to this sooner or later with a professor as a partner. "Okay, let's hear it," she said skeptically.

"Maria, the only thing we've got to work with right now is the fact that all of our women are professionals who live in Miami."

"And who are total strangers," she added.

"Which means that they have to be connected in some way they're not aware of."

"Such as?"

He cradled the phone against his shoulder. "I don't know … maybe they all belong to the National Organization of Women. They could be members of a right-to-life or environmental protection group. Jan could have gotten hold of some list of professional women Robert has."

"But they've all seen the Compusketches," she reminded him. "None of them know anyone who looks like that."

"He may own a business they all use. It could be anything—a restaurant, a book store, a travel agency." Nine Lives roamed into the room and bounded onto his lap. "The link is there, I promise you. We just have to find it."

"You think we can do that just by having them fill out a questionnaire?"

"I'm not talking about them filling out anything."

"Then what …"

"People who've been through this kind of emotional trauma aren't good at remembering small details, especially with a couple of cops sitting across from them, pressing for answers. I'd like to give them each a tape recorder to keep for a few days, along with a list of maybe ten or fifteen questions to think about in their spare time."

"Just sort of free associate, huh?"

"That's right. We need to learn everything we can about each of them. Where they grew up and went to school. Every place they've ever lived or worked. Their professional achievements. Stores they shop at. Business services they use. Clubs and civic organizations they belong to. Charities they've been active in." He interpreted the several seconds of silence that followed as at least tentative interest. "Well, what do you think?"

"I don't know. Let me sleep on it."

* *

By morning, Roth had managed to pare the topics he wanted to cover with the victims down to nine key questions. Sosa finally agreed to the unorthodox investigative measure. With the help of McNees and Walker, they got the questionnaire and a cassette recorder to all five of the Wake-Up Rapist's victims by the end of the day. Each questionnaire would be transcribed and analyzed as soon as it was completed; in the meantime, there was little they could do except hope for a break in the case.

CHAPTER

53

Several days later, another envelope addressed in peacock-colored ink and bearing a Palm Beach postmark appeared in Roth's mailbox. He put on a pair of latex gloves and opened it carefully. Instead of a letter, this time there was a three-by-five card and a Polaroid picture of several objects on a redwood picnic table. The card said simply:

P.C.H.

April 7

3 a.m.

His eyes moved to the calendar on his desk; it was already March 29th.

*   *

Not surprisingly, the latest offering had been wiped clean before being sent. The meaning of the terse note was all too clear. Jan Nasargiel planned to attack another Miami professional woman, whose initials were P.C.H., on the seventh, at his usual "wake-up" hour. They sat in Sosa's office, grappling with the latest clue. The photograph showed three items side by side on the table. They recognized the first one right away. It was the alabaster replica of the *Pieta* that Jan took from Sister Kearney. Next to it was a copy of the front page of the *Miami Herald*. It was Wednesday's paper. Roth recalled the headline:

73 PERISH IN COLUMBIAN JET CRASH

The third article was a lacy, black, garter belt. Its straps hung just over the edge of the table.

"I'm lousy at puzzles," Sosa groaned. "I used to go nuts trying to do Rubik's Cube with my brothers. Why did he send us this?"

"We're supposed to figure out who P.C.H. is from the things on the table."

"Fat chance! We may as well try to pick next week's winning Lotto number."

"Don't be so pessimistic," he urged, scooting his chair closer to hers. "Since the statue is first, let's start with it."

She folded her arms on her desk and put her head on them. "We've spent so much time talking about the damn *Pieta* that I feel as if I was there when Michelangelo carved it!"

"Come on, what do we know about the statue, besides the fact it's Italian?"

She shrugged. "Nothing we haven't already talked about."

He stood and walked to the window. "He must have had a very specific reason for making the *Pieta* the first thing on the table."

"Well … the nun was his first victim."

"No, something else."

She bit her lower lip and looked at the picture again. "Sister Kearney told me that her parents gave her the statue the day she took her vows as a nun."

Roth's eyebrows rose inquiringly. "That would have been … what … fifty years ago?"

"More. I think she was eighteen when she entered the convent."

"Maybe that's why the statue is first—because it's so old," he mused.

They turned their attention next to the newspaper shown in the picture. After trying to locate a copy of Wednesday's paper in one of the CID offices, Sosa sent the SBU secretary to the *Herald* to get one.

"While we're waiting for her to get back, let's see if we can figure out what the garter belt means," Roth suggested.

"Jan obviously burglarized P.C.H.'s home and took it as a fetish."

"Women have all kinds of personal things in their dressers and closets. Why take a garter belt instead of, say, panties or a bra?" he asked.

"Something like this is for a special occasion."

"A hot date?"

"No. Too intimate for that. You wear this kind of lingerie for a man you're emotionally involved with. I wonder if it was a gift from her lover."

"Or her husband?"

"All of the victims have been single so far," she reminded him. Besides, most husbands aren't that romantic."

"That's not true! I bought Sara lingerie all the time." The words were past his lips before he could stop them. Her eyes sparkled with merriment.

"Why, Dr. Roth. I never thought of you as a *Victoria's Secret* kind of guy."

They read every article on the front page of Wednesday's *Herald* as soon as the secretary returned with a copy of it—even the weather and stock market summary in the header. They could find nothing that shed light on the strange collection of objects on the table. It was hard to imagine two things more dissimilar than Michelangelo's *Pieta* and a frilly garter belt.

Sosa traced her pencil slowly in a circle around the date beneath the newspaper headline. A light dawned in her eyes. "I think I see it!"

"What?"

"David, the clue doesn't have anything to do with what's in Wednesday's *Herald*. It's the *paper itself!*"

"What do you mean?"

"It's *new*—the statue is *old*." She held up the picture triumphantly and said, "Something old ... something new."

"Something borrowed, something blue!" he added, finishing the wedding rhyme.

"Robert is telling us that P.C.H. is about to get married," she said. "The garter belt is 'something borrowed.' It must have been part of her honeymoon trousseau."

"If that's true, her name and address will be on the marriage license application." They slapped their palms together in a 'high five' salute.

"I thought you said you were no good at puzzles."

"I lied! I'm a friggin' genius!" she laughed.

A moment later, she looked at the picture again. "Something old, something new, something borrowed ... but what the hell is *blue*?"

They had exactly ten days to answer to that question.

CHATPER

54

The lights of a lone car knifed through the darkness in front of Jan's apartment. He drew back the curtain another inch and watched until its tail lights disappeared at the end of the block. Even though the street looked deserted, he was uneasy. The cops had been to Steel asking questions and showing the sketch of him. His hands coiled into fists.

"Why the fuck did I send that letter?" he said aloud. He began pacing the one-bedroom apartment like a caged animal. Kurt Mueller told him he never should have written Roth. If only he'd known Kurt at the time, it wouldn't have happened. He swiped the air in frustration. Fucking idiot! At least he could have postmarked the goddamn thing from somewhere besides Delmar. The bar where the two cops had been nosing around was only four blocks from the apartment.

He started to light a joint and stopped. No! No more dope! Kurt had made that clear. If he smoked and Kurt found out about it—which he would—he'd kick his ass up around his ears. Nothing got by him, man. Nothing! He was, hands down, the smartest mother fucker Jan Nasargiel had ever met. He didn't understand a lot of the things Kurt said or the stuff he gave him to read, but that didn't matter. The guy knew what he was doing. He was totally in control of everything.

They had only known each other a week. He was sitting in a booth in the back of Steel late one night, nursing a Schlitz, when Kurt just popped up out of nowhere and introduced himself. Jan liked him right off. After they'd downed four or five brews, he told him about the women and what he was doing. Mueller laughed approvingly and said, "We'll finish the rest of the bitches together." He had actually said 'we.' It blew Jan's mind!

Mueller spent that night with him at the apartment. The next morning, Jan showed him the portions of Roth's book he had underlined. "You think you know torture?" his new friend said dismissively. "Just wait until we do the next one."

They were a team now! With his balls and Kurt's brains, they'd be unstoppable! The thing that impressed him most about Mueller was how quickly he'd managed to offload the Jesus freak. The little prick left the very night Kurt moved in. He was gone. G-O-N-E. No more listening to him whine and snivel. No more letters to the cops. He'd interfered with every single bitch Jan had done. If he'd been around a little longer, he could have really fucked things up!

He pulled off his Garibaldi boots and dropped them on the floor. Kurt had been worried about the Rolls biting them in the ass. Jan explained that he'd scrubbed the front seat and mats real good to get all the blood out and then covered the car with a tarp before locking it inside a storage garage in Hialeah. He'd even used a case-hardened, steel padlock on the door.

Kurt didn't care. He said that the car was evidence. It had to go. A murder had been committed in it, for Chrissakes! Even though both the niggers were dead, someone might have seen him driving it. A car like that stood out. As much as he hated the thought of giving up the Rolls, he knew Kurt Mueller was right.

The way Kurt got rid of the car was nothing short of genius! He read in The Islander *one night that local environmental groups had been complaining about marine life gradually disappearing from the Palm Beach Inlet because of the dwindling number of natural coral formations. The State Division of Wildlife had agreed that an artificial reef was urgently needed in the narrow finger of water that separated Palm Beach from its poor sister, Riviera Beach.*

Kurt called the Palm Beach Maritime Society the next day and offered to donate the nearly new Rolls-Royce as the town's first artificial reef. There were only two conditions: the identity of the donor had to remain confidential, and there could be no publicity about the 'Rolls Reef' until after the car was actually sunk. The movers and shakers on the island were so excited about the project they nearly came all over themselves.

Kurt said that even if word got out about who owned the car no one would be surprised by such a generous gift coming from Peter von Hausmann III. He was already at the top of every list of contributors to charities all over the world—everything from Save the Fucking Pandas to Children of Darfur and the American Cancer Society. The Original Soft Touch. That was the way Kurt described him. When he wasn't on his knees praying for lost souls, he was writing checks to everyone and anyone as Director of the Lois von Hausmann Foundation.

Ever since his mother's death in November, Peter had been busy trying to give her fortune away to worthy causes. The Rolls had belonged to Lois. So did Casa Serena, a thirty-room, oceanfront mansion on the island. It was already on the market, along with her hundred-foot yacht, Enchantress, and the Gulfstream jet she bought not long before she was diagnosed with breast cancer. Old Sackcloth and Ashes could never have let himself enjoy any of mama's toys.

Jan about split a gut laughing when Kurt told him that the car he had cut up the nigger whore in was going to become a home for nurse sharks and barracudas. That was what Kurt called 'irony.' He said, "Let the cops try to find any blood or fingerprints on that Rolls after it's been in a couple hundred feet of salt water for even five minutes." God, it felt good to have someone around who was not only smart but who appreciated what he was doing.

Kurt was so careful about everything. The police computer sketch of him had been all over the tube and the newspapers. It was a real good likeness. Too good! Kurt had him dye his hair brown and start growing a mustache. He bought him a pair of cheap glasses with clear lenses and insisted he wear them whenever he left the apartment.

He also liquidated a few of Mr. Holier-than-Thou's investment accounts. He had taken 6.5 million in cash—exactly the amount the do-gooder turd gave to charities last year. Hell, with as much money as he had, he'd probably never even miss it; and, if he did, what was he going to do—go to the cops? The 'Mad Money', as Kurt called it, was tucked away in safe deposit boxes at four Miami banks. The cash was their insurance; if anything went wrong, they could get out of Dodge with it in a hurry.

He smashed a palmetto bug that was scurrying across the stove and wiped his hand on the peeling wallpaper in the kitchen. What a shit-hole to wake up in every day! He opened the refrigerator and got a beer. Whenever he got low over being stuck in Delmar, Kurt reminded him that they'd be living like Saudi princes as soon as their work was done. Kurt had plans. Big plans. Jan couldn't believe his ears when he told him what he was planning to do in Miami. It was totally awesome!

He closed his eyes and rolled the cold can across his forehead. He felt lousy … achy … he'd had some kind of flu for nearly a week now. Chills. The runs. Night sweats. No big deal, but he hadn't been able to shake it. He looked at his watch. Kurt wouldn't be back for another couple of hours. There was still plenty of time to take the bike out on the Saw-grass Expressway and open it up. Feeling the Harley under him at full throttle was damn near as exciting as shoving his cock in the ass of some cute guy he'd just picked up at a bar.

After draining the can, he crushed it and tossed it in the sink. He eyed the keys to the bike for a long moment. No! Kurt had said not to leave, so that was out. If Kurt Mueller had ordered him to stay right where he was until hell froze over, well that's just what he'd do.

Steel was too hot to go back to. That saddened him. He'd really miss the place. The guys there had become like brothers to him. No matter. There was a gay bar in South Beach that he'd been spending time at ever since he got to Florida. It was an SM bottle club that was open all night. He'd take Kurt there to celebrate right after they did Number Six, as he called her.

He sat at the cracked Formica counter, studying the pictures he'd taken of the next woman. The truth was that he was getting pretty damn good with the 35mm camera, especially the telephoto lens. He would have given anything to see the look on Roth and Sosa's faces after the cops got the pictures of them he sent. He'd shot the photos of Number Six from down the street when she stepped out of a new Lexus in her driveway. Nice wheels for a cunt. Especially, a spic. He raised an *imaginary camera to his face: click ... click ... click. He'd nailed her with the Canon three times before her ass was off the seat. He looked at the high cheekbones, the olive skin and the corona of black hair that framed her face. Kurt was right. You could spot a non-Aryan right away if you knew what to look for. He went to the fridge and got another beer. Mongrels. That's what Kurt called women like Number Six.*

One night, the owner of Steel *gave him a magazine called* The New Order. *An article in it described how thousands of pregnant wetbacks slipped across the border each year to have babies that white Americans wound up paying for. He took a long swallow of beer and belched. Well, Paloma Hidalgo wouldn't be adding to the welfare rolls. That was for sure. This bitch had dropped her last egg.*

He scratched a match and touched it to the corner of the photo, grinning as it began to blacken and curl. He couldn't wait to watch Kurt Mueller work.

modus operandi - way doing something
forensic signature - documents burt mark
Corpus delicti - concrete evidence
   such as corps

— John wayne Gacy
— David Berkowitz
- Theodore Bundy
- Randy Kraft.

CHAPTER

55

"Oh, my! Another happy couple!" the clerk at the marriage license bureau gushed. Before either Sosa or Roth could reply, she shoved an application form across the counter. "Now, if you'll both just fill out ..."

"Look," Sosa said abruptly, "we're not a couple, and we're not especially happy at the moment."

Roth showed her his ID.

"Is anything wrong, officers?"

He managed a polite smile. "We'd like to see your marriage license applications for the last few months."

"Of course, but it's going to take you a while," she piped. "Miami seems to be the marriage and honeymoon capital of the country right now." She led them to a room that held ledger books containing the names of all recent applicants for marriage licenses. A male clerk soon lugged in a banker's box filled with the forms that went with them. Roth opened one of the ledgers and scanned the maiden names on the first few sheets.

Henry ... Haggerty ... Huerta ... Hartley. Plenty of 'H's, but no P.C.H.

"I had no idea so many people get married down here every week," he said, turning one of the pages.

"Half of them will be divorced in the next few years," Sosa said cynically.

Was she really that down on marriage? "Lots of people stay married," he observed.

She glanced up from the ledger in front of her. "Yeah? Well, I sure don't see many of them in this job. Most of the cops I know are already on their second or third marriage. I know a few who've been down the aisle six or seven times. Staying solo is a lot safer, believe me."

He thought about telling her how much he and Sara were still in love after almost fourteen years together, but he didn't.

Something old, something new, something borrowed, something blue.

The wedding rhyme kept running through his mind. Why was there nothing blue in the photo he sent them?

They were both in a dark mood by the time they left City Hall. The day after receiving the latest clue, they put out an appeal on every radio and television station in Miami, as well as in the *Herald,* asking any woman with the initials P.C.H. to immediately contact a hotline number that had been established. Two women responded to the media blitz, but neither fit the professional victim profile: one worked in the mail-sorting section of the post office, and the other was a groom at the race track in Hialeah.

*   *

A friend of Roth's who was a criminal profiler at ViCAP provided him with the name of Cyril Wilkins. The FBI had used the eighty-six-year-old cryptologist a number of times to help decipher encoded messages sent by violent criminals. Wilkins was a retired chief inspector with the Royal Canadian Mounted Police in Winnipeg. As a young RCAF officer in London during the war, he was part of the team at Bletchley Park that finally cracked the German Enigma Code.

Roth overnighted all of their case files, along with a copy of the photograph and note they had just received, to Wilkins. After examining everything, the cryptologist was convinced that figuring out the significance of the missing part of the wedding rhyme was the key to locating the Stalker Sadist's next victim.

Despite his age, the Canadian proved indefatigable, calling often to ask questions and clarify various things he found in the records. On the afternoon of April 6th, he phoned with the disheartening news that the last part of the rhyme continued to elude him. "If I only had a little more time," he told them.

That was something they had just run out of.

CHAPTER

56

After tossing several items he had no intention of buying in his shopping cart, he followed the woman through the supermarket to the wine aisle. Paul Masson Chardonnay. He smiled to himself, knowing exactly what she would select before she reached for the bottle. Few details of her life had escaped his attention during the past weeks; he knew everything about her, from the kind of face cream she used to the names of her parents and the date the payment on her Lexus was due. It was amazing how much you could learn about a person from their trash. He had taken hers late one night from a plastic bin in front of her house, and then sorted through it at the Delmar apartment.

The other women left their places for substantial periods of time each day. This one worked at home and was seldom gone for more than an hour at a time, which made getting a look at the interior of the house a challenge. When he finally got inside, one of the first interesting things he came across was a stack of love letters from her fiancé. They were bound with a yellow ribbon and tucked in the back of her dresser. He read all of them. In one, the overseas pilot she had been living with out of wedlock told her how bad he felt about talking her into an abortion the year before. Men were inherently weak when it came to sex. The pregnancy had been her responsibility! Knowing that an unbaptized little soul was condemned to roam limbo for eternity because of her lust angered him.

She and her lover apparently shared a fascination with pornography. The hall closet was filled with sex videos of all kinds. Such filth! He supposed that she modeled risqué outfits for the pilot like the garter belt he had taken from the bedroom. Her fiancé's frequent trips meant that she was alone most of the time. Well ... she wouldn't be tonight. "Excuse me," he said politely when his cart brushed hers in the cereal aisle. Blessed is the bride that the sun shines on. Blessed is the corpse that the rain falls on. Better to marry than to burn, Paloma.

CHAPTER

57

The Miami Police Department had just doubled the reward being offered under its Cash for Tips program to $50,000 for information leading to the arrest of the Wake-Up Rapist. By the night of the anticipated attack, everything humanly possible had been done.

Sosa and Roth left the police garage with an armada of vehicles drawn from various law enforcement agencies. All leaves and vacations at MPD had been cancelled. The usual number of patrol units in the city was being tripled between midnight and seven. In addition to all the members of Sosa's unit, Captain Wilcox had every available CID detective on the streets: men and women from Homicide, Robbery, Burglary, and Auto Theft—even the Juvenile Unit. There were close to eighty investigators in all. The department's two Bell Jet Rangers were being supplemented with helicopters from other agencies that would be circling the city from midnight on.

Even with the formidable array of law enforcement resources being focused on Miami, the result was nothing more than a blind giant stumbling about in the darkness, waiting for a blow to land and having no idea where it would be struck.

Sosa and Roth were dressed casually in jeans, sports shirts and tennis shoes. That night the *Exxon Valdez* carried a twelve gauge shotgun with a round of double-ought buckshot already chambered. They cruised slowly through the downtown area, monitoring the scrambled interagency channel that was being used by the Task Force.

They pulled into the first of five sprawling residential developments they had been assigned to cover. Roth trained the beam from a portable spotlight on parked cars and the yards of houses, watching for any kind of suspicious movement. The minutes passed. *12:30 ... 1:15 ... 1:25.*

Sosa's hands tightened on the wheel. "There isn't a cop out here who doesn't realize this is nothing but a death watch," she said. "The worst part is thinking about what he's going to do to her before he kills her."

Grisly images from the Appendix of *Patterns of Sexual Violence* forced themselves into Roth's mind: mutilation, asphyxia, acid, electrocution. He wondered what Jan had in store for P.C.H.

New numbers kept appearing on the car's clock.

2:27 ... 2:51.

"0300 hours ... KMA 247," the dispatcher finally said, giving the time and the department's FCC identifier.

The radio became as quiet as a tomb. *He would be inside now. Standing beside her bed.* Roth shut his eyes, trying to stop the tape that was running in his head.

3:22. Still nothing. *3:37.*

He allowed himself a fleeting moment of hope. *Maybe ...* Seconds later, his nerves were jolted by the sound of a high-pitched emergency tone.

"2391 and 2316," the dispatcher said, summoning two patrol units. "Take a burglary in progress at 1545 North Azure Lane. Reporting party advises suspect is running south toward Hampton Drive at this time."

Azure Lane ... Azure!

"Maria!" Roth shouted. "That's him. *Azure Lane is what's blue!*"

She slammed on the brakes, made a U-turn and jumped the concrete median. The Ford accelerated sharply as he snatched his radio off the seat.

"714 to all Task Force Units! That's our suspect at the B & E on Azure Lane!"

"Air One copy," the pilot of one of the Jet Rangers said over the sound of his rotor blades.

Roth turned on the red and blue strobe light and put the siren on YELP. Another alert tone was followed by the dispatcher's voice.

"All units ... Azure Lane burglary suspect is a WM, six feet ... wearing a windbreaker and a ski mask. We're getting reports now that he's running east through yards on Wiley. All units use extreme caution. Reporting party advises suspect is Signal Zero with a pistol."

Roth braced himself against the dash with both hands when the car slid into a turn. "How far away are we?" he yelled over the siren.

"Only eight or nine blocks!" Sosa said, alternately riding the gas and brake as she cut in and out of traffic. His body strained against the seatbelt when she swerved over a double yellow line to pass a string of cars. Out of the corner of his eye, he watched the speedometer creeping steadily higher. Units from all over the city were now converging on Azure Lane. The radio became a jumble of voices.

Sosa cursed when a delivery truck pulled into their path, cutting around it with a sickening squeal of tires.

"He's probably headed toward Lake Powell!" she said. "We might be able to cut him off if we go through the park!"

Several blocks later, she made a right turn onto Felton and hit her high beams. A dark figure was running down the middle of the street a half block ahead of them.

"714 Miami!" Roth cried. "We have the suspect running south on Felton toward Lake Powell!"

The *Exxon Valdez* began swallowing the pavement that separated them from their quarry. Roth was fumbling with his seatbelt release when the shape in front of them suddenly stopped running and spun toward them with a shiny object in his hand.

"*Gun!*" Sosa yelled, jamming the brakes. The word slammed into his consciousness. He caught a glimpse of blue eyes behind a ski mask just before Sosa jerked him onto the seat and threw herself on top of him. A bullet struck the windshield with a loud pop, transforming it into a tangle of silver spider webs. The car yawed violently to the right and went into a slide. His fingers dug into the seat at the sound of more shots and the whine of a slug ricocheting off metal. Shards of glass and pieces of reflector from the strobe light rained down on them. The Ford bounced over a curb, plowing into a mailbox and coming to a stop with its siren still piercing the night.

Sosa kicked her door open and jumped out with her Glock. "You son of a bitch!" she screamed, firing eight times rapidly into the darkness. She lunged back inside the car and grabbed Roth's shoulder.

"Are you hit?" she said urgently.

He opened his mouth and gulped air. He tried to speak but nothing came out.

"David, are you alright?"

He managed to nod.

She located her radio on the floor amid pieces of windshield glass. "418! Shots fired! Shots fired on Felton!" she gasped. It took her a moment to catch her breath and continue. "Suspect is in the woods by the lake!"

The alert tone sounded again. "All units ... shots fired! Officers need assistance on Felton Drive, south of Lawrence by Lake Powell. 418, do you need EMS?" the dispatcher said shrilly.

"Negative ... negative on injuries," Sosa replied. She crouched in the break of her open door, squinting into the dark stand of slash pines and palmettos bordering the lake. "Responding units, we need a perimeter east and west of the lake," she said, ejecting the partially-spent magazine from her weapon and quickly reloading. Roth could hear the sound of a police chopper approaching and started to raise his head.

"Stay down!" she ordered. He flattened himself on the seat again, the sweat streaming down his face. A wave of nausea coursed through him when he looked up and saw the bullet hole on the right side of the windshield. It was exactly where his head had been before she yanked him onto the seat. He raised himself with shaking hands just high enough to see over the dash. Lights were coming on in houses up and down the block. A number of residents watched cautiously from windows and doorsteps.

"418 ... Miami, I need K-9 out here ASAP!" Sosa said tensely. One of the MPD dog handlers replied that she was close by. Red and blue lights now appeared at the other end of the block. A helicopter swooped low overhead, turning night into day with a three million candle power search-light. Its thermal imagining system swept the woods, searching for signs of life. Within minutes of the shooting, eleven patrol units and four un-marked cars were parked on what had been a quiet residential street. An auburn-haired officer in her mid-twenties soon arrived in an SUV that had

POLICE DOG–KEEP BACK! lettered on it. She opened the canine 'bail out' window hurriedly and put her German Shepherd on a short lead.

"Come on, Thor! Find him, boy! Find him!" The dog brought its snout close to the ground and began sniffing. Its ears perked up immediately, and it began to strain against the leash. Its handler moved cautiously into the woods behind the dog with her gun in hand. A dozen officers fanned out on either side of her, with five-cell flashlights and weapons at the ready.

Roth sat with his legs hanging outside the car and his head down, still trembling. Sosa bent over him and put her hand on the back of his neck. "Just take some deep breaths. You'll be okay."

A young patrolman jogged toward them. "Hey, Sarge, it looks like you hit him!" he said excitedly. "The dog's got a blood track going into the woods."

An ugly black skid trail extended from the center of the street to the curb the *Exxon Valdez* had jumped before coming to rest with its front wheels on a well-manicured lawn. It was no longer just an over-the-hill CID clunker, but part of a crime scene.

A couple of evidence vans soon arrived. One of the technicians began 'painting' the unmarked SBU vehicle and the area around it with a video camera. Another drew a yellow chalk line around the half-empty ammo magazine beside Sosa's open door and photographed it. Two other ET's searched the ground with flashlights, looking for ejected shell casings from both the police weapon and that of the suspect; each time they found one, they placed a numbered orange cone next to it and snapped a picture.

Roth's legs still felt rubbery. He walked over to where Sosa was talking to Jim McNees on her cell phone. "McNees and Walker are at the victim's house on Azure Lane," she told him.

"What about the woman?" he said apprehensively. "Is she ..."

"She's okay. Some minor injuries, but she's mostly just shook up. EMS is going to transport her to Mercy."

As soon as the uniformed patrol zone commander arrived, she went to him and handed him her gun. They spoke for a minute before he opened the trunk of his car and sealed it in an evidence bag. She returned to where Roth was now standing, watching the evidence crew work.

"David, listen to me. Wilcox will be here in a few minutes. He's going to place me on administrative leave."

"What?" he said incredulously. "Why?"

"I just shot someone."

"But he tried to kill us!"

"That doesn't matter. The Shooting Review Board will have to do a full investigation. It'll probably be pretty much routine, but ..."

"Making you go on leave at a time like this is outrageous!" he fumed. "A child could see that this shooting was justifiable!"

She made a calming gesture. "That's just the way the system works. By the way, the board will want to talk to you."

"Why?"

She hesitated for a moment before replying. "When an officer fires and his or her partner doesn't, they want to know why," she said bluntly.

He felt his face flush. "Maria, I ..."

"Just tell them you didn't have a clear shot, and that'll be the end of it."

A clear shot? I never even drew my gun. I was hugging the seat with my eyes closed.

"I'll probably be off-duty for at least a week. I want you to keep working the case while I'm gone."

He could see the glint of flashlights deep in the woods. "But you wounded him. He may be bleeding to death out there right now."

"I hope he is ... but, until I see him in handcuffs or on a slab at the morgue, we've got to operate on the assumption that he's still at large and dangerous."

"What do you want me to do?"

"Hitch a ride to the motor pool with one of the uniform guys and pick up another car. Then go to Mercy ER and interview the victim."

"I've never done an interview by myself. Wouldn't it be better to send McNees and Walker?"

"I would have asked them if I thought it was," she said sharply. "I want you to do it."

He nodded without speaking.

"Tomorrow, you can follow up with the evidence techs. See if they found anything on Azure Lane that might help us."

A black Crown Victoria with a flashing emergency light pulled to the curb moments later. It was Captain Wilcox.

"Where are you going now?" Roth asked.

"Back to the SBU to start writing this up. I've got several hours of paperwork ahead of me."

He gathered everything he would need for the interview from the trunk of the *Exxon Valdez* before it was towed to the police garage: a clipboard, report forms and a cassette recorder, along with Sosa's camera.

CHAPTER

58

On his way to the motor pool, he peeled off the Kevlar vest, feeling as if he'd just shed twenty pounds. The Chrysler they issued him had a loose muffler and nearly as many miles on it as the *Exxon Valdez*. After arriving at Mercy Hospital, he slung the camera case over his shoulder and headed for his first one-on-one interview with a victim.

He found Paloma Consuelo Hidalgo seated on the edge of an examining table in a white hospital smock with tiny blue flowers on it. She was a slim-hipped woman in her mid-thirties, with small breasts and slender legs. Her bare feet dangled several inches above the floor. A man stood beside her, gently stroking her long black hair.

"Miss Hidalgo, I'm Detective Roth." *Gutless Detective Roth*, he thought bitterly. He ran a hand across the stubble on his face, realizing that he didn't look much like a cop the way he was dressed. The salmon-colored pullover shirt he had on was badly soiled. Only the Miami police shield clipped to his belt said that he was what he had just claimed to be. The man beside Paloma Hidalgo extended his hand.

"I'm Brad Garrity, Paloma's fiancé."

He had a grip like a vise. Garrity was a tan, fit-looking figure in his early forties with close-cut, salt-and-pepper hair and blue eyes with crow's feet. Roth thought he detected a hint of a Texas accent in his voice. An American Airlines jacket with two stripes on the sleeves, denoting the position of first officer, was draped over the back of a chair.

"Did you get him?" Garrity asked expectantly.

"Not yet, but we will. My partner wounded him."

"Yes! Yes!" Garrity exulted, punching the air with his fist as if his team had just scored a touchdown.

"Did you hear that, baby?"

Paloma Hidalgo stared vacantly at her lap without responding. Her upper lip was split, and her right cheek was beginning to swell. Roth said gently, "Do you feel up to talking with me for a few minutes?"

"I ... I guess so," she said quietly.

He marked a cassette and slipped it into the recorder before drawing up one of several plastic chairs in the room. It occurred to him that he must smell awful: *stale sweat and fear.* He had read somewhere that a person's body releases a special pheromone when they're scared shitless. Why had Maria sent him out to conduct an interview this important? After what just happened, he was surprised that she was still speaking to him.

He learned a great deal over the next half-hour about what happened on Azure Lane. The media blitz hadn't reached the sixth professional woman on Jan Nasargiel's hit list because she was in Tampa, getting ready for the wedding that was to take place at her parents' home there on Saturday. That was why there was no record of her at the marriage license bureau in Miami.

Paloma Hidalgo explained that she had moved to the city a year and a half before because it was convenient for Garrity, who flew primarily overseas flights out of Miami. She told Roth that she was a sculptor and worked out of a studio in her home. All of her family and friends were in Tampa. Like many artists, she kept mostly to herself when her fiancé was traveling. She didn't take the *Herald* and rarely watched television or listened to the radio.

Roth was relieved to learn that she hadn't been raped. The only reason she was still alive was because her soon-to-be husband's scheduled flight from La Guardia to Madrid was cancelled at the last minute; Brad Garrity had deadheaded back on a red-eye from New York, intending to surprise her. The Wake-Up Rapist had apparently entered the townhouse not long before he arrived.

The thirty-four-year-old woman said that the masked intruder threatened to kill her if she screamed. She described how he took a black garter belt she thought was in her dresser drawer from his gym bag and threw it at her. Her lower lip quivered as she went on. "He made the room dark. Then he told me to take off my pajamas and put on the garter belt."

"Do you remember his exact words?"

"Yes." She sniffed and dabbed at her nose with a Kleenex. "'Put it on, whore!' I asked him to please not hurt me. That's when he hit me in the face with his fist." Her body began to heave with sobs. Garrity put his arms around her, and she buried her face against his shoulder.

"Just take your time," Roth told her.

She swallowed hard. "He wanted me to put on black stockings with the belt. When I told him I didn't have any, he hit me in the mouth with his gun and called me a lying cunt. He went to the dresser drawer where I keep my lingerie and took out a pair of black hose. I put them on, but my hands were shaking so badly that I had trouble fastening the snaps. That made him madder."

Roth moved the recorder a little closer to her. "Then what happened?" he probed.

"He put a piece of tape over my mouth and made me lie face down on the bed. After he finished tying my wrists and ankles to the bedposts, another man came in the room."

Roth looked up from his notes. "Another man?"

"I couldn't see him because my face was against the pillow, but I could hear the two of them talking."

Robert must have gotten out again and tried to stop Jan, just as he had during the other assaults.

"What did this second man do?"

"He said, 'No, not the knife! Use the *lighter* first. Let's see how the bitch likes her meat cooked.'" The blood drained from her face. "The second man began laughing. He told the first man to turn the flame up higher. I could feel the heat when he brought it close to my shoulder." She put her face in her hands and began to cry.

"Shhh. You're safe now, Paloma," Brad Garrity said soothingly. "Everything's going to be alright."

"Couldn't this second person have been the man with the mask just trying to disguise his voice?" Roth asked.

"No!" she said emphatically, shaking her head. "His voice was completely different ... much deeper. The first man called him Kurt."

My God! It's another alter!

Before leaving the ER, Roth spoke with the resident on duty. She had a nurse come in and slip the smock over the victim's right shoulder. The R.N. carefully lifted the dry dressing that had been put on, exposing two, badly blistered, third-degree burns that had been treated with silver sulfadiazine. Roth photographed the weeping areas of charred flesh and also took several pictures of the victim's split lip and swollen cheek. He wondered if Paloma Hidalgo realized how lucky she was to be alive.

CHAPTER

59

Roth winced at the bright morning sun like Bela Lugosi in an outtake from *Dracula*. As exhausted as he was when he left the hospital, he was too wired to sleep. He had heard over the air on his way to the ER that the intruder left his gym bag behind when he fled Azure Lane. There was a chance that it might contain information about the latest alter. In a few hours, the bag would be on its way to the Florida Department of Law Enforcement lab for analysis. He wanted to get a look at what was inside it before then.

After stopping at Denny's and wolfing down a Grand Slam Special, a large orange juice and enough high test to keep himself going a little longer, he headed for the evidence room on the first floor of the police building. He signed himself in on the chain-of-custody log, noting the exact time the technician on duty retrieved the bag from a locker and turned it over to him.

He took it to a small room and put on a pair of latex gloves before unzipping it. The ET who had transported the bag from the crime scene had already made a detailed inventory of its contents:

1 small scissors
1 Ronson-brand lighter
1 five-ounce can butane lighter fluid
1 Vancenase inhaler

Vancenase. The asthma. He had forgotten about that.

1 box 9mm ammunition (23 rounds)

243

Nine millimeter? All of the women except Paloma Hidalgo had described their assailant's weapon as small and dark. The police had been assuming it was probably a .22 or .25 caliber blue steel semiautomatic. The sculptor insisted that the gun she saw was large and shiny. Until he opened the gym bag, Roth had attributed her claim to emotional stress. He dumped several bullets from the box into his hand. They were for a pistol almost as powerful as the one in his shoulder holster. Why had the Wake-Up Rapist suddenly switched guns?

His eyes returned to the inventory list:

1 tube K-Y lubricant
3 pairs latex gloves
1 roll 3M duct tape
1 wire cutter
1 Bearcat-brand programmable scanner

He clicked on the handheld scanner and immediately heard the crackle of radio traffic from the north side patrol frequency that included Azure Lane.

1 'Slim Jim' lock pick set
2 screw drivers
1 pry bar
1 'Tru-Thro'-brand seven-inch knife

He touched the serrated edge of the blade with a gloved finger, realizing he was holding the knife that was used to butcher Amber Semple.

1 spool copper wire

The garrote that Peaches Brooks was strangled with probably came from it.

4 ampoules of ammonia

To keep Paloma Hidalgo conscious while Jan and his new playmate burned her alive, inch by inch.

He came to the final entries on the inventory sheet:

1 magazine
2 books

Reading material as the alters sat in their car, waiting for 3 a.m.? He opened the magazine first.

The New Order
Winter Edition

It appeared that few minorities had escaped the wrath of contributors to the glossy, twenty-five page publication: Jews, Blacks, Asian Americans, and Latinos. From the looks of it, there was plenty of hatred to go around. Beneath the magazine was a paperback copy of William L. Shirer's *The Rise and Fall of the Third Reich*. He thumbed through it briefly, and then rummaged in the bag until he located the second book, a hardback that was bound in brown leather. Four words were embossed in gold letters on the front:

Mein Kampf
Adolf Hitler

Shock flew through him when he opened the book. It was in *German*. He stared at the three publications, reflecting on their significance, and the multiple personality's apparent ability to understand German. Then it hit him. "Heidelberg," he whispered. The Wake-Up Rapist hadn't found out about the *palimpsest* through a source at either the Vatican or the Archives. The elaborate safeguards established by the Church to assure that the heretical document never became public hadn't broken down in Rome. Someone at the German monastery where the papyrus scrolls were deciphered must have told the man they were after about the Gospel of Matthias and copied the seven lines of Chapter 9: Verse 31 for him. *But who? And why?* He bit his lip reflectively. What possible motive would anyone at St. Stephens have had for sharing such a secret with an outsider? Certainly it wasn't done for money. Every man at the Trappist monastery had chosen poverty as his lot in life.

What would a wealthy American from Palm Beach have been doing at a remote German monastery at the same time a team of Vatican archivists was there translating a two-thousand-year-old set of papyrus scrolls? Even if, by a remarkable coincidence, the rapist had visited St. Stephen's for some reason while Monsignor Garofalo and his colleagues were in Heidelberg, how could he have known what they were working on, especially in light of the secrecy that surrounded it? And how would being able to speak German have helped him learn anything about the *palimpsest* in a place that had been ruled by silence for centuries?

He began leafing through the copy of *Mein Kampf*, reading its passages as easily as he could Hebrew. Many sentences had been underlined. The handwriting in the margins appeared very different from that on the letters sent by the host personality and the alter ego Jan Nasargiel. The longhand notes were entirely in German. They expressed approval of the author's views on such subjects as 'preserving the purity of Aryan blood' and dealing with 'the Jewish problem.'

Steel!

In his mind's eye he saw the Nazi banner on the wall of the skinhead bar they had staked-out uneventfully for three nights. It had to be one of the Stalker Sadist's haunts!

His thoughts were interrupted by the ringing of his cell phone. It was Sosa. She couldn't sleep and wanted to know how the interview with Paloma Hidalgo had gone. He filled her in on everything that had happened that morning.

"Good work! Now get some rest," she said. "That's an order!"

After he hung up, he took off his glasses and rubbed his eyes, realizing he was close to crashing. He was about to put the copy of *Mein Kampf* back in the gym bag when a business card fell out of it:

The Reich Warehouse
613 W. Dearbourne St.
Chicago, Illinois 60602

He jotted an 800 number and e-mail address before turning the card over and reading the back of it:

World's Largest Collection of German War Memorabilia: Medals. Uniforms. Weapons. Equipment of The Third Reich. No replicas. Certificate of Authenticity with every purchase

CHAPTER

60

It was nearly 10 a.m. by the time he got home. He turned off the ringer on his bedroom phone and immediately fell into a deep, dreamless sleep that lasted until mid-afternoon. After a long, hot shower, he picked up the *Herald* from the lawn and saw the headline:

MIAMI COPS IN SHOOTOUT WITH WAKE-UP RAPIST

"Make that 'cop' in the singular," he murmured. He began reading the article:

Late last night, Miami Sexual Battery Unit Sergeant Maria Sosa and her partner, Detective David Roth, cornered a man suspected of at least six assaults on professional women in the metro area, as well as two murders in Riviera Beach. A police spokesman reported that Sergeant Sosa fired her service weapon eight times at the fleeing suspect after he shot at them on Felton Drive. The suspect, though apparently wounded, was able to escape into the woods. A police K-9 unit followed a trail of blood but lost it at the water's edge. Officers speculate that the injured suspect may have drowned trying to cross the deep lake. A police dive team arrived at mid-morning to begin a thorough search of the water, though a citywide manhunt continues.

He arrived at the office late that day. Every face he saw had the same accusatory look. The sidelong glances of the workers in CID concealed a single unasked question: *Why didn't you fire?*

'Because I was too goddamned scared!' He knew that his inaction had nothing to do with his lifelong pacifism—nor could it be explained by any

lofty reverence for human life. The simple truth was that the confrontation at Lake Powell had exposed him for what he was: a coward.

It was already evening in Lyon. He placed a call to Interpol's twenty-four hour intelligence hotline there, introducing himself to the accented female agent who came on the line and explaining that he needed the assistance of a criminal investigator in Heidelberg as soon as possible. Within minutes, he had the name of Chief Inspector Ernst Kettler of the Heidelberg *Polizei.* Since it was too late to reach him by phone, he sent an e-mail, saying that he urgently needed help in conducting an investigation at St. Stephen's Monastery.

His next call was to the Chicago Police Department's Criminal Intelligence Unit. He requested that they check the sales records of The Reich Warehouse, stating that he was interested in any shipments of German war memorabilia to South Florida since November—the month when the Wake-Up Rapes began.

CHAPTER

61

Chief Inspector Kettler responded to Roth's request with a phone call the following day. The two men discussed the case in German for nearly a half-hour. While Kettler was eager to help, he pointed out that St. Stephen's had been largely cut off from the outside world for hundreds of years. Visitors to the Trappist monastery were rare. Even if the Wake-Up Rapist had been on its grounds for some reason in 2002, too much time had passed, he said. The likelihood of anyone recognizing his face from one of the Compusketches was small at best.

Roth agreed. He knew the monastery was a long shot when he called Interpol; still, it was a lead that needed to be checked out. As soon as they hung up, he scanned all eleven Compusketch variations on the suspect's possible appearance into his computer and e-mailed them to Kettler.

*   *

After a full day of searching the dark waters of Lake Powell, the dive team abandoned its efforts. The sergeant who supervised the search speculated during a television interview at the scene that an alligator could have wedged the Wake-Up Rapist's body in its lair at the bottom of the lake. A few days later, a specially trained cadaver dog from the state police barracks in Homestead was brought in. The animal stood in the bow of a police boat as it made ever-narrower circles on the still water, sniffing the damp air with a sense of smell 10,000 times greater than its handler. In addition to the cadaver dog and a sonar tracking device, an instrument in the boat continuously sampled the air quality just above the water, searching for telltale chemical signs of organic decomposition. Even the slightest trace of gas from a decomposing body would have registered on it, as well as provoked a frenzy of barking and scratching by the dog. The animal remained silent.

CHAPTER

62

As much as Roth had dreaded appearing before the Shooting Review Board, he was in the room barely twenty minutes. He did exactly what Sosa told him to, answering the question of one of the deputy chiefs about why he didn't fire by explaining that he didn't have a clear shot at the running suspect. It wasn't exactly *a lie. It was impossible to align your sights on anything when you were cowering on the front seat of a car.*

*   *

On Friday morning, he went to the State Police lab and met with Hiram Meeks in the Firearms Identification Unit. He was a man in his fifties with stooped shoulders and a low, white forehead.

"Oh, yeah ... you're Maria's partner," Meeks said tonelessly.

"I was hoping you might have gotten some prints from one of the shell casings on Felton Drive."

"'Fraid not. The heat generated in the breach when the weapon was fired toasted whatever latents were there."

"I know the gun was a nine millimeter. What else can you tell me?"

Meeks located a folder that contained notes, diagrams and photographs of the shooting scene at Lake Powell. A total of four bullets had entered the cavity of the Ford Taurus, he explained. Three of them were recovered inside the car. Unlike the soft-nosed lead police ammunition Roth and Sosa were carrying, their assailant had used armor-piercing military surplus bullets that were capable of penetrating the body of a vehicle with very little deformation.

All three ballistics specimens were in excellent condition. The firearms examiner said that the counterclockwise spin of the bullets and their angle of pitch against the lands and grooves of the barrel had produced a kind of ballistics fingerprint—a series of striations that were unique to this particular type of weapon.

He had patiently translated the scratches on one of the recovered slugs into an alphanumeric code and entered it into the FBI's NIBIN (National Integrated Ballistic Information Network) system in Washington. The FBI computer compared the markings with the class characteristics of all known types of weapons in its vast database. The results were unequivocal: the bullets fired at Sosa and Roth came from the barrel of a nine millimeter Einheit Luger semiautomatic. Roth had heard of Lugers, but none with the prefix *Einheit.*

"My friend, you were nearly killed by an antique," Hiram Meeks said. He paused to tear open a pack of peanut butter crackers. There hasn't been an Einheit manufactured since 1944," he added, munching a cracker. "That was the year when the Allies bombed the factory in Stuttgart that made them."

"Just what is an Einheit Luger?"

"A very special gun," he replied, holding one of the armor piercing slugs between a thumb and forefinger. "The Einheit was created in 1939 by Hitler to commemorate the role of his secret state police in the rise of the Nazi party. A thousand of the pistols were supposed to be produced, one to symbolize each year of the Thousand Year Reich Hitler envisioned. Nazi war records reveal that only 619 were actually assembled and shipped to Berlin."

Meeks brushed some crumbs from his lap and continued. "Every Einheit pistol was handmade. I've only seen a couple over the years. Truly superb craftsmanship."

Roth said wryly, "You tend to lose sight of that when you're on the wrong end of one."

"The Einheit was nickel-plated with a black swastika in a red circle engraved on its ivory grips," Meeks continued. "Just below the swastika were the twin lightning bolts of the SS and the letters G.S."

G. S.: Geheime Staatspolizei. The Gestapo, enforcement arm of the SS, the infamous Ministry of Justice. Roth looked up from the notes he had been making. How he had grown up hating those words! It was the Gestapo that arrested his uncle's entire family and sent them to Buchenwald. By the time they realized what was happening in Germany, it was too late to get out; the firestorm had already begun. Only Roth's father, Samuel, managed to escape.

"Hitler personally presented the Einheit Lugers as special gifts to Gestapo officers and prominent members of the party who had won his favor. The fact that the Führer himself chose an Einheit as his personal weapon made owning one quite a status symbol in the Nazi pecking order."

"How do you know so much about this particular gun?"

Meeks smiled. "Firearms are my hobby as well as my profession. Someone paid a pretty penny for the pistol these bullets came from. I'd give anything to have it."

"I'd settle for just one good latent fingerprint off it," Roth sighed.

Meeks removed a book entitled *Famous Firearms* from a shelf and showed him a picture of an Einheit Luger.

"I still haven't told you the most interesting part of the weapon's history," he said, drawing his brows together. "As you know, Hitler and his mistress committed suicide in the Führerbunker as the Russians closed in on Berlin."

"By swallowing cyanide, as I recall," Roth added. "Their bodies were burned."

Meeks nodded. "Hitler also shot himself. Russian troops found a single spent nine millimeter cartridge beside his bed."

"From his Einheit Luger?"

"Presumably, though the pistol itself was never found. The speculation is that one of the Russian officers took it as a souvenir."

The firearms expert leaned forward with his hands on his knees and said intently, "Somewhere out there is an Einheit Luger with the number '1' engraved above the silver Reich Eagle on its frame. Whoever has it is sitting on a fortune."

Roth thought of the shooting at Lake Powell, suddenly struck by the absurdity of a Jew nearly being killed by a seventy-year old Nazi weapon. Why had the Wake-Up Rapist gone to the trouble of acquiring it?

CHAPTER

63

Roth spoke with Maria at least a couple of times each day while the Shooting Review Board completed its investigation. As everyone had expected, Chief Crenshaw officially declared the shooting at Lake Powell justified. Sosa would be returning to duty the following Monday. Until then, Roth was on his own.

He shook his head in frustration when he saw the FDLE lab report on the contents of the yellow gym bag. None of the items in it had yielded a single fingerprint—not even the heavily annotated copy of *Mein Kampf* or the business card from The Reich Warehouse. Everything had been either wiped thoroughly or handled with gloves. The newest criminal persona had obviously tapped into his host's intelligence, anticipating the possibility of having to abandon the bag and its incriminating contents in an emergency. Henry Stafford was right when he said that their best chance of catching the Wake-Up Rapist would come from the alter ego Jan doing something reckless.

McNees and Walker were running down one of the few viable leads provided by the gym bag. While the number of South Florida stores that carried Bearcat-brand programmable scanners was huge, only eight sporting goods shops stocked 'Tru-Thro' commando knives. Even though the knife had been carefully cleaned, the lab found traces of human blood that had seeped into the juncture between the blade and handle. If a sales clerk recognized the face depicted in one of the Compusketches, and the Stalker Sadist had been careless enough to use a credit card when he bought the knife, McNees and Walker would have his name and address. Roth doubted that was going to happen, unless they got awfully lucky.

A detective from the Chicago Police Department's Criminal Intelligence Unit had gone to The Reich Warehouse the day after he called. CPD faxed him copies of all sales receipts for the period in question. The apparent interest of south Floridians in German war relics was surprising: The Reich Warehouse had made a total of twenty-four shipments to the Miami area since November. Two *Waffen SS* uniforms went to the Drama Department at Miami-Dade Community College. He remembered reading that the college was staging a production of *The Diary of Anne Frank. So much for that one.*

In early November, a person identified as G. R. Gilmer in Sunrise paid ninety-seven dollars for a 1939 ten mark commemorative coin of the Teutonic Order. *Probably a collector.* There was no way to know how many of The Reich Warehouse's customers were just people with an interest in war memorabilia and how many were crypto-Nazis with copies of *The New Order* on their coffee tables. Most of the purchases appeared to be for inconsequential items like medals, coins and military insignia.

He continued examining the sales slips. A Hitler Youth knife and scabbard had been sent to Allen Bartels in the Miami suburb of Coconut Grove; Kenneth Denton of Homestead ordered a Kriegsmarine U-Boot-Waffen (U-Boat Service) belt buckle with the inscription, 'Wir segeln gegen England (We sail against England)!' He was willing to bet Denton was a maritime war buff. He thumbed rapidly through the remainder of the slips. His pulse quickened when he came to the last item in the stack. A 1939, nine-millimeter, Einheit Luger pistol, described as 'in mint condition,' had been sent via UPS from The Reich Warehouse to Tony's Gun and Pawn in *Delmar* a few days before the shooting.

"Delmar!" he exclaimed, pounding a fist into his palm.

The receipt indicated that Tony's Gun and Pawn paid $6,000 for the World War II pistol. Someone in Delmar, who wasn't put off by the price, had obviously been in a hurry to get hold of the commemorative Nazi weapon.

For the first time, they had a paper trail that could lead straight to the Wake-Up Rapist. Under Florida law, whoever purchased the Einheit Luger from the gun shop would have to produce positive ID, as well as leave a fingerprint for a police background check, before they could take possession of it. In his excitement, he started to phone Maria to tell her what he had discovered, but decided not to. He wanted to run this down by himself and hand her a major breakthrough in the case, something to make up for what happened at Lake Powell.

CHAPTER

64

Tony's Gun and Pawn was located in a seedy section of Delmar. The one-story, stucco structure, with burglar bars on its windows and doors, was sandwiched between a windowless adult book and video shop called PORNORAMA and a strip joint with the tongue-in-cheek name of THE ORE HOUSE.

A stuffed grizzly with bared teeth loomed just inside the door. What looked like the heads of Bambi's parents were mounted prominently on the wall on either side of it. The display area inside the gun shop was immense and bright. Roth could hear faint popping sounds coming from an indoor shooting range on the other side of a thick glass partition. Several men with ear protectors and goggles were firing at human silhouettes like the ones he had trained on at the police academy.

A large assortment of pistols and revolvers with price tags on their trigger guards was displayed on shelves beneath a long counter. Behind the counter was a rack of rifles and shotguns that ran the entire length of the store. The gondolas in the center of the room were filled with sporting and hunting equipment: fishing poles, back packs, tents, camouflage clothing, hunting bows with razor sharp arrows, lanterns and camping stoves. The place was Walmart with a flavor of lethality.

Roth walked up to one of two clerks behind the counter. He was a slightly-built man of about sixty with conspicuous false teeth and an ill-fitting toupee that looked a little like a dead squirrel.

"Hep ya, neighbor?" the man said cheerfully.

"I'd like to speak to the owner."

"You're lookin' at him. I'm Tony Clayton."

"I'm interested in a German Luger."

"Well, you come to the right place," the man beamed. "Happens that I got a couple in stock right now." His expression changed as soon as Roth took out his badge.

"A 1939 Einheit Luger was shipped to you from Chicago last week."

Tony Clayton licked his lips. "Yeah, but I don't have it no more. Sold it."

"Who to?"

A film of perspiration appeared above the owner's upper lip. "Uh … I don't rightly recollect his name."

Roth's posture stiffened. "I'd like to see your firearms disposition log, please," he said officiously.

The man cleared his throat. "I'll be glad to show it to you, Officer, but that particular sale isn't on it." The clerk at the other end of the counter walked over and started to say something.

"Not now, Norm! Goddamnit! Can't ya see I'm busy?"

Roth knew what the answer to his next question would be before he asked it. "Did you ID the buyer and run a background check on him with the state police?"

Clayton swallowed hard. "I'll be honest with you, Officer … I didn't."

"Why not?"

"Well…," Clayton began uncomfortably, "ya see, this fella was kind of in a rush. I said I'd have to do some checkin' on the computer. Tell ya the truth, I didn't know what the hell an Einheit Luger was when he come in. I wasn't sure I could locate one."

Roth leaned on the counter. "He must have left a name and phone number for you to call if you found one."

"Nope. He said he'd come back in the morning to see if I'd had any luck. When he showed up, I told him I'd found one in Chicago, and I could let him have it for sixty-five hundred. He offered me seven grand to skip the forms and the three-day waiting period. I says, 'No way! I could lose my firearms license!' So he says 'How about eight thousand in cash up front?'" Clayton ran a hand across his mouth. "Guy opened an envelope right where you're standin' and just started peelin' off new hundred dollar bills."

Roth noticed the dampness on the glass counter. The gun shop owner's bony hands were sweating profusely. He paused to shake a cigarette out of a pack and light it. "Hell, I didn't see no real harm in it, especially since he's a regular."

"What do you mean 'a regular'?"

"He comes in here to shoot all the time. Usually at least once a week with his buddies. They all ride big bikes."

"Harley-Davidsons?" Roth asked, with interest.

"Yep. Harley Hogs. Every one of 'em."

'Steel' again.

Clayton raised his nicotine-stained fingers and took a deep drag on his cigarette. "I got some full automatics I keep in the back," he volunteered: "Uzis, MP-5's, SKS's." He blinked rapidly several times. "They're all legal, of course. I got ATF permits for 'em. This guy and his friends are always rentin' 'em to fire on the range. Them boys love to shoot!"

I'll just bet they do.

Roth wondered how many of the Aryan brothers from *Steel* came to Tony's Gun and Pawn regularly to vent their hatred on the paper men. He kept a poker face, considering his next move with the gun shop owner.

"Officer, most of the time, I follow the law real close. I really do!" Clayton said plaintively.

"I won't sell a gun to just any punk or nigger who walks in off the street and wants to buy one. Nosiree!"

Roth's eyes roamed around the store. "Are you telling me that you don't have any paperwork *at all* on this sale?" he said sternly.

Clayton shook his head. "Mister, we don't see that kind of money in here very often. I figured I could skip the red tape just this once. I mean, hell, a guy doesn't pay that kind of dough for a gun to kill his old lady or knock over a 7-11, right? This was a collector's item."

Anger welled in Roth's throat. "Your goddamn collector's item nearly blew my head off!" he said in a voice loud enough to draw the attention of several people in the shop. He showed Clayton the original Compusketch. The gun shop owner put on a pair of reading glasses with unsteady hands.

WANTED FOR MURDER, RAPE, ARMED BURGLARY
AND MAYHEM

"Holy shit!" he croaked.

"Is this the guy who bought the Einheit Luger?"

Clayton studied the Compusketch for a long moment. "That's him, al-right, but his face is thinner than this here. He's also started wearin' a mustache and glasses lately. I noticed last time he come in that he'd dyed his hair brown. I was kiddin' him about blondes having more fun."

"What else do you remember about him?"

"Well … let's see…," Clayton said, squinting at the fluorescent ceiling light. "He had a cold last time he come in. Kept sniffin'."

Maybe the AIDS is beginning to kick in. He hoped so. "Tony, I'm going to level with you. You're in a world of shit right now! All it's going to take is one call to ATF, and they'll padlock this place within twenty-four hours."

Tony Clayton brought a hand to his chest. "Please, mister. I'm getting angina. I gotta sit down."

Roth followed him to a chair in the back of the store. Clayton took a small, white pill from a prescription bottle and put it under his tongue. Roth waited a few moments, letting him twist slowly in the breeze, then placed a hand on his shoulder. "You know, I might be able to let you slide on this."

Clayton looked up expectantly. "Could you, Officer? Please?"

"Well, that depends on you."

He wrote his cell phone on the back of a business card. "I want you to call me right away if he comes back in. You can reach me at this number anytime, day or night."

"You bet!" Clayton said, with obvious relief.

Oh, no. You're not getting off that easy.

"I'm going to have to make a report on this," Roth intoned menacingly. "Whether or not I file it and send a copy to ATF is up to you. I want this guy's name! I want to know where I can find him. Understand?"

Clayton nodded weakly.

Roth left Tony's Gun and Pawn in high spirits. While he hadn't found the Wake-Up Rapist yet, they were getting closer. He now had an extremely well motivated pair of eyes and ears in Delmar.

CHAPTER

65

Roth was watching the countdown on a chicken pot pie in his microwave when his phone rang. The call had been automatically forwarded from his voice mail at the SBU.

"David!" Inspector Ernst Kettler said excitedly, "We found the connection between your suspect and St. Stephen's!"

"What?" Roth said, taken off guard by the news. He listened anxiously while Kettler recounted his visit to the monastery earlier that day.

"The Abbot didn't react to the first few Compusketches, but as soon as I came to the one that showed the suspect with no hair and a beard, he said, 'Why, that's Brother Tobias!' It seems your man joined the Trappist Order under the name of Peter Dietz and was at the monastery for almost two years." Roth had found a pen and was searching in a drawer for something to write on. "Dietz told the Abbot that he had just taken his degree in classical languages at the University of Heidelberg and wanted to become a Trappist friar. When I mentioned that the man in the Compusketch was an American, the Abbot shook his head. He said that Dietz spoke perfect German, with no trace of an accent."

"They didn't verify what he told them?" Roth said in amazement.

"The Abbot said that they accept anyone, without question, who comes to them. The life of a Trappist brother is so hard that they take it as a sign from God whenever a man seeks to join the order."

St. Stephen's Monastery was as harsh a world as one could imagine, completely devoid of pleasures of the flesh. What more perfect setting could there be for an *anhedonic*?

"The Abbot told me that they all felt especially blessed by the arrival of

Peter Dietz because he could read and write both Greek and Latin. Most of the brothers at St. Stephens work in its fields and vineyards. Since Dietz had a background in classical languages, he was assigned to the manuscript room. The monks there taught him the techniques used to excavate and restore papyrus codices."

And how to read and write Aramaic Estrangela. The Aramaic passage had been a major clue to the identity of the Stalker Sadist all along, and one that they had missed. He located a tablet and began scribbling notes as Inspector Kettler continued.

"The Abbot said that while Dietz was there, St. Stephen's received a set of scrolls that was of particular interest to the Vatican. Several archivists were sent from Rome to study them. Brother Tobias worked closely with them in the manuscript room for months."

"Did Dietz understand Italian?"

"Yes. He's fluent in it, as well as several other languages, though outsiders would have had no way of knowing because of the Rule of Silence the Trappists observe."

Monsignor Garofalo had said that he and the other two priests never discussed the *palimpsest* outside the manuscript room. The Italian linguists would have felt comfortable talking in their native tongue in the presence of a mute German monk who did nothing but scrape pieces of papyrus each day. That was how Dietz found out about the Papal order to seal the gospel once it was translated. How furious he must have been! All of his painstaking work excavating the Aramaic subtext of the Gnostic gospel had been for nothing. The world would never see the biblical treasure he had helped unearth. He felt betrayed by the very Church he had given up a life of luxury to serve. That must have been when he decided to leave St. Stephen's and returned to the states. The pieces of the puzzle were slowly coming together.

"The Abbot told me that Tobias disappeared shortly after the Vatican linguists left. It's the only time in over three hundred years that a brother has deserted the order."

He didn't leave St. Stephen's empty-handed. Peter Dietz, or whatever his real name was, either removed Chapter 9, Verse 31 from the scrolls or copied the controversial passage before the Vatican archivists returned to Rome.

"I think you'll find this most interesting," Inspector Kettler continued. "Brother Tobias' duties included locking the *palimpsest* and its translation in the safe when the linguists finished their work each day."

How many times must Dietz have slipped back into the manuscript room after the Italian translators and the other monks were asleep to look at the object that had been the center of his life for so long? It was undoubtedly while studying ancient codices at the monastery that he also became familiar with the myth of the avenging angel, Nasargiel.

Roth's initial elation over Inspector Kettler's phone call was short lived. While he now understood the connection between the Aramaic scripture and the criminal case, knowing that the man they were after spent two years at a Trappist monastery in Germany still didn't explain the wave of torture, rape and murder he had inflicted on south Florida after returning home. Nor did it account for the newest alter ego's apparent interest in the Nazis. He thought of the intense spirituality that must have characterized the life of Brother Tobias at St. Stephen's. What could have happened to produce such a radical change in him?

CHAPTER

66

Roth and Sosa had reason to celebrate. Not only were they making progress on the case, but her promotion had just come through. She would be returning to the Sexual Battery Unit as Lieutenant Sosa. For the first time since Sara's death, Roth had met a woman he desperately wanted a relationship with; yet, the chances of that happening now seemed more remote than ever. Aside from the department's fraternization rule, he doubted that she would ever consider seeing him on a personal basis after what happened at Lake Powell.

He had sent Henry Stafford the transcript of his interview with Paloma Hidalgo, along with a translation of the handwritten notes he found in the pages of *Mein Kampf*. They needed to talk with him about what to expect from the new alter ego that had surfaced.

Roth decided to arrange a dinner meeting that weekend with Maria and the Staffords; while it wouldn't exactly be a date, at least it was a way to spend some time with her in an off-duty setting. The presence of the dean and his wife would confer an aura of legitimacy if anyone happened to see them together. The Rusty Pelican on Virginia Key seemed like the perfect setting; he reserved a table overlooking the water for Saturday night.

*   *

He had never seen Maria look lovelier than she did when he and the Staffords picked her up at her condo. She had on heels and a sheer lavender and black silk dress that accented the olive hue of her bare shoulders.

Several couples were on the dance floor at The Rusty Pelican when they arrived. The running lights of yachts sparkled on the water of Biscayne Bay while brightly-colored fish darted between sharp pieces of coral in a huge iridescent aquarium. Roth and Maria settled on Lobster Thermador, the house specialty, and sipped chilled *Veuve Clicquot* champagne while a tuxedoed waiter tossed a Caesar salad beside their table.

During dinner, Roth told Stafford about the ascetic life the man they were after had led in Germany for nearly two years as Brother Tobias. The psychoanalyst listened attentively, and then said, "The isolation and enforced silence of the monastic lifestyle enabled him to control his sexuality for a time, but the defense mechanism collapsed when he became angry at the Church and left St. Stephen's." He paused while the waiter refilled their champagne flutes.

"Dr. Stafford," Maria began.

"Henry, please," he said.

She smiled. "Henry, why has this second alter ego appeared?"

"Ah, yes," Stafford said, "it's quite common in cases of a multiple personality for an alter to appear that is the diametric opposite of the host. Maria, during our first meeting, you mentioned *The Three Faces of Eve*. You'll recall that Eve White was a model wife and mother, while her alter ego, Eve Black, was a promiscuous alcoholic. That kind of polarization of the parts of a multiple personality is fairly typical. We see the same kind of dynamic here between the host personality and this new alter ego. Kurt is Brother Tobias turned inside out, so to speak. The monk's decency and spirituality have been transformed into an especially vicious form of sadism in the new persona."

"Wasn't Jan brutal enough?" Sosa asked. "Why was there any need for a more sadistic alter?"

Their waiter reappeared with a second bottle of champagne and placed it in an ice bucket.

"Jan had apparently begun to realize his limitations. He was afraid of being caught because of his own ineptness and the clues the host personality has been providing the police. He needed an ally to help him get rid of Peter Dietz— the person we've been calling Robert. The newest alter, Kurt, is strong and clever enough to protect him. That's why he unconsciously created him."

Sosa seemed perplexed. "But why all the Nazi stuff?"

"Judging from the magazine David found in the bag and what he learned at the gun shop, Jan has apparently been hanging out at the skinhead bar, *Steel,* for some time. That must be where he was first exposed to neo-Nazi propaganda. Keep in mind how naive Jan is. He would have readily accepted anything his new acquaintances at the bar told him without questioning it. *Steel* became a kind of cocoon in which the alter ego of Kurt incubated. The new persona gradually absorbed the neo-Nazi propaganda, integrating it with the host's knowledge of German language and culture. Kurt emerged from his chrysalis just before the attack on Paloma Hidalgo as a synthesis of Third Reich ideology and the host's intelligence."

"That's scary," Sosa observed.

"Indeed, it is," the psychiatrist agreed, declining the waiter's offer of a dessert menu. "*The New Order* magazine in the gym bag is just the kind of low-brow, hate stuff Jan would be comfortable with, but the copy of *The Rise and Fall of the Third Reich* reflects a more refined intelligence. I found the notes Kurt made in *Mein Kampf* fascinating from a psychiatric standpoint."

"In what way?" Sosa asked.

"The new alter ego is apparently obsessed with Hitler. Studying his autobiography so closely, and even going to the trouble of acquiring the same kind of pistol he carried, is an indication of how much he identifies with him."

The analyst added a dash of cream to his coffee and stirred it. "What happened during the attack on the Hidalgo woman concerns me," he said pensively.

"Why? He's done a lot worse things," Sosa pointed out.

"Jan stalked each of his victims and collected background information on them before he attacked them," Stafford replied. "I don't think Kurt really knew anything about Paloma Hidalgo, except that she was someone he wanted to torture and kill."

"You don't think he was going to rape her?" Sosa said.

Stafford shook his head. "Rape is Jan's aberration. He was the one who tormented her with the garter belt and stockings. You'll recall that, as soon as Kurt 'came out' that night, the sexual overtones of the attack stopped, and the torture began. The new alter's brand of sadism has nothing to do with sex. It's far more virulent than anything we've seen up to now."

"What's happened to Robert or Peter Dietz—the host personality?" Roth asked.

"I'm afraid he's gone."

"Dead?" Roth said, immediately struck by the absurdity of his choice of words.

"Perhaps. In any case, he may never have the strength to come out again. It was all he could do to stand up against Jan. He's no match for Kurt." He turned to Roth. "David, I'm afraid you're no longer dealing with an inept brute that goes around anally raping and torturing women. You've got a highly intelligent, sadistic killer on your hands now."

Maria said, "But, if Kurt is now in control and he's not into rape, maybe the attacks on the professional women are over."

Stafford leaned forward and clasped his hands. "I only wish that were true. You see, both alters share their host's compulsiveness. Kurt will probably feel the need to finish what Jan has started."

"By torturing and murdering more women?" Maria supplied.

Stafford nodded.

The lights in the room dimmed as a female vocalist joined the band in a mellow rendition of *Unforgettable*.

"You said before that we should concentrate on catching Jan," Sosa said. "Do you still believe that, even though Kurt seems to be running things?"

"Yes, even though Kurt is now the executive of the personality, I doubt that he's going to be able to control Jan for long."

Elise Stafford pushed her chair back. "Come on, Henry … that's enough shop talk. How about dancing with your wife?"

Roth drained his champagne glass and watched the Staffords walk onto the dance floor. He was beginning to feel a slight buzz. No matter. The dean was the designated driver tonight. He spotted a woman walking between the tables selling long stemmed roses and signaled her, selecting a red flower from the assortment of colors and handing it to Maria.

She smiled. "This is just too pretty not to go on my desk at work, even if Fladd and Cochoran plant a bug in it."

He motioned toward the dance floor. "We can join them, if you like, unless you think you'll get in trouble with the department."

"I'm not a cop or a supervisor tonight, just a lady out for dinner with some friends." She stood and reached for his hand as the band started playing *The Days of Wine and Roses*. He felt himself break out in goose bumps on the dance floor when he put his hand on the small of her bare back.

"I didn't know you liked to dance," she said.

I don't. I just wanted an excuse to hold you again.

"Sara was a great dancer. She used to kid me about having two left feet."

"You're doing great," she said, resting her head against his shoulder. He led her slowly around the floor, listening to the music. The song they were dancing to gave way to another, then another, and another. He held her in his arms without speaking, savoring the nearness of her.

Only a few couples were now left on the floor. She took off her heels, taking ever smaller steps with him in her stocking feet.

"I've been trying to think of a way to thank you," he finally said.

"For what?" she said dreamily, with her eyes closed.

He touched his forehead with a finger. "I'd have a nine millimeter hole there right now if you hadn't pulled me down on the seat."

"We're partners. You'd have done the same for me."

Would I? Or would I have just cared about saving my own ass?

"They should put me on administrative leave more often. I can't believe all you've gotten done while I've been gone. You're a natural detective, David."

"Oh, sure. I may not be much in a firefight, but put me in an office where it's nice and safe, and I really shine!"

"Stop it! Why do you keep beating yourself up over that night? Don't you think I was scared, too?"

"You did the job," he said sullenly.

"That wasn't the first time someone's shot at me." She gazed up at him with her dark brown eyes. "Look, you're a university professor. You have zero street experience, and only half the training of a rookie. What did you expect to do if somebody tried to kill you—charge out there with your gun blazing like Rambo?"

"Everybody in CID wonders why I didn't fire. We both know the reason."

She stopped dancing and put her hands on her hips. "Is that what this is about? You think I'm ashamed to have you as a partner?"

"Aren't you?" he said, meeting her eyes.

"For a smart guy, you can be so damn dumb sometimes! You really want to know how I feel about you?" She took his face in both hands. Then, right there on the parquet dance floor of the Rusty Pelican in front of the Staffords and thirty or so complete strangers, *she kissed him*—not a sisterly peck on the cheek, but a deep, lingering, sensual kiss squarely on the lips. She pressed her body against his while her tongue probed the inside of his mouth.

He stood there, too dazed to move.

CHAPTER

67

The newest lieutenant in the Criminal Investigation Division looked every inch a successful young police executive when she arrived at the SBU Monday morning in a navy blue suit and white blouse. She stopped by the ladies' room to check her makeup.

Oh, Christ, what was I thinking? She squeezed her eyes shut as the memory of Saturday night returned. If Fladd and Cochoran from IA got wind of her little maneuver on the dance floor, they wouldn't be intimidated by another display of righteous indignation.

Shit! She had always been so careful about everything she did, both on and off duty. The day she first put on a uniform, she realized she was crashing an all male club. Only two kinds of women exist in the minds of most male cops, she told herself: *Madonnas and whores.* There was nothing in between in the double standard world she was part of. For CID's only female lieutenant to be French kissing a subordinate officer in a room full of witnesses could hardly be reckoned as a shrewd career move.

Roth wasn't her type, she reminded herself. He wasn't really that good looking. She had always been drawn to stereotypically handsome men. There had been several of them over the years; everyone said that the brooding Latin hunk she married was a dead ringer for Antonio Bandaras.

She lingered in front of the mirror, still trying to sort out what happened at The Rusty Pelican. Despite her initial reaction to Roth, his gentleness and sensitivity had gradually drawn her to him. She heard the sadness in his voice whenever he spoke of Sara or Jacob; a part of her wanted to cradle him in her arms and take all the pain away.

His intelligence was a major turn-on for her. So was the fact that he knew so much about her field. She wasn't patronizing him when she said he was a natural detective. Even without the experience or training of the other investigators she'd worked with, he was the best partner she'd ever had. Not that she'd ever want to see him directing traffic downtown during rush hour; he was far too spacey to ever be a street cop. She had been around him long enough to realize that he lived in his head much of the time. She sighed. He wasn't even Cuban, for Chrissakes! She could hear her mother: "Madre de Dios! Miguel! She's fallen in love with a Jew!"

Love.

Was that what it was? She had known something was going on between them ever since that night on the stakeout. He looked at her differently after that. His clothes suddenly improved. He kept finding excuses to come to her office and call her after hours about the case. His body language also changed; she noticed how he always pulled his chair close to hers during their meetings. Sometimes, he brushed against her ever so slightly when he leaned over her desk to see what she was working on; recently, he had taken to touching her arm when he was making a point. A woman could read the signs.

She was so used to men hitting on her. Any other cop would have been all over her the first time she responded with obvious flirtation to his subtle advances. Roth's shyness was as endearing as it was unique. He reminded her of a kid on a first date, trying to summon the courage to put his arm around a girl. She guessed that was why she finally made the first move. She brought her hands to her face. What a move it was! That was the cop in her—too many years of having to take charge of situations.

A discrete affair was one thing. She knew now that she wanted that with him, despite the risks; she sensed they would be great lovers. But this guy wanted more—a lot more. She could see it in his eyes. *Commitment. Marriage. Kids.* She had decided years ago that none of that was in her future. Hal Wilcox would be retiring before long. As the ranking female in CID, she would have a good shot at his job. After that, the sky was the limit: Major, Deputy Chief. Miami had never had a female chief of police. She could be the first.

* *

Later that morning, she found Roth by the copy machine. "Hi," she said a little too casually.

"I need to talk to you." She could see by the expression on his face what he had read into her remark.

God, no! Not about that!

"Alvin has a new lead for us."

"Oh…," he said, sounding relieved.

She knew that nothing between them would ever be the same after Saturday night. They were still partners, but everything else had changed. They were already *involved*; it was only a matter of time before they wound up in bed.

On the way to her office, she said, "Remember the red handkerchief Laura Kelce saw in the rapist's pocket?"

"Yeah. Why?"

"Alvin was out all weekend checking SM bars in different parts of the city. He called me last night and told me about a place in South Beach called The Back Door. Passive gays there are known as '*bottoms.*' They wear a yellow handkerchief in their right front pocket when they're cruising. Can you guess what color handkerchief a *top* wears?"

"Red!"

"Ten to one the condom Jan used on Laura Kelce came from The Back Door."

CHAPTER

68

The *Exxon Valdez* had just come back from the city garage.

"Hey, check it out," Sosa said expansively. The windshield had been replaced and there was no trace of the gaping hole one of the armor-piercing slugs had punched in the hood. A fresh coat of blue paint masked the orange peel texture of the old paint job.

"Looks like we're getting a new car, piece by piece," she observed

"Yeah. Maybe next time he can manage to hit the engine."

They drove to The Back Door that afternoon. After circling the place several times, they sat in a parking lot across the street, watching it with binoculars. A number of men were already lined up in front of the building, waiting for the bottle club to open.

"We haven't had exactly great luck with bars so far," he reminded her. "How do you want to work this?"

"What do you mean 'we'? I'm a woman. I can't walk into a place like that. You're going to have to go."

He looked at her aghast. "You … you … expect me to *cruise* an SM bar?"

"Have you got a better idea?"

"Alvin's gay. Why not send him in there?"

"He doesn't know any more about the SM scene than we do."

He picked up the Nikons and focused them on the bar. "Look at the way those guys are dressed! They'd make me as a cop the moment I walked up."

She started the car. "Not after we make a few changes in your wardrobe. Dr. Roth, we're about to retrofit you for the leather scene."

* *

They went to the Ocean Mall where Roth tried on a pair of tight, black pants in the stall of a department store dressing room while Maria waited on the other side of the partition.

"Do they fit?" she called out.

He sucked in his stomach and buttoned the front. "Yeah, as long as I don't breathe. Don't you think I'm a little long in the tooth to pass as a *bottom* at a place like The Back Door?"

"Stop worrying. You'll be fine. Here, try this on."

He caught the dark 'muscle shirt' she threw over the partition. The cut-off sleeves and thin straps were designed to expose the wearer's arms and chest.

"What's this?"

"Just put it on. It's part of your undercover ensemble."

"Forget it! This looks like something an addict would wear," he protested, tossing it back over the partition.

"Come on, David … do you want to catch this guy or not? Don't make me pull rank on you." He mumbled an expletive and put the shirt on. That afternoon they bought some other items that would help him pass as a patron at The Back Door: a pair of boots, a yellow scarf they could transform into a handkerchief for the front pocket of his jeans, a gaudy zircon pinkie ring and a bracelet. On the way back to the police department, they stopped at a novelty shop and picked up a paste-on tattoo of a snarling, black panther.

"*Ay, macho hombre!*" she teased, after pasting it on his arm.

"Knock it off! All I need now is to have my hair dyed orange, and I'll look like Ronald McDonald's kinky brother."

She glanced at her watch. "We've got to get back to CID. I still have to get some equipment for tonight."

After returning to the Sexual Battery Unit and picking up the 'wire' he would wear inside the club, she appeared at his office with a roll of white adhesive tape and a pair of scissors. "Take off the shirt," she said matter-of-factly after closing the door.

"What?"

She rolled her eyes. "Come on ... don't get all modest on me. I need to show you how this thing works."

He peeled off his shirt and draped it over the back of the chair. Her skin tingled. It was the first time she had seen him with his shirt off. She had no idea he had so much hair on his chest. His upper body was firm and lean. She held a piece of tape between her teeth and pressed the wafer-thin transmitter against his chest; after taping it to him, she plugged in a microphone that was about the size of an M & M. "These units work really well. I'll be able to hear anything you say, even if it's just a whisper, though we won't have any way of communicating."

"What do I do for a gun?"

"Gun? I thought you were a pacifist?"

"I am. I just want to make sure I remain a live one."

She pulled up the leg of her slacks, exposing an ankle holster that held a Beretta .380. She handed him the holstered back-up gun and he strapped it to his ankle.

"I look like an asshole!" he said as she checked the transmitter wire that snaked to within an inch of his low collar.

She stifled a laugh. "That's really sort of the idea."

CHAPTER

69

Patrol units had been alerted at roll call that two detectives would be conducting surveillance in the area of The Back Door. If Sosa and Roth needed backup, they'd have plenty of it within minutes.

The lot in front of the bar was full by the time they arrived. They parked at a defunct used car dealership across the street that served as overflow parking for the club.

"Remember," Maria cautioned, "if you spot him, just say 'It's hot in here,' and I'll call the cavalry. We don't want to try to take this guy by ourselves."

"Don't worry. You're talking to a professor, not a cop." He opened the door and started to get out. She reached over and put her hand on his arm.

"David ..."

"Yeah."

"Be careful in there."

The Oriental bouncer at the entrance was in his mid-twenties with a shaved head and the build of a Sumo wrestler. He motioned Roth inside with the others, remaining as expressionless as a Buddha.

The cavernous room beyond the heavy wooden door was easily twice the size of *Steel*. Fifty men or more packed the smoke-filled interior. Some sat at the bar while others stood in small clusters, drinking and talking. Dancers on the floor gyrated to the sound of acid rock. Their bodies appeared as surreal freeze frames beneath a mirrored mobile that spun on the ceiling. Roth made his way through the crowded bar, still feeling as if he had COP stamped on his forehead.

Some of the men he saw wore metal rings in their nipples and ears or had studs in their tongues and nostrils. A number were shirtless, while others wore tank tops. Nearly all of them wore tight pants similar to the ones he had on. Everyone had either a red or yellow handkerchief sticking out of the right front pocket of their pants. He sat at the only available seat at the laminated pine bar between two other men. When he leaned forward to order a beer, the adhesive tape tugged at his chest, reminding him of Maria's presence at the other end of the wire. The kiss at the Rusty Pelican still had him off balance. At first, he was ecstatic. Then, he started thinking about *why* she kissed him. Maybe it was just the champagne and music. He began to wonder if she felt sorry for him because of the funk he had been in ever since the shooting—a princess kissing a frog. Well, if she was trying to cheer him up, she had only made things worse. He was half-crazy with desire for her now. When she taped the microphone to his chest, it was all he could do to keep from …

"Hi!" a baritone voice behind him said.

He turned and saw a muscular man of about thirty wearing a black leather vest and jeans. A cigarette dangled from his lips, and prominent veins snaked down both of his tattooed arms. The needle marks on them stood out like the stars on a summer night.

"Buy you a beer?" he said, with a blast of fetid breath.

"Thanks. I've already got one."

The man propped his foot on the brass railing. Roth spotted the red handkerchief in his pocket out of the corner of his eye. "You're not a real friendly bitch now, are you?" the *top* said. He grinned, exposing badly stained, chipped teeth. "You know, maybe you just need a little discipline from the right guy," he said, toying with a pair of handcuffs on his belt.

"I'm waiting for someone," Roth told him, studying the bottle in his hands.

The *top* reached over and snatched the yellow handkerchief out of his pocket, tossing it on the bar. "Hey, man, if you're not looking to get fucked, don't show colors!" A moment later, he stormed off.

Roth dug a five-dollar bill out of his pants and paid for the beer, realizing he had just violated some bizarre rule of SM courtship. A drunken *bottom* was stumbling toward the door of the men's room, zipping his fly, when he stepped inside. He splashed water on his face at a grimy basin and dried it with his yellow handkerchief. The coin machine on the wall immediately caught his eye.

BUTTMASTER CONDOMS
75 cents

Jan's brand.

A little after one, the bouncer at the front door stamped the back of his hand so he could go outside and get some fresh air. He walked beyond earshot of several men on the sidewalk and gazed into the darkness of the parking lot across the street. "I think we're in the right place," he whispered. "But I'm not sure Kurt is going to let Jan come out and play."

Maria's flashlight blinked twice in acknowledgement. Business was still booming around three as he watched a couple of *tops* shoot a game of eight ball. He turned at the sound of a familiar laugh behind him. It was the same laugh he had heard on his voice mail the day Peaches was killed. Jan Nasargiel was sitting at the bar with his arm around the waist of a shirtless man in his mid-twenties. Roth recognized him immediately from the Compusketch, even with the chestnut-colored hair, mustache and glasses. A white bandage on his left bicep attested to the wound Maria had apparently inflicted on him. Before Roth could react, Jan spotted him, springing to his feet and toppling his stool. The bottle he was holding slipped from his fingers and shattered on the floor.

"Police!" Roth shouted, dropping to his knee and jerking the Beretta from its holster. A moment later, Jan bolted toward the rear of the bar with Roth running after him.

"It's him! Maria, it's him!" he called out. The multiple personality darted nimbly between tables, knocking over chairs as he ran.

"Stop or I'll shoot!" Roth threatened, knowing it was a bluff. There was no way he could fire in a place this crowded.

Jan stumbled but quickly regained his footing. Roth had closed to within four or five feet of him when someone thrust a boot in his path. He pitched forward, breaking his fall with his hands. The pistol skittered across the floor like a hockey puck, disappearing under a cigarette machine as the bar exploded in a tumult of angry voices.

"It's a fucking cop!" someone shouted. "Kill the cocksucker!"

Roth ducked when a bearded man at one of the tables threw a bottle that narrowly missed his head. He lost precious seconds groping for the gun; just as he felt its grips, a beer mug crashed into the cigarette machine beside him. He turned and saw Maria pushing her way through the crowd with her gun out. She keyed her radio, calling for help as a hail of bottles and beer mugs rained down on them. They reached the door to the parking lot just in time to see a tall figure jump on a black Harley and roar into the street with his lights off.

Maria radioed the bike's direction of travel breathlessly while they sprinted toward the *Exxon Valdez*. The motorcycle was already a couple of blocks ahead of them by the time they reached the car. Roth hit his shin on the passenger door, cursing as he jumped inside.

Screeching into the street, they saw Jan's brake light cutting on and off as he swerved around cars.

A mile later, two solid lines of traffic blocked the road ahead of them, bringing the two detectives to a dead stop with their siren wailing. Far in the distance, the motorcycle shot down an alley and disappeared.

Maria threw her radio on the seat in frustration. "Goddamnit! I told you not to try and take him alone!"

"I ..."

Her lips thinned with anger. "You didn't even use the codeword!"

"If you'll just shut up for a minute, I'll tell you what happened!" The words came out harsher than he intended. She looked as if he had just slapped her. "He *made* me and started running before I could do anything!"

"Oh ..."

He grasped her arm. "Quick! We've got to get back to the bar!"

"Are you crazy? Do you want to start a riot?"

"Maria, he was holding a bottle. He dropped it when he ran!"

"Oh, Jesus!"

"They were back at the SM bar within fifteen minutes, this time escorted by a phalanx of uniformed officers with nightsticks and pepper spray canisters at the ready. The bartender had shoved the fallen bar stool aside and was getting ready to sweep the remnants of Jan's bottle into a dust pan.

"Get away from that!" Sosa shouted. Roth quickly put on a pair of latex gloves and began placing the dark brown fragments in an evidence bag.

"Hurry!" Sosa urged.

"I am!" he told her, stretching to reach a piece of glass under the stool Jan had knocked over. Even with nine, heavily armed cops around them, missiles were being hurled from different parts of the room. Roth ducked when something shattered a bowl of pretzels on the counter above him. He knew they were in trouble when he heard a uniformed sergeant ask for more units. Tense minutes followed as the contingent of officers held the screaming crowd at bay.

"That's the last of it!" Roth finally announced. "Let's get the hell out of here!"

They ran through the parking lot to their car. "For someone with AIDS, Jan didn't exactly seem to be at death's door," he puffed, jumping in on the passenger side. "He tore through that place like a running back with the Dolphins."

"Shit! I must have just nicked him at the lake."

On the way downtown, he held up the plastic bag, inspecting the pieces inside against the lights of passing cars. "What do you think the chances are of us getting a usable latent off any of these?"

"Fifty-fifty ... at best."

He brushed pieces of pretzel from his shoulders and hair. "Well, I guess my cover at The Back Door is blown, so to speak ... no pun intended."

She laughed. "Do you realize that's the closest you've ever come to telling me a joke?"

"It is?"

"Maybe you're starting to lighten up, huh?"

"Maybe ... just a little," he grinned, adding, "I'm sorry I yelled at you."

She made a careless gesture. "It was my fault. I should have listened to what you were trying to tell me. It's no big deal. All coupl ..." she looked suddenly flustered. "All partners have friction."

Couples. She started to say couples! The slip of the tongue meant the kiss on the dance floor was more than either champagne or sympathy! The next move was his. *So, what am I waiting for?*

He mustered his courage on the way to the SBU. As soon as the metal gate at the police garage rolled open he decided to go for broke.

"I've been thinking. Maybe we could get together at my place this weekend to sort of take stock of where we are with the case."

"Your place?"

"Well ... we wouldn't have all the distractions of the office. Phones. People. It's hard to get anything done there sometimes. We could maybe throw a couple of steaks on the grill and ... uh ..."

Moron! Did I really say that? Of all the stupid ... His mouth was filling with cotton balls. It had been too many years since he had come on to a woman. He'd forgotten how!

She drove up the ramp without responding. He searched her profile anxiously, looking for some reaction but seeing none. Finally, he said clumsily, "Of course, I realize that you may already have plans or think that ..."

"What time Saturday?"

CHAPTER

70

They got lucky. Very lucky. All the shards of glass Roth collected from the floor at The Back Door were badly smeared except one. The triangular-shaped fragment contained a thumb print that yielded a total of fifteen *minutia points*—just enough to try for a fingerprint match through the AFIS computer.

Within minutes of entering the appropriate sequence of codes for the unique pattern of tiny ridge endings, bifurcations, directions and contours, a fingerprint technician at the state crime lab called with word that they had a *hit*. The print from the bottle matched fingerprints on file with the FBI in Washington.

Their initial excitement was tempered by an awareness that the print from the piece of glass could belong to the bartender or someone else who touched the bottle before the multiple personality. A fax with a name and physical description soon followed:

PETER NICHOLAS VON HAUSMANN
WM/ 6' 170/ BLD/BLU/ DOB 11-15-78

"Peter von Hausmann ... Peter Dietz ... or Brother Tobias," Roth said jubilantly. "Take your pick."

"Son of a bitch! We've got him!" Maria exclaimed. Henry Stafford's prediction had been right; Jan Nasargiel had finally made a disastrous mistake.

They examined the *rap sheet* that chattered over the fax a few minutes later. It reflected only a single arrest for von Hausmann:

L&L/ MPC 2712.6
Boston P.D.
5/14/00
Nolo contendre /Prob

The occult legalese of the printout said that their suspect was arrested by the Boston Police Department in 2000 for violating Section 2712.6 of the Massachusetts Penal Code: *lewd and lascivious conduct in a public place.* He had apparently entered a plea of 'no contest' to the charge and was placed on probation.

Now they knew why the Stalker Sadist had been so careful about never leaving any fingerprints at the scene of his crimes. Within a half hour, they received a color copy of Peter von Hausmann's driver's license from DMV along with his address:

955 North Oceanic Blvd., Palm Beach, Florida 33482

Roth studied the finely chiseled features on the license photo. The picture was remarkably close to the description Peaches Brooks gave them, right down to the cleft chin, piercing blue eyes and confident thrust of the jaw.

* *

Stakeout teams from the Palm Beach Police Department quickly converged on Peter von Hausmann's barrier island residence. To describe 955 North Oceanic Boulevard in Palm Beach as a 'home' would be a gross understatement. *Casa Serena* was one of the island's best-known residences. The imposing 15,000 square foot, three-story structure afforded a spectacular view of the ocean. Twelve-foot ficus hedges and high iron gates obscured it from the prying eyes of sightseers roaming the island.

Sosa and Roth set about obtaining arrest warrants for von Hausmann, realizing that with his financial resources it would be almost impossible to keep him from fleeing the country and becoming an international fugitive once he discovered the police knew he was the Stalker Sadist. Because of the extreme flight risk involved, the superior court judge who signed the warrants ordered them sealed at Lieutenant Sosa's request. Even with the confidentiality measure, it was only a matter of time before some aggressive reporter with either the mainstream press or one of the tabloids learned the identity of Miami's Wake-Up Rapist. Peter von Hausmann's name and face would then be splashed on the front page of every newspaper in south Florida. They had to find him before that happened.

* *

The arrest report from Boston PD's Vice Unit revealed that Peter von Hausmann III was taken into custody for 'indecently touching' a male undercover officer in the men's room of a bar called The Rocket in an area of Boston known as 'The Combat Zone.' The report listed his occupation simply as 'Student, M.I.T.'

Roth phoned the arresting officer, Ron Lazzio, who was now a sergeant assigned to burglary.

"What kind of bar is The Rocket?" he asked.

"Heavy leather," the Boston sergeant replied. "One hundred percent SM."

"I know it's been a while, but do you remember this guy?"

"Oh, yeah. Real well. Most of the people you pop in places like that are maggots. The names and faces begin to run together after a while. This guy was different. You could tell right away that he didn't belong down in the zone. He was a college type, very quiet and polite, even after we arrested him. I remember he started crying when I put the cuffs on. He said it would kill his mother. He begged us to let him go. It was strange. On the way downtown, he started whispering to himself in the back seat. I asked what he was saying. He was reciting the *Confiteor* in Latin."

"What's that?"

"It's a prayer Catholics say when they go to confession. I've been Catholic all my life, but that's the first time I ever heard anyone say it in Latin. He kept talking about how he was going to hell, saying that he didn't deserve to live. I told him that he'd just made a mistake, that he had his whole life ahead of him. I really felt sorry for the guy. "

"Anything else about him you can recall?"

"My partner and I were worried that he might try to off himself in the jail, so we had him put on a suicide watch that night. I remember he called an uncle who's a lawyer in Palm Beach right after we booked him. The next day, the uncle flew in and got a local shyster to bond him out. I think the guy took a *nolo* plea and got probation. That was the last I heard of him. What did he do, honk another cop?"

"Worse," Roth replied. "Much worse."

*   *

A check with the Registrar's Office at the Massachusetts Institute of Technology revealed that Peter von Hausmann was a senior with a split-major in Mathematics and Computer Science at the time he was arrested. Roth spoke with the professor who had been his academic advisor. He recalled von Hausmann as an outstanding student with a 4.0 average who had inexplicably dropped out of school in 2000, only weeks before he was scheduled to graduate *summa cum laude*. He had no idea what had become of him.

CHAPTER

71

Saliva obtained from the broken beer bottle at The Back Door yielded a DNA banding pattern that matched that of the Wake-Up Rapist perfectly. Things were beginning to make sense. Von Hausmann had apparently dropped out of college and gone to Germany to become a Trappist friar as atonement for the sexual sins that led to his arrest in Boston. A combination of guilt and the fear of facing his mother apparently drove him to desert the life of wealth and comfort he had known.

Once the former monk returned to south Florida from Germany, the sadomasochistic sexual impulses must have surfaced again. His conscious mind couldn't accept the prospect of returning to a series of one night stands in leather bars. That was when the first alter ego, Jan Nasargiel, emerged and began cruising south Florida nightspots like The Back Door. While Roth and Sosa still had many unanswered questions, the most important thing now was to find Peter von Hausmann III.

* *

The two detectives soon learned that von Hausmann had become the best-known philanthropist in the history of Palm Beach following his mother's death the year before, contributing millions of dollars to a wide variety of charities. He was a virtual recluse who never appeared in public or allowed himself to be photographed. Nor did he grant interviews. He had even declined to attend the dedication of a new wing at St. Mary's Hospital he had built in memory of his mother.

Aerial photographs of von Hausmann's estate taken by a Palm Beach County Sheriff's helicopter indicated that the ten-acre property was deserted. The outline of the huge house loomed forebodingly against the backdrop of the sea. Its Olympic-sized swimming pool was covered with dark green algae, while the tennis court was littered with branches and leaves, and the once well-tended gardens were overgrown with weeds.

Roth sat in the *Exxon Valdez* with Sosa, watching the front gate of *Casa Serena* with binoculars. The initials, *VH,* on a rusted coat of arms were etched into one of two marble columns at the entrance. A steel chain and lock held the tall iron gates together.

"What a creepy place," Sosa said. "Reminds me of the Bates Motel."

"Yeah, except that Norman's gone, and I don't think he's coming back."

Arrangements were made for Palm Beach PD to continue round-the-clock surveillance of *Casa Serena* on the off-chance that von Hausmann might return. On the way back to Miami, Roth received a call from Palm Beach police chief Ray Miley.

"I wonder where the hell he could be," Miley said. "I'd always heard that he never left *Casa Serena* after his mother died."

Oh, no. He left, sometimes.

CHAPTER

72

Two days later, Roth and Sosa visited Palm Beach's only newspaper to see what else they could learn about Peter von Hausmann. It was there they discovered that his mother, Lois Daniels von Hausmann, had died of a virulent form of breast cancer called invasive ductal carcinoma *one week* before the Wake-Up Rapes began. A front-page story in *The Islander* described how the widow of international shipping magnate Peter von Hausmann II had successfully managed his business for over a quarter century after his death. Running her name on the Web led to a number of major articles in places like *Fortune* and *The Wall Street Journal.*

"What now?" Roth asked, after they left the paper.

"I think it's time we paid a visit to the uncle."

They made an appointment to meet Edgar Daniels late that afternoon at the law offices of Miles, Archer and Daniels, a silk-stocking firm that enjoyed the reputation of having some of the country's most successful personal injury attorneys. Roth phoned Henry Stafford, who agreed to drive up from Miami and join them.

* *

A secretary explained that Daniels was in a meeting but would be with them shortly. She led Sosa, Roth and Stafford to a tastefully appointed conference room. Fourteen, high-backed, leather chairs were arranged around a polished walnut table with lozenge-shaped green lamps. A pen and tablet were neatly aligned in front of each seat. Roth guessed that strategies on a great many high profile cases had been plotted here by the partners of Miles, Archer and Daniels. The pendulum of an old Regulator clock marked the passing seconds with sharp clicks.

Edgar Daniels entered the room in a well-tailored, charcoal gray suit, backlit by the ocean across the two-lane highway. He was a wintry little man in his late fifties with hard eyes and wispy gray hair. He introduced himself in a businesslike voice that betrayed concern.

"I assume you're here to tell me that Peter has been arrested again," he said resignedly.

"No," Maria replied. "Do you have any idea where he is?"

The attorney shook his head. He peered at them warily from behind his glasses, obviously curious as to the reason for their presence.

"What do you want with him?" he asked.

"He's hurt some people," Roth answered.

"Peter? That's preposterous. He wouldn't harm a fly. He's the gentlest person I've ever known."

"When was the last time you saw him?" Sosa asked.

"At his mother's funeral in November."

Dr. Stafford's eyebrows slanted in a frown. "How did he seem then?" he inquired.

Daniels' face darkened. "He was in a terrible state. He showed up drunk."

"Does he have a drinking problem?" the psychiatrist asked.

"I'd never known him to take a drop of liquor before then."

"Besides being intoxicated, was there anything else about him that day that was unusual?"

Daniels took a deep breath and let it out. "He made quite a scene at the cemetery. He threw himself on the coffin and wouldn't let them lower it. When Father McHugh tried to comfort him, he pulled away and cursed him. He shouted that we were all fools, that the Church was nothing but lies."

"Had you ever heard him express anger toward the Catholic Church before?" Stafford asked.

"Never! He was very religious, even as a child. He always wanted to become a priest. I think he would have if it hadn't been for Lois. She was dead set against him entering the seminary. That's why he went to M.I.T.

She insisted that he study something practical. His father had started out as an engineer."

The psychiatrist adjusted his glasses. "What was Peter's relationship with his father like?"

Daniels' eyes wandered toward the ocean. "There really wasn't any. He died of a heart attack when the boy was only four or five. I doubt that Peter has much memory of him."

"Did his mother ever remarry?"

"No."

"How did she and Peter get along?"

"The two of them were very close, perhaps too close."

"In what way?"

"You'd never know it to look at him today, but Peter was in frail health when he was growing up. He had severe asthma. Lois was afraid to let him do things, like go to school with other children or roughhouse with them. She was worried he might get hurt. He was her only child." He fingered the fob on his gold watch chain. "So, she arranged for tutors to come to *Casa Serena*. He took all of his education right there."

Roth was beginning to understand the genesis of Peter von Hausmann's hostility toward professional women. His mother apparently micromanaged every aspect of her son's life. From what he had read about her, she ran von Hausmann International with the same kind of intrusive iron will.

"Peter was truly a wunderkind. He was inducted into MENSA when he was only nine with a recorded IQ of 165. By the time he was twelve, he'd mastered a half dozen foreign languages. When he was around sixteen he beat a former national chess champion who was visiting *Casa Serena*. Lois was so proud of him. She insisted that he excel at everything he did. My sister was a woman who had no tolerance for any kind of failure."

"What about his friends when he was growing up?" Stafford asked.

"He really didn't have any, except for his tutors and the staff at *Casa Serena*," Daniels said sadly. "I know my sister loved him, but she was too overprotective." He paused, as if searching his memory for an example. "I remember when he was a child, how frightened he was of the summer thunderstorms that rolled in off the ocean. He couldn't sleep during them unless Lois took him to her room and let him spend the night in her bed."

A fatherless boy with an overpowering, unconsciously seductive mother. How terrified he must have been of displeasing her! The role that Lois von Hausmann had played in her son's castration anxiety and resentment of professional women was a powerful one. *She was smothering him. That's why he picked a college so far away from home.*

Sosa said, "Maybe you can fill in some gaps for us. We know about his arrest in Boston just before graduation. What happened to him after he dropped out of M.I.T.?"

"No one knows. He vanished for nearly two years. Lois was frantic. She hired some of the best private detectives in the country, but they couldn't find any trace of him."

That was why he used the name Peter Dietz at St. Stephen's and made up the story about having just graduated from the University of Heidelberg. He didn't want his mother to find him.

"One day, he just showed up back at *Casa Serena*. He refused to say anything about where he'd been or what he'd been doing."

Stafford's eyes narrowed. "Did he seem different after he returned?"

"Oh, yes. Everyone noticed how sullen and distant he was. He began doing peculiar things."

"What sorts of things?" Stafford asked.

"One of the maids came across a traffic citation from the highway patrol while she was cleaning his room. Lois couldn't believe it. The ticket was for driving over a hundred miles an hour on the Interstate at two in the morning—on a motorcycle, of all things! He said it belonged to a friend in Miami. Lois was afraid he'd kill himself in an accident. She made him swear that he'd never ride it again. We all tried to talk him into going back to M.I.T. and finishing his degree, but he wouldn't consider it." He paused to collect his thoughts.

"Sometimes, he'd seem like his old self for a while. Then, without warning, everything about him would change. He began staying out at all hours and bringing unsavory characters home with him. Rough-looking men. Lord knows where he found them! He'd have violent outbursts of temper if we tried to talk to him about what was happening."

"Did anyone try to get him into therapy?" Stafford asked.

"Many times, but he wouldn't go." Edgar Daniels shook his head. "His language was so vile sometimes. It didn't matter who was around. There were periods when he would vanish for days at a time. No one had any idea where he was. When he was home, he seldom left his room. None of us ever saw him at mass again after he returned to the island."

Dr. Stafford leaned back in his chair. "Are you aware of anything in his background that was especially upsetting to him?"

Daniels went to the window and angled the blinds to reduce the glare. He stared at the ocean for a long moment. "When he was a child, Peter had a piano tutor for several years named Phillip Gaston. He was a young Austrian chap who was very popular in Palm Beach. He came to *Casa Serena* twice a week to give him lessons."

On a nineteenth century French Erard.

"Gaston was a gifted pianist, but very eccentric. He insisted on never being disturbed for any reason during Peter's lessons." His voice grew ominous. "One afternoon, a new governess happened to walk into the parlor. She found Gaston and Peter ..." Daniels' eyes shifted to Maria. He was visibly uncomfortable at the prospect of saying what he was about to in the presence of a woman, even if she was a detective.

"Well ... he was *buggering* the boy."

"Can you be more specific?" Stafford said intently. "It's very important that we know exactly what happened."

Daniels returned to his chair and sank heavily into it. "Peter was lying naked, face down, on the sofa. Gaston had gagged him and tied his hands behind his back. He was having anal intercourse with him."

There it was! The moment when young Peter von Hausmann first began to associate sexual pleasure with the infliction of pain.

"Lois was out of the country on business at the time. That was so typical," Daniels said bitterly. "The company always came first. The boy was really raised by a succession of governesses."

"What happened after the rape?" Maria asked.

"Gaston was arrested. Peter had to testify at the trial. It was very hard on him." The muscles in his face tensed. "The day before he was to be sentenced, Gaston hanged himself in his jail cell. Peter was devastated! He blamed himself. I don't think he ever really got over it."

He went to a corner of the room and opened an artfully concealed liquor cabinet. He held up a decanter that was half-filled with brandy. "I realize it's a little early," he said awkwardly, "but, if you'll indulge me ..."

He poured two fingers of brandy in a glass and took a long swallow. "Lois never forgave herself for allowing Gaston to be alone with Peter so much of the time. Besides the piano lessons, he had also started doing things like taking him to the movies and on camping trips. Peter was so shy. Lois thought it was good for him to get out from time to time with a responsible adult." He sighed. "I'm afraid we were all taken in by Gaston."

He drained his glass and put it down. "When the police searched his apartment, they found torture equipment along with pornographic pictures he had taken of children. There were a number of photos of Peter."

He sighed heavily. "My sister was never able to accept the fact that she had unwittingly played a part in the formation of his...." He paused, lowering his eyes " ... condition," he added in a subdued voice.

"Even after his arrest in that dreadful bar, she insisted that he must have been entrapped by the police." He twisted a cufflink absently. "She sent me to Boston with marching orders to find the best criminal lawyer in the city and fight the charges."

"Did you?" Roth asked.

Daniels wagged his head. "Peter would have none of it. He insisted that everything in the officer's report was true. He said he deserved to be punished. I tried to persuade him to call his mother after we got him out of jail, but he wouldn't. He said he needed time to think. The day after he was placed on probation, he disappeared."

Daniels' face was slightly flushed from the brandy. "By the time he returned to Palm Beach, Lois had already been diagnosed with cancer. He never left her side for the next four years. The day she died, he let the entire staff go and moved into her room. He's been alone at *Casa Serena* ever since."

No. Not really alone.

Roth listened attentively while the psychiatrist explored other areas. It didn't take a classically-trained psychoanalyst like Henry Stafford to realize what had happened: von Hausmann's anger at being deserted by his domineering mother, through her death, had been displaced onto other professional women in a series of sadistic rapes committed by his alter ego, Jan. That much was now clear. But, there were other things Roth still didn't understand. The most nettlesome one was why the Wake-Up Rapist was attacking professional women so far from his home. The question kept rolling around in the back of his mind, demanding an answer.

He scanned his notes. "Mr. Daniels," he said abruptly, "do you know if Peter ever visited Heidelberg?"

"Why ... yes," he replied, visibly surprised at the question. "He spent a semester there during his junior year. The Math Department at M.I.T. had an exchange program with the University of Heidelberg."

Inspector Kettler had mentioned that St. Stephen's Monastery was nestled high in the hills above Heidelberg. Peter must have gazed longingly at it during those months in Germany, imagining himself safely behind its walls, beyond the reach of his mother and insulated from the compulsion that drove him to SM bars like The Rocket.

"Peter has always had a great fondness for Germany," Daniels told them. "His grandfather emigrated from Berlin to New York in the early 1900's. He started a small shipping company that his son inherited. After the death of Peter's father, Lois took over as CEO of von Hausmann International. She was the one who really built it into what it is today. She left Peter all of her stock in V.H.I.—close to half a billion dollars' worth."

A smile tipped the corners of his mouth. "Peter never had any interest in business. He had me liquidate all of his shares and set up a non-profit foundation in Lois' name shortly after she died. He seems determined to use his entire fortune to relieve suffering throughout the world. That's all very commendable, of course, but...," he stared at the backs of his hands, letting the sentence trail off.

Roth asked, "Did Peter ever talk about Hitler and the Nazis?"

"Oh, yes, quite often. He despised them for what they did to the Jews, as well as to Germany. I remember he visited the concentration camp at Dachau during the summer he was in Heidelberg. He called me late that night, crying." The lawyer's voice dropped to little more than a whisper. "He kept saying, 'How could they have done it? How could they?'"

"One of his first acts, after establishing the Lois von Hausmann Foundation, was to donate a million dollars to the Holocaust Memorial Fund, and another million to the Jewish Anti-Defamation League. The letter he sent with the checks said that, while he realized nothing could ever compensate the Jewish people for the suffering they had endured, he believed that every person of German ancestry had an obligation to do whatever they could to assure that the world never forgot what the Nazis had done."

Daniels met the eyes of his visitors unflinchingly. "Whatever his personal failings may be, Peter is a man of boundless compassion. He would never harm anyone."

Edgar Daniels was right. Violence was as abhorrent to the Wake-Up Rapist's host personality as it was pleasurable to both of his alter egos.

They were about to leave when Henry Stafford said, "Mr. Daniels, I know you care deeply about your nephew. He needs professional help badly. If we don't find him soon, I'm afraid that both his life and the lives of others will be in great danger."

"I understand," Daniels said solemnly. "I'll contact you immediately if I hear anything."

CHAPTER

73

Kurt sat at the kitchen table polishing the Reich eagle and swastika on the old Luger with a soft white cloth. He burnished the pistol's nickel surface until it gleamed as brightly as it must have on the day the Führer presented it to a Gestapo officer or a high-ranking member of the Party. After loading it, he cradled the gun in his hands, as if it were an icon. For perhaps only a few seconds, the object he was holding had been in the shadow of Greatness. He closed his eyes, feeling the weapon's power surge through him. His thoughts were almost entirely in German now.

He was better today. The flu or whatever it was had passed. The injury to his left arm was also healing nicely. He peeled back one of the adhesive strips that held the bandage on his arm in place and inspected the ugly scarlet furrow that the policewoman's slug had plowed in his flesh. A fraction of an inch deeper and it would have shattered the bone.

"Bastard hure (Mongrel Whore)!" he cried.

Going to the medicine cabinet in the bathroom, he opened a bottle of isopropyl alcohol and slowly poured half of it directly onto the exposed wound. It pleased him that he didn't even flinch, though the pain was exquisite. He could just as easily have been pouring cool water on his arm. The secret to mastering any kind of pain, he had learned as a boy, was simply not minding its presence.

He had read somewhere that the experience of childbirth over thousands of years left females better equipped to cope with physical suffering than males of the species. He wondered how Maria Sosa was at *handling pain. She would need to be strong. Very strong. Soon, she would be in such agony that she would welcome death when it finally came.*

CHAPTER

74

The muffler on the cobalt-blue Miata snarled as Maria climbed quickly through the gears. She usually drove with the top down, but after spending two hours having her hair styled she wasn't about to arrive at Roth's house looking like she'd tangled with a Yazoo mower.

The idea of a weekend meeting to discuss the case didn't even pass the giggle test. She had tucked a latex condom in her purse along with her off-duty gun before leaving home. They both knew what tonight was about. The lime knit top she was wearing showed just enough cleavage to assure the undivided attention of her dinner companion. Sexy but demure. That was the look she was after when she prowled the shops at the mall earlier that day.

Drinks. Small talk. Dinner. She reflected on the time-honored hurdles that had to be vaulted before they got to the real reason for their little get-together. Men and women had been playing variations of the same game for thousands of years. While she usually relished the minutiae of courtship rituals, she was conscious tonight of an imperious longing to feel the scholar's naked body against hers. She told herself that this would be just another in a long line of brief affairs, though nothing about it felt that way.

Never go to bed with a cop. That had always been Rule Number One in her career. Tonight, she was about to violate it for the first time. The fact that Roth wouldn't be on the force much longer provided the rationalization she needed. She sat in the car for a couple of minutes after pulling into his driveway, anxiously checking her makeup.

For all the times she had been here to pick up her partner and drop him off, she had never been inside his house. She saw the bashful look on his face when he answered the door in a pair of cream-colored Dockers and a blue Calvin Klein sports shirt. She noticed the pale band of skin where his wedding ring had been. It was the first time she had seen him without it on.

He stood in the doorway, looking at her.

"Well … are you going to invite me in?"

"Of course!" he said, stepping aside awkwardly.

The living room showed signs of a woman's touch. Lacey white curtains hung in the windows. An antique knitting table sat between a pair of high-backed, English wing chairs covered with chintz. Silver and china service had been set for two on a dark mahogany dining room table. *Sara's pattern.*

They sipped wine in the living room until the steaks were ready. Once the meal was on the table, he dimmed the lights, lit a candle, and slipped in a Cole Porter CD.

Very cozy. Nice start, she thought approvingly while he refilled their glasses with Cabernet Sauvignon.

She noticed a picture on the china cabinet showing a bearded man with a yarmulke in a dark suit at the railing of a ship. Beside him was a willowy woman with white hair. "Your mom and dad?"

He nodded.

"You look a lot like him, just taller. Do you have any brothers or sisters?"

He shook his head and handed her a basket of bread. "How about you?"

"Three brothers and one sister, plus assorted uncles, aunts and cousins. They're all in Miami." Cole Porter segued from *Night and Day* to *In the Still of the Night* on the stereo.

"What's it like to be part of such a large family?"

"Total chaos, but I love it. Every time I see my mother, she reminds me that I'm the only spinster in our clan."

"Being single at your age hardly makes you a spinster. You still have plenty of time."

"I'll drink to that," she smiled, raising her glass.

"*L'cha-im.* To life!" The rims of their glasses made a pinging sound when they touched.

After dinner, she helped him rinse the dishes and stack them in the sink. "Am I going to get the cook's tour?" she asked, drying her hands.

"Sure, but there's really not that much to see." She followed him onto the back porch. He switched on a light, revealing a lush garden filled with yellow shrimp plants, blue plumbagos, angel's trumpets, and bright red bougainvilleas. A birdbath stood in the center of it.

"Oh … it's beautiful!"

Beyond the garden, was a small, kidney-shaped swimming pool ringed by palm trees. "We put the pool in right after we bought the place."

On the walkway near the shallow end, she saw the outline of a child's handprints in the cement. A date and initials were below them. *J.R. Jacob Roth. What was it like to have a child die? And his wife and the baby, too. How did he get through it without losing his mind?* Still wearing a ring after four years. He must have had it so bad for her.

Nine Lives appeared and began circling her legs with its tail in the air.

The cat began purring when she picked it up. "Hey, I think he likes me!"

"He likes everybody. You could be walking off with the TV, and he'd jump on top of it, begging to be held."

Back inside the house, he led her into the master bedroom where a colorful quilt was spread on an antique double bed. A maple rocking chair and a full-length dressing mirror stood on either side of it. She touched one of the bed's ornately carved posts. "This is lovely. It must be very old."

"It belonged to Sara's great-grandmother."

Sara again. She could feel her presence everywhere.

She moved her hand on the bedpost to where it brushed his. He held her eyes for a long moment.

"Have I told you that you look really lovely tonight?"

"You have now," she smiled. "Thanks."

"I … uh … haven't shown you my study yet."

She had tried to imagine what his study looked like during their after-hours phone conversations about the case. It was the only room she had been in that had a distinctly masculine flavor. A roll-top desk sat in the middle of the cedar plank floor. Next to it was an old world leather globe imprinted with signs of the Zodiac. The floor to ceiling bookcase was filled with hardbacks. A rolling ladder on a track gave her the feeling of having just entered a library.

"How about some cognac?"

"Sure."

While he was gone, her eyes moved across the rows of books. *Descartes. Pascal. Dante. Virgil. Aristotle.* She touched her chin inquiringly when he returned with two short-stemmed goblets. "Everything here seems to be philosophy. Where's all the crime stuff?"

"At the university," he replied, handing her a glass. "I started out as a philosophy major. It's still my first love."

She put her drink down and took a volume from the shelf.

"Good choice," he said. " Thomas Aquinas has always been one of my favorites."

"What's the *Summa Theologica*?"

He stepped behind her and turned a couple of pages. "It was Aquinas' attempt as a medieval scholar to reconcile religious faith and reason. He developed a series of logical arguments for ..."

"For what?"

He put his hands on her shoulders and turned her gently toward him. "I don't want to talk about philosophy tonight."

"No?" she said in a silky voice. "Oh, that's right. We're supposed to be discussing the case, aren't we?"

He braced his hands against the bookcase, encircling her in the cage of his arms.

Her body tingled when his lips grazed her cheek. "If I kiss you, are you going to throw me on the ground the way you did Vincent?"

"There's only one way to find out. If you're really worried, I've got some cuffs in my purse."

The *Summa Theologica* tumbled from her hands as their mouths found each other. They kissed hungrily against the bookcase for several minutes, all the longing that had been building inside them suddenly released. He slipped the straps of her blouse over her shoulders and began fumbling with the back of her bra.

"The snap's in the front!" she said breathlessly.

He clung to the shelf, running his tongue around one of her nipples, while trying to support her back with his other hand; inexorably, gravity had its way. They slid to the floor, dislodging a copy of Homer's *Illiad* and Hume's *Essay on Human Understanding* on the way down.

The bedroom, like the condom in her purse, may as well have been miles away, given the urgency that consumed them both. A button popped off his shirt as she hurriedly undid it. He unzipped her skirt, pulling it off along with the blue lace bikini panties, and began kissing her thighs. She was wet by the time his mouth reached the dark triangle between her legs. For the next half hour, their bodies ebbed and flowed in the rhythm of lovemaking. He moved slowly, tentatively inside her at first. She wrapped her legs around him, coaxing him deeper with her hips. Toward the end, she shifted astride him, throwing her head back with a sharp cry of pleasure just before he came. Afterward, they lay entwined on the floor, still breathing hard, their bodies damp with sweat.

He touched her cheek with the back of his hand. "Did I hurt you?" She nuzzled her head against his shoulder.

"No. It's just been a while. I'm a little sore. *Tue tienes un pene muy grande!*" she whispered.

He propped himself on an elbow. "What does that mean?"

She giggled. "I'm not going to tell you."

"Come on. That's not fair. I don't speak Hebrew around you."

She made a zipping motion on her mouth.

"Alright, you asked for it!" He sprang onto her, digging his fingers into her ribs. She flailed from side to side, laughing hysterically. "Better tell!"

"Okay! Por Dios! Stop! You'll make me pee!"

He knelt over her, pinning her wrists to the floor. The sight of his naked body looming above hers and the strength of his grip delighted her.

"I said that you have a *huge cock*! For a guy your size … well, it was a pleasant surprise."

He rolled onto his back, putting his hands behind his head. "All Jewish men have large *shlangs*," he said casually. "You didn't know that?"

"You've got your stereotypes mixed up. That's supposed to be black men!"

His face broke into an easy grin. "Listen; with all the negative stereotypes Jews have been saddled with for centuries, whenever I see a positive one, I go for it."

Later that night, they watched stars in the clear subtropical sky through a roof window above the antique bed and fell asleep in each other's arms. It was nearly two when she awoke.

"It's late. I should go."

She went to the study and began gathering her clothes in the faint light from the hallway. He wrapped his arms around her waist, kissing her neck as she sleepily fastened her blouse.

"Don't go," he said plaintively. "I make a great Denver omelet. We can have breakfast in bed in the morning and read the Sunday paper."

Is that what you and Sara did?

"Sounds like you want to play house, David." Their eyes met and held.

"I do, with you."

CHAPTER

75

He usually spent a great deal of time thinking about what kind of trophy he would take from each woman's home. It had to be just the right thing to memorialize the coming event. Hours sometimes passed during his pre-attack burglaries as he went through drawers and closets, vacillating between different objects. Today was different. He knew exactly what he wanted the moment he saw it. With the others, he had taken care to leave no sign of his presence during the fetishistic burglary, fearing that they might run, but he wanted this woman to know he had been in her home and was coming for her soon. He stared at the open drawer beside her bed, masturbating over it until ejaculate pulsed from his body.

He had followed her through the mall the afternoon before, all but invisible in the throng of Saturday shoppers. That evening, he trailed her again to the house where she spent the night. He was about to leave her apartment with his prize when he was startled by the sound of a key in the door. He hadn't expected her home this early! Moving quickly to the bedroom closet, he stepped inside and shut it, watching Maria Sosa through one of the louver slits when she entered the room. She took off her earrings and began undressing, draping her skirt over an easy chair at the foot of the bed. He clutched the loaded Glock he had taken from her nightstand drawer, thrilled by the opportunity that had just presented itself. He would kill her with the very gun she shot him with.

She tossed her bra in a hamper and slid her panties over her hips. His chest began to tighten the moment he saw her naked groin. The gate of hell itself! He squeezed his eyes shut, fearing an asthma attack. When she looked again, she had moved into the bathroom. He could hear *the sound of water splashing in the tub through the open door. Easing out of the closet, he crept across the carpet. He was less than six feet from her now, his heart hammering in his chest. She was in the tub with her back to him and her feet propped on either side of the running faucet, singing softly to herself in the mist of steam. He raised the Glock and pointed it at the back of her head, imagining the water turning scarlet when the slug slammed into her brain. No. Wait! People in the building would hear the shot. He was on the nineteenth floor. The police could be here before he was able to escape. Besides, it was too quick a death. He wanted her to die slowly, and he wanted Roth to watch. That would take some planning. He took his finger off the fetish's trigger and backed quietly out of the apartment.*

CHAPTER

76

Maria Sosa glanced at her watch and took a last swallow of coffee. It was almost eight. She was running late this morning. A cry escaped her lips when she opened the drawer beside her bed. The black leather holster that should have held her Glock was empty and covered with stains that gave off a faint chlorine like odor. *Semen.* "Oh … my God, no!

*   *

The burglary of her home and the theft of her service weapon was itself a kind of rape. She felt violated, defiled by the bizarre nature of the crime. There was no mistaking the message of the fetishistic burglary at her condo: von Hausmann wanted her to know that he had targeted her too for torture and death, and that being a cop wouldn't stop him from getting her.

The members of the SBU were gathered in the briefing room for their regular weekly meeting when she entered. She couldn't stop thinking about the Glock and what von Hausmann might do with it before they got him. Losing a gun to a crazed killer had to be every cop's worst nightmare. Looking around the room, she wondered if the stress she was under was beginning to show. Every detective in the room was conditioned by training and experience to pick up on subtle signs of a person's emotional state. They were all watching her closely.

She made eye contact with Roth for an instant, and then looked away with a twinge of guilt. They had spent every night together at his home since the burglary at her place. She could easily have stayed with any number of girlfriends who were cops or even with her family, but she wanted to be with him. On days like today, she berated herself for starting the affair, knowing at the same time she was powerless to end it. She was already falling in love with Roth. She'd been a cop long enough to appreciate how dangerous the emotions churning inside her were. It didn't matter that he would be leaving MPD soon. None of this should be happening, not in a job where lives were at stake.

They both knew that the sensible thing to do was to put their personal relationship on hold until he was back at the university; but, the chemistry between them was too strong to allow that to happen. She thought of the night they first made love at Roth's home. While he was probably the last guy on the planet she'd worry about contracting an STD from, suppose she got pregnant? She tried to reassure herself that the chances of that happening from a single unprotected act of intercourse were small. Damn! She had always been so careful when it came to contraception— until that evening.

A knocked-up, unmarried new lieutenant in charge of the Sexual Battery Unit? Even with a police administrator as liberal as Chief Crenshaw, that would be pushing the envelope. If Cochran and Fladd from IA found out that Roth was her lover, the whole "fraternization rule" issue would resurface with a vengeance. It would be bad enough if he were assigned to another division, instead of being a high profile subordinate working directly for her. If their relationship was discovered, she could forget the lieutenancy and her hope of succeeding Wilcox as head of CID. She'd be lucky to wind up riding a desk as a uniformed sergeant in the records division when the shit storm was over.

CHAPTER

77

St. Andrew's Catholic Church in Palm Beach was nearly empty. Rows of ivory-colored candles flickered beneath statues of the Blessed Virgin, the infant Jesus and St. Joseph in three of its alcoves. A large, redwood crucifix hung suspended above the marble altar. Bright sunlight streamed through stained glass windows on either side of the aisles. A few people waited patiently in line to enter one of two cubicles to have their confessions heard. A lone man knelt in one of the pews with his head bowed and his hands clasped in prayer. When the last of the penitents had left, he walked quickly into the confessional.

Kneeling, he made the sign of the cross when the window slid open. Even in the subdued light, Peter von Hausmann recognized the familiar profile and receding hairline of Father Timothy McHugh. He had been coming here to tell his sins to him since he was a small boy.

"Please, bless me, Father, for I have sinned. It has been ... almost five years since my last confession," he said a halting voice. He suddenly stopped speaking. Sobs shook his body.

The priest brought his face closer to the window. "What's troubling you, son?" he said, in an Irish brogue undiminished by nearly fifty years in the states.

"Father, I've done terrible things ... unspeakably evil things." He buried his hands in his face.

"Whatever you've done, our Lord will forgive you. His compassion is infinite. Remember how he forgave his enemies, even as he hung dying on the cross."

The confessional was silent for several seconds. "Father, it's me. Peter ... Peter von Hausmann."

"Peter! Where have you been? I haven't seen you since ..."

"I need your help!"

"What's wrong?"

Peter drew the back of his hand across his nose. "There's a woman named Rhonda Buckner in Miami Springs who's going to be tortured and murdered on May 11th."

"How do you know this?" McHugh said gravely.

"The person who's going to do it told me. He plans to kill a lot of other people around the same time"

"Good Lord! Have you called the police?"

"I can't," Peter gulped.

"Why not?"

"He ... he won't let me."

"Who won't?"

There was no reply.

"I'll take you myself," McHugh said determinedly. "We'll go right now."

Peter brought his face close to the window. "Father ... you don't understand! Please, I don't have much time," he said urgently.

"What do you want me to do?"

"Get hold of Detective David Roth at the Miami Police Department. Tell him that the person they're after is Kurt Mueller. He lives in Delmar at the Regency ... Oh, God!"

"What's wrong, Peter?"

A groan escaped Peter von Hausmann's lips. He closed his eyes and pressed his fists against his temples. "Oh ... oh, Father!" he cried in anguish.

"Still (Silence)!" Kurt Mueller's voice roared an instant later.

The alter rushed from the confessional and tore back the velvet curtain that separated him from where the priest was sitting. Father McHugh was able to raise his arthritic frame only a few inches before Mueller seized him by the throat and slammed his head hard against the wall. He grabbed the green and white stole around the priest's neck, quickly twisting it into a noose.

"Sterbe (Die)!" Mueller commanded, in a guttural voice.

Father McHugh's eyes grew wide with fear. He clutched at the strong hands around his throat, staring uncomprehendingly at the familiar face. The alter kept increasing the pressure of his improvised garrote until the elderly priest's body went limp. As soon as McHugh's lifeless form slumped to the floor, he bolted from the confessional, knocking down one of two women who had just entered the church with baskets of flowers. Moments later, he burst through the double doors and disappeared into the street.

CHAPTER

78

The call from Detective Alexandra Green with the Town of Palm Beach Police Department came as a surprise.

"We had a priest strangled at St. Andrews Church on Saturday," she told Sosa." The lab got two good prints from the kneeler in the confessional booth. They match Peter von Hausmann."

*   *

Detective Green and her partner were waiting for Sosa and Roth in an unmarked, beige Chevy when they pulled up in front of St. Andrew's Church. She was a tall, red-haired woman of about forty with an intense, angular face. She and her partner, a stocky man in his thirties, led them into the church. All of the crime scene tape had been removed. The only sign of Saturday's tragedy was a large picture of Father McHugh, surrounded by flowers, in the vestibule.

Green took them to one of two cypress confessionals at the rear of the church.

It was Roth's first time inside a Catholic Church. He bent and examined the area where Father McHugh's body was found. Faint chalk marks were still visible on the floor where it had been.

"We've got two witnesses who came in right after the murder. They both ID'd von Hausmann from a photo line-up as the person who ran from the Church."

Roth roamed down one of the side aisles while Maria spoke with the Palm Beach detectives. He paused beneath a Station of the Cross that showed Jesus being scourged by a Roman soldier with a whip. A look of agony was etched on his face, and his back was covered with bloody stripes. *Pain*, Roth realized, was the common denominator of all three parts of Peter von Hausmann's personality.

After Green and her partner left, Maria sat beside him in one of the pews and showed him the homicide report Green had given her. "Now what is he doing?" she said. "Declaring war on the clergy?"

Roth pondered the latest murder in the case. "He's always been so careful about never leaving his prints at any crime scene. Why, all of a sudden, are they all over the place at a homicide?"

Maria looked back at the confessional booth. "This has every sign of being a spontaneous killing. The fact that he used one of the priest's vestments to strangle him must mean that he came here without a weapon. He didn't even try to hide his face, knowing every cop on the island is looking for him."

Roth gazed at the high, vaulted ceiling. "Neither of the alters would have done anything this reckless. Not even Jan. They wouldn't have any reason to kill the priest, unless ..."

"Unless what?"

"Unless he found out something that was a threat to them. Peter must have gotten out somehow and come here for absolution. He told Father McHugh about the alters. That's why they murdered him."

How strange it was to refer to one person as 'they.'

Roth said, "Now that he realizes we have his prints and know who he is, he may try to leave the country."

"His passport has been revoked, and his picture is at every customs checkpoint," she reminded him.

He looked at the effigy of Christ on the cross above the altar. "That won't stop him from running if he wants to. It all depends on how determined he is to get you and the other women."

CHAPTER

79

Roth found the connection he had been searching for in the response of the six professional women to a single item on his questionnaire. *Describe any publicity you have received as a result of events in either your personal or professional life.*

Curiously, every victim had something written about her in the *Miami Herald* during the year before the Wake-Up attacks began. Roth and Sosa quickly obtained copies of the articles from the *Herald's* Web site.

One story was entitled '*Miami's Mother Teresa*' and dealt with the contribution of Sister Kearney's rescue mission to helping the city's poor. It provided an account of her long missionary career that included information about the murder of her two fellow nuns in Africa.

Another article praised Principal Georgia Griffin for starting an after hours adult literacy program at her school. The courage of Coast Guard Lieutenant Diane Whitaker was recounted in a story that told how she and her crew risked their lives by bucking gale force winds to rescue a family of Cuban refugees after their boat capsized in a storm off Key West. It also mentioned that her father had been a Navy jet pilot who was killed when his plane was shot down near Hanoi.

The rapid rise of Paloma Hidalgo as one of the country's most promising bronze sculptors was discussed in a story called *In the Footsteps of Auguste Rodin*. The smiling face of Dr. Nina Pulaski appeared in a brief piece announcing her appointment as the first female Chief of Staff at St. Joseph's Hospital. Laura Kelce's most recent CD, "Chopin by Moonlight," was featured in the Entertainment section of the paper a few weeks after the Pulaski story.

Sosa finished thumb tacking the last of the articles to the bulletin board in her office.

"Every one of these women is a hard-driven overachiever, just like Peter's mother," she observed. "It doesn't take a shrink to see how these stories would have pushed a hot button in this guy's brain. The death of his mother must have triggered all the rage that had been building inside him for years."

Roth folded his arms, studying the collection of articles on the board. "But why would a Palm Beach recluse pick his victims from newspaper articles about women in a city nearly a hundred miles away. There's something here we're missing."

*   *

They met with the *Features* editor of the *Miami Herald* in his office the following morning. Matt Chambers was a portly man with an iron-gray beard and a harried look.

Sosa told him, "We're working a case involving six Miami women who've been victimized by crimes. Interestingly, all of them have had stories written about them in the *Herald* sometime during the past year."

Roth caught a sudden glimmer of interest in the editor's eyes. "What kind of crimes are we talking about?"

"Oh, nothing very newsworthy," Sosa replied offhandedly. "Just some residential burglaries."

Roth had noticed that she didn't mention they were sexual battery detectives when she showed Chambers her ID.

She handed him the articles and said, "Most of these appeared months apart. We're curious about their connection to the break-ins."

He put on his glasses and scanned the stories.

"Any of them look familiar?" Sosa asked.

Chambers shook his head. "Hell, we run some kind of *Community Features* piece on a woman just about every day."

Roth said, "We were thinking you might have done a story on these ladies as a group, maybe something where you showed their pictures together."

Chambers turned to his computer and entered each name.

"No. Nothing," he reported.

"Are you sure?" Maria said.

"Absolutely!" He took a swallow from a can of Fresca. "I'm a real control freak when it comes to knowing what's going on in my shop. Even when I'm out of town, I proof and sign off on each article by e-mail or fax before it runs. Every *Features* story that's been in the *Herald* for the past fifteen years is here in my database." He bit a crescent out of a half-eaten cheese sandwich on a paper plate.

"This thing really has us baffled," Maria told him. "These ladies live in different parts of the city and have completely unrelated jobs. The *Herald* stories seem to be the only thing they have in common."

Chambers licked a bit of cheese off one of his fingers. "Hmm ... could be a stringer wrote a single story about all of them."

"What's a stringer?" Roth asked.

"That's what we call freelance reporters who scavenge through our copy, looking for things they can recycle into fresh articles. It happens all the time."

Chambers stifled a belch. "A stringer could have pulled all these off our Web site, just the way you did, and cobbled them into a story that your burglar happened to read."

"Who would buy something like that?" Maria asked.

"Just about anybody in the media business: TV, radio stations ... smaller papers out in the 'burbs." He scratched his paunch. "I'd say *Florida Daily Times* is a good possibility. They're notorious stringers. Just about everything they print has been chewed up and spit out at least once by somebody else."

"Is that a magazine?" Roth asked.

"Hardly," Chambers snickered. "We call it the 'Slick Sheet' around here. It's part of that Buick-sized hunk of crapola that winds up in your trash can each week after you finish sorting through the Sunday paper. It's an advertising supplement that goes to newspapers all over the state. You know—tire discounts at Pep Boys, group cruises to the Bahamas, stuff like that. We carry it, too. Their hook is usually some kind of human interest story on the front page."

"How do we get in touch with them?" Maria asked.

"They're located in a strip center on U.S. 1 in Miami Shores." He retrieved the number from his PDA and gave it to them. "It's a real ma and pa operation. The people who own it, Al and Betsy Ambrose, are nice enough— though neither of them is in any danger of winning a Pulitzer any time soon."

CHAPTER

80

It was mid afternoon when Maria finally reached Betsy Ambrose at *Florida Daily Times.*

"Did you happen to do a piece on professional women in Miami sometime last year?" she asked directly.

"Uh-huh. I think it was last summer. Why?"

Maria's pulse quickened. She picked up a pen. "Tell me about it."

"Well ... it dealt with the careers of ten Miami women who've done outstanding things with their lives."

Ten. Maria underlined the number. *Six down—four to go.*

"How did you learn about them?"

"I believe it was through the *Herald's* Web site. Of course, we didn't use anything except their photos. All the writing was our own," she added, a little defensively.

"Do you remember what the story was called?"

"I'm trying to think ... just a minute." Maria heard her say to someone in the background, "Hey, Al, what was the name of that piece we did last summer on the professional gals?"

"On Their Own and On The Move in Miami," a muffled voice replied.

Maria was already writing the name of the article by the time Betsy Ambrose repeated it.

"Do you know if *Florida Daily Times* is carried as an advertising supplement by the *Palm Beach Islander?*"

"Sure is," Ambrose responded, adding proudly, "and twenty-three other papers throughout the state."

"Did you interview these ladies?"

319

"Lord, no! We don't have the time or money to do things like that. There's just the two of us here."

"What can you recall about the women?"

"Well, I know one was a Catholic nun. Another was that pianist. We have some of her music. Oh, what's her name ... Laurin ..."

"Laura Kelce," Maria supplied, adding quickly, "Can you fax me a copy of the story?"

"I wish I could. The computer drive it was on got zapped by lightning during that last bad storm we had. Wiped out everything in our system."

"You must have hard copies of it."

"Of course. I've also got it backed up on a disk. The problem is, we moved recently. Most of our stuff is still boxed up."

"We really need to see that article. How about if my partner and I come over and look for it?"

"Sure, but you're talking about going through maybe fifty boxes," Ambrose warned.

"We'll be there within the hour."

*   *

It was nearly 1 a.m. when Roth backed down a ladder from the loft at *Florida Daily Times* carrying a banker's box full of papers. Seventeen similar boxes were scattered on the floor. He put it down with a groan and stretched. "It's comforting to know that I may have a future with Bekins if criminology doesn't work out." He cut the packing tape on the box with a pen knife and shoved it across the floor to Maria. He was halfway back up the ladder when she jumped up with an envelope.

"David ! I've got it!"

They sat next to each other studying the *Florida Daily Times* story. Ten female faces appeared in a row on the front page below the headline, "On Their Own and On the Move in Miami." Six of them belonged to the professional women who had been attacked so far.

"Meet Peter von Hausmann's next four victims," Maria said, reading the names aloud: "Yvonne Aronson, Terri Johnston, Rhonda Buckner and Rita Emmons."

"But which of them is next?" Roth puzzled. "He hasn't been attacking them in the order the pictures are shown here."

They spent the next hour carefully studying the full page article, trying to learn everything they could about the remaining four women. The story told how Yvonne Aronson had turned Miami's Museum of Natural History into a major tourist attraction shortly after becoming its curator. It also chronicled the mercurial rise of Rita Emmons from an assistant fashion editor at the *St. Petersburg Times* to her present position as president of *Woman's Life* magazine, a Miami-based publication with 2.5 million readers nationwide. Terri Johnston was applauded for transforming the Miami-Dade County Special Olympics into a model for cities all over the country. *Florida Daily Times* recounted how Rhonda Buckner took over a small nursing home that was started by her late husband and built it into a chain of twenty senior care facilities spanning the entire southeast.

"Look at the date on the story," Roth said.

Sunday, November 4

"That was just three days after the death of von Hausmann's mother," he pointed out. "He must have seen the article in the Sunday supplement of *The Islander* and gone ballistic. Jan attacked Sister Kearney the following week."

The article mentioned that all ten women were Miami residents.

"Now we know why all of the attacks were inside the city limits," he said.

Maria's jaw dropped.

"What is it?"

"I see what he's doing!" Her finger skipped back and forth along the line of faces. "First, Bridget … then Diane, followed by Georgia, Laura. Nina … and Paloma. He's attacking them alphabetically by their *first* names."

"Shit! How did we miss that?"

"It was easy. As cops, we get used to thinking of victims by their last names. They're *Kearney, Whitaker,* and *Pulaski* to us, not *Bridget, Diane and Nina*. Every police report I've ever read starts with the victim's last name in caps. That's what we focus on. This is the only time we've seen the victims as a group with their first names beside their pictures."

"His last victim was Paloma," Roth said. "The Tampa police have her at a safe house, so there's no way he can get to her again to finish what he started. That means Rhonda's next." He drew a circle around the face of the CEO of Senior Care, Inc.

A shadow of concern crossed Maria's face. "Her first impulse will be to get out of Miami when we tell her she's been targeted. If she does, he'll know we've figured out his victim sequence."

He began putting the lids back on the storage boxes. "Would you stay and help us if you were her?"

"Are you kidding? You don't know how much I want to run right now!"

CHAPTER

81

The following morning, Maria placed a call to Rhonda Buckner at her office in the AmeriFirst building, telling her she was a detective with the Miami Police Department, and that it was urgent they meet as soon as possible. Buckner wanted to know the reason for the call, but Maria insisted it would be best if they spoke in person. She agreed to meet Sosa and Roth that afternoon at a nearby sandwich shop. They couldn't take the chance of having her come to the department or them going to her home. Von Hausmann would likely be watching her by now, building momentum for his next attack.

Roth recognized Rhonda Buckner the moment she stepped into the foyer of the restaurant. She exuded the confident air of an executive in her conservative, gray business suit and black leather heels. She was a striking, statuesque woman with a cupid's bow mouth and high cheekbones. Blue eyes and blond hair complimented a creamy, unlined complexion that made her look at least ten years younger than the age listed in the story. She reminded Roth of the pictures he had seen of Lois von Hausmann.

Maria drew her to one side, displaying her badge and ID before leading her to a table in the patio area well away from other customers. Buckner slid onto the seat opposite them.

"Okay, now what's all this cloak and dagger business about?" she asked, in a butterscotch drawl.

"We're sexual battery detectives," Maria told her.

"I don't understand. Why do you want to talk to me?"

"I'm sure you've heard of the Wake-Up Rapes," Roth said.

"Sure. Who hasn't?"

Maria said bluntly, "We believe that the man who's been committing them has selected you as his next victim." Rhonda Buckner's face blanched when she saw her picture in the article with a circle around it.

"He's attacked six of these women so far," Roth said.

Panic was building in her eyes now. She twisted the opal ring on her left hand nervously. "I … I have family up north. I can …"

"Running from this guy isn't an option," Maria said. "He followed one woman all the way to Rome and back before assaulting her." She reached across the table and put her hand on Buckner's. "Don't worry. We're not going to let anything happen to you. We know who he is, and we're very close to getting him."

She inclined her head toward a table where McNees and Walker were seated. "Those two men are also officers. We'll have a team like them with you from now on until we arrest him."

Rhonda Buckner was close to tears. "I read that he…." She paused and swallowed hard, " … that he mutilates his victims."

Roth nodded, realizing that they needed to play down the horror. *Cutting. Blinding. Burning.* He was sure she'd bolt out the door if they told her that the Stalker Sadist was also after the police lieutenant who was talking to her. *Goddamnit!* She had a right to know everything, including the certainty that she would die a slow, horrible death if he found a way to get to her. If he was determined and crazy enough to break into the home of the lead cop on the case, what would keep him away from this woman? The assurances they were feeding her bothered him.

"What do you want me to do?"

"Just go about your life each day as if nothing has changed," Maria said. "That's important. He'll be watching you closely."

"When is he …"

"We aren't certain of the exact date yet," Roth said. "If he follows his pattern, it'll be sometime between the fifth and the ninth."

Her nostrils flared in anger. "That's just great! You want to use me as bait, but you don't even know when this is going to happen!"

Roth said, "We know you're scared."

"Scared? I'm fucking petrified!" She opened her purse and removed a pack of Virginia Slims. Her hands were shaking so badly that Roth took her gold lighter and lit the cigarette.

They spent the next half-hour trying to allay each fear she raised. Suppose he decided not to wait until next month and just grabbed her off the street? What if they tried to arrest him, and he began shooting? The two SBU detectives worked together like tennis partners, striking down each concern with glib answers that flew across the table like fast, low returns over a net.

"Your officers could lose me in traffic. Then I'd be …"

"That won't happen," Maria said. She removed a shiny metal disc about the size of a dime from her purse. A narrow chain was attached to it.

"You'll wear this around your neck. It's a tracking device that's tied to a global positioning satellite. Our communications center will always know your location, within a few yards, from the moment you leave here. If you press the button on it, an alert goes out on all our frequencies, giving the nearest street coordinates."

Roth jumped in. "You'll never be alone for a moment from now on. We'll have one officer inside your house each night and another watching the outside."

She seemed to relax a little. By the time the meeting was over, she had agreed to remain in Miami and cooperate with them. Roth watched her leave the restaurant, feeling like a used car salesman struggling with a residual sense of decency after sticking someone with a lemon. If von Hausmann killed her, he wondered how he would be able to live with himself.

CHAPTER

82

Roth was in his robe and slippers in an easy chair in the living room, listening to drops of rain ping against the window panes. He glanced at the clock on the mantle, noting that it was almost 3 a.m. and wondering where von Hausmann was right now. Earlier that day, he spoke again with Peter's former academic advisor who mentioned that von Hausmann had been president of the chess club at M.I.T., and also wrote a term paper during his sophomore year on combinational game theory and chess that won the Dean's Award for Creative Scholarship. The advisor faxed Roth a copy of the paper. Most of it was mathematical gobbledygook that he couldn't begin to understand. He recalled that von Hausmann's uncle told them how Peter had beaten a chess champion as a teenager. He reached down and ran a hand across Nine-Lives' back as Maria entered the room in a pair of silk pajamas.

"What are you doing up so late, amado?"

"Thinking about chess," he said absently as she sat on his lap. He told her what he had learned during his conversation with von Hausmann's advisor.

"What does chess have to do with catching this guy?"

He scratched his head. "Maria, this character is so methodical and systematic in everything he does. I believe he's approaching these attacks like a chess game. Each 'move' is predetermined by an alphanumeric system of some kind that he's worked out. We've discovered half of it."

"The first name sequence."

He nodded. "Now that we know the order of the victims, we have to figure out how he's picking the dates of his 'moves.'"

"What he's doing has always seemed totally random to me. He hits on both odd and even days and weekends as well as weekdays. I've never been able to see any order to it."

"I promise you, there is one. If the attacks were random, they wouldn't be confined the way they are to a five-day period each month," he said, gently stroking her hair.

"Whatever he's doing to come up with the attack dates is generating only single digit numbers on the calendar," he observed.

"Let me get this straight. We're supposed to figure out what kind of system an M.I.T.-educated mathematician is using. I had enough trouble just getting through high school algebra."

"It may not be that difficult," he said, leaning his head against the back of the chair. "Jan set up the attack system long before Kurt appeared. Nothing he does is that sophisticated. The way he's coming up with the assault dates might be as simple as what he did with the first names."

He turned the issue over in his mind for a moment. "Tomorrow, let's make up a spreadsheet with every number on the women that von Hausmann would have had access to: DOB's, addresses, zip codes—everything. He could be doing something like using the first number on their license plates or the last digit of their phones to get his assault dates."

"You're talking about a lot of numbers."

"I know, but if we can't figure out the system, we'll have to do a full-blown stakeout at Buckner's house every night between the fifth and the ninth."

"Okay, we'll give it a try."

She brought her lips close to his ear and guided his hand beneath her pajama tops. "Feel like fooling around?" she asked in a sultry voice.

He took off his glasses. "Hmm ... stay out here with Nine Lives thinking about the case or go to bed with you? Tough choice," he said, kissing her deeply.

CHAPTER

83

The next day, they took Roth's laptop, along with the case files and the *Florida Daily Times* article, to the briefing room and began the tedious task of setting up a spreadsheet on the women.

Late that evening, they were still scrutinizing the rows of numbers. He finally tossed the spreadsheet on the table with a sigh. "This is hopeless. It looks like I was wrong about Jan doing something simple."

"Maybe what we need is a numbers whiz of our own," she threw in.

"It wouldn't do any good. The potential combinations of these figures are infinite. He could be doing something with prime numbers or cube roots that Einstein couldn't spot if he had a hundred years to look for it."

At least the next woman on von Hausmann's list was as safe as the Miami Police Department could make her. McNees and Walker were at Rhonda Buckner's house tonight, one of them inside and the other watching the house from across the street until dawn. Another surveillance team would trade places with them in the morning, trailing her throughout the day from a discrete distance when she left home.

It was almost midnight when they got ready to leave.

Maria said, "I still can't believe that what he was doing with the first names was right there, staring us in the face the whole time."

Her words struck him with full force. "Have you ever heard of *Ockham's Razor*?" he asked, picking up the *Florida Daily Times* article again.

"What's that?"

"It's a principle of logic that says to always look for the simplest explanation of a thing first. If you hear hoof beats, think horses—not zebras. We've been looking for a goddamn zebra in these rows of numbers!" He balled up the spreadsheet and tossed it in a wastebasket.

"What do you mean?"

"It would never occur to Jan to do anything as involved as use a digit from the women's license plates or ZIP codes." He hunched over the *Florida Daily Times* story, running his eyes down the columns of print. "If this is where von Hausmann first saw the victims' names, it must also be where Jan got the numbers for the attack dates."

"*Quiero*, the only numbers in the story are the victims' *ages*. That was one of the first things we checked," she said wearily. "Sister Kearney is seventy-one and she was assaulted on November 8th. The last time I looked, there weren't seventy-one days in that month."

71 ... 71 ... He squeezed her hand. "Seven and one is eight! That's the date he raped her. He's *adding* the digits in their ages to get his attack dates! Look! No combination of numbers in the ages of any of the victims ever adds up to less than five or more than nine. That's why the assaults always fell between the fifth and the ninth. Buckner is forty-seven, so he'll do her on May 11th."

"Where do I fit into this? I wasn't in the story. Why the hell is he after me—because I shot him?"

"It's not just that. You're a professional woman who's trying to control him. That's what his mother did all those years at *Casa Serena*."

* *

The upper level of the police garage was nearly empty by the time they left the building. Their footsteps echoed through the concrete structure on the way to the car. Maria had just put her key in the door when Roth swept her hair to one side and kissed the back of her neck.

"David! The cameras!" she said urgently. The nearest pole-mounted surveillance camera swept a pie-shaped portion of the garage with a soft whir, stopping just short of where they were standing.

"You've made me too observant. We're in a blind spot in Big Brother's eye," he said, putting his arms around her waist.

"You're awful!" she said, shoving him away. "Next thing I know, you'll try to get me on the back seat."

He drew her close to him. "Have you ever made it in a police car?"

She laughed. "You think I'd tell you if I had?" She looked at him for a long moment. When her period started earlier that day, she felt a sense of relief commingled with disappointment.

CHANGE CHAPTER

84

On Monday, Roth and Sosa attended a briefing with twenty-one other officers on the upcoming stakeout at Rhonda Buckner's home. Lieutenant Paul Fitzharris, a buzz-cut man in his late thirties, spoke first. As the department's SWAT commander, he would be the on-site supervisor of the operation. He used a PowerPoint to display an aerial shot and close-ups of Buckner's house on Cutler Court.

"Boys and girls, this is about as sweet a stakeout situation as you could ever hope for. Her place is at the end of a cul-de-sac. He's got just one way in and one way out."

After studying the enlarged photograph on the screen, Roth said, "What about the canal behind the house?"

"I wouldn't worry about that. It's at least fifteen feet deep and thirty feet wide. It's also full of gators. This is their mating season. It'd take a braver bastard than me to dog paddle across it. He used a laser pointer to indicate the rear of the property on one of the photos. "Even if he managed to get across the canal, there's a forty-five degree slope going up to the house. I don't think a goddamn gorilla could climb it. The whole incline's overgrown with Spanish Bayonet and Bougainvillea. Some of the spikes on that shit are over an inch long. You may as well try to wade through a field of razor blades!"

Fitzharris explained that the SWAT team would be concealed in the dense foliage around the two-story house. He and Captain Wilcox would be parked down the block in a van with dark-tinted windows, which would serve as the operation's mobile command post. The same police resources that were deployed citywide on the night Paloma Hidalgo was attacked would now be concentrated in the five-block area surrounding the cul-de-sac. Marked patrol units and a department helicopter would remain well outside the area until the order was given to move in. On the night of the stakeout, Cutler Court would be transformed into a Venus flytrap, waiting to spring shut. The stakeout plan called for Sosa and Roth to be stationed inside the house with Rhonda Buckner. Von Hausmann would be arrested by SWAT the moment he set foot on the property. Roth was relieved at his assignment. There would be no danger of him losing his nerve again the way he had that night at the lake.

CHAPTER

85

Rhonda Buckner kept a scheduled dinner engagement with a couple of out-of-town business clients before returning home around ten. The entire police team was already in place when her burgundy Mercedes pulled into the driveway. Roth watched the filaments of her tail lights die from where he was crouched in the living room. Moments later, the garage door rolled shut.

"All units on Tango Seven perimeter ... the sparrow's in the nest," Lieutenant Fitzharris said over the scrambled tactical channel.

The tension of the officers increased as the hours passed. Everything had to come off as flawlessly as a shuttle launch—from start to finish. Something as simple as the sound of a snapped twig, a barely audible cough or a burst of static from a radio that hadn't been turned down, could mean failure.

Roth knelt on the carpet, watching the street through a small opening in the drawn drapes. A lone car appeared on the block just after midnight and was quickly swallowed by one of the garages. A little after two, he unsnapped his gun when a dog began barking and chased something across the yard.

There were no other signs of movement on Cutler Court as three o'clock approached. His mouth went dry when the secondhand on his watch swept past three. The hour came and went. So did four. Then five. Around six, lights began to turn on in other houses. A few minutes later, his ears registered the hydraulic sound of a trash truck making its rounds.

Lieutenant Fitzharris' voice finally came over the air, giving the order to stand down.

Maria leaned over the upstairs railing. "What happened?" she asked. "Why didn't he show?"

Roth took off his ballistic vest and dropped it on the floor. "I don't know."

CHAPTER

86

100.8°

Kurt Mueller put the thermometer on the nightstand and sat up in bed. He'd been gulping aspirin every few hours for nearly two days and still had a fever. He hugged his arms and shivered, unable to believe that he was sick again. The recurring nature of the malady puzzled him. If it was like last time, he'd feel fine in another day or two. He'd just have to ride it out. He couldn't risk leaving the apartment to visit a Doc-In-a-Box clinic or an ER, not with the police looking everywhere for him.

He never left the apartment now unless it was absolutely necessary. When the boy from the Winn-Dixie arrived with groceries every couple of days, he slipped the money through the mail slot and had him leave the bags on the mat. Whenever he had to leave the apartment, he drove with great care, realizing that he would have to kill any cop who stopped him.

He glared at the calendar on the wall. The return of his illness had forced him to cancel his little visit with Rhonda Buckner on the eleventh. That annoyed him. While he had no interest in the other women on Jan's list, Buckner reminded him so much of Peter's mother. A primitive rage rose in him when he thought of her rushing to her precious luncheons and conferences, too busy for anything or anyone outside herself. He couldn't wait to see the look on her face when he told her what he was going to do to her before he killed her.

CHAPTER

87

Roth and Sosa were exhausted after the stakeout at Rhonda Buckner's. The following weekend, they rented a cottage on a remote stretch of beach at Captiva Island. It was far enough from Miami to afford them a relaxing weekend without having to worry about being seen by anyone from the department.

Late that afternoon, they walked along an expanse of sugar-white beach, holding hands. Sandpipers darted across the hard pack while seagulls squealed high overhead.

"I told my parents about you last night," he said.

"What did they say?" she asked anxiously.

"My mother wanted to know if you were Jewish."

"Oh, God … what did you tell her?"

He grinned. "I said that, with a name like Maria Teresa Sosa, how could you be anything else?"

They laughed. "I want my family to meet you next Sunday. Everyone gathers at my parents' house for brunch after mass. Can you come?"

"Think if I brush up on my Spanish you can pass me off as Cuban?"

They swam out to a sand bar and stood in shoulder-deep water, watching the lights of a cruise ship on the horizon. She put her arms around his neck. "Let's just stay here and never go back!" she said wistfully.

Back at the cottage, they made love and listened to the murmur of the surf until they fell asleep. Late that night, Maria had a dream. In it, she was in a gown at her OB-GYN's, with her feet in stirrups waiting for her annual Pap smear. Instead of the doctor, Peter von Hausmann entered the room in a white lab coat carrying a gym bag. She tried to move but couldn't; her arms and legs were tied to the examining table. Her Glock was on a stainless steel lab tray only a few inches from her fingertips, but she couldn't reach it. She screamed for help but no one came. "You're really going to like this," he smiled, opening the bag and reaching inside.

"No ... no!" she cried, jolting upright in bed. Her face was damp with perspiration.

Suddenly, Roth's arms were around her. He held her close as she lay there in the darkness, trying to get the dream out of her mind.

CHAPTER

88

The weekend at the beach ended too soon. On Monday after work, Roth had just stopped at the market to pick up some things when his cell phone rang.

"Detective Roth!" a man's voice said in a tense whisper.

"Yes ... ?"

"It's Tony Clayton at the gun shop. The guy you're looking for just walked into my store!"

"Stall him!" Roth instructed. "We'll have officers there right away." He disconnected Clayton and dialed 911, cautioning the dispatcher to put the call out on one of the scrambled channels. Delmar was at least twenty minutes away. He ran from the store and jumped in his Volvo. Pushing it as hard as he dared, he cut in and out of traffic, sounding his horn at intersections amid the curses and shouts of other drivers. He could hear Maria's voice on the air over the yelp of her siren. She was nearly as far away from the gun shop as he was. Two patrol cars radioed their arrival at Tony's Gun and Pawn within seconds of each other.

Be careful ... for God's sake ... be careful, he mentally coached the officers who were about to go inside.

A couple of minutes passed before one of the cops came back on the radio. "Miami, be advised suspect is GOA."

Gone on arrival.

Roth hit the steering wheel in frustration. Marked cruisers were crisscrossing the streets around the gun shop by the time he reached it. He found Maria inside, talking to Tony Clayton.

Clayton eyed him like a dog expecting to be beaten. "Detective, I did my best to keep him here. I really did. Something must have spooked him. He was gone when I got off the phone."

"What did he want?" Roth asked.

"Another gun," Clayton told them, flicking his cigarette ash. "An AK-47 this time."

"A *Kalashnikov*?" Maria said, her voice tinged with concern.

The gun shop owner coughed convulsively. "Now that's some serious firepower. Slap a thirty-round magazine in one of those babies, and you got yourself an awesome weapon! I told him I'd have to check in the back to see if I had one in stock. That's when I phoned you."

Maria shook her head disgustedly. "Why do we still let people buy things like that?"

Tony Clayton set his jaw defiantly. "The First Amendment says folks got a right to bear arms."

"That's the Second Amendment," she responded acidly.

"Well ... whatever. The point is that it ain't illegal to sell them."

"That doesn't make it right," she volleyed.

"Did he say anything else?" Roth asked.

"No, sir." Clayton took a fresh cigarette from a pack and lit it with the stub of the one he was smoking. "Damned if his hair wasn't blonde again."

Maria stood beside the open door of her car after leaving the gun shop. "What does the new alter want with an AK-47?" she wondered aloud.

"I don't know, but it sure doesn't have anything to do with the women in the article."

CHAPTER

89

Roth felt the covers being jerked off him. "Wake up, Detective! Time to hit the bricks," Maria said. She was standing naked beside the bed with a cup of coffee. He sat up and rubbed his eyes, gazing at the dark shadow of her pubic hair. The sheets still held the scent of her. He put down the coffee she gave him and ran his hand along the inside of her thigh.

"I can think of a lot more interesting things to do today than play policeman," he said, pulling her onto the bed. She touched his swelling groin and smiled.

"Hold that thought until tonight. I have to leave early and pick up a few things at my place before I go to the office."

"I'll go with you," he said quickly, reaching for his glasses.

"I'll be fine," she assured him. "Don't worry. I'll have a marked unit meet me at the condo."

He caught her reflection in the bathroom mirror as she stepped into the shower. Each day he was more aware of how much he loved her. If anything happened to her....

* *

That evening after dinner, they sat in the living room discussing the case. Roth said in a troubled voice, "The AK-47 just doesn't fit. A modern, Eastern bloc assault rifle is a far cry from a 1939 Einheit Luger." He thought of the Patty Hearst case back in the seventies and the shootout in L.A. between members of the heavily armed Symbionese Liberation Army and the police. Was that what the newest alter was planning: to go out in a pyrrhic blaze of gunfire when he was finally cornered?

Maria said, "I keep wondering why he didn't show up at Rhonda Buck-ner's that night. Maybe he knows we're on to what he's doing."

Roth shook his head. "I don't think so. Whatever kept him away from her on the eleventh, I believe he's still going to come after her." He reminded her of the photos of Lois von Hausmann they had seen. They were both struck by the remarkable resemblance between the next woman on the Wake-Up Rapist's list and Peter von Hausmann's mother. They could have been sisters: they were close to the same age, with the same nose and mouth, the same high cheekbones. Even the color of their hair and the way they wore it were almost identical. He pointed out, "Not only do they look a lot alike, but Rhonda Buckner took over her dead husband's business and built it into a successful corporation, just the way Peter's mother did. She's bound to touch a raw emotional nerve in him. I believe he'll be drawn to her like a moth to a flame."

She drew up her legs on the couch.

"But why go after her, or any of the other women on the list for that matter, when there are plenty of other professional women down here he can assault without the risk?" she asked.

He leaned forward and clasped his hands. "Because compulsion is what drives this guy."

CHAPTER

90

On Wednesday morning, Maria was supposed to testify on the fifth floor of Miami-Dade County Superior Court in an old case that was finally being tried. She walked briskly across the street to the Hall of Justice, discovering when she arrived that all the elevators were tied up on the upper floors. She glanced at her watch. The judge who was hearing the case was a stickler for punctuality and she was already several minutes late. She had climbed a couple of flights when she suddenly heard a noise behind her. A short cry escaped her lips. She turned quickly with her gun half out of its holster, startling an elderly black maintenance man. Moments later, she leaned against the wall and drew a deep breath, realizing for the first time just how scared she was.

* *

She got back from court in time to take the one hundred sixty-first call to come in on the Wake-Up Rapes Hotline. Most of the people who phoned in tips were well intentioned enough, though a few were crackpots. The face depicted in the well-publicized Compusketch had been reported being seen all the way from Seattle to Buffalo.

"I think I know where you can find the man you're looking for," a woman's voice said.

"Uh-huh." Maria replied, only half-listening. She opened the logbook they used to record calls coming in on the taped line. "Okay. Let's start with your name."

"Joan."

"Joan what?"

"Do I have to give my last name?"

"No. It's just that we get a lot of anonymous tips. It's better if we know who we're talking to." Her eyes shifted to the caller ID display: PAY PHONE (305) 871-8420.

"I understand there's a twenty-five thousand dollar reward if you catch him because of what someone tells you."

"It's more than that now. It went up again on Monday."

"Okay ... my name is Saldano. S-A-L-D-A-N-O. Joan Saldano. I manage the Long Leaf Apartments in Delmar."

There had been no mention in the media of any connection between the Wake-Up Rapist and the downscale suburb. Maria spotted Roth walking past her office and waved him inside. *'DELMAR LEAD - LONG LEAF APARTMENTS,'* she wrote hurriedly on a notepad.

"What do you have for me, Joan?" she said eagerly, motioning for Roth to pick up the extension.

"Uh ... well, we had a bathtub overflow on the fifth floor last night from a stopped-up drain. It did a bunch of water damage to the units below. I needed to get in touch with the guy in apartment six this morning to see if his place was okay. He doesn't have a phone and he didn't answer when I knocked, so I let myself in. I'm legally allowed to do that as manager, you know."

"Go on."

"When I got inside, I saw all these newspaper clippings about the Wake-Up Rapes taped to the kitchen wall."

"What does the guy in apartment six look like?"

"Nice looking. Probably mid-twenties. Tall. Well-built. Blond."

"You haven't seen the stuff we've been putting out on TV and in the newspapers about these crimes?"

"Yeah, but I never really thought much about it. The only time I saw the guy up close was the day he checked in. He gave me a couple of months' rent in advance. Paid cash. Sometimes, I see him coming and going on his motorcycle late at night."

Maria flashed Roth a thumb's up.

"When I was in the apartment I noticed a rifle on the couch." The two detectives glanced at each other.

"What kind of rifle?"

"Um … I don't know much about guns. It looked like something you'd see in a war movie. I remember there was a curved piece of metal sticking out of the bottom of it."

A Kalashnikov.

Maria put her hand over the receiver. "Call SWAT!" she mouthed.

Roth put down the phone and rushed from the room.

"There was a piece of paper with some names written on it beside the rifle."

"Where are you right now, Joan?"

"I'm at a coin phone in the Delmar Mall. I was afraid to go home."

"Just stay where you are. I'll have a car pick you up right away," she said, reaching for her radio.

"I'd rather not do that. Can't we just meet somewhere?"

"Sure … you name it."

"How about the Greyhound Station at five. I'll be out back where they load the busses."

Sosa checked her watch. It was only three fifteen.

"Why can't we meet now?"

"I … I can't. I've got to go."

"Wait a minute! How will I know you?" she asked.

"I'm twenty-seven with medium-length brown hair. I'll have on a pair of light blue slacks and a white blouse." The line went dead a moment later.

Roth was back in her office within minutes. "I told Lieutenant Fitzharris what we've got. SWAT should be set up on the place in the next half hour. Walker and McNees are already on their way over there."

"I think we've got him," Sosa said, her heart still pounding.

*   *

Lieutenant Fitzharris sat at one end of the chief's conference table, monitoring the transmissions of his SWAT team at the Long Leaf Apartments through a headphone tucked in one ear.

"What's the situation out there?" Chief Crenshaw asked.

Fitzharris explained to Captain Wilcox and the other detectives assembled in the room with Sosa and Roth that he was certain the suspect's apartment was empty. His team had scanned the walls with a DETEX 'flashlight' shortly after they arrived. Even though the curtains were drawn, the instrument's sixteen-degree radar beam and signal processor would have picked up even faint signs of respiration, as well as the slightest bodily movement inside.

The chief's hands coiled on the table. "I don't want a barricaded gunman situation out there," he said firmly. If you can arrest him out front, fine, but if he so much as farts ..." The chief let the sentence trail off. Fitzharris nodded understanding.

CHAPTER

91

At twenty minutes to five, Roth and Maria headed for the Greyhound station seven blocks away for their meeting with Joan Saldano. He inched along in heavy traffic, wondering how the multiple personality would react when he returned to the apartment and found himself surrounded by heavily armed police. He turned into the bus station and began searching for a parking place while Sosa clutched her hair into a pony tail and fastened it with a barrette.

The Greyhound station was filled with late afternoon travelers as the SBU detectives walked slowly along the loading platform, watching for anyone who matched the description of Joan Saldano.

"She's late," Sosa said worriedly after ten minutes had passed.

"She'll be here," he assured her.

The engines of two of the five gleaming blue and silver busses idled noisily. A line of travelers stretching halfway to the depot waited to board them as announcements blared from a speaker on the side of the building. People filed past them and disappeared into one of the busses: young soldiers and sailors; elderly couples; women with small children. The mode of travel for the poor and near poor.

They scanned the faces on the platform as the boarding line briefly came to a stop. A girl of about four with blond hair tied in ribbons held a teddy bear close to her as she looked up at Roth and Maria with emerald-green eyes.

"What's your bear's name, sweetheart?" Maria asked.

The child pressed against the leg of a pretty woman in her mid-twenties with the same striking eyes, hooking a finger on a baby tooth and looking at the ground.

"It's alright, Julia, tell her."

"His name is Boo," she said shyly, swaying from side to side.

Maria touched the child's soft hair. "Where are you and Boo going, Julia?"

"To Semma … to see Grandma."

"Julia, say Selma," her mother told her.

"I just did, Mommy," she protested. "Semma!"

A ripple of laughter came from the people around them.

"I want one just like her," Maria said. "First, a girl, then—"

Her body suddenly lurched backward, as if an invisible fist had struck her. The echo of the rifle shot registered in Roth's mind an instant after the slug ripped into the left side of Maria's chest. As she was falling, a second bullet struck the forehead of the woman with the child. Her skull exploded like a watermelon dropped from a great height onto the pavement, spraying Roth with blood and gray brain tissue. She crumpled like a rag doll onto the tarmac. Reflexively, he threw himself on the ground and covered his head.

Crraacckk. Craacckkk. Craaackkk. Craacckkk.

Bullets lashed the loading platform around them. The front of Maria's linen jacket was crimson. He grabbed one of her arms and dragged her behind a large, terra cotta planter. People everywhere were screaming and running.

Craackk. Craackkk. Craackk. Craackk. Beeeyowww. Beeeyoww. Ricochets whined through the air, shattering the windows of parked busses and making hollow sounds as they punched holes in their aluminum sides. He pressed his face against the hot tarmac. His fingers clawed helplessly at the ground, as if he might dig a hole deep enough to swallow them both. For a few seconds, everything around him was spinning and blurred.

A moment later, he hit the panic button on his radio. As soon as he pressed it, a computer-generated alert tone sounded, followed by the dispatcher's voice.

"714 … what's your emergency?" she said anxiously.

He raised his head just high enough to see the muzzle flashes that were coming from the parking garage across the street. He ducked when a bullet chipped the planter, spraying him with plaster.

"Miami to 714!" the dispatcher shrilled. "Do you copy?"

He bent over Maria. Blood was coming from her nose and mouth and she was trying to speak. In the panic that engulfed him, he didn't recognize the badge number coming over the air as his. "Maria's been shot!" he yelled into the portable. "People are hurt! We need help!"

Craackk ... craackk ... cracckk ... beyoww ... A bullet skipped off the pavement a couple inches from his left knee. "We ... we've got a sniper ... !" he gasped. "He's firing from the top of the parking garage on McAllister!"

He dropped his radio and drew the Glock, bracing it on top of the planter with unsteady hands. The pistol recoiled and flashed repeatedly as he fired at the top of the garage. He emptied the magazine and was about to reload when he realized that the shooter was easily seventy-five yards away—almost twice the effective range of his service weapon.

Bodies were strewn everywhere on the loading platform; some were writhing in pain. Others lay motionless, twisted in grotesque positions. A man of about twenty in a khaki Marine uniform crawled several feet toward one of the busses before two shots flipped him on his back.

Craackk ... craackk ... crackkk ... craackkk ... crackkk. A stream of bullets stitched the depot's plate glass window. Roth's pulse raced when he saw the child Maria had spoken to. She was standing beside the body of her mother, screaming hysterically. He jumped to his feet and ran to her. She flailed wildly in his arms when he grabbed her and sprinted toward the cover of the nearest bus.

"Take her!" he said, thrusting the girl at a heavyset woman who was huddled behind one of the bus tires. He crouched and ran back onto the platform, yanking the wrist of an elderly black woman who was sprawled on it. After dragging her to cover, he crawled to a man who was lying face down. When he turned him over, he saw that most of his head was gone. He dove behind a pillar as bullets sliced the air around him.

Suddenly, the shooting stopped. *He's reloading.* He seized the opportunity, moving to a bus driver who was crying in pain and holding his bloody thigh. After getting him behind a bus, he made his way back to where Maria was lying. His hands were skinned and bleeding.

She clutched his shirt frantically. "I ... I ... can't ... breathe. Her eyes were wide with fear.

"Help's on the way!" he told her, choking back tears.

Crracck ... crraack ... craacck ... crraack.

"Miami ... we need EMS and SWAT here now!" he shouted into the radio, suddenly realizing that the SWAT team was miles away in Delmar.

The dispatcher said something that didn't register as he rolled up his jacket and put it under Maria's head. He pressed his hand against the wound, trying to stop the flow of blood that kept seeping through his fingers. *Oh, God!* There was so much of it. Each breath she took seemed more labored than the last. She was slipping into unconsciousness.

He took her face in his hands. "Maria, keep looking at me. Don't ..." Her eyes suddenly became vacant and glassy. She wasn't breathing. He covered her mouth with his and blew, tasting the metallic flavor of blood, then interlaced his fingers and began a rhythm of chest compressions and breaths. *One ... two ... three ... four ...*

"Breathe for me, Maria! Please breathe!" he pled, knowing she couldn't hear him and that brain death was only a couple of minutes away. Suddenly, she coughed and began breathing.

Police cars and ambulances were now streaming into the parking lot. Two paramedics ran to Maria while EMS crews triaged the other victims scattered across the tarmac. Her skin was cold and pale when Roth let go of her hand and stepped back to make room for the medics.

One of the paramedics located a faint, rapid pulse in Maria's neck and quickly put a blood pressure cuff on her arm. "We've got a collapsed lung," he reported moments later. The endotracheal tube they placed down her throat began to suck red fluid. "Better get Trauma Hawk on the way, stat," the paramedic said. "She's too critical to risk a ground transport in all this goddamn traffic!"

A police helicopter was already overhead, its blades slapping the humid air above the parking garage. The paramedics hurriedly placed Maria in military, anti-shock trousers and inflated the rubber bladders in the legs and abdomen. Roth watched them place a cervical collar on her neck to keep her airway open and guard against the possibility of spinal injury.

Ambulances were still arriving. The bus platform looked like footage of a terrorist attack on the evening news. TV crews scrambled out of vans with satellite uplink equipment on their roofs and began unpacking gear, while uniformed officers kept the large crowd of onlookers back. An evidence team was already busy cordoning off the area around the depot with crime scene tape.

Minutes later, a Trauma Hawk chopper glided into the bus station lot as the paramedics attached an EKG strip to Maria's chest and carefully transferred her to a gurney. Roth started to follow them to the helicopter when he felt a restraining hand on his arm.

"Homicide's on the way," a uniformed lieutenant told him. "You'll have to wait for them! They'll want to ..."

He jerked away. "She's my partner!" he said with a catch in his voice. "I have to stay with her."

The lieutenant hesitated for a moment, and then nodded. "Okay. Go ahead. They can talk to you at the hospital."

Roth ran to where the waiting helicopter sat with its blades violently churning the air and jumped aboard.

CHAPTER

92

Lieutenant Maria Sosa's blood pressure was close to zero by the time she reached Mercy Hospital and was rushed into emergency surgery. Roth and a number of other officers kept a vigil in the lobby beyond the operating room. His white shirt and tan slacks were covered with rust-colored bloodstains. He stared numbly at the cuts and gunpowder residue on his hands.

Images from the bus station kept floating in and out of his mind: the little girl with the blond curls and the teddy bear; the bodies on the tarmac and the ground receding when the Trauma Hawk lifted off from the parking lot; the look on Maria's face as she fought for each breath.

The memory of the day his wife and son were killed came crashing down on him. Tears welled in his eyes. *Oh, please … no! Not again!* He rushed to the men's room and knelt in one of the stalls, retching. His hands were shaking when he returned to the waiting room; he kept pressing them against his legs, trying to control the tremor.

Captain Wilcox arrived within the hour with Miguel and Carmen Sosa. The CID commander had gone directly to the home of Maria's parents as soon as word of the shooting reached him. Roth introduced himself awkwardly, not knowing what to say. His throat drew into a knot when Maria's mother put her arms around him and began to cry. Before long, Maria's sister and brothers began arriving with their families.

Hours passed with still no news of her condition. Roth kept going over the events leading up to the shooting in his mind—dissecting it all, trying to make sense of it. Jan was incapable of the kind of methodical planning it had taken to draw them into the trap. How had Kurt persuaded the woman who called herself Joan Saldano to become an accessory to murder? She had to have been carefully coached before she made the call.

The massacre at the Greyhound station hadn't taken any great skill. Maria had told him the day von Hausmann tried to buy the Kalashnikov that even an average shooter with a rifle and a six power scope would have no trouble grouping shots in a circle the size of a tea cup at a hundred yards.

Why am I still alive? The question kept intruding itself into his thoughts. He recalled the number of times he had abandoned cover to run or crawl back onto the loading platform. Each time, he had exposed himself to the sniper's fire. Von Hausmann let him live for some reason.

He looked up when he felt the weight of a hand on his shoulder. It was Sgt. Joe Akervik, his nemesis from the police academy.

"If there's anything you need ..." Akervik said. "Anything at all ..."

"Thanks," Roth replied in a voice that was just above a whisper.

Forty-five minutes later the department chaplain arrived and asked if he wanted to join him for a prayer in the hospital's non-denominational chapel. Roth explained that homicide was on the way and he needed to wait for them. After the chaplain left, he closed his eyes and tried to remember the words to an old Hebrew prayer he had learned as a child.

A couple of homicide detectives got off the elevator a few minutes later. One of them, a weary-looking Latino, handed Roth his bloody jacket and radio. The men from homicide shared what little they knew at this point. Officers had swarmed through the parking garage, searching for the sniper, while Maria was being airlifted to Mercy Hospital. A total of forty-seven spent 7.62 X 39 military surplus cartridges and an empty magazine were found on the roof. The assault rifle they came from could have been purchased at any number of gun shops in the Miami area. Eleven people were killed outright at the Greyhound station and another thirteen seriously wounded. Men. Women. Children. The shootings appeared to be completely random.

Within minutes of Roth's frantic call for help, SWAT kicked in the front door of what proved to be an empty unit at the Long Leaf Apartments. The elderly couple who managed the building had never heard of anyone named Joan Saldano.

A gray-haired man in a black suit and Roman collar got off the elevator while Roth was talking to the detectives. As a young priest, Father Juan Aguilar had baptized Maria. Now, he had come to administer the last rites of the Catholic Church to her. He embraced both of her parents and said something in Spanish to them before being led by a nurse through the double doors.

The hospital lobby crackled with police radios that had been turned down. Every few minutes, another cop arrived and asked the same question that was on everyone's mind: Was she going to make it? Police and family members converged on a man in a green surgical smock as soon as he emerged from the operating room; a white mask dangled against a semicircle of sweat on his chest. The thoracic surgeon explained that Maria had survived the ordeal. The operation had lasted nearly six hours and took a total of ten units of blood. While she was still in critical condition, the worst was over.

A nurse led Roth and the Sosas to the recovery room where Maria had been taken after surgery. Carmen Sosa wiped tears from her eyes when she saw her daughter. A cadaverous pallor had replaced the normal luster of her skin. A respirator made a pulsing sound as it cycled oxygen into her lungs and waveforms drifted across a radium-green oscilloscope monitor. After several minutes, the nurse returned and pointed at her watch. Roth remained beside the bed for a minute after Maria's parents left. He bent and kissed her forehead. "It's going to be okay…," he whispered, wondering if it ever would be.

CHAPTER

93

McNees and Walker drove Roth back to the bus station to pick up the *Exxon Valdez* that night. It was almost two a.m. when he got home. As soon as he pulled into the driveway, he noticed that the front door was ajar. At first, he thought he hadn't slammed it hard enough and the wind had blown it open. Then he saw the Star of David that was scratched on the oak surface of the door. He drew his gun and moved onto the porch, carefully entering the house and checking each room and closet. A handwritten note was on the kitchen table:

> *Jude! Rache ist Süß. Ich hoffe doch dass sie gelitten hat bevor sie starb! (Jew! Payback is hell, isn't it? I do hope that she suffered before she died!)*

Now he knew why von Hausmann hadn't killed Maria with a head shot, the way he did the little girl's mother. The multiple personality wanted him to watch her die slowly and painfully. He had obviously taken careful aim with the single shot he fired at her from the parking garage. The surgeon explained that the chest wound had created a *hemothorax*. Blood was being drawn into the pleural cavity between her lung and chest wall, making each breath she took excruciating. The agonizing death von Hausmann had planned would have happened if she had reached the hospital just a little later. Roth started to dial the department and stopped, holding the receiver until the dial tone was replaced by a series of beeps. His mind returned to the child at the bus station. For the rest of her life, she was condemned to watch an endlessly rewinding horror film of her mother's head being blown apart. He stared numbly at the note.

Sooner or later, von Hausmann would be caught. But, what then? *An alter isn't real. It's just a shadow cast by the dominant personality.* Henry Stafford's words came back to him. If he and Maria couldn't help but think of Peter, Jan and Kurt as three separate entities, a jury would likely do the same thing. After hearing the poignant story of Peter's rape as a child, they would learn how he had committed the entire fortune his mother left him to helping others and even banished himself to a monastery in an effort to control his sexual demons. In the end, jurors might well feel sympathy for him, even while despising his alter egos. Any inclination they had to punish him would be tempered by an awareness that nature had already meted out a terrible sentence in the form of AIDS. He could be found not guilty by reason of insanity and eventually be released from psychiatric confinement. Then—in a week, a month, or a year—one or both of the alters would re-emerge and resume killing. The blood of innocent people would be on Roth's hands for not putting an end to the violence when he had the chance.

The note slipped from his fingers and fluttered to the floor. It surprised him that he felt neither bitterness nor anger, only a black emptiness roiling in the core of his being. He knew at that moment that he was going to kill Peter von Hausmann.

*   *

By the following morning, Maria had improved enough to be moved to the Intensive Care Unit. While she was still unconscious and tethered to the respirator, the physician Roth spoke with said that her vital signs were continuing to improve. Since she was clearly the main target of the bus station shooting, two uniformed officers were posted outside her door at all times.

CHAPTER

94

It was the first time Roth had been back to the department since the shooting. Detectives who had barely spoken to him before now pumped his hand warmly and clapped him on the back. The front page *Herald* story of the shootings was prominently displayed on the CID bulletin board. His voice mail held a number of messages from national news organizations, including *Good Morning America, CNN, Newsweek* and *60 Minutes*. All were eager to interview the professor-cop who had risked his life to save others from the sniper.

He went to communications and got a copy of the tape that contained the conversation between Maria and 'Joan Saldano.' Back at his office, he listened closely to it, again and again. Only a few seconds of the tape hinted that something was wrong. When Maria mentioned that the reward had just gone up, 'Joan' didn't ask by how much. In her eagerness to follow the new lead, Maria hadn't picked up on it. Afraid of losing the woman's cooperation, she never pressed her when she insisted she couldn't meet until five o'clock. Von Hausmann obviously wanted to wait until the loading platform was packed with late afternoon travelers before starting his killing frenzy.

If the call had come from a man, they both would have been wary, especially with the new alter's sudden interest in assault rifles. They took the bait because the lead came from a woman who had information about what police call *discrete details*—things about a crime or suspect that haven't been made public. Whoever Joan Saldano really was, she established immediate credibility by describing someone who looked like the man they were after, lived in Delmar and rode a motorcycle. It all went exactly the way von Hausmann had planned, except for one thing: Maria was still alive.

CHAPTER

95

The killings at the bus station completely dominated the next meeting of the Wake-Up Rapes Task Force. *When and where? How many casualties?* Those were the questions on the mind of every cop in the room. Security had already been increased at what were regarded as high-risk locations: shopping centers; Miami International Airport; the coliseum and the downtown courthouse complex, as well as at all major hotels and recreational facilities in the area.

The four remaining professional women on von Hausmann's list never came up at the meeting. Dr. Stafford's opinion mirrored that of the ViCAP profilers who were present. Everyone was certain that von Hausmann's next crime would involve another act of mass violence—everyone except David Roth. He was now more convinced than ever that von Hausmann would continue to regard Rhonda Buckner as an item of unfinished business. A single line from the former M.I.T. student's term paper on combinational game theory in chess stood out in his mind:

> 'The key to checkmating an opponent is a series of precisely determined, contingent moves that keep him off balance and unable to anticipate the direction of future attacks.'

If the police were expecting another mass homicide at any moment, Kurt would confound them by reverting to the individual assault pattern Jan had devised. He would be in no hurry to begin killing strangers again. Watching the police attempt the impossible task of safeguarding the entire city would only appeal to his sadism. He would savor the feeling of power that came from holding so many lives in his hands. The torture

and killing of Rhonda Buckner on the eleventh would catch the author-
ities off balance, just as the Greyhound attack had. After her murder,
while they rushed frantically to protect the remaining women on the list,
von Hausmann would bring his assault rifle back into play in another
grisly attack.

Check and mate in two moves.

There was no way to know where the next sniper event would be. Children playing on a school ground during recess. Sports fans rising in the
stands to cheer their team. Shoppers going to and from their cars at one
of the area's busy malls. Even with every effort being made to protect the
public, the metro area remained a "target rich" environment.

Roth and Maria had been about to propose a second stakeout to Wilcox
when the bus station shooting took place. He had no doubt that the captain would readily agree to another major stakeout if he told him what he
thought was going to happen. The problem was that such an operation
would only lead to von Hausmann's capture, not his death.

Wilcox walked over to him after the meeting. "What do you think about
ending the surveillance on Buckner?" he asked.

"I don't see any reason to continue it," Roth replied without hesitation.
"The Wake-Up attacks are obviously over." He felt a stab of guilt at providing another cop with disinformation, but he had to make sure that no
one got to von Hausmann before he did.

He went immediately from the meeting to Rhonda Buckner's office to
tell her that the protection she had been receiving was about to end. She
was alarmed at first. The stress she had been under showed on her face.

"I'm tired of being afraid." She opened her purse, exposing a Walther
.380 automatic. Her jaw tensed. "I know how to use this," she said determinedly. "If the son-of-a-bitch comes near me, I'll kill him!"

Roth barely slept that night. Knowing the chance he was taking with
Buckner's life tormented him, but he needed her in that house during 'the
darkness of the third hour' on the eleventh. What he was planning had to
seem like a last minute idea. He would call her on the tenth, explaining that
he wanted to watch her home that night, just as a precaution, since it was
exactly one month after the attack date they had uncovered. It was dicey

as hell to wait so late to talk to her, but he had no choice. If she had time to think, she'd probably panic.

If that happened ... He wondered how many more people von Hausmann might kill before he was caught.

CHAPTER

96

After the stakeout on Cutler Court, Roth knew the area around Rhonda Buckner's home reasonably well, but there were still a few details he needed to work out. He went to the house one afternoon while she was at work to check out the burglar alarm she had installed after learning she was to be the rapist's next victim. Von Hausmann would have to disable it before entering. *How long would that take?* He located the alarm panel on the side of the house and inspected the key aperture. He knew very little about burglar alarms but guessed that von Hausmann would need at least five minutes, maybe ten, to deactivate this one. He paced off the distance from the alarm to the corner of the house; it was just over twenty-six feet. In his mind's eye, he began to choreograph what would happen that night.

He would be parked out of sight down the block from midnight on. The steep, thorn-infested slope in the back meant that Rhonda Buckner's assailant would have to approach the house from the street. Once von Hausmann arrived, he would give him enough time to begin working on the alarm before moving to the corner of the house. He shielded his eyes from the bright sunlight, studying the short distance that would separate him from his prey.

While he was a lousy shot, he would have the advantage of surprise and close range. Sixteen bullets in the Glock meant sixteen chances to kill Peter von Hausmann. The concrete wall he would be firing from would afford good cover and he would be wearing a bulletproof vest with steel inserts in it. Even if von Hausmann got off a couple of rounds, it wouldn't matter unless he was lucky enough to hit him in the head or throat.

He would open fire without warning while von Hausmann was pre-occupied with the alarm. As he began shooting, he would yell, *'Police! Drop the gun!'* He had read enough about the unreliability of lay witnesses to be confident that Rhonda Buckner and her neighbors wouldn't be certain which came first—the shots or the shouting.

Plausible deniability. That was all he needed. Any doubt about the shooting would be resolved in his favor, if only because the man he was going to kill was a dangerous felon who had shot a cop.

Around midnight, he would radio dispatch that he was on a surveillance at Buckner's home. His apparently spontaneous decision to watch the house of a woman he felt could be in danger might later raise some questions, but it was clearly within his discretion as a detective. With Maria in the hospital, the most anyone could accuse him of was using poor judgment by not informing Captain Wilcox. *What the hell can they do? Suspend me? Fire me?*

He walked around the outside of the house, grappling with a dilemma: while he didn't want anyone to know what he was planning, he needed a cop inside with Rhonda Buckner, just in case something went terribly wrong. With his newfound popularity in CID, it would have been easy to find a detective to help; yet, telling anyone in criminal investigation about the stakeout would mean that word of it would inevitably reach Wilcox. Once the captain found out what was happening, he would insist on a full SWAT call-out. Then, there would be no … *ambush.*

He brought a hand to his forehead. *My God, what am I doing?* How many times had he told his classes at the university that freedom in any democracy begins to die when the very people charged with enforcing the law begin violating it. He had always believed that. Damnit! He still believed it. His mouth went dry. The state of Florida executed people for what he was about to do. It was known in the parlance of the law as *'murder with special circumstances: lying in wait with a premeditated intent to take the life of another human being.'* Being a cop only made it worse.

His only chance of not committing a capital felony that night would be if von Hausmann made a threatening move before he killed him. Then, it wouldn't be murder. He clung to the thought like a drowning man grabbing at a piece of floating debris.

The eleventh was now only five days away. He returned to his plan. It was essential that he shoot von Hausmann while he was at the alarm box. Bullets entering his body from either the front or side would be consistent with his claim that he fired in self-defense when he saw a gun. If he only managed to wound him, and had to finish him with a coup de grace while he was on the ground, powder fouling and stippling from lead particles seared into his skin would tell the medical examiner what really happened. Ballistic evidence that the fatal wound was inflicted at close range would be supported by the testimony of neighbors who would recall hearing two distinct bursts of gunfire separated by a few seconds. If that happened, Dr. David Roth could well face criminal prosecution for murder.

CHAPTER

97

Maria had been off the respirator for several days now and her condition had been upgraded from *critical* to *stable*. Instead of being asleep or floating in a netherworld of painkillers, the way she had during most of his visits, she was fully awake today. The room was filled with flowers from friends and members of the department.

She managed a faint smile when she saw him. He took her hand in both of his and kissed it.

"You gave us quite a scare," he said, pulling up a chair.

She tried to touch his face but the IV line kept her from moving her arm more than a few inches. "Umm … I've been so out of it … what day is today?" she asked in a thick voice.

"Friday … the sixth."

Her face clouded. "Is the stakeout set up for the eleventh?"

"There isn't going to be one. Rhonda's gone. I guess she went up north to stay with her family. You can hardly blame her after all that's happened."

She winced from a spasm of pain. He elevated the bed slightly, easing another pillow behind her head. He had never lied to her about anything; but he had to now. Just knowing what he intended to do would make her an accessory to the crime.

He told her that Homicide had now virtually taken over the investigation.

She stared blankly out the window. "I can't believe I was so stupid. I should have known the call was a set-up."

They discussed the possible motive of von Hausmann's accomplice and the search that was underway for her. He held a straw to her mouth while she drew a sip of water past her parched lips.

"Just get some rest and don't worry," he said, smoothing the hair back from her face. We'll get him, I promise you."

*   *

On the way home from the hospital, it occurred to him where he could find the help he needed for the eleventh: *Frank Bailey*. The SBU detective who had talked him into the professor-policeman project had recently been transferred to the citywide D.A.R.E. (Drug Abuse Resistance Education) program. He now worked directly out of the school superintendent's office on the north side of the city, far from both Captain Wilcox and CID.

He reached his former student at home that night. After answering his questions about how Maria was doing, he came to the reason for his call.

"I need your help, Frank."

"Sure. Just name it."

"I've got a hunch our guy might come after a woman named Rhonda Buckner at 3 a.m. on the eleventh. It's a real long shot, but I still need someone inside the house with her from midnight to sunup while I watch the street. Can you give me a hand?"

"No problem," Bailey assured him. "I've got some time off coming. I'll just take the eleventh as a comp day. But, why not get more help out there? Two guys aren't enough to handle something like that."

He was right, of course. "It isn't worth calling the troops out for," he said casually. "The truth is that, with Maria off the case, I don't have any other leads to follow right now."

Bailey was silent for a couple of seconds. "Okay, but why don't I cover the front and you take the inside?"

Cops are so careful. Any detective would have made the same offer to someone as inexperienced as he was.

"Believe me, if I really thought this guy was going to show up, that's just where I'd want to be," Roth told him, adding, "This lady happens to be very attractive. I don't think you'll mind babysitting her."

He made arrangements to pick him up at his home at eleven on the night of the surveillance. "By the way," he said, matter-of-factly. "If you talk to Maria, I wouldn't say anything about this. Her doctor wants to keep her mind off work right now. Also, better not tell anyone in CID. I'm really not supposed to be doing anything on my own."

"Gotcha."

CHAPTER

98

Frank Bailey would run outside when he heard the shots. By the time he reached the spot where Roth would be standing over von Hausmann's body, the Einheit Luger would either be in the dead man's hand or on the ground beside him. Bailey would wonder why Roth hadn't radioed as soon as he saw von Hausmann approaching the house. He had that covered. He'd put a dead battery in his portable just before he got out of the car.

* *

That afternoon, he answered his phone at the SBU and heard a woman crying hysterically.

"Ma'am ... please ... calm down. I can't understand you!"

"I did it!" she sobbed. "I'm the one you want!"

Now he recognized her voice from the tape. It was *Joan Saldano*. The caller ID indicated the call was coming from a Motel Six on Orange Blossom Trail in Orlando, one hundred and fifty miles away.

"I ... I got all those people killed!" she slurred.

Drunk.

"I just want to die!"

"Who are you? Why did you set us up?" he asked, trying to control his anger.

"Look, mister, I'm a drunk and a whore, okay? But, I'd never hurt anybody. You've got to believe me!"

"Why don't you tell me your first name, so we can talk."

"Randi ... It's Randi Keller," she blurted, giving him more than he'd expected.

He jotted the name down. "Who did you make the call for, Randi?"

"A guy I met in a bar." He heard her blow her nose. "The bastard lied to me. He told me he'd been dating this cop, and that she'd just dumped him for some other guy. I didn't believe him at first. He was such a hunk! I'm thinking, who'd drop a guy like that? He told me Sosa was working some big rape case down there."

"The Wake-Up Rapes."

"Yeah."

"You hadn't heard of them?"

"No. I'd only been in Miami a couple of days. I cruise bars and convention hotels in the bigger cities. Excuse me, I need a cigarette." He heard the flick of a lighter followed by the sound of smoke being blown against the receiver. "The North American Petroleum Association had a convention going on in Miami Beach. I figured I'd spend a week there. Those guys are pretty good tippers."

"What did he want you to do?"

"Call Lieutenant Sosa and tell her I had information about the guy she was looking for. It was all supposed to be a big joke. He said he just wanted to let her cool her heels at the bus station for an hour or so. I didn't know that he ..." She began crying again. He waited for her to compose herself. "At first I told him no. In my business, I make it a practice to stay as far away from cops as I can. He said he'd give me four hundred bucks to make the call. I thought he was just bullshitting, but he gave me half of it right there in the bar. He said I could have the rest after I made the call. I was supposed to meet him the next day at a coin phone in the Delmar Mall. He had everything he wanted me to say all written out for me to study. Christ, he must have spent an hour going over it with me ... all this shit about me seeing the newspaper clippings and a rifle and not being able to meet Sosa until five o'clock!"

She sniffed loudly. "When a guy offers a woman like me four hundred bucks, he usually wants something more than a phone call. I was smashed by the time we left the bar. I offered to blow him in my car right there in the parking lot. He said he didn't have time. Kind of hurt my feelings. I mean, I'm no dog!"

"Uh-huh."

"I saw what happened on the news. That's when I got scared and left Miami. I … I know I'm going to prison."

"No, you aren't, Randi! Listen to me! You didn't have any idea what he was going to do." He moved to the edge of his chair. "You're not guilty of anything but giving false information to a police officer. That's only a misdemeanor. You'll be looking at probation if you help us."

"Really?"

"Yeah, but I need to get you to someplace safe right away. Everyone who's seen this guy's face so far is dead."

"Shit!"

He put her on hold while he called the Orlando Police Department and arranged to have her placed in protective custody. After returning to the line, he kept her talking until OPD officers arrived at her room. Homicide detectives from his own department would soon be peppering her with questions about the man who had paid her to phone Maria.

CHAPTER

99

Roth spoke briefly with the two uniformed officers posted outside Maria's room. He was surprised to find her sitting up in bed, brushing her hair, when he entered. The ten-page narrative he had written on the bus station shooting was on her lap.

"Who smuggled you that?"

"McNees and Walker. They just left."

"You're supposed to be resting, not working."

She motioned for him to close the door, and held out her arms. After gently kissing her, he told her about his conversation with Joan Saldano, *a.k.a.* Randi Keller.

"I hear that the chief is recommending you for the department's Medal of Valor," she said.

"I don't deserve it. They should give it to you."

"For what? All I did was get shot." She peered down the front of the hospital gown. "I'm going to have a nasty scar," she fretted.

"Hey, I'll bet my appendectomy scar is bigger. I'll show you mine if you'll show me yours," he teased.

"It's not funny!"

He raised her chin with his fingertips. "Do you really think I care about that? Sara had a cesarean with Jacob. You'll have a lot bigger scar if you ever have one of those."

She smiled. "Having babies is something the Sosa women do easily." Here she was, talking about having children again, just the way she had been moments before the shooting. It was as if starting a family together was already a given, though they had never spoken of marriage. He had never even told her that he loved her, not even when their naked bodies were entwined. Perhaps it was because he had lost the only other woman in his life he had said that to.

A few days before the shooting he had bought a nearly colorless marquis solitaire. Not long after Maria was admitted to the hospital, he badged his way past the guard in the lobby of her condo on the pretext of picking up some things to take to her. He found her college ring in a jewelry box and had the solitaire sized to it, still worried that he was moving too fast. What if she said no?

The department couldn't keep a police guard on her indefinitely. She would never be safe as long as Peter von Hausmann was alive. As strong as his resolve was to kill Miami's Wake-Up Rapist, he grew increasingly edgy as the eleventh drew closer. Unwanted images of von Hausmann kept forcing themselves into his mind. He saw him in his monastic robes, laboring over the papyrus scrolls that contained the lost Gospel of Matthias. He thought of his contributions to the Holocaust fund and his efforts to relieve poverty and misery throughout the world. Sometimes, he envisioned him on his knees in Father McHugh's confessional, begging forgiveness for the crimes committed by the deranged splinters of his psyche. Peter's goodness seemed as boundless as the evil of his alter egos.

CHAPTER

100

Rhonda Buckner was surprised by Roth's phone call on the tenth, but she accepted his explanation for the sudden, two-officer stakeout at her home that night. He told her that he and Bailey would arrive a little before midnight. For the first time since he made the decision to kill von Hausmann, he was beginning to have doubts about whether the multiple personality would appear on Cutler Court. Suppose Kurt didn't share Peter's Oedipal rage toward his mother? Regardless of what happened, there was no turning back now.

*　*

Before leaving the house that evening, he changed into a pair of jeans, a polo shirt and running shoes. He sprinkled talcum powder liberally on his chest before putting on the Kevlar vest. Maria had told him that it lessened the sweating during long stakeouts. She had taught him so much about being a cop in such a short time. He strapped on his shoulder holster and slipped into a dark-blue vinyl "bust jacket" that had **POLICE** lettered on the front and back.

He started to reach for the handcuffs on his dresser and hesitated. *You don't need handcuffs for a dead man.* It occurred to him that not carrying any on a stakeout was just the kind of thing a homicide investigator might later pick up on. He grabbed the cuffs, looped them on his belt and left the house.

CHAPTER

101

Maria was sleeping soundly when he got to the hospital. There were so many things he wanted to tell her. He realized there was a chance he might never see her again. A few days before, he had made her the beneficiary on his life insurance policy. Both of his parents were well provided for, and he had no one else.

He took the solitaire from its box in his pocket. She stirred slightly when he slid it on her finger. He couldn't afford a diamond when he asked Sara to marry him; they were lucky to have enough to eat while he was finishing his doctoral dissertation. He had planned to buy her a diamond eternity ring for their fourteenth anniversary. She was buried wearing the plain gold band he gave her on their wedding day.

The clock on the wall lurched forward another minute. He kissed Maria's forehead and slipped quietly out of the room.

CHAPTER

102

Roth knew that both of Frank Bailey's children were small. He was taken aback when a teenaged-girl came to the door. "There's been an accident. Mr. Bailey is in the hospital. His wife is there with him. I'm watching the kids."

He rushed to the car and phoned dispatch on his cell. The operator he spoke to explained that Bailey was on his way home from work late that afternoon when he responded to a robbery in progress call. Someone had broadsided his unmarked car in an intersection and he was being kept overnight at the hospital for observation because of a possible concussion.

It was too late to find anyone else now. He stopped by the SBU and grabbed Maria's radio from its charger before going to Cutler Court.

Rhonda Buckner looked apprehensive when she opened the door and saw him standing there alone. "Where's the other officer?"

"Something came up at the last minute. He's not going to be able to make it," he said, trying not to sound concerned. He motioned toward a large banyan tree on the other side of the street, several houses away. "I'm going to be parked right there, watching the house until dawn," he said, handing her the extra radio." If you need to talk to me, just key the mike like this." The portable made a clicking sound as one of the repeater towers picked up the test signal and relayed it to headquarters.

"See this little button on top?"

She nodded nervously. "If you press it, you'll have more cops on your doorstep in a couple of minutes than you can count." She gripped the radio tightly with both hands.

"Why don't you lock up now and set the alarm."

He heard her throw the deadbolt behind him when he started down the walkway. Twenty minutes later, lights in the house began to go off. There was nothing to do now but wait. The *Exxon Valdez* was well concealed by the banyan's low hanging canopy of thick leaves. He sat inside it, going over a mental checklist of his preparations.

A one-officer stakeout for a psychotic killer. He tried not to think about it. His eyes moved restlessly back and forth between the house and the street. By 2 a.m., they burned with fatigue from trying to penetrate the darkness beyond the lone street light at the end of the cul-de-sac. A little before two-thirty, he flinched when he heard Rhonda Buckner's voice come over his radio.

"Detective Roth?"

"I'm right here. What is it?"

"I ... I can't sleep."

"I know it's hard, but try to get some rest. Everything's fine out here."

The tactical channel remained silent until a few minutes before three when a burst of static suddenly came over it. "Fucking thing!" he blurted, suddenly aware of how tense he was.

3:12. Nothing.

Fear drifted over him like a fog. He swallowed hard, struck by the realization that he was completely alone.

3:20. He squinted into the darkness, thinking for an instant that he saw something move in the bushes across the street. Probably just a gust of wind or an animal, he decided, listening to the din of crickets coming from the subtropical foliage.

"Detective Roth!"

It was Rhonda Buckner again.

"Yes?"

"S ... Someone's in the house. I can hear them downstairs!" she whispered urgently.

The canal! The dark ribbon of water behind the property suddenly flashed in his mind. '*The key to checkmate is keeping an opponent off balance ... unable to anticipate the direction of future moves.*'

"Quick! Lock yourself in the bathroom!" he told her, jabbing the panic button on his radio. He drew his Glock and jumped out of the car. The house seemed miles away. His chest felt as if it would burst as he raced toward it. When he rounded the corner, he saw the window beside the alarm panel standing wide open. A shadow was moving up the staircase. The Glock bucked in his hands as he fired at it, the sound of his shots splitting the stillness of the night. An instant later, a slug ricocheted off the window frame next to him as the figure on the stairs fired back.

He could hear running upstairs followed by the sound of someone kicking a door. A scream of pure terror reached his ears as he climbed through the window. He took the stairs two at a time, with the gun in front of him. It was as if the weapon was a feral force with a will of its own, straining at its leash, eager to spit its remaining venom.

Rhonda Buckner's bedroom door was open when he reached it. Curtains billowed into the empty room through an open window. He rushed to the bathroom door and grabbed the locked knob, jumping back when a bullet tore through the door, missing him by a couple of inches.

"It's Roth! Don't shoot!" he cried. A moment later, the door opened. Buckner was still holding the gun with both hands. The smell of cordite from the Walther's blast still clung to the air.

"Are you hurt?" he asked urgently. Her face was ashen. She shook her head and began to cry.

He ran to the window just in time to catch a glimpse of someone jumping from the roof to the lawn. Hurriedly holstering his pistol, he clambered onto the roof. Halfway across the steep shake incline, he lost his balance and landed hard on his back. He clung to the storm drain for a couple of seconds before dropping into a tangle of bushes in the yard below.

Von Hausmann was already running down the street by the time Roth got to his feet. The humid night air seared his lungs as he ran after the masked figure. A cold jolt of adrenaline hit his bloodstream when he caught up with von Hausmann in the middle of the block and brought him down with a tackle, skinning an elbow on the pavement.

Von Hausmann spun toward him with a roundhouse punch that drove him backwards.

Sparks of pain shot across his face when a second blow bent his glasses. His younger adversary was several inches taller and had a good twenty pounds on him. They thrashed at each other in the street now. Rage burned in the multiple personality's blue eyes like flames as he cursed in German. The alter managed to break free long enough to pull the shiny Einheit Luger tucked in his waistband. Roth grabbed the barrel with both hands and held on with all his strength as von Hausmann forced the muzzle closer to his head. He could feel warm blood from a gash on his forehead trickling down his face. Just as the Luger was about to slip from his grasp, he seized a split-second opportunity, driving his knee hard into von Hausmann's groin. A sharp cry of pain emanated from the mask, and the antique weapon clattered onto the street. Roth sprang on von Hausmann's back when he lunged for the pistol, catching his throat in the crook of his arm. Von Hausmann clawed frantically at his forearm with both hands, making choking sounds as the carotid restraint hold on his neck grew ever tighter. Roth kept the pressure on, even after von Hausmann stopped struggling and went limp. The blood to his brain had been cut off. He would be dead within a couple of minutes.

"You son of a bitch!" Roth shouted, letting the pent-up hatred surge through his veins like molten lava. He could hear sirens in the distance. There was still enough time. *Kill him! Do it!*

A moment later, he released his vise-like grip and the multiple personality wheezed and coughed, still groggy from lack of oxygen as Roth cuffed his hands behind his back.

His glasses rested crookedly on the bridge of his nose and he was still breathing hard from the struggle.

"You're under arrest."

"Hey, suck my dick, mother-fucker! Get off me!" von Hausmann yelled in a completely different voice.

Jan!

He pulled off the ski mask and saw the face of the man he and Maria had been after for so long.

A marked cruiser slammed on its brakes ten feet away, blinding him in the glare of its lights. A few minutes later, the knot in his stomach eased when he watched Jan being dragged, still kicking and cursing, to one of the marked police units that now filled the street.

The woman who had nearly become the multiple personality's latest victim walked over to him from a crowd of people gathered on the sidewalk.

"Oh, my God! I … I nearly shot you."

He put an arm around her and hugged her without speaking.

CHAPTER

103

The sun was just beginning to rise when he drove over the Intracoastal Waterway and saw the city skyline. He thought of how close he had come to killing von Hausmann. No one would have questioned a death resulting from the misapplication of a neck restraint hold by a rookie. He could have gotten away with it.

Why did I stop? He knew only that, just as he was about to kill Peter von Hausmann, all the hatred he felt toward him suddenly drained from his being.

He looked at the dark, choppy water below the bridge, wondering what would happen now.

On the way to the station, he heard over the tactical channel that a stolen car had been located parked on a street behind the canal. In the trunk was a loaded military style assault rifle, several magazines of ammunition, and a news clipping about a Pearl Jam concert that was to be held the following day in Miami. How many people would have died and been injured at the packed event if von Hausmann had made it there with his assault rifle? A rubber raft with a paddle was found beached on the sandy bank behind Rhonda Buckner's property and a duffle bag was located next to the house; inside it were heavy workman's gloves, canvas coveralls and a pair of climbing crampons that had enabled von Hausmann to ascend the inhospitable slope without being cut by its thorns.

* *

Captain Wilcox was waiting for Roth when he arrived at the Sexual Battery Unit. The division commander was bleary-eyed and wearing a

379

rumpled, short-sleeved shirt and slacks. A shadow of whiskers covered his face.

"Has he said anything?" Roth asked.

"Not a word. He fought like a wild man all the way down here. The guys in the cruiser had to put flex cuffs on his ankles to keep him from kicking the windows out. As soon as he got here, he just went quiet all of a sudden. It's really weird."

"Where is he now?"

"We've got him locked in Interview Four. McNees and Walker are watching him through the one-way. We let him make a call to his uncle in Palm Beach right after they brought him in. He's on his way here now." Roth had expected the captain to say something about his solo stakeout, but he didn't.

He stopped by the SBU and removed two items from one of the Wake-Up files before going to where Peter von Hausmann was being held. The prisoner was seated at a drab, metal table; cuts and abrasions on his face and flecks of blood on his shirt attested to his scuffle with Roth. His left hand was cuffed to a U-bolt that was anchored to the floor. He looked up when Roth entered the room.

"Who are you?" von Hausmann asked, as if seeing him for the first time.

"My name is David Roth. I'm a police officer."

Von Hausmann's eyes moved around the empty room. "Is ... is it over?" he asked, in a subdued voice.

"Yes," Roth replied simply.

Peter von Hausmann lowered his head.

The man seated at the table wasn't the person who had just tried to kill him. He was looking at the reclusive ex-monk, whose plea for help had first come in the form of a cryptic biblical passage. The handcuffed figure looked up at him.

"Did I...." He stopped speaking, as his voice began to break.

"You didn't hurt anyone tonight." Von Hausmann stared at him with a vacant look.

"Jan ... Jan Nasargiel!" Roth said loudly. Von Hausmann appeared startled. Roth stepped closer to the prisoner and spoke again, trying now to summon the newest alter ego.

"Kannst du mich hören (Can you hear me)?" he asked in German. Von Hausmann's head slumped on his chest as if he were asleep.

"Kannst du mich hören?" he repeated.

Silence.

"Kannst du dich mir gegenüber nicht offenbaren und deinen Mann stehen? (Can't you come out and face me like a man?). Du bist sehr mutis, wenn du dich hinter einem Gewehr versteckst und Frauen, Kinder, und alte Leute erschie Ben kannst (You're brave enough when you're hiding behind a rifle shooting women, children and old people)!"

Von Hausmann's eyes snapped open. "Was willst du denn (What do you want)?" he demanded.

Roth thought he detected a trace of Bavarian in the German.

"Wie heißt du (What is your name)?"

"Müller. Kurt Müller."

"Sprichst du Englisch (Do you speak English)?"

Von Hausmann's lips twisted into a cruel grin. "As well as you, Jew-boy!" He crossed his legs and stared defiantly at his captor. "You must be feeling very pleased with yourself, *Roth*," he sneered. "Roth … Stein … Goldman. There are still so many of you. You breed like roaches!"

Roth glared at him without speaking.

"The Final Solution wasn't ambitious enough. Next time, we—"

"There isn't going to be a next time for you!"

The alter threw back his head and laughed. "Come now, are you really so foolish as to believe that a jury will ever convict poor Brother Tobias of anything?" He rolled his eyes. "Mea culpa … mea maxima culpa" (Through my fault … through my most grievous fault)!" he said, in Latin. A peel of laughter filled the room. "You know, people like Peter are just too decent for their own good. He hasn't changed a bit since the day I met him. I guess you can take the monk out of the monastery, but you can't take the monastery out of the monk, eh?" He slapped his leg with amusement. "We really *are* a multiple personality, you know. We're quite insane."

"Yes. I know."

Mueller clapped his hands. "Bravo for you, Roth!" he said mockingly. "What a clever little *Juden* you are!" He leaned back, balancing himself on the back legs of his chair. "Jan and I have a very active interest in Peter's welfare. You see, whatever happens to one of us happens to all of us."

Roth held up a color photo of Bridget Kearney's battered face. "Remember her?"

The alter shrugged. "Suppose I do? So what?"

He removed the Department of Public Health report on Sister Kearney from an envelope and tossed it on the table.

"Was ist das (What is this)?" the alter frowned. He scanned the one page document indicating that the Dominican nun was HIV positive. His lips parted as he looked up at Roth, his face a mask of disbelief.

"Nein! Nein!" he cried.

CHAPTER

104

Roth burst into Maria's room at Mercy Hospital. "We got him!"

She stared at him agape. "How?"

"It's a long story."

He told her everything over the next half hour, including how he had planned to kill Peter von Hausmann.

She put her arms around his neck and kissed him. "David … David, what am I going to do with you?"

"Hey, nice ring," he said.

She held out her hand. "Looks like I got engaged while I was asleep."

"Lucky guy. Anybody I know?"

"Oh, it's so beautiful!"

"Can I take that as a yes?"

She smiled. "I'll marry you the day you leave the department, if you want."

Leaving the department.

He touched the cut over his eye. The life of a university professor had its advantages. Even the most difficult students didn't try to kill you.

"I'm afraid you're going to need some stitches."

He inspected the gash and several strawberry abrasions with a mirror she handed him. "I coulda been a contendah!" he said, in his best Marlon Brando voice. They both laughed.

"I love you, Lieutenant Sosa."

Her eyes filled with tears. "I love you, too, Detective Third Grade Roth."

His brief career with the Miami Police Department was almost over. No more chasing multiple personalities or worrying about IA finding out about his affair with his supervisor. Even in his joy, he couldn't escape a trace of melancholy. David Roth liked being a cop.

*   *

By Fall semester he was back on campus in the Memorial Building auditorium, teaching Victimology 3666 just as he had for so many years. He opened his notes and looked out at the sea of undergraduate faces, running a hand over the unfamiliar salt and pepper stubble of his new beard. Everything seemed so different now. Even though he was no longer a police officer, vestiges of the role remained with him. The night before he dreamt he was back at the academy pistol range firing at one of the human silhouette targets. Suddenly, the paper man in his sights morphed into Brother Tobias. The robed figure came off its frame and began walking toward him holding a large bloody crucifix with both hands. He fired again and again, watching the slugs tear into the body of Peter von Hausmann.

A tremor passed through him as he stood at the podium. No one beside the police lieutenant he was about to marry would ever know the real reason he had gone to Cutler Court that night. Murder. His awareness that he went to Rhonda Buckner's home to kill another human being still seemed surreal, so foreign to everything he had ever believed. He wondered what had happened to the man he was and if he would ever again be that person. Even as he began his lecture, his mind kept drifting back to the things he had seen and done the past six months. He recalled the mutilated hands of Laura Kelce swathed in bandages, the pleading face of the blind Dr. Pulaski, the lifeless body of Peaches Brooks sprawled on her bed, staring up at him with unseeing eyes.

"Violence is about far more than statistics," he said, gripping the podium. "In this class we're going to consider what it does to the lives of other human beings and what we can do to stop it."